B. Hill

D1047571

Dear Reader,

They say that people are the same all over. Whether it's a small village on the sea, a mining town nestled in the mountains, or a whistle-stop along the Western plains, we all share the same hopes and dreams. We work, we play, we laugh, we cry—and, of course, we fall in love . . .

It is this universal experience that we at Jove Books have tried to capture in a heartwarming series of novels. We've asked our most gifted authors to write their own story of American romance, set in a town as distinct and vivid as the people who live there. Each writer chose a special time and place close to their hearts. They filled the towns with charming, unforgettable characters—then added that spark of romance. We think you'll find the combination absolutely delightful.

You might even recognize *your* town. Because true love lives in *every* town . . .

Welcome to *Our Town*.

Sincerely,

Leslie Gelbman
Editor-in-Chief

❖ ❖ ❖

∞ OUR • TOWN ∞

CANDY KISS

GINNY AIKEN

JOVE BOOKS, NEW YORK

CANDY KISS

A Jove Book / published by arrangement with
the author

PRINTING HISTORY
Jove edition / September 1996

The Putnam Berkley World Wide Web site address is
http://www.berkley.com

ISBN: 0-515-11941-5

A JOVE BOOK®
Jove Books are published by The Berkley Publishing Group,
200 Madison Avenue, New York, New York 10016.
JOVE and the "J" design are trademarks
belonging to Jove Publications, Inc.

PRINTED IN THE UNITED STATES OF AMERICA

10 9 8 7 6 5 4 3 2 1

To my five heroes:

George Ivan
Gregory Alex
Geoffrey Nicholas
Grant Adrian
and
as always,

George

ACKNOWLEDGMENTS

I extend my heartfelt thanks to five very special women. To Peggy Stoks, for the hand in the dark. To Karen Rose Smith, for the sympathetic shoulder. To Donna Grove, for the world's best critiquing. To Linda Hyatt, my agent, for her unwavering faith. And especially to my wonderful editor, Judith Stern Palais, for making my dream come true.

A special thanks to the Classic Caramel Company of York, Pennsylvania, especially to Lisa Magill, for their help with the promotion of this book.

❖ 1 ❖

*Lancaster County,
Pennsylvania
1894*

IT WAS ALL over before Dulcie Kramer realized it was happening. What a disaster! And all she'd wanted was to make a living for Granny K and herself.

One moment she was snapping the reins, urging her old horse, Molly, to pick up her pace. The next, a skunk was scuttling away from a tangle of blackberry brambles. Molly neighed shrilly and bucked.

"Oh, Molly," Dulcie wailed, "this isn't the time for you to get frisky. It's not as if the skunk sprayed or anyth— Phew!"

Molly reared up, jerking her head from side to side, and with another panicky squeal broke the worn leather that bound her to the buckboard.

The wagon tilted behind Molly, and Dulcie tried to move her weight to the opposite side, hoping to counterbalance it. Her efforts only gained her a longer, more awkward flight from the wagon and a graceless, painful landing in the brambles. Now, instead of being nearly to Lancaster, she lay on the side of the road, eyes tearing and nose running from the successful efforts of the skunk. And Molly had abandoned her.

Dulcie's temper soared. "You traitor, you! How dare you leave me behind?"

Wiping her eyes, Dulcie glared in the direction the horse had gone. In the distance, she saw Molly's beamy behind making short shrift of the velvety green pasture. Another neigh reached her ears, faintly this time.

"Just you wait till I get home, you prune-tempered nag. And why did you recover your long-lost youth only after dumping me?" Dulcie winced as she reclaimed her skirt from the grasping blackberry vines and snagged a finger on a bramble. "Ingrate. Look how fast you ran off. It's been more than five years since we last saw that much sass from you." Dulcie swiped at her streaming eyes. "Wait till I come around with an apple or two. I won't be so quick to share with you."

Molly's treachery, however, was the least of Dulcie's worries. Not only was she alone on the road, her buckboard on its side, wheel broken, horse vanished, but also her ankle was throbbing, and she could feel it swelling as the seconds rushed by. She could neither ride the now-departed Molly, even if she were able somehow to climb on with her injured leg, nor walk the rest of the way to Lancaster. She couldn't return home, for that matter.

So, there she sat.

And teared.

And sat.

A movement on the rolling field across the road caught Dulcie's eye. Blinking away the veil of moisture that blurred her vision, she focused despite the hovering foulness and saw a cow, a placid-looking beast with a black-and-white mottled hide. A sharp bleat brought the bovine to a stop, and a calf approached in the wake of the sound.

More cows soon dotted the lush, green pasture behind the whitewashed fence. Moments later, their clumsy offspring swarmed around the grand ladies. As Dulcie's senses tried to cope with the assault they'd received, she watched the beeves through her tears. One of the cows plodded close to the fence, glanced at Dulcie, then lowered her head for a bite of green. As she chewed, the bovine stared at Dulcie, seeming to ponder the ramifications of her predicament. When two more beasts converged at the fence, Dulcie felt oddly like their morning entertainment. But there was nothing entertaining about the putrid stink of skunk or the pain in her ankle.

Would that it were market day. Then Dulcie could hope to appeal to any of the local Amish farmers who once a week took the fruits of their labor to market in Lancaster. If she weren't mistaken, her audience behind the fence was part of Joseph Hochstetter's herd. Surely Mr. Hochstetter, a member of the deeply religious, separatist denomination, would offer to help, perhaps take her into town.

But no. Today was Monday. Not market day. No Amish dairyman would be headed to town, his plain black buggy bearing rich cream, yellow butter, and fresh milk.

Dulcie twirled a finger around a curl that had escaped her hairpins, a habit she'd had since early childhood. What was she going to do? It was still early, and this back road to Lancaster was not as popular as the Columbia Pike. The way her luck was running, she could be sitting here a very long time. She pressed the hem of her blue cotton skirt to her drippy eyes, sniffled, feeling distinctly sorry for herself, then took another look at her surroundings.

"Hmmmm . . ."

Not ten feet away lay the remains of the buckboard's wheel. Maybe she could crawl over and reach that one spoke that hadn't shattered into overlarge toothpicks. It might work as a cane.

Hiking her skirt to her thighs, Dulcie rose on her knees,

then crawled her way to the ruined conveyance, favoring her hurting ankle. A finger's length away from her goal, she heard hoofbeats approaching, accompanied by the most skillful use of invectives she'd ever heard. Being Granny K's relation, she'd heard prodigious use of such language since she was knee-high to a gnat, as the old scamp would say, and considered herself eminently qualified to judge.

Turning toward the approaching rider, Dulcie craned her neck to see what was coming her way.

"... damn it all to hell!"

Fighting the fumes in the air, Race Langston tried to protect his eyes with his handkerchief. Zephyr was balking—and who could blame the horse when the stench of skunk had robbed the world of breatheable air.

For a moment Race considered using the mishap as an excuse for aborting his mission, but soon discarded that option. Milton Hershey was nobody's fool. His father's long-time friend would see clear through such a flimsy excuse.

There was no avoiding it. Race had to go to Everleigh, find that Mignone Kramer woman, and buy her secret recipe for—of all things—French candies. It came down to paying the woman for her cooperation. An outrageous waste of a new attorney's day.

Zephyr snorted, shook his head, then began to turn. Race fought to keep the animal on the road to Everleigh, no easy feat as he held his handkerchief to his nose. Stuffing the white fabric into his breast pocket and tightening his grip on the reins, Race made out what looked like an overturned wagon and a blue blur of jerky motion. Most likely the wagon's unfortunate passenger.

The closer he came, the more his eyes burned. Cursing the skunk, Race clamped his eyelids shut, then opened them quickly, hoping to see what was happening only a few yards away. Zephyr seemed curious, too, as he quit trying to turn and went forward—at a dismally slow, if understandably cautious, gait.

The splotch of blue coalesced into what at first resembled a swaying Cupid's heart. Then Race made out a mass of golden hair. He blinked. Was it a woman? Seconds later, he caught sight of well-turned feminine calves trailing the valentine-shaped posterior. What a pleasing sight! If only his eyes didn't burn and tear so much. He'd love to see well enough to fully appreciate the view.

He quickly sobered when he saw the woman drag herself closer to the fallen wagon. It looked as if she'd been injured in the accident. And she seemed to be alone.

With his knees he guided Zephyr closer, then dismounted near the victim of the accident. "Might I be of assistance, ma'am?"

"Oh!" she cried, and lost her precarious position on all fours. She tumbled to the grass and, through his tears, Race saw the blue of her skirt puddle on the grassy roadside. She brought the bottom of her garment up to her face and dabbed at her streaming eyes. A froth of white underskirt still covered her legs. Moments later, brilliant sapphire eyes peered up at Race.

"Wh—who are you?"

He downscaled his estimate of the lady's age. "Race Langston, miss. I'm an attorney from Lancaster. I was on my way to Everleigh on business. The skunk's poor manners made me stop. *My* good manners urge me to help you."

Again those blue eyes blinked, squinted, then stared through more sparkling drops. "I'd best not detain you. My . . . companion . . . went to find help. I'm sure she— *he'll* be back shortly."

"I can't just leave you here, hurt and alone." Then Race caught the flicker of fear that crossed her features. And he again adjusted his assessment of her age. She was little more than a girl, perhaps all of eighteen or nineteen, if one chose to ignore the childlike way she kept tweaking a lock of her shiny blond hair. Although he felt fairly certain that her appealing facial contortion was in essence a frown, and despite his impaired vision, not to mention his hampered breathing, Race admired her pursed lips and blushing cheeks.

Hoping to reassure her, he offered, "You have nothing to fear from me. As I said, I'm a member of the bar, an officer of the court. All I want is to help you."

Another dab of the skirt's hem to her eyes, and Race got a good look at her purpling, swollen ankle. "There, see? That looks nasty. Please allow me—"

A graceful hand waved his words aside. "*Do* not let me detain you," she urged. "As I said, my . . . companion should be right back."

The minuscule hesitation in the young lady's speech proved Race's suspicion that she was lying. As an attorney, it was crucial for him to be keenly attuned to the way people spoke. Small clues often meant the difference between a win or a loss in court.

He also had no doubt that if he confronted her, she would most likely become more adamant in her fiction. "Very well, then, I'll stay with you until *he* returns."

White teeth caught a rosy bottom lip. A pair of diamond drops slipped into the dimples in her cheeks. Race sucked in a lungful of putrid air, his eyes overflowed, and an oath escaped his lips.

A muffled chuckle followed.

"So," he went on, wiping his eyes with his wrist, relieved by her humor, "my tears amuse you?"

As the skirt came up to the blue eyes again, the golden

curls shook from side to side. "It's just that I always thought Granny K was the world's best cusser."

"Oh. I see. You appreciate my talent."

"Something like that." Dulcie shifted, seeking a more comfortable position. It seemed none could be found, since the pain in her leg was sharp.

Another minor adjustment to her hips.

Another stab of pain.

Another tear.

The man shook out his handkerchief. "Here, let me at least bind up that ankle. This cloth wasn't helping against the skunk's fumes, and would probably do more good as a bandage."

"Oh, I couldn't trouble you. It's not really that bad. See?" Holding her breath, Dulcie flexed her foot and wished the half-witted idea had never occurred to her. She moaned in pain before she could stop herself.

"Indeed," the young attorney answered, a droll note in his voice.

"Really. You don't have to put yourself out—"

"Of course I don't have to. But what sort of human would I be if I could help someone but spared myself the effort? Especially if my help would ease her pain."

She shrugged.

"Would *you* ignore another's misfortune?"

Dulcie felt her cheeks warm. "No."

"So there! Neither can I. Let me see that ankle."

Before Dulcie could react, strong, warm hands pushed her skirt and petticoat up to her knees, baring her to Mr. . . . What was his name?

Oh, yes! Mr. Langston. Dulcie narrowed her gaze. The not-one-bit-timid Mr. Langston. The one who took hold of the situation and played it to his best advantage. Just as he was playing with her leg.

Mr. Langston's fingers pressed gently into the swollen spot.

Fresh tears popped into Dulcie's eyes, these having nothing to do with the effects of the skunk spray and everything to do with her sore leg. A rough finger dabbed the moisture away.

The gentle friction against her cheeks brought warmth to Dulcie's skin. She caught her breath when he repeated the gesture, this time despite the lack of further tears. Heat rushed to her cheeks, her temples, even her earlobes.

Embarrassed but curious, Dulcie blinked a couple of times, then studied her companion. A quizzical expression filled his features, and Dulcie wondered if Mr. Langston had also felt that odd vibrancy she'd just experienced.

Then he shook his head, set her foot on his lap, and flicked open a pocketknife.

Dulcie gasped. Good heavens! She was alone with a stranger on a deserted road. He had a weapon. The blade was shiny, catching the sun on its edge. Would she be dismembered . . . ravished?

Fear filled her throat. Her hands chilled as he rasped his thumb over steel. At least her death would be swift. Dulcie cried for help—in vain, strangled as she felt. Her heart pounded. Her stomach quaked. Her head spun.

Toppling to her elbows, Dulcie jerked back up when she felt a tug on her boot. Another pull, and a second button flew off. Relief nearly drowned her. Her foolish suspicion made her cheeks blaze. "Oh, dear."

Mr. Langston glanced her way. "Yes, it's a shame. They're nice shoes, but it can't be helped. If your ankle continues to swell inside the leather, you might find your circulation hampered."

At least he couldn't know she'd thought him a murderous deflowerer! Especially since he'd only ruined her shoe.

But a shoe was a weighty matter these days. Life was difficult. Maman was dead and buried no more than eight weeks. The little money she'd left was swiftly fleeing, as Dulcie worked to ease her grief and sought to keep Granny K and herself fed. Now they'd have to spare money to buy her new footwear. Her funds were meager indeed.

". . . and I think that should do it," said Dulcie's rescuer, patting his handiwork. His voice dragged her back from her thoughts, and she allowed herself a smile.

"See that?" he said. "You're even smiling. I knew the handkerchief would be just the thing."

"You really didn't have to—"

"Oh, no. We already discussed that. Think up another topic while we wait for your *companion* to return."

Dulcie flushed. "Uh . . . er . . . um . . ."

Mr. Langston's deep brown gaze bored into Dulcie's guilty conscience. At least, that was where she felt it. And from the way her cheeks burned, she was sure he knew she'd been stretching the truth. If he only knew how far!

The thought of Old Molly plodding back to offer Dulcie assistance was more than she could handle. A smile curved her lips.

Mr. Langston smiled back.

The poor man might spend eternity here if he was determined to wait for Dulcie's recalcitrant steed. A vision of Molly, with her spreading girth and grizzled muzzle, waddling to the rescue, sword drawn to down all foes, made Dulcie chuckle.

Mr. Langston peered quizzically at her.

Old Molly, her champion, her knight who needed no white horse, but heaven help her should a skunk appear!

The absurdity proved too much for Dulcie, and her laughter chimed out. She laughed long and loud, as she hadn't since well before Maman's brief, final illness. She laughed until tears streamed from her eyes. Until the certainty that her mother could see her this very moment, could share her daughter's laughter, took root in Dulcie's heart.

She laughed until she caught sight of Mr. Langston's alarmed expression. "Oh . . . dear . . ."

Between chuckles, she tried to explain her outpouring of emotion, but it seemed the silliness had freed a certain part of her heart, a part that wasn't yet ready to be restrained. Dulcie waved toward Everleigh. "You—you know . . . there is no . . . companion. But my horse did . . . run off. . . ."

With laughter and descriptive words, Dulcie painted a picture of her day's misadventure that immediately wiped the trepidation from Mr. Langston's attractive features.

As she came to the end of her tale, Dulcie glanced again at her companion. He really was attractive, more so than any other man she'd ever known. Not that there was any great abundance of appealing males in Everleigh to compare him with, but still, coffee-dark hair, deep eyes, and finely carved features such as Mr. Langston's deserved feminine appreciation.

As she pondered the strong line of his jaw, she noticed it was moving. "Oh, dear," she said, then bit her lip. He'd been speaking, and she had no idea what he'd said! "Excuse me, could you please repeat that?"

A straight eyebrow rose. Brown eyes scanned her face. "As I was saying, you're still here, in the middle of the road, with a damaged vehicle and no horse. Injured, as well."

"Well . . . I *had* been trying to reach that spoke over there. I figured I could use it as a crutch to get back home. Everleigh's not too far."

"Nonsense! I was headed for Everleigh on business. I can get you there."

"But Mr. Langston—"

"Please call me Race. Mr. Langston is my father."

Race, she thought. What an unusual name. Perhaps it was handed down in his family generation to generation. She decided to test it. "Race . . ."

A broad smile appeared on his face. "Thank you, and what shall I call you?"

"You're welcome, and I'm Dulcie." She certainly didn't need to tell him her full, given name. To be named after a character in some ancient book about an eccentric Spanish nobleman who went through life tilting at windmills was not something Dulcie was wont to share.

He didn't respond immediately. A moment passed. Then another. He took a visual voyage of her face, and she felt his gaze as if it were a touch. "Sweet," he finally murmured, "from the Latin, *dolce.*"

"Close," she muttered. Figures! It was just her luck to be rescued by an attorney, someone who had obviously spent years studying. Latin must have been a part of his training. And from the Latin, it was just a hop to the Spanish Dulcinea, Don Quixote's glorified peasant.

To change the direction of the conversation, she accepted his help. "Since you were going there in the first place . . ."

"Absolutely. It will be a pleasure."

"But how?"

Mr. Langst—*Race*—took a good look at his enormous chestnut. Then he glanced back at Dulcie. "Shouldn't be too bad. Here. Let me help you up."

Moments later, Dulcie found herself high atop the horse Race called Zephyr, both her legs draped over the beast's left side. Then with fluid ease, Race mounted behind her, to surprisingly minor objection from the animal.

They discussed the differing temperaments of their steeds, laughing at stories Dulcie told of Molly's antics. They fell silent for a while. They shared the quiet beauty of the day,

enjoying the good fortune that had brought them to that
fateful spot at just exactly the right time.

Dulcie took in a deep breath of summer-scented air that
scarcely bore a hint of skunk. She wondered if this stroke
of luck presaged a change in her circumstances. Maybe, despite today's fiasco, she could start all over, produce new
samples. The ones she'd made this morning were splattered
all over the road. Great, big, rich, brown blobs of Maman's
secret recipe bonbons. Melting in the sun partway to Lancaster. Not earning any much-needed income.

There wasn't much she could do about what had happened, and she certainly wasn't about to waste the apparent
interest her companion was showing in her. She sighed. The
exhalation brought her flush against Race's chest. She stiffened at the contact.

"No, no," he said, "please lean back. It will jar you less
if you brace yourself against me during the ride."

Pinpoints of heat danced over Dulcie's flesh. She'd best
not get too interested in her companion, though. He was
from Lancaster, an attorney. She was a country girl from
Everleigh. Not exactly a perfect match.

But there was nothing to keep her from enjoying today.
It was nice to speak with an intelligent, caring gentleman.
It was a pleasure to respond to his smiles. It was wonderful
to ride home on his horse, his strong arms protecting her.

As they approached Everleigh and Dulcie caught sight of
the familiar surroundings, she wondered if anyone would be
outside at this time. It would be a tad embarrassing to have
to explain the predicament that had led to her unseemly
mode of transportation.

"Tell me where to turn," Race said, smiling.

That smile scattered all of Dulcie's cares. Maybe most of
them. And maybe Granny K's cackling cronies were busy
cooking right now. If they ventured out, their inevitable cu-

riosity might dim the luster of riding home on Race's horse. Maybe . . .

In all honesty, she was virtually riding on his lap. And *that* was something she could ill afford anyone seeing!

She straightened, using the need to direct Race toward her home to pry herself from the warm support of his body. "When you go past the square, you must turn right. Then follow that street, and we're the last home at the edge of the woods."

Race nodded, then glanced both ways. "Everleigh looks nice."

"It's fine, I guess. It's home. Lancaster is just more . . . *more*."

"Sometimes more isn't all that pleasant."

"Must be better than ordinary."

Race cocked an eyebrow and eyed his lapful of blond beauty. "Can't be too ordinary, if it's where you live."

Rose tinted her cheeks. She lowered her eyelashes, then met his gaze. "Why, Mr. Langston, I believe you're flirting."

"With you? But of course!"

Race was charmed. Purely and simply charmed. Dulcie was indeed young, but not *too* young for his twenty-five years. She felt warm and sweet against him, her blue eyes sparkling with what looked like interest. He hoped so. He was certainly interested in her. He'd hate to think all she felt was gratitude for his earlier rescue.

He caught her looking up at him and smiled. She blushed again and smiled back. That didn't look like gratitude. The expression on his companion's face looked exactly the way he felt inside. Enchanted, entranced, enthralled.

What a delightful way to forget an unpleasant task.

❖ 2 ❖

FOLLOWING DULCIE'S INSTRUCTIONS, Race turned Zephyr down the lane to his right. Tall evergreens tangled with maples and oaks, shading half the road from the midday summer sun. As he breathed deeply, appreciatively, the scents of rich, damp soil and lily-scented woman twined into an intoxicating blend, covering the lingering odor of skunk.

Race glanced about him and smiled with pleasure. Everleigh was a quaint village, not really a town. With its simple homes and their colorful flower beds, this quiet side road suited it. Around the sturdy structures of stone, brick, and whitewashed clapboard, a multitude of blossoms tried to outdo each other. Red, gold, pink, green. Every house had its own blanket of blooms, all adding to the rich scent in the air.

Still, the fragrance of lilies teased his senses; Dulcie's smile warmed his insides.

A sharp cackle of laughter caught his attention, and Race looked in the direction it came from. At the end of the lane, on the porch of a small white clapboard house, he saw movement.

"Vill ya lookit that?" cried a raspy voice. "Dulcie-girl's brought herself home a man!"

The outrageous statement flew with a billow of smoke off the gingerbread-trimmed porch of the house. Race blinked, wondering if his eyes had sustained some sort of lasting damage from the encounter with the skunk. Surely that wasn't Dulcie's home, was it? Well, the tidy little house wasn't the problem; the person on the porch was.

Race glanced at Dulcie, who'd said hers was the last house on this back road, then again at the apparition chuckling and waving a corncob pipe. In his arms, Dulcie squirmed, then sat bolt upright.

"Granny, hush! He doesn't even know you—"

"Yit!" finished the wizened goblin, then burst into more peals of dry, mischievous laughter. Race was more than a bit puzzled. Stunned was more like it.

"Oh, dear," Dulcie moaned, then stiffened in his arms so that he feared they'd both plop off Zephyr if either dared breathe. Before he could so much as think of what to do, Dulcie went on. "I'm so sorry, Mr. Langst—"

"Race."

Dulcie's earnest blue gaze met his. "You must excuse her, R-Race. She meant no offense. Granny K is eccentric, but she's really good as gold. Most of the time."

"Granny K? The one you said was the world's best cusser?" He really should have paid more attention to Dulcie's words earlier, certainly more than he'd paid her physical attributes. "*Your* grand*mother*?"

Dulcie sniffed and made to slide down Zephyr's left flank. As the beast danced sideways in protest, Race grasped Dulcie's arms to hold her still. "If either one of us wants down from here, we're going to have to grant Zephyr some concessions. I go first. Once I'm on the ground, I'll help you off."

"Fine. And if you must help me down, then you're going to have to grant me one concession. You will explain the meaning of your pointed question about, yes, my grand-mother.''

Race frowned. He hadn't meant to offend. It just seemed incongruous to link the Delft-porcelain beauty of Dulcie to the downright strange person on that porch. Especially difficult was the notion that they were blood relatives. He stole another look at Granny K.

A steady stream of smoke climbed skyward from her pipe. Thin lips curved up around the stem. Cloudy eyes, older than history, catalogued his every move. Race knew he was being judged, and his judge was a female Methuselah in faded denim trousers! Bare feet poked out from under the wash-bleached cloth, the knobby-boned toes curling over the lip of the porch step. A salt-glazed crock stood at her side.

As if his scrutiny were a trigger, the old woman swooped down. With her left hand, she swung the jug over her shoulder, with her right, she aimed the smoke from her pipe away from her face. Then with relish she glugged down a healthy measure of whatever she had in the crock. Race was uncomfortably certain it was moonshine.

''D'ya want some?'' With one faded blue eye closed, she peered at him.

Race stiffened. ''N-no!'' he managed, his voice cracking with shock. Another salvo of cackles poured from Granny K's twig-thin self.

Dulcie's voice pierced through his complete discombobulation. ''Mr. Langston, please! If you would be so kind as to trouble yourself and help me down from this great beast of yours, I could perhaps persuade her to behave herself.''

With alacrity, Race reacted, easing the formerly warm and pliant woman, now stiff and icy, off his horse. ''Please do whatever it takes . . .''

''If you must know,'' she said in that snippy voice when

he set her down a few inches away, "very little is needed. *I* can speak with her. *You* must stop gaping at her. She's not some curiosity. She's just an elderly eccentric, with her own personal brand of uniqueness."

"Please don't let my presence keep you from what you must do with your grandmother. I have business in Everleigh, after all." With an index finger Race tapped his brow. "Good day."

As he nodded her way, the *unique* Granny K frowned, or so he thought. With that many wrinkles it was hard to tell what was a frown and what wasn't.

"Damn and blast it, Dulcie-girl!"

Yep, thought Race, it had been a frown, all right.

Granny K continued. "Choo don't even knows how to hang on to 'im now's ya got him here. Ach! A body's gotta do it all hersel'."

Hoping to head off any further contact between her grandmother and the scared-off Race Langston, Dulcie headed for the porch. Seconds later, her injured leg crumbled under her. Strong arms caught her from behind, steadied her, helped her regain her balance. "Thank you," she said, meaning it.

"Dulcie . . ." he began hesitantly.

Wishing to die of mortification, she shook her head. "Please, this has been a difficult day. And I've kept you from your business, as you yourself said. You've been most kind. Do accept my apologies for my grandmother's incorrigible behavior."

Granny K plunked down her jug, then sucked loudly at her pipe. "Yer doin' it agin, Dulcie-girl," she muttered, hobbling down the porch steps. "Looks like y'ain't never gonna yerself hitched get. Choo still have that conjuring bag I made? Unt how 'bout the red yarn . . . ?"

At Granny's comment, Dulcie's stomach clenched in fear. She glanced behind her to see if Race had caught the gist of what her grandmother had said. But aside from a befuddled look on his face, he seemed to have missed the significance of her words.

Dulcie took a painful step toward her grandmother. Lowering her voice, she said, "You know you can't talk Pow-Wow like that when there are other people around, Granny. They don't understand your Hex-Craft. Please watch what you're saying."

"Vatch how yer losing the only decent man come 'round here sniffin'," Granny returned.

Dulcie shook her head. "Now that's not a nice way to say you dislike Kirk Schleinbaugh."

"Schleinbaugh, slimebaugh! He's got dirt under 'is fingernails unt more dirt deep in 'em beady eyes. I kin smell bad oozin' from 'im. Vant I should take some a' his hair, maybe make an amulet to pertect you from 'is dirty hands?"

"Hush!" Dulcie urged her grandmother, despite bearing little hope of derailing Granny K's current train of thought. What could the elegant, obviously wealthy, well-educated Lancaster attorney be thinking by now?

Dread in her middle, Dulcie turned toward Race. A look of horror filled his face. "Oh, dear. Now you've gone and done it, Granny!"

"Ain't done nuthin' yit!"

"A-a . . . mu . . . let?" Race mouthed the word as if it were alive and writhing on his tongue.

"Oh, don't pay her any mind," Dulcie urged, pasting a smile on her face. "She loves to shock people."

Race's eyebrow cocked up. "Really, now. What would make you say such a thing?"

The sarcasm edging his words struck Dulcie wrong. "Years of experience, something you lack. Now, if you're done insulting my grandmother—"

Her words were cut off by Granny's gnarled fingers and

rough palm over her lips. "Phe-ew! Ya stink a' skunk, Dulcie-girl! Unt choo there, choo jist vait, ya dressed-up pup. Cain't leave 'til ya beg my leave. Ain't ready to be begged jist yet. Vat's yer name?"

Despite her frail appearance, Granny was a wiry little thing. In dismay, Dulcie caught the dazed look on Race's face. She tried to shake loose of Granny, but her grandmother clung tenaciously. She ended up prying each knobby finger off her mouth.

As she turned to chastise Granny, she saw just how much the elderly imp was enjoying herself. A cautious smile spread slowly, and she hobbled two steps to the side to lean against the latticework supporting the porch railing. It should prove entertaining to watch the dashing Mr. Race Langston in Granny's clutches.

Race cleared his throat and said his name. A wary expression then crept onto his features. Dulcie could almost hear his agile attorney's mind trying to anticipate Granny K's next move.

After drawing deeply, and with the bowl in her hand, Granny jabbed her pipe stem perilously close to Race's nose. "Race? Vat the diebil kinda name izzat?"

Race ran a finger between his collar and his neck. "A family name."

"Unt vat kinda race choo runnin'? That's my grandbaby choo vere tight holdin' on that horse o' yourn."

A sheen appeared on Race's forehead. "Oh, no, ma'am, nothing of that sort. Her horse was spooked by a skunk . . . turned the wagon over on its side. I—I couldn't leave Dulcie on the roadside, injured as she is."

Dulcie bit her lower lip to keep from laughing.

After a long silence, Granny narrowed her eyes. "Couldn't ya've hitched yer horse to th' buckboard? Choo vouldn't've had her so much to handle."

Red circles blazed on Race's prominent cheekbones. "The wheel," he blurted out, then turned beseeching eyes toward Dulcie.

But was she ready to show him mercy? she wondered, remembering the rasp of his hand against her stockinged leg. She shivered deliciously, despite herself. No, he could sizzle in the heat of his conscience for a moment or two more.

"Vat wheel you speakin' 'bout?"

Race stretched his neck, and again sent a finger around his collar. "The wagon wheel, ma'am—"

The pipe again waved near Race's nose. "No more o' that 'ma'am' stuff. Call me Granny K. Ever'body does."

"Ah—yes. Fine—uh, Granny K."

"Vat wheel? Or didja think I'd *fergess* it?"

"No, no, ma—Granny K! The wagon wheel broke when the horse took off. I couldn't leave Dulcie on the roadside."

Granny lipped the stem end of her pipe. After a series of sharp puffs, she let out a curling swirl of smoke that then hovered over her steel-gray head. Dulcie glanced back and forth between the two.

Oh, dear. Race looked to be growing more and more uncomfortable under Granny's scrutiny. And he had been a gentleman. Most of the time, he had.

And he was so strong . . . and handsome . . . and his touch . . .

From beyond her pleasant distraction, Dulcie heard Granny mumble something under her breath. Sounded just like one of her Pow-Wow spells, one that invoked supernatural help or protection. Then the old rascal laughed again and winked at Dulcie; it seemed Race had passed some sort of test.

Heading toward the house, Granny said, "Come on in. Ve're havin' Dulcie's best stew fer dinner. Ve got plenty fer big fella like you. Let me fetch ya some tomaty juice. Choo kin vash off some a' that skunk.''

With difficulty, Granny started up the porch steps. Before Dulcie could even take the first one, Race intercepted and closed the distance to grasp Granny's bony elbow, steadying her on her way up.

Hmmm . . . And in spite of Granny's antics. A gentleman after all.

Race followed the two women inside. At first his eyes had trouble with the muted indoor light. Soon, however, he adjusted and began to study his surroundings. A small parlor was to his right; a staircase led upstairs at his left. He stepped into the parlor and caught the scent of flowers before noticing the vase full of red and white roses on the mantel.

A wide forest-green settee sat under the front window. A small table nearby held a cloth-shaded, prism-bedecked lamp. A spindly chair with a wine-red heart-shaped back came next, and Race made a point to remember to avoid it altogether. He'd hate to break such a delicate piece of furniture with his large frame.

Leaded stained glass in the small hexagonal window above a gilt-trimmed antique spinet caught the rays of the summer sun, turning them into puddles of ruby, sapphire, topaz, and emerald. Lace festooned the other window, and the delicate white webbing of antimacassars frosted every conceivable surface.

From somewhere in back of the room, Granny called out. ''Choo hungry?''

Race's stomach grumbled. ''I'll say!''

''Come on in here *instanter*. Ve nothin' fancy have, but last time I looked, there vas plenty enough. Vash up here in the kitchen.''

Race followed the sound of the raspy voice, keeping an eye on Dulcie, who still limped a bit. By now his curiosity was getting the better of him. As beautiful and enchanting as Dulcie was, her eccentric grandmother added a dose of the unpredictable to the occasion. And the grandmother? He could well understand her caution when it came to a beauty like Dulcie. There were men out there who'd think nothing of taking advantage of her. But Race wasn't like that.

Oh, he appreciated feminine beauty as much as the next fellow, and Dulcie's leg had certainly been a delight to check for further injuries. . . .

He slipped his index finger inside his collar again and gave the celluloid-stiffened contraption another loosening tug. He cast a wary look around, feeling all knobby-kneed and of elephantine proportions, hoping his long limbs didn't topple over any of the bric-a-brac that littered curios, furniture, and shelves.

Walking through it, Race observed that the cluttered, overdone elegance of the parlor didn't seem to match either of the home's two residents. Dulcie's blue dress looked fairly plain and serviceable, and Granny K's garb . . . well, Granny K wore men's clothes. Neither woman appeared sufficiently extravagant for him to think she was the one who'd chosen the furnishings.

As Race proceeded to the dining room, he noticed that it too matched the parlor. In that quick glance he had the impression of ornate dark furniture and a sparkling chandelier.

In the kitchen, Granny stood by the cast-iron stove, her back to Race. "That's better! Choo kin sit my table down, unt tell me about yersel'."

Great. Just exactly what would she want to know now? Race wondered. Nothing seemed too farfetched for the outspoken woman. But aside from causing him embarrassment, there didn't seem to be too much harm in Granny K.

When she turned, however, Race felt his stomach crash to his toes. In her arms, the old woman cradled a shotgun, muzzle aimed right at Race's privates.

"Wait!" he cried. How in hell had he landed in this madhouse?

"Oh, Granny," said Dulcie with a tired sigh. "Put that thing away! Poor man doesn't even know you're all bark and no bite."

"Ain't no such thing! If I don't like vat I hear, and I kenn he's still after free milk, I'll help the vemen of Lancaster County and cut 'im down to size!"

"You have it all wrong—"

"It wasn't at all like—"

Dulcie and Race stopped speaking and glared at each other, then started again.

"Me first! She's threatening my—"

"I'll go! I know her better—"

Suddenly Granny turned and stomped to the kitchen door, opened it, and pulled the trigger. The shot rang louder than anything Race had ever heard, certainly louder than anything he hoped to hear again in his long, healthy existence. As his ears rang with the echoes of the shot, he fell silent. Dulcie had nothing more to say.

Granny patted her gun and smiled. "Much *besser*! Go on, vash yer hands."

Race took a cautious step forward. He understood her message. She meant business. But was he safe? He hadn't done anything . . . much. Touching Dulcie's leg surely wasn't worth dying for. Was it?

Could he get past the old woman and out that kitchen door after washing up? He had to get out of here.

As he approached, he saw Dulcie reach for Granny and confiscate the aged imp's toy. Then she plucked the corncob pipe from behind Granny's ear. "Here! Go back to this foul old thing," she said, shaking her head. "At least you can't maim anyone with a pipe and tobacco."

"Y'ain't tried Herbert Miller's tobaky yit!"

"And I swear on Maman's Bible that I never will."

Race smiled, a rather weak and wobbly excuse for a smile, but at least he could feel some relief. And just in case Granny availed herself of a long knife or some other weapon, he went and did as she'd ordered, washing his hands at the chipped white porcelain sink with what looked and smelled like smashed tomatoes. He then rinsed with clear water, and dried his hands on the towel Dulcie gave him. Leaning close, he whispered, "Thank you for saving my—"

"Shhh!" Dulcie hissed, her cheeks heating hotter than the sun outside.

Race leaned closer, and Dulcie caught a whiff of some citrusy scent mixed with the lingering miasma of skunk. "I was going to say 'skin,' " he said with a mischievous wink.

Dulcie's earlobes grew hot. "Never mind. Just don't set her off again. Answer her questions, eat your stew, and before you know it, you'll be back in Lancaster."

"We'll see if she goes that easy on me." Now that the gun was safely hidden who-knew-where, Race could almost see the humor in the actions of the protective, albeit drastically so, grandmother. Almost.

Dulcie's smile proclaimed years of experience, as she'd said, with her grandmother. "She'll play off whatever you give her," she added.

"Unt she ain't deaf yit!"

Race smiled.

Dulcie sighed.

Granny ladled stew.

Outside, Old Molly neighed and stuck her muzzle through the curtains on the kitchen window. As she thought of tend-ing to Molly despite her sore ankle, Dulcie scowled.

"Now, you behave yourself, Granny, while I see to Molly." With a final, stern look at her grandmother, Dulcie started toward the door. Her ankle, however, had other plans. It buckled, and had it not been for Race's immediate rescue, she would have fallen at his feet. "I'm so sorry," she said. "I seem to do nothing but require assistance."

Race helped her to a chair at the table. "And I'm glad to do the honors. What should I do for your horse?"

"Oh, dear. You really don't have to bother. I suspect she'll see herself into her shed. She's never been known for skipping meals."

"But you'll need help to settle her with water and feed. Let me at least do that for you."

At his words, Dulcie caught Granny's frown deepening. "Yes, yes," she hurried to say. Granny settled back and continued serving stew.

While Race was gone, Dulcie begged Granny to stop her fooling. "He's really a nice man, and he never did anything improper."

Granny waved her pipe. "Saw 'im holding choo on 'is lap. I'd say that's bein' too familiar."

"How else would he have gotten me home?"

"Don' know, don' care. He vas touchin' unt smilin'. Now vat's he next gonna do? Take ya behind a barn someveres?"

Dulcie rolled her eyes heavenward, praying for added patience and assistance. "We don't have a barn, Granny. And we'll probably never see him again after today. Especially after you turned your shotgun on him."

Granny cackled. "Skeered 'im goot, didn't I?"

"And who wouldn't you have?"

Granny turned her faded blue gaze on Dulcie. Narrowing those tired old eyes, she peered at her, and Dulcie felt as if nothing in her heart or her mind or her soul remained her own.

"Hush, now, Dulcie-girl," Granny said in a rare, soothing tone. "I'm not all *ferhoodled* yit. I may be old, unt I may be tired, but I'm more'n a little *bissel* prudent. I saw 'is eyes on ya. An' I saw yours on 'im. I vanta see vat 'e's made of. Think he'll come back ven 'e's mit Ol' Moll done?"

Dulcie held her breath. It never would have occurred to her to think Race might bolt once given the chance. Surely he wouldn't sneak away. Not without a proper farewell and thank-you, another chance to capture his face in her memory.

Moments later, when the kitchen door swung open, Dulcie let her breath out in relief. And pleasure. She was glad for another opportunity to speak with him. Even if later, when he returned home, he forgot all about the country girl with the cowardly horse and the crazy grandmother.

And she was glad for the pleasure of his company during the meal. She fervently hoped that for the rest of his visit the focus remained on the food and not the events of the morning. Or any other farfetched topic her grandmother thought to test him with.

Granny obliged. As she was often fond of doing, she regaled Race with reams of Pennsylvania German jokes and country anecdotes, sprinkling her tales with the oftentimes hilarious words peculiar to the people of the Lancaster area.

After Dulcie served Race a thick wedge of buttermilk pie, she went for the pot filled with fragrant coffee. "Cream, sugar?" she asked.

As the meal ended, talk turned to plans for the buckboard, still back where it was felled by the skunk. "I'll send one of the Miller boys with Old Molly after the wagon," said Dulcie. "If he takes his time, he should be able to bring it back to Everleigh. Ev Draubaugh can fix a wheel as well as he can shoe a horse.''

Granny's penetrating gaze landed on Dulcie. ''Vere did this happen?''

Dulcie knew what was coming, but saw no way to avoid it. ''On the old road to Lancaster, down by Joseph Hochstetter's lower pasture.''

''Hell a'kitin'! Vy d'ya do somethin' so stoopid fer, Dulcie-girl? Choo shoulda taken th' Columbia Pike.''

Patience, please, Dulcie prayed. ''There's less traffic that way. I didn't want Molly rattled by other horses. My samples could get damaged bouncing on that old wagon. They would never have looked right.''

''Ain't looks vat's gonna sell 'em! It's the taste vat'll do it. 'Sides, I figger they got slung out ven Moll ran.''

Dulcie nodded, then went on to further explain her position. As the two women debated, Race's thoughts wandered. Love clearly cemented the relationship between the two. And despite Granny's peppery comments, it was obvious they regarded each other with great respect, as well. He took it all in and wished he'd had the opportunity to experience something similar in his own home. But, no. His family was far more ''proper''; they didn't go head to head on issues that mattered to them, trivial or otherwise.

What freedom the two women had with each other! Race smiled wistfully.

A glance out the kitchen window startled him. He pulled out his pocket watch, and the gold hands of the timepiece verified what he had seen. It was late. Sunset drew close. He should have left hours ago. He'd had a duty to perform, one he'd gleefully cast aside in favor of pursuing his instant attraction to Dulcie. A duty he hadn't wanted to carry out in the first place. One he'd had dumped in his hands as a result of his father's entrepreneurial naïveté.

But it was clearly too late to seek the Everleigh confectioner, that Kramer woman, tonight. He'd have to speak with Milton Hershey and explain what had happened. Maybe he'd be able to persuade the successful candy manufacturer to seek another representative for this particular affair. Someone with far less personal interest in it than Race.

He slipped his watch back in its pocket and cleared his throat. "Ladies, if you'll excuse me for interrupting . . . I really must be on my way. Time has flown, and I should leave. It's been a pleasure—"

"Not all, it ain't!" Granny's words were punctuated with cackles. "My gun at yer—"

"Granny!" cried Dulcie.

"Madam!" echoed Race.

"There's that 'ma'am' horse *misht* agin! I'm Granny K, I said. Unt vat's a matter now? Cain't call things vat they are?"

"For goodness' sake, Granny! You know better," Dulcie said, limping to her grandmother's side and handing the rascal her jug. "Here, take this and your pipe out back. I'd say you've done enough today. You've earned yourself a rest."

"Ach! I'll git all the rest a body needs soon enough. But I'm a mite dry, all right." She popped the fat cork that sealed the crock, swung it over her shoulder, and took a long drink. She then offered some to Race.

He refused.

Granny shrugged. " 'S yer loss." The old eyes crinkled at the corners. The wrinkles on her brow looped even lower. She studied Race for long seconds.

The back of his neck began to itch.

She waggled her pipe stem toward him. "Don't choo get friendly like sayin' my Dulcie g'bye. Granny'll know vat youns up to."

Race swallowed hard. "Yes, ma'am—er, no! I mean—

Hell, I don't know what I mean!'' Then he flushed and turned to Dulcie. ''I beg your pardon. My language . . .''

He allowed the apology to drift off when he caught sight of the laughter dancing in Dulcie's blue eyes. He shook his head. He shrugged. He had no notion quite how, but that sprightly old woman had filled him with the fear of God. Although he'd been wondering about it since he'd first glimpsed Dulcie's rosy mouth, he knew that no matter how alone they were during their farewell, he wouldn't steal a taste.

The memory of that gun barrel aimed between his legs cooled any ardor he might have entertained. And more's the pity, he thought, stealing another glimpse of the plump lips that were smiling all too knowingly at him.

Race lifted his hands in surrender. ''I'll be a model of propriety, ma—*Granny K*.''

Opening the door, Granny chuckled wickedly once more. ''I'll say ya vill! Ain't a dumb hair on yer head, is there?''

''Not a one,'' he answered with humor.

In the doorway Granny turned. ''He'll do, Dulcie-girl. This one'll do jist fine!''

❖ *3* ❖

As HE THOUGHT over his eventful day, Race let Zephyr set a comfortable pace back to Lancaster. To be sure, the morning had ended on a sour note. He'd been summoned to that uncomfortable meeting with Father and Milton Hershey, and the two friends had roped Race into handling a delicate negotiation for the wealthy candy maker.

Then, on his way to Everleigh to find the confectioner—that Mignone Kramer woman—fate, in the form of a smelly skunk, had intervened. Remembering, Race laughed out loud. Hard to believe something so foul as a polecat could have led him to the most enchanting young lady he'd ever met.

From the pleasant province of his thoughts, Race took note of the sights and sounds of the season. To the tune of summer crickets, fireflies danced down the road. As dusk deepened, the rolling green of the fields and pastures turned dark, somber, as if to say that today's ball was over and the musicians and dancers should return home. But the crickets didn't mind the night, and the fireflies provided their own illumination. Summer waltzed onward.

Race's spirits seemed to dance just as the creatures of the countryside did. Just for the joy of it, for the pleasure of having met a delightful young lady who'd captured his imagination, his thoughts, his interest. Better yet, it seemed he'd struck her the same way, too.

Although he was on his way home now, Race knew he'd return to seek out Miss Dulcie . . . what was her last name, anyway?

Mentally thumbing back through their various conversations, Race found a void where Dulcie's full name should have been. Had her presence addled him so much that he'd failed to ask her name?

Never before had this happened to him. He'd always been a methodical man, knowing that bit by bit, detail by detail, an attorney built a case, making certain that all pertinent information was at his fingertips. Such attention to particulars came naturally to him, and he'd learned to use it to his advantage in his chosen field of expertise. That he should forget to ask something so elementary as Dulcie's name, especially since she'd so appealed to him, was uncharacteristic and daunting, to say the least.

Well, he knew where she lived. And he would have to return to Everleigh to find the lady confectioner—unless he found a way to persuade Milton Hershey to do his own negotiating. At least Race could console himself with the exciting prospect of seeing Dulcie again, even if he was forced to carry out Mr. Hershey's bidding.

But tonight was a different story altogether. He still had to report the unproductive outcome of his trip. Letting the reins slacken further, Race allowed Zephyr to slow his pace yet again. He'd speak with Milton Hershey soon enough.

As Race strode into the vestibule of the Langstons' fine brick residence, he removed his ruined summer suit jacket. Dust, grass, mud, and some thick brown stuff had stained the cream-colored linen. He paused and looked at himself in the cherry-framed mirror at the base of the sweeping stairway. When he saw his loosened tie hanging askew, the dirty smudges on his face, and the mussed brown curls on his head, he laughed.

Running a careless hand through his hair, he caught the gleam of excitement in his eyes. Yep! It sure looked as if Miss Dulcie . . . Oh, hell! What the devil was her name?

No matter. He'd make sure that was the first thing he asked her when he saw her again. And he would make certain *that* happened soon.

As he began to go up the stairs, the library door opened. He muttered a curse under his breath. As he'd feared, Horace was waiting for him. "Hello, Father," Race said, slinging his jacket over one shoulder.

"Son." With deliberate motions, Horace Langston III stood aside to usher Race into the room. "Well?"

Race dropped the jacket on a cordovan chair near the door. "Not much to tell, sir."

"Not much? What does 'not much' mean?"

Unable to meet those worried, questioning eyes, Race turned away. Absently he sat on his jacket, then struggled to pull it out from under him. "What I mean is . . . well, let me tell you just how complicated it was to find Mignone Kramer."

Father's eyebrows furrowed. "How can that be? I was under the impression that Everleigh was little more than a cluster of homes on various crisscrossing country lanes. Surely there aren't so many residents there that you couldn't track her down?"

Race again tried to get comfortable. "Yes, Everleigh is just as you say. Something happened on my way there however, . . ." His voice trailed off, but as soon as he noticed the sudden alarm on his father's face, Race hurried to relate the afternoon's events.

"As I'm sure you can now see," he said in summation, "I couldn't just leave that young woman on the roadside. She was injured. Or did I already tell you that?"

With an exasperated sigh, Horace began to pace. "You have provided me with every minor detail regarding the buckboard, the young lady with her shiny blond hair, her tearing eyes, her swollen ankle, and I really don't want to hear another word about the skunk. I can smell it from here." Horace's voice grew louder, worry creasing his temples. "Did you carry out Milton's business?"

After another twitch in search of comfort, and taking the time to fortify himself with a deep, calming breath, Race answered obliquely and on a faltering note. "I—I had to help the young lady with her horse once I took her home."

"Horse? What horse?"

"Why, the horse that panicked and overturned the wagon. It eventually returned home, and had to be fed and watered. I couldn't just leave Dulcie to tend to the horse, her leg injured and all. Besides, her grandmother is old and walks with a limp. It was—it was— Oh, yes! It was my Christian duty to assist two ladies in need."

Horace scrubbed his forehead with the knuckles of his right hand. "Son," he said in a strained, subdued voice, "I have *never* heard you dither so. This young lady must be something quite remarkable. She has turned you into a babbling, lovelorn swain."

Walking around the enormous oak desk, Horace sat in his well-worn leather chair. Leaning forward, he took his pipe from its stand, struck a match, and brought fire to the aromatic bits in the bowl. Moments later, the essence of fine, brandy-flavored tobacco filled the room.

With the pipe in his hand, Horace released a curl of smoke. Remembering Granny K, Race struggled to smother a chuckle. Her "tobaky," as she'd called it, would never scent a room like this rich blend did, but she clearly got as much pleasure from her crude mix as his father did from his.

"Race!"

"Yes, sir!"

"Nothing in this disaster is even remotely humorous. And I expect you to handle yourself in a suitably circumspect manner. Now, I want an answer, and none of your vague evasions this time. A simple yes or no will suffice. Did you or did you not obtain Mignone Kramer's signature on the contract you wrote for Milton this morning?"

Swallowing hard, Race shook his head. "No, sir. And I realize that this matter is nothing to laugh at. I just remembered an amusing moment from this afternoon." At his father's progressively stormier expression, Race tried to reassure him. "Look, I'll contact Mr. Hershey right away. I can explain what happened, and perhaps even persuade him to stop insisting that I—personally—handle this negotiation. I'd much rather he take care of his own contract."

"And I'd prefer never having had to appeal to Milton in the first place, but personal preferences mean nothing now. As we discussed earlier today, this is a matter of great importance. To me, as well as to Milton. It's not unusual for him to want an attorney to protect his interests during delicate bargaining. And furthermore, you must know how desperate my situation is. Should your grandfather Richter learn of the failed venture . . ."

As his father's voice wavered then faded, Race narrowed his gaze. "How much money are we talking about, Father?"

"The amount is immaterial to—"

"The amount is most certainly *not* immaterial. I deserve to know what I'm buying with my services."

"Thousands, son, thousands."

"I assumed it would be a large amount, Father. *Precisely* how large is it?"

Horace ran his hand over his mouth, muffling his response. "Ffyetsansdhls."

"Fifty thousand dollars! Why would you think you could take fifty thousand dollars' worth of profit from Grandfather Richter's store, invest it in some cockamamie scheme, and not have him notice if the deal went sour? Are you mad?"

Red-faced, Horace cleared his throat and wiped his damp brow with a soggy-looking handkerchief. "Show some respect here, Race. I'm still your father, and a failed business venture doesn't permit you to behave disrespectfully."

"I meant no disrespect, sir. I'm just stunned." Race shook his head, still trying to understand his father's motives. "Why? Why did you do this?"

Horace strode to the window that in daytime overlooked his wife's rose garden. Over his father's shoulder, Race saw the older man's reflection in the glass. Pain scored harsh lines around his mouth.

"Pride, I guess," Horace said, his voice low, defeat in the tone. "I've spent my life working for your grandfather, and Edward has made no secret of what he thinks of me. After marrying your mother, I felt driven to do his bidding, to support his actions, to manage his empire. I did all this in the hope of changing his opinion of me. With no success, son. And a man's spirit can stifle, he can turn desperate if he's never able to prove himself worthy on his own merits." With a futile wave, Horace turned from the window. "Pride, son. A very shallow reason. One that invariably makes a man a fool."

The slump of his father's shoulders illustrated how devastating this failure was. Race had never seen him look so broken. Horace had always held himself erect, never wavering in his movements, a distinctive confidence underscoring his every word. It was hard to believe it had all been a façade. But that was how it seemed. His father had bared his soul, he'd given Race a rare glimpse inside his heart. He'd revealed the pain he'd felt for so long as a result of his powerful father-in-law's rejection. It was an extraordinary moment, one where Race felt uncomfortably as if he were the parent and Horace the child.

Approaching, he placed an encouraging hand on his father's shoulder. "I understand," he said, and he did. Somewhat. "The only reason I agreed to take on Milton's business was to help you. Even if I can't persuade him to execute his own frivolous negotiation, I'll do what I can on your behalf. It's just that it seems such a waste of time. I'm eager to establish my practice, to find clients. I've studied so long, and now that I'm through, I want to practice law. I don't want to look for some farmwife out in the country. Buying a recipe for chocolate candies seems a ridiculous waste not only of time, but also of those years of study."

The entire ordeal had left a sour taste in his mouth. He'd recently begun acquiring clients. Once he fought—and won—their legal battles, he'd be sure to receive referrals. He could ill afford to squander his time chasing down cooking instructions. Besides, he'd found Dulcie, and he'd rather spend what spare time he had with her.

But his father was his father. And Edward Richter was a most intimidating man. Race couldn't let his father down. "I'll see what I can do with Milton. Perhaps my lawyerly arguments will sway him. It's worth a try."

"I doubt it. Milton is one determined cuss. Honest as they come, and a harder worker I've never known. But he's like a dog with a juicy bone. Once he gets his teeth into something, he's not likely to surrender. Certainly not without a fight."

With a confidence he didn't feel, Race sought to reassure

his father. "I've been known to turn stubborn when there's a need. Seems to me this is one of those times."

With a sigh of obvious relief, Horace clapped him on the back, and without further comment, left the room, leaving Race to contact Milton Hershey on his own. Dread in every step he took, Race approached the telephone on the wall.

Funny, he thought, staring at the contraption. He would never have suspected his father's feelings of failure. Horace had always known just what he wanted, and had always made certain he achieved his goals. As with the telephone, for one thing. Despite the suspicion and alarm voiced by many, Horace had subscribed to the telephone service as soon as it became available in Lancaster, almost twenty years ago. Race could still remember the arguments between his father and grandfather. Horace had contended that the machine was here to stay. Edward Richter had sworn it was no more than a toy, a newfangled whim that would lose favor soon enough. Of course, Horace had been proven right. His decisiveness and instincts regarding commerce had always been on target.

Could the stroke six months ago have damaged some portion of Father's brain? Could that have brought on the urgency that must have fueled the need to invest recklessly? Race hoped not. Dr. Murdoch had assured the family that Horace's stroke had been the mildest he'd ever seen. He was certain that with peaceful rest, his patient would make a full recovery.

Perhaps Father's contact with his own mortality had scared him enough to make a poor judgment. He'd repeatedly proven himself in business during the past thirty years. Hadn't he?

Well, no matter what had motivated Horace's thinking, he had taken action, and the results had been devastating to the tune of fifty thousand dollars. Milton had agreed to help his friend; he would cover the default, not only for the sake of friendship, but to keep Horace from being accused and charged with criminal intent. Fifty thousand dollars represented a monumental level of error. Grandfather Richter's prejudice could get the better of him. He might resort to the police, have Father charged with felonious theft.

Above all else, that possibility had to be avoided. Father's health wouldn't weather such a storm. Race had no alternative but to do whatever it took to safeguard his father's physical well-being.

He squared his shoulders. At least now, at this awkward moment, Race could take advantage of modern technology. Telephoning Milton was preferable to arguing with the older man face-to-face. And this call was bound to become an argument the moment the operator made the connection.

After placing his request, Race fidgeted with a pencil he'd picked up from his father's desk. Not that he expected to write anything, but he was nervous, anxious to end this business. He wanted to put this all behind him, as he had more promising activities with which to fill his time. Like getting to know Dulcie a whole lot better.

Milton's brisk "Hello" interrupted Race's fantasy.

This was it. "Race Langston here, sir. I'm afraid I must report no success on your negotiation. I encountered a mishap and was detained for the better part of the day. After such a delay, I felt it in poor form to try to approach Mrs. Kramer in the evening."

A long silence followed his statement. Race tapped the pencil against the wall. He then twirled it between his fingers. He dropped the instrument. When Mr. Hershey remained silent, Race bent to retrieve the pencil.

"And how do you intend to address that failure?" asked Mr. Hershey.

Jerking upright, Race cracked his forehead against the

wooden telephone cabinet where it protruded at least six inches from the wall. At the stab of pain, he dropped the earpiece, which then hit the wall with a loud report.

A crackling noise came over the swinging receiver, reminding Race of a metronome gone amuck. Milton's irritated voice followed the sounds.

"Sorry, sir," said Race when he'd retrieved the fugitive earpiece. "It couldn't be helped. Today's mishap involved a matter of principle. As to your interests, might I suggest that you use your regular attorney to plead your case in this situa—"

Loud and emphatic rejection of Race's suggestion roared into his ear. Holding the offending gadget away, Race winced as Milton grew more dogged in his arguments.

When Mr. Hershey fell silent, Race ventured, "I understand your wish for privacy in this matter, and I even agree that eliminating potential competition is a sound business practice. What I can't understand is why you're so determined to have *me* do your negotiating."

More crackling came over the line.

More arguments followed, and Race's ear rang still more. "Well, yes, sir, I do appreciate the vote of confidence your insistence on hiring me represents. But surely you can trust your regular attorney. Wyatt Adams is a fine man, and I would trust him with even the most ticklish business. Besides, I've only recently set up practice. Wyatt is far more experienced."

The line fell silent.

Race waited. And waited.

Then, "It's a matter of friendship," came over the telephone. "Your father indeed helped me out at a lean moment, but not before extracting a promise to repay him as soon as my efforts produced results. Which I did. Likewise, I want to help him now. And I, too, expect repayment. At this time, however, I'm not asking for cash. I've decided that availing myself of your services will suffice."

The very same argument the two older men had used on Race earlier in the day. "You already expressed those sentiments—"

"But I obviously failed to impress upon you that I have personal reasons. Don't you feel equal to executing a simple contract of sale? Must I assume that Horace's son isn't a capable attorney? Where are your principles?"

Race's pride was stung. "Of course I'm capable! As far as my integrity, sir, an attorney's honor is everything."

"Well, then . . ."

Race remembered his father's words. *"A man's spirit can stifle, he can turn desperate if he's never able to prove himself worthy on his own merits."* "Mr. Hershey, I'll move heaven and earth to obtain Mignone Kramer's signature on that contract. Her secret chocolate bonbon recipe will be yours in no time."

After Race left, Dulcie helped Granny in the kitchen, but ended up shooing her away. "Now you take yourself to your rocker on the porch. My ankle's not so bad that I can't finish. And here, take your pipe, I certainly don't want it."

"Ever'one gots 'is pleasures. Some's like fancy choclet, me, I like my pipe."

Dulcie laughed. "You don't fool me, Granny! You like chocolate as much as the next person. I caught you stealing some whenever Maman set them out to cool."

Granny chortled. "Unt she alvays pertended she didn't kenn vere to dey'd gone."

The two women exchanged sad looks.

"Ach, Dulcie-girl, I miss yer maman, even mit 'er persnickety Frenchy tastes."

Dulcie swallowed the lump in her throat. "Me, too," she whispered.

The memories flew at Dulcie, and she welcomed them. Yes, Maman had been as fussy as they came. Still, she'd been so cheerful and kind that everyone had accepted her, whimsical tastes and all. And despite the fact that Everleigh was not a center of fashion, the local matrons had consistently strived to follow in Mignone Kramer's footsteps when it came to style.

Since the small white house at the end of Willow Lane retained so much of her mother's spirit, Dulcie was unwilling to weed out the more modish and elaborate adornments that Mignone had considered *de rigueur,* absolute essentials. The constant reminders of her late mother made it seem as if she were still with them.

A tear rolled down Dulcie's cheek. Granny's gnarled finger wiped it away. "Now don'choo fret. Things gonna vork out. They alvays do."

Dulcie shrugged and turned back to the sink. Swishing a cup through sudsy water, she said, "I don't know, Granny. I just wish I'd finished teacher's college before Maman died. She would have loved to see me graduate, and I could have found a position teaching school, just as I always dreamed of doing. But with Maman gone, I have to earn our keep, I haven't the time or the money to finish school. What little money Maman left is mostly gone."

Nodding, Granny struck a match and lit her pipe. "All's gonna vork out. I cast the runes. Unt I kin make 'nother conjuring bag, this one mit cinquefoil for money."

Dulcie's fears had her seeing red. "There! You see? You don't watch what you say. If Race Langston puts two and two together, who knows who'll come around after you. You have to keep your spells and Pow-Wow magic secret.

There are many who won't put up with witches and magical healing.''

"Unt vat izzit I do mit my magic, Dulcie-girl? I helps them vat fer help comes. I give 'em herbs for their aches unt a spell fer their healin'.''

Dulcie sighed tiredly. They'd argued this same point for years. Ever since Dulcie had really listened to the chants her father's mother offered at any sort of need. And no one could miss the herbs hung to dry from the rafters in Granny's room. But not everyone was willing to accept the ways of some of the older Pennsylvania Germans, especially anything relating to the art of Pow-Wow, Hex-Craft.

She returned to her chore. "I know, Granny. I know what you do, why you do it, and even that you feel you must. Go on, go rock in your chair. I'll come keep you company as soon as I'm done here.''

Nodding, Granny sucked on her pipe and took steps toward the front of the house. "Oh! Cain't *fergess* my jug. Give it me, my rheumatiz is me stiff makin'.''

Dulcie scooped up the crock from where Granny had stowed it under the kitchen table. "Here, it feels full. Go on, I'll be right with you.''

Washing the last of the dirty dishes, Dulcie allowed her thoughts to return to the events of the day. And it *had* been a most unusual day. First, she'd risen at the crack of dawn to cook up a batch of Maman's special secret-recipe bonbons. The owner of the store Dulcie hoped to rent wanted to taste her product before committing to lease her the space.

She was certain that with his first taste of the chocolates, Mr. Eby would be happy to do business with her. And Dulcie was at wit's end. She saw no other means of supporting Granny and herself. Certainly not here, so close to Lancaster and York. Many qualified, trained teachers were available.

Although she could probably find a teaching position out

West, where schoolteachers were needed and qualifications were less rigorously scrutinized, Granny's health was poor. The strain of moving so far and to a place so foreign could easily be the end of the irascible, cantankerous scamp. Having just lost her mother, Dulcie wasn't willing to risk Granny. As eccentric and outspoken as she was, Granny was also loving, generous, caring, Dulcie's only living relative, and she would do anything for the old woman. Surely if Dulcie went into business for herself, it wouldn't pose too great a hardship for Granny K.

Dulcie stood on tiptoe to set the salt-glazed milk pitcher back on the cupboard shelf where it belonged. Yes, selling Maman's marvelous bonbons should prove lucrative. There were many successful businessmen in Lancaster. Their families could well afford the luxury of handmade, French-style candies. Every time Maman had made the delicacies at a friend's request, she'd been well paid for her labors. Dulcie wanted to do the same, only on a greater scale.

She would be following in Maman's footsteps. For the last fourteen years, ever since Papa died, Mignone's design and dressmaking skills had kept the small family fed and housed. Maman had even earned enough to allow Dulcie to pursue her wish to become a teacher.

But now Maman was gone. And her savings were nearly gone, too. It was up to Dulcie to use what she had available to care for Granny and meet her own needs. She couldn't teach without credentials, and she couldn't sew to save herself. The only marketable asset she could bank on was the secret recipe for Maman's bonbons.

As she closed the kitchen window, Dulcie heard Old Molly snuffling in the shed. "And if it weren't for you, you cowardly nag, this morning's batch of candy wouldn't be decorating a pasture halfway to Lancaster."

Oh, just the thought of those beautiful candies, wasted

when the buckboard had overturned, was enough to make Dulcie ill. Worse yet was the memory of Molly trampling them in her escape. Not to mention watching her investment melt into the grass.

Now Dulcie had no alternative but to withdraw another sum from the fast-depleting account at the bank in Columbia, buy more of the costly ingredients, cook up a new batch, and get herself back to Lancaster. All in time to persuade Mr. Eby that she would indeed be a profitable tenant. She dearly wanted the small shop that comprised the vacant half of his storefront building. Mrs. Eby's fancy millinery thrived next door.

Renting from Mr. Eby made good business sense. The shop was situated at the north end of Queen Street, near the railroad station. Although it was a fairly long walk downtown to Penn Square, the horsecar route ran right out front. Besides, Dulcie should be able to take advantage of the brisk business generated by Mrs. Eby's hat shop. And if those ladies had the money to afford extravagant head coverings, they would surely treat themselves and their loved ones to Mignone Kramer's Sweet Secret Chocolate Bonbons.

Bolstered by her plans, Dulcie hung the kitchen towel to dry from a peg on the wall above the sink. Maybe . . . maybe she would even see Race every once in a while. Although Lancaster was a good-sized town, Queen Street was a major thoroughfare, and coincidences did happen on occasion.

Turning out the gaslight, Dulcie went to the front porch where her grandmother sat rocking. "You know, Granny," she said, "I think you might be right. Everything could very possibly turn out well. I'm prepared to do whatever it takes to make a smashing success of Mignone Kramer's Sweet Secrets Confectionery."

*   *   *

After promising Milton Hershey that he'd do his best to find Mignone Kramer and negotiate the acquisition of the lady's secret chocolate bonbon recipe, Race worked on a file he'd brought home from his office. Hours later, he went to bed. But he didn't go to sleep.

No, his mind kept taking him back to Everleigh, to a tantalizing horse ride, Dulcie in his arms. Although he wasn't crazy about having to buy the confectioner's cooperation for Milton, Race was glad for the excuse to see Dulcie again so soon.

Tomorrow he'd return to Everleigh. He'd obtain Mrs. Kramer's signature on the appropriate line. Then he'd be free to pursue the powerful attraction between Dulcie and him.

❖ 4 ❖

WHEN RACE FINALLY fell asleep, dreams came swiftly, and how sweet they were! Dulcie reigned in the vivid scenes his mind produced during his rest. When he awoke, however, a certain physical discomfort added to his wish to again see the lovely accident victim.

Rushing through his morning bath and the attendant grooming, Race was soon ready to tackle the morning's most urgent business. He was no happier about having to persuade some Pennsylvania German farmwife to sell him her family secret than he'd been before. The whole thing felt . . . oh, inappropriate, somehow. There was, of course, nothing illegal about the job Milton Hershey had hired him to do, but something about it didn't sit right with Race.

Still, he'd given his word. To Mr. Hershey, as well as to his father. Damned if he'd let anything keep him from performing on that contract. With his wide boar-bristle brush, he made certain his naturally undisciplined hair was as docile as he could get it. A critical look in his washstand mirror showed him a well-dressed young businessman with a fanciful sparkle in his eyes.

Dulcie . . .

Yes, he'd take care of the Mignone Kramer matter in no

time. Then he'd have most of the day to spend with the lovely Dulcie. Business came first.

As he again considered his father's current problems, Race's curiosity about the failed venture continued to grow. "What in the world could he have lost fifty thousand dollars on?" he asked his reflection.

But he got no answer. Until his father was willing to divulge additional details of his investment fiasco, Race would have to remain in the dark.

With a spring in his step, he ran down the stairs and, whistling a lively tune, he left the house, pleased to note the perfect summer sky streaked with the occasional wispy strand of clouds. It even smelled good outside today. Not like that clever polecat who'd so cannily played Cupid yesterday.

Thinking of the mischievous mythological infant and his accurate arrows, Race smiled. It was just like a child to bring about wonders using the simplest, most unlikely things.

As he approached the carriage house, he saw the Langstons' driver in the doorway. "Morning, Harris!"

"Good one it is, Race, my boy— Oh, pardon me, *Mr. Langston*." A wink and a grin accompanied the unnecessary apology. Harris had had as much to do with shepherding Race through childhood as his mother had, and far more than his father. "Zephyr is frisky and full of sap today. Make sure you work him good, now."

"Excellent! I've a business matter I want to finalize as soon as possible. Zephyr's good mood will only help."

"Business, son?"

Race's collar grew uncomfortable. "Of course," he hurried to state, stretching his neck. He then mounted his horse in one smooth motion. "I've been retained by father's friend Mr. Hershey."

"Hershey?" asked Harris. "The one making the chewy milk caramels?"

"That very one."

"I heard he made it big with his Lancaster Caramel Company. Who would have thought a body could—with only sugar and milk."

"You have a point there, Harris. But no matter how rich he's become, he hired me, and I have a job to do."

Harris's sharp black eyes narrowed. "Business, you said . . ."

"Yes!"

Silence. Then, "That's not *all* you're planning for today. You've got a woman sparkling in your eyes. I'm too old to be lied to, and I know you too well. There's a woman in there somewhere, and I'd bet she's a looker, too."

Race's shoulders bounced with his sheepish laughter. "I've never been able to fool you. I don't know how you do it, but you always know what I'm up to. You're a good man, Joshua Harris. And I'm lucky to know you."

"Ah, son, the pleasure and good fortune's been mine all these years." A knobby, large-palmed hand surreptitiously caught a drop of moisture before it spilled from the confines of Harris's eye. "Now, get on with that important business you've got with Mr. Hershey. And if he's giving away his candies, I'm always ready to take!"

"Hmmm . . . that's a good idea. I'll stop by the factory and buy a box of the fancy, chocolate-covered ones. I'd bet Dulcie will love them."

"Dulcie, eh?"

"Yes, well . . ."

A deep belly laugh rumbled out. "I knew it, my boy, I knew it!"

"I'd best be on my way, then, since I want to buy flowers, too."

"Flowers *and* candies? Must be something special, that Dulcie of yours."

Race weighed the term. It felt right. "That Dulcie of mine . . ." he echoed. With a smile and a flick of the reins, Race turned his horse toward town. "Yes, that Dulcie of mine is special, all right. Candy-sweet, she is."

Zephyr took off, carrying Race to buy sweets for his sweet.

Anticipation grew in leaps and bounds as Race got nearer to Everleigh. He had the worst urge to set aside the matter of the Kramer woman again and go visit Dulcie. But this was highly uncharacteristic of him. He was used to getting his work out of the way in a swift and efficient manner. That way, when he took time for sport or other entertainment, he had no reason to worry. His conscience had always been well developed, but today it was falling down on its job.

Once on the Columbia Pike, Zephyr overtook various carriages and wagons. He was a fast horse, and Race seemed to be the only one traveling on horseback this day. He wanted to waste no time in reaching Everleigh. He wanted to be done with Milton Hershey's business. Leaning forward, he patted the animal's muscular neck.

His affectionate gesture imperiled the bouquet of pink tea roses he'd bought for Dulcie. He'd had the florist's assistant wrap the delicate blooms in a sheet of waxy green paper, then he'd looped a length of cord around it all and affixed it to his saddle. Unusual, yes, but so far, successful. He should have taken the rig, but he much preferred the freedom he experienced on horseback.

Looking ahead, he smiled. *"Yes!"* He was almost there.

The sight of the first houses on the outskirts—if the smattering of houses at the edge of town could even be called that—of Everleigh had him pressing into Zephyr's sides with his knees, urging him to pick up his already brisk pace. Time to get to work. Soon enough the time for pleasure would arrive.

Where would he find Mignone Kramer? he wondered. With critical eyes, he studied his surroundings. To his right, two plump matrons in voluminous white aprons were exchanging confidences over the boxy cut of a privet hedge. On the front porch of the large stone house to his left, three little girls held dolls in their laps and teacups in their hands. Down the street a ways, a woman lugged a heavy-looking basket to a clothesline strung between two sturdy saplings in her yard. A silky-haired, yellow-colored dog trotted down the street, skirting the neat front lawns.

Race liked what he'd seen on his two visits to Everleigh. The town was peaceful, yet brimming with life. And there was none of the tension he so often sensed in Lancaster. Smiles abounded; frowns seemed rare. At least, none was evident on any of the folk he could see.

But Granny K . . .

Now there was a woman who knew when to laugh and when to frown! Even the challenge she posed for Race was exciting. He'd have to stay on his toes, lest she become irritated again and shoot him in the—

"Hey, mister!"

Cheeks heating, Race looked down at the boy who'd called to him.

"Where you goin'?"

Perhaps this rascal could point him in the right direction. "I'm looking for Mrs. Kramer's house. Do you know where it is?"

The boy screwed up his nose, narrowed his eyes, and drew his white-blond brows together. "Strange," he muttered. Then with a shrug he answered, "Look there. Down

Willow Lane. It's white, with a porch.'' With that, the helpful scamp took off.

Race pulled on the reins, and Zephyr responded. For a
stallion, the animal was a joy to ride, well trained and su-
premely tractable. But once Race found himself on what the
boy had called Willow Lane, his smile faded, and a strange
shiver wormed through his gut. This street eerily resembled
the one he'd taken to and from Dulcie's home last night.
Although he'd thought himself too busy with his thoughts
to retain many of the details of the path he'd followed, he
suddenly recognized a lush weeping willow, and he was
certain he'd passed the house with those fat blue flowers
hiding what leaves the shrub might have.

Race was *awfully* near Dulcie's home.

In fact, up ahead the lane turned to the right and . . . before him stood Dulcie's white house with a porch. Dread
filling his heart, Race turned every which way seeking just
one more white house with a porch. There was none other.

He tried again.

To his right, he saw a tall redbrick house flanked by a
pair of evergreens. A few yards farther back stood a field-
stone cottage with sharply pitched eaves. Across from that
one, behind a luxurious maple, he made out a gray-painted
Queen Anne–style house, heavily embellished with ginger-
bread trim and ornate balustrades. And a blue bungalow
with dormer windows filled the corner. There was no other
white house with a porch on Willow Lane.

''Damn and blast!''

There was only one conclusion to arrive at. Mignone Kramer's house and Dulcie's home were one and the same.
Since he'd never asked Dulcie for her full name, and she'd
introduced her grandmother as simply Granny K, there was
a distinct possibility that one of them could be the woman
he'd been sent to buy out.

But that was too grim a prospect. Race carefully sifted through all sorts of scenarios. Some were too ludicrous to consider. Others, as grim as they were discouraging. The best option he could come up with was the slim chance that Mignone Kramer might be a distant relative of Dulcie's and her grandmother's.

Something deep inside told Race he wasn't about to get so lucky.

Great. In order to help his father, he had to persuade that Mignone woman to sell him her recipe, and Mignone could very well turn out to be Dulcie's middle name. If not hers, then perhaps Granny K's. How many Kramers could there be in a village the size of Everleigh?

And all Race wanted was to get to know the lovely Dulcie.

Reviewing his options again, Race felt the urge to turn Zephyr around and beat a hasty retreat back to Lancaster and Milton Hershey. On the heels of that wish, he felt his attraction to Dulcie wrestle with his need to run. He weighed both wishes, but remained undecided.

His decision was made for him when Dulcie opened the black front door to the Kramer home. *"Damn!"*

Stepping out on the front porch, Dulcie was surprised to find Race just beyond the hitching post outside. Warmth skittered through her body, filling her with a novel form of pleasure. "Race! How nice."

For a moment, Race hesitated. Then Dulcie watched his cheeks redden, and she could have sworn he'd diverted his gaze. It seemed as though he didn't want to look at her, or perhaps he didn't want *her* to see too much in his eyes. How odd!

"Yes, well . . . I . . . um . . . had to return on business, and . . . ah . . . I wanted to see how you were doing. Your ankle! Yes, how your ankle is doing."

Strange. She hadn't noticed him being so tongue-tied with her yesterday. Surely he wasn't now feeling uncomfortable in her presence? With a generous smile, she approached the porch steps. "See? I'm hardly limping anymore. And the swelling has gone down."

Race dropped his gaze to her leg, frowned, then cast a wistful look over his shoulder. He sighed, then faced Dulcie again. A strange expression gave his features a . . . grim cast. *What on earth . . . ?*

Before Dulcie could think of something to say to break the awkward moment, Race swung his leg over Zephyr's rump and dropped heavily to the ground. "I see," he said, then frowned. Yet again. "Tell me, what *is* your name?"

Oh, dear! Had he begun to put two and two together? Was he arriving at the embarrassing connection to the fanciful Spanish *Don* and his lady love? Suddenly Dulcie felt unable to meet Race's piercing brown stare. "Why . . . I told you. My name is Dulcie. As I said yesterday."

Race nodded, but his frown deepened. "Yes, yes. But what is your *family* name? You know, your father's last name."

Dulcie's held-in breath poured out in relief. "Oh, that. Why it's the same as Granny's. She was Papa's mother. I'm Dulcie Kramer."

Dismay narrowed Race's brown eyes. "Is there something wrong with *that*?" she asked, his strange behavior beginning to irritate.

"No, no. Of course not," he said, but his cheeks lost their normal fullness, as if drawn within. "Here," he added, "let's take a seat on the porch."

What on earth was this man up to? she wondered. Perhaps she'd find out sooner if she humored him a bit. She no longer feared him, as she had out on the roadside when he'd tried to assist her. She knew he meant her no harm;

she felt safe with him. But what did she really know of him? Who was this Race Langston? As Granny had remarked, what kind of name *was* Race? And what sort of business had brought him to Everleigh?

Dulcie sat in her favorite hickory-twig rocker, its wide seat feeling more like a welcoming maternal lap than a span of joined branches. She gestured for Race to take Granny's more severe, slat-backed chair.

Silence lengthened the moment. Dulcie sought answers to her questions, but after studying Race's remarkably attractive face, she found herself admiring his fine looks and entertaining a greater curiosity about the man.

"So, what brings you to—"

"Just what *is* Granny's na—"

Both stopped. Both looked away. Barely audible apologies were exchanged. Then Dulcie deferred to her caller.

He nodded. "I realized late last night that I'd forgotten to ask Granny's name. I feel strange calling her Granny."

"Why? That's what everyone calls her. It's what she likes."

"I understand. But I still feel uncomfortable not knowing who I'm speaking with."

"Oh, but that's silly. By asking you to call her Granny, she was letting you know she liked you."

Race's eyebrows drew close. "I suppose I should be flattered, but I find it remarkable that she keeps her identity secret." With narrowing eyes, he went on. "Stranger still is your refusal to reveal her name!"

"Why, that's the most ridiculous thing I've ever heard! Granny's name is no secret because everyone knows her given name is Ermentrude."

Race collapsed into his chair.

"Now what is so devastating about my grandmother's name, sir?" she asked, growing impatient.

A sudden smile sliced away Race's unreadable expression. "Why, nothing, of course. Nothing at all." He crossed his legs, settled into the straight-backed chair, then leapt up. "Before I forget, if you'll excuse me for a moment, there's something I need to get."

Leaving her dumbfounded, he ran to Zephyr, grabbed a conical, green-paper–wrapped bundle with one hand, and a brown-paper parcel with the other. With a spring to his gait, he loped back to the porch.

"Here," he said, extending the packages toward Dulcie, pride streaming from his erect posture, pleasure from his glowing gaze.

Moments later, Dulcie was even more surprised. Within the green paper lay the most exquisite pink tea roses she'd ever seen. "Thank you, Race. I've never seen any more beautiful than these."

Race smiled, dark eyes focused on her face. "I have."

Blushing, she opened the brown bundle. "Oh!"

Race watched Dulcie's pleasure vanish as she studied the chocolate-covered caramels with what seemed like . . . dismay. Or was it perhaps disappointment? "What is it?" he asked. "Don't you like caramels? Chocolate?"

With a sharp bob of her head, she turned her beautiful blue eyes to meet his own. "No, no. I . . . I adore chocolate, and caramels are wonderful."

Race felt relief. That soon changed to concern, however, since Dulcie's expression continued to reflect worry. "Does your ankle hurt? Has something happened to Granny? Your crazy horse?"

A faint smile tipped the corners of her lips. "I must agree with you. Old Molly is a strange one. I'm amazed by your stallion. He's so obedient, so calm."

Race cast a glance at Zephyr. "He's used to me. His dam was my mother's favorite mount."

"Was?"

"Mm-hmm. She died this past winter. It's especially nice to have her firstborn." How had they gotten to discussing Zephyr? Race loved his gentlemanly beast, but this wasn't getting him any closer to Dulcie, much less Mignone Kramer. "Have a chocolate caramel. Go ahead, do."

Dulcie opened the box of elegant caramels, then proceeded to study the treats. After a period of scrutiny, she lifted the fancy box, peered at the back, eyed the lid inside and out, then looked again at Race. "Are these from the Lancaster Caramel Company? Milton Hershey's company?"

Race nearly groaned. Seemed he couldn't escape the man! "The one and only. Why do you ask?"

Dulcie's gaze flew back to the candies, her cheeks warming to a rosy flush. "Oh, nothing," she said vaguely. "No reason . . ."

Damn and blast! She was behaving in a most peculiar manner. True, he had just met her. Yesterday, in fact. But whereas most people ate candies, she merely stared and glared at the damn things. That odd sensation Race had felt yesterday around the eccentric Granny K was back, raising the hairs on the nape of his neck. These Kramer women were most unusual. Would the elusive Mignone prove to be the same?

One thing was certain: Milton Hershey and his foolish contract refused to let Race pursue his own interests. Instead of spending the day trying to figure out why Dulcie was so different from any other woman he'd ever met, Race felt guilty because he still hadn't carried out Milton's bidding.

And there was no better time than the present to do so, he thought. "Dulcie? Do you know a—"

"Vell, light my vhiskers unt tan my hide! If it ain't Mr. Race agin." A flag of smoke rippling in her wake, Granny popped out the door and swooped down on the two on the porch.

And damn again! "Hello, Mrs.—"

"Fer heav'n sakes," Granny yelped, waving the smoking bowl of her pipe dangerously close to Race's nose. He backed away in a hurry.

"I tol'choo yeste'dy ta call me Granny like ever'one else do. Vat I gotta do fer to remind you?"

"I'm sorry. I . . . forgot."

"Bad memory, eh? Vere choo last night reading?"

"For a while," Race said.

"Ya musta left last night a book open. If ya vant to 'member, ya keep closed the book. Unt put it yer pillow under."

Book? What book? "Excuse me?"

"Ja. That's how to remember. 'Speshly vat choo read."

Dulcie stood. "Oh, Granny, Race doesn't know about your stories and superstitions. He's from Lancaster."

Granny stuffed the mouthpiece of her pipe between her teeth, puffed a couple of times, and studied Race. "Looks like other men ta me. He gonna 'member or *fergess* same's Dutch man."

"Yes, of course he is. But he's never heard those stories of yours."

"Vat stories? I tell 'im vat to do fer to 'member. Not a story." Granny stepped toward Race and peered up at him. "D'you vant stories fer to hear? D'you vant again dinner mit us eat'n?"

Before giving him a chance to answer, Granny spied the chocolate-covered caramels and the flowers. "Choc'let! Flowers! I tol'choo, Dulcie-girl, this one vants free milk from my heifer." Turning toward Race again, she waggled bony fingers before his face. "You vant I should git my gun agin?"

"No!" Race cried, his life speeding past him. "I was just leaving—"

"Agin?" asked Granny. "Dulcie-girl, even if he's a *bissel* fast, Race bein' 'is name, dis one's better'n Schlimebaugh. Now don'cha go eatin' the last piece bread, choo don' vant old maid to stay."

"Granny!" Dulcie cried. "First you bring out one of your favorite superstitions. Then you threaten Race—again! Now you're mortifying me—and him—with that old-maid stuff." Placing a hand on Granny's back, she prodded the old lady toward the front door. "Here, take the flowers and go to the kitchen. They should be put in a vase with water."

"Shur, shur. Granny fer *Wasser* go." With a pointed stare at Race, she lifted her chin. "Choo better not light no fire my Dulcie mit."

"N-no!" he stammered.

"Goot!" Turning, she grabbed the roses and went for the door. "De choc'let! I'll take de choc'lets." Holding the box high over her head, Dulcie spun away from her grandmother. "We'll keep the chocolates."

Then sadness etched the aged face. "Ach, Dulcie-girl . . . too bad yer maman ain't yit here. She woulda love de choc'lets. Nobody love choc'let more'n she did. I sure do miss that Mignone of ourn."

Race's stomach turned a flip. Mignone Kramer was Dulcie's late mother?

That meant the owner of the secret recipe was dead! Who had the blasted thing now? Could Mignone have died keeping her secret? And if no one had the recipe, couldn't Race simply drop the entire matter, now that Milton Hershey would no longer need to fear the competition?

"Come on inside, Race," Dulcie said from the doorway. "I have a pair of scissors in the parlor. I'll have the candy box open in no time."

"Mignone Kramer," he said, respectfully following the two women inside. "What an unusual name. And she was . . . Dulcie's mother? My condolences."

Excitement began to grow. He'd have to see what he could learn through some discreet questioning. And while investigating the whereabouts of the bonbon recipe, he would be spending time with the unique Dulcie Kramer. Yes! That was exactly what he would do. Step one was to get himself invited to share another meal with the Kramer women.

❖ 5 ❖

ONCE INSIDE, DULCIE paused in the middle of the parlor. "Thank you," she said, replying to Race's offer of condolences. Although she still felt the sadness of loss, she no longer suffered the agony of grief. "Maman was so alive, so determined to succeed, so busy. Her absence is harder to accept because of the kind of person she was."

Dulcie fell silent. Then, "I miss her all the time. So does Granny."

"I kin talk fer myself. Unt I miss Mignone, too."

Silence again descended. Dulcie noticed the rare tear sliding down Granny's weathered cheek, then felt one of her own fall on her hand. This wouldn't do, she thought. They had a guest. She cleared the lump from her throat. "Like Granny said, Maman loved chocolates."

Race lifted his head in a sharp bob, his eyes homing in on Dulcie's own. "Had a sweet tooth, did she?"

"Um-hmm," Dulcie murmured, surprised by the sudden urgency in Race's voice. Was he going to start acting strange again? Was he going to ask more inane questions? Or would he settle down to talk calmly, the way normal people did?

Time would tell, she thought. "Maman not only loved

them, she made the most luscious chocolate bonbons you've ever tasted.''

Race's forehead creased. Even before he spoke, Dulcie realized he harbored questions. Earlier they'd talked about Granny's name and his horse. Was he about to start discussing something silly like the ingredients in her mother's candies? She decided to wait him out, and didn't have long to wait.

"So she was a confectioner, right?"

"Well, no. Maman was a dressmaker. She just loved to make bonbons."

Race seemed to take a moment to digest that information. He *was* getting strange again. With a quick glance, Dulcie noted that Granny had relit her pipe and was leaning against the jamb in the kitchen doorway. Her pale blue eyes were beamed on Race, seeming to seek what secrets he hid. So she wasn't the only one who found his questions odd.

"I . . . see . . ." he said slowly. "She was a dressmaker by *vocation* and a candy maker by *avocation*."

Dulcie struggled to keep from rolling her eyes. "Not exactly, Race. My mother was a wonderful dressmaker. Her mother, my other grandmother, who died before I was born, was a confectioner in France. She taught my mother a lot about the art, and Maman especially liked making rich chocolate treats. Is that clear enough?"

With a surge of satisfaction she watched a flush appear on Race's neck, then seep upward until his cheeks burned red. "Why of course . . . I mean— Yes, it's clear."

"Do I need my gun agin?" asked Granny from her vantage point. "Or kin I go dinner make?"

"Yes, Granny," Dulcie said in relief, not certain that Granny hadn't yet discovered her latest hiding spot for the shotgun. "Go cook. We'll follow as soon as you call us."

Turning to Race, she asked, "You'll stay for dinner, won't you?"

Like sunshine after a summer storm, Race's face lit up with a smile. "I'd be delighted!"

"Well, then, let's take a seat." Dulcie led her guest to the settee. "I wouldn't recommend you sit anywhere else. I'm afraid Maman's furniture wasn't built to hold a man your size."

"I noticed that last night. I felt like the proverbial bull in a china shop."

"I can promise the sofa will hold you. Some of Granny's sewing-circle cronies probably weigh more than you do, and it's held them for years," she said, perching on the edge of the settee's left side.

Taking a good portion of the right side, Race said, "I'd hate to cause trouble."

Trouble? she thought. He was definitely causing trouble! Why, with that dazzling smile and his glowing eyes, he was wreaking havoc with Dulcie's breathing. Not to mention the rapid patter of her heart!

Dulcie glanced at the roses. Granny had set them on the dining-room table in a cut-glass vase. She looked at the box of chocolate-covered caramels. Granny had already filched one. Seeming not to do so, she dared a quick peek at Race, then dropped her gaze when she spied him studying her.

Dulcie's cheeks heated. A shivery thrill spun through her body. Although at times Race seemed strange, he was attractive and well educated. He also seemed intelligent, and was obviously wealthy. Altogether he was a most flattering suitor for any young lady. And perhaps that was why it seemed so strange that he'd returned, displaying such interest in her, a simple young woman from a tiny town like Everleigh.

Could he possibly be as attracted to her as she was to

him? The thought made her heart again pick up its beat.

"So . . . tell me more about those chocolates of your mother's."

"Again? You're still discussing the bonbons?"

"Why, yes. I too love chocolates. As you can see, I chose chocolate-covered caramels for you since I like them so much. Do tell me about your mother's specialties."

With a frown, Dulcie stood. "Very well. I'll tell you about the chocolates. Maman learned to make candy from her mother. She was also a gifted designer and a fine seamstress. When my papa died, I was only four, and Maman had to find a way to support our small family. Granny has always lived with us."

Feeling nervous because of the way Race kept his gaze fixed upon her, Dulcie began to pace. "On special occasions, she'd make for us the candies Grandmère Suzette taught her to make. Of those, her favorites were the chocolate bonbons. Mine and Granny's, too."

"Hmmm. Did she ever think of opening a confectionery?"

Dulcie spun around at Race's words. She searched his face. Why would he ask *that* particular question? Was there a problem with being a confectioner?

"I don't believe she ever did," she answered cautiously. "She made enough money from her dressmaking. It was sufficient for the three of us. She was even paying for my education. I was studying to become a teacher."

"So, is that what you do?"

"No, I have yet to finish school. I don't have my teaching certificate. Since I'm now responsible for Granny, this house, even Old Molly, I must earn a living. I can no longer pay for school, nor can I take time for classes or studies. At least, not as much as I'd need to."

Sudden alarm filled Race's face. Why? She hadn't said

anything wrong, had she? Before she had a chance to formulate a discreet question, he leaned closer. "So how *do* you earn your living?"

"I don't. Yet." Uncomfortable under his close scrutiny, she inched closer to her end of the settee. "But I've had a splendid idea. And that's why I was on my way to Lancaster yesterday."

"Yesterday," Race repeated, his voice a strained croak. He coughed. "You were headed for Lancaster yesterday because you'd had a splendid idea for earning a living?"

"Yes, but—"

"And what *was* that splendid idea?"

Before answering his question, Dulcie flung a bewildered look in Race's direction. A rather discomforting look, if he did say so himself. He'd obviously been more ham-handed than he'd intended in his questioning. When she continued to study him, that odd, itchy sensation returned to the back of his neck. Although he couldn't say why he felt the way he did, Race was miserably sure he already knew what Dulcie's answer would be.

And he damn well hated it. Damn that Milton Hershey, too!

Dulcie's pert nose rose a couple of inches in the air. "Why, I was on my way to present my future landlord with samples of my wares. I'm going into business. I'm going to become a con—"

"—fectioner," Race moaned, not giving Dulcie the opportunity to finish the damnable word.

"Why, yes! Don't you think that's a marvelous idea? Especially since Maman's secret recipe is my inheritance."

Damn and blast! How could this possibly be happening to him? Dulcie, sweet, sassy Dulcie, was the person he had to finagle the accursed recipe from. The situation could hardly have been worse. "A . . . fine," Race started, then had to gulp, "idea, if I do say so myself."

"Dulcie-girl!" called Granny K from the kitchen. Race exhaled in relief as Dulcie answered the summons.

Now what was he going to do? He'd promised his father he'd do Milton Hershey's bidding. Then he'd turned around and sworn to Milton himself that he'd obtain the recipe in no time at all. All Race had wanted was to finish the transaction in the shortest length of time so he would be free to court the lovely Dulcie Kramer, who then turned out to be none other than the new owner of the blasted recipe!

Just what was he going to do next?

". . . unt den dis one," said Granny, as Race clapped his appreciation of her last joke. She smiled and went on. "A city salesman stopped at a Dutch country inn unt asked the owner: 'Can choo give me a room unt bath?' Says the owner: 'Vell, I can give you room, but you have to take yer own bath.' "

Again, Granny chortled at her own wit. Race couldn't help but join her. Not because her stories were particularly funny, but because she got such joy from the telling.

Race made another production of checking his pocket watch. He'd been doing this for the past half hour, but each time Granny had come up with another story he *had* to listen to. Not only had he taken his midday meal with the two Kramer women, but he'd also spent the afternoon mucking out Old Molly's shed!

Then Granny wouldn't hear of him not staying for supper. After the meal was cleared away, she'd begun regaling them with scraps of folk wisdom and silly jokes. Race hadn't had the heart to stop her. But once again, dark had come, and he was still at the Kramer home. And although this time he'd actually found the owner of the chocolate recipe, he hadn't found a way to broach the subject with her.

"I really must be on my way, ladies. I never expected to bother you so long."

"Ain't no bother. Yer alvays vellcome."

"Thank you, Granny. And Dulcie, your peach pie was as wonderful as the one you served last night."

Dulcie's cheeks pinkened with pleasure. "I'm glad you enjoyed it. And thank you for all the help with Molly."

Wryly, Race glanced at his clothes. Yet another ruined summer suit. This one, as the other one, he considered a fair trade for the time he'd spent with Dulcie. "I know how thankless a horse can be. And you did injure your ankle yesterday."

"It's much better today. You're very kind, although you needn't have done it."

"It was little enough, since I got to enjoy your company. But really, I must be running al—"

Pounding on the front door cut off Race's latest attempt at farewell. In her animated limping gait, Granny trotted to answer the knock. A hefty woman stood on the porch, wringing her hands in obvious distress. Moments later, Granny led the new arrival up the stairs, both women firing forceful bursts of Pennsylvania German dialect. Neither paid the least attention to Race and Dulcie.

"I'll see you out," Dulcie murmured. "Granny will be busy for a while."

On their way to the porch, Race felt pinpricks of excitement in his gut. This would be the first time he'd been alone with Dulcie since he'd brought her home yesterday. He couldn't count the time they'd spent cleaning Molly's shed as time alone together.

Would she shy away if he tried to take her hand? He hoped not. He had an irresistible urge to again feel her warmth, to touch her soft skin, to breathe the faint essence of lilies mingled with her unique, personal scent. He caught her hand in his.

"Oh!" she said on a soft, breathy sigh. But she didn't pull away. In fact, he could swear she returned his firm clasp with her slender hand.

Still in silence, he led her down the porch steps. A full summer moon glowed in the rapidly darkening sky. Crickets chirped, fireflies again waltzed, and from somewhere not too far away, a bullfrog added his rich bass to the other singers of the season's song.

Gathering Dulcie's fingers in his other hand, Race pressed her palm to the crook of his elbow. The motion brought her closer to his side. Turning, he found himself right where he most wanted to be, scant inches away. "It's been a pleasure meeting you, you know."

She turned her luminous eyes toward his, then quickly fanned her lashes down and lowered her head. "For me, too."

Her response came as soft as a whisper, a nervous catch within the faint sound. Race smiled. It seemed she was as affected by his nearness as he was by hers. "Dulcie . . . ?"

"Yes," she answered, still staring at his hand holding hers.

"May I come back again? To see you, of course."

A soft nod was followed by a murmur of assent. But still she kept the beauty of her eyes hidden from his. Race reached a finger to her chin and tilted her face toward the light of the moon.

"Ah, yes," he said, finally able to gauge her response as changing expressions flitted over her features, to see the beauty of her eyes, to guess at her feelings from what he saw mirrored in the blue depths.

Their gazes caught and held. Dulcie nipped her bottom lip with her teeth. Race searched her face to find something, some hint that she would welcome further intimacy. He found nothing but her simple pleasure in his company, her enjoyment of his touch. He found innocence.

The delightful scent of lilies teased his senses, softer than the moonlight's touch. The gentle delicacy of the fragrance he'd already come to know as Dulcie's own filled him, making him more light-headed than fine brandy would. Around him the night swirled in, and darkness surrounded them. The light of the moon flowed down, seeming to light only them and the shrub that offered seclusion. The silver glow illuminated Dulcie's eyes, her blushing cheeks, and caught in the golden strands of her hair.

Race had never seen a more beautiful or enticing woman. He knew he never would. "Sweet," he whispered against her lips.

Then he brushed a fleeting kiss against her mouth. He held his breath. He sighed in relief when he felt her smile against his own. Pressing into the soft flesh of Dulcie's lips, Race relished the silky smoothness of her, her welcoming warmth.

He again tested her lips, breathing in her fragrance, imprinting his mouth with the fullness of her lips. As he'd suspected all along, Dulcie was a heady experience, flinging his most prudent, most cautious thoughts to the winds of emotion. He filled his heart with the sound of her response, her quickened breathing, the vaguest hint of a murmur. . . .

Heaven! he thought. Dulcie was a sweet heaven he'd been fortunate enough to find on earth.

Then, to his surprise, she pressed her lips more fully against his. Dulcie's hesitance, her tentative touch, went far to suggest that this was probably her first kiss. And she wanted more! The knowledge went straight to his heart, inciting the most extraordinary surge of tenderness Race had ever felt.

He kissed her yet again.

When the roiling sensations began to sift through to a very masculine, but most inappropriate part of his anatomy, Race reluctantly released her lips. His breathing was erratic, his cheeks felt hot, his body thrummed with electric impulses, all of them impelling him toward Dulcie.

And yet it was too soon to feel so strongly about a woman he'd just met. This had never happened to him before. Although he'd always appreciated beauty, he was a serious sort, not given to the aimless pursuit of whatever pretty face or enticing shape happened to catch his eye.

It only confirmed what he'd begun to discern from his first meeting with the enchanting Miss Dulcie Kramer. She was . . .

"Intoxicating," he whispered at her temple as he held her in a close embrace. "Like fine wine . . ."

With great reluctance he released her, then noticed her discomfort. The moon lit up her golden hair, but as she kept her head low, all Race could see of her face was the heightened color of a blush at her temples. He again tilted her face to the moon.

"There's nothing to be ashamed of," he said. "Do you regret my kissing you?"

A gentle shake of her head rubbed her chin against his palm.

"Then why won't you open your eyes?"

"I . . . can't."

"Why not?"

Because I might kiss you again, Dulcie thought, fighting to smother inappropriate urges. "I—I just can't."

"Will you open them if I return tomorrow?"

Of course I will! I'm not stupid, after all. Dulcie nodded. The movement loosened his hold on her face, and she quickly took advantage of the moment. She backed away.

If Granny and Mrs. Oberholtz were to come out and find them so close together, even touching, there'd be the devil to pay. Maybe even a round or two of Granny's shotgun would be fired.

"I think," she said hesitantly, "it would be best if you went home. I dare not think what Granny might do if she found you still here with me. . . ."

A quick peek upward revealed Race's face paling in the moonlight.

"The shotgun!" he exclaimed.

"The shotgun!" she echoed.

Turning, he beat a hasty retreat to the shed, where they'd left Zephyr earlier in the day. "I can return tomorrow. Would you like that?"

Dulcie's heart began a faster cadence. Three days in a row! "Of course," she said, following him.

He led Zephyr out by the reins, and she watched his every move. There was a solid elegance in each gesture Race made. Strength was broadcast in the sturdy width of his shoulders, the length of his pace, the firm control he maintained over his horse. His coffee-colored hair shone in the glow of the moon, and his dark eyes flashed his appreciation when he glanced back at her.

"Of course I'd like to see you again," she repeated unnecessarily, but if he could so easily confess his interest in her, she owed him at least the honesty of her feelings.

"Well, then, I will," he said, mounting. "Pleasant dreams, sweetheart."

As he urged Zephyr down the lane, Dulcie mouthed his last word. *Could it be true? Could I possibly become his sweetheart?*

What a wonderful thought! But her more practical side urged her not to get her hopes up too high. After all, he belonged in Lancaster, in elegant surroundings, in the courtroom doing battle against injustice. She, in turn, belonged to the countryside, in a kitchen concocting bonbons, in rural Everleigh.

A world of difference separated her from Race. Only time would tell if they'd be able to overcome it. Still, she had the memory of tonight. Her first kiss. And in the moonlight. From the most fascinating, most attractive man she'd ever met!

When she could no longer see him on the lane, Dulcie wrapped her arms around herself, embracing the sensations Race had brought to life. The excitement of his touch, the warmth of his kiss.

She spun around in circles no more dizzying than what she'd just experienced in Race's arms. She could very easily be falling in love. . . .

She slowed her rotations. She came to a stop.

She *was* falling in love. And it posed a great risk. Could they ever have a future?

Only time would tell.

Once again Race found himself returning home with his spirits crawling through a pit of gloom. This time, the worst had come to pass. Not only was he committed to helping his father, but he'd also promised Milton Hershey he'd get the recipe and obtain the owner's cooperation. In other words, he'd vowed to take Dulcie's inheritance from her.

A bitter taste filled his mouth. He felt like a heel. Especially since he'd found much to like about Dulcie. And his interest had nothing to do with carrying out a business transaction.

No, to Race, Dulcie represented nothing but pleasure and joy.

But how was he to proceed? What could he tell his father? How could he explain his position to Milton Hershey?

After those kisses, Race knew he felt too much for Dulcie to be able to back away. He knew this was special, if for no other reason than because he'd never felt this way before. And he feared that in time his feelings for the lovely Pennsylvania German girl could easily deepen into something more lasting.

A man would be a fool to walk away from feelings of such great promise. Race had never considered himself a fool.

He'd never thought himself a coward, either, but his reluctance to face his father and Milton Hershey was beginning to rankle. Had he lost all confidence in himself? Perhaps Horace had been speaking of Race, too, when he'd commented on the loss of pride frustration gave rise to. If that were the case, was he man enough to pursue a young lady who was full of dreams, of vision for the future?

"Well, damn and blast! Of course I am." Nothing would make him walk away from Dulcie so easily. Nothing.

In order to ensure success, the first thing he had to do upon arriving home was to confide in his father and obtain his help in persuading Milton Hershey to hire himself another representative.

Yes, indeed, Race had a plan he could put in action immediately. He had plans for tomorrow. He had plans for his future. And those plans included his law practice and a beautiful blue-eyed blonde.

Impatient to carry out his plan, Race dismounted Zephyr as soon as they reached the elegant, redbrick Langston home. He'd whistled a tune on his way there, but now his thoughts fought each other for position. First things first, though. "Harris! Curry Zephyr for me, please. I'm in a rush."

"A bit tardy returning from business. Or was it perhaps Dulcie who kept you so late?"

Race chuckled. "Both, believe it or not."

"Anything can happen, given the opportunity. So, I do believe it."

"Good night, then," called Race.

" 'Night."

Climbing the front steps, Race noted that the house was unusually dark. It wasn't much past nine, yet the only lights he could make out seemed to be in the upstairs hallway. "Strange."

In the vestibule, he confirmed what he'd seen outside. The parlor and his father's library were dark; even the kitchen was silent. Had his parents planned an outing for this evening? They would normally have told him, so perhaps something had come up while he'd been in Everleigh with Dulcie.

But Harris hadn't mentioned anything. Whatever it was hadn't called for a vehicle.

Removing his filthy jacket, Race loosened the knot in his tie. Again whistling his merry tune, he took the wide, curving steps two at a time. He felt great! He'd decided on a course of action, and he was on his way to set it in motion. After a quick bath to remove the musk of horse and hay from his skin, he'd go down to wait for Horace. Then, once he had his support, he'd telephone Mr. Hershey and bow out of his plans.

"Race?" His mother's voice came as a surprise. Especially the strain he heard in her tone.

"What's going on here? Why are all the lights out? Is it . . . Father? Again?"

"Yes, and no, son," she said, raising her hand to his cheek. Mother was tall for a woman, but beside Race, she appeared fragile, frightened. He slipped his arm around her shoulders.

"How is he?"

She trembled. "Dr. Murdoch is with him. He requested silence, so I let Maudie and Pearl leave once they finished in the kitchen. He also suggested indirect lighting. But you're right. It's dark. Too dark. I guess I went too far, but there's been little to do, and I felt such a need to *do* something, anything. Even turn out the lights. To help Horace however I could."

Race wrapped his other arm around his mother, offering comfort, as he sought the same for himself. "Was it another str—"

"Hush! Don't even say it. It was only chest pains, but seeing that he's miraculously survived the stroke six months ago, I dared not take any chances."

In her anxiety she'd uttered the dreaded word. And although Race was glad Horace hadn't had another stroke, he couldn't discount the seriousness of his father's condition. Chest pains. His heart.

Fear fighting disappointment and romantic urgings, Race understood that his hope of winning his father's support in refusing Milton Hershey's business would come to naught. Romance was soundly outweighed by the need to keep Horace well.

A peaceful, worry-free recovery was crucial. As apprehensive as Father had been about Grandfather Richter's reaction, should that accursed investment be revealed, Race knew that rehashing the matter would further try his failing health.

He'd have to persuade Mr. Hershey to negotiate his own contract. He would have to appeal to Milton's sense of friendship, his spirit of mercy, in view of Horace's condition. Race would even offer to pay back the sum, regardless of how long it took him to earn it.

Although his feelings for Dulcie had begun to deepen, they would have to be set aside. He had to trust it would only be a temporary setback, for he now knew he could easily fall in love with her.

❖ 6 ❖

SUNSETS SURE LOOKED different through tears, Dulcie thought, sitting on the top porch step, knees hugged to her chest. Especially when you were alone. And you'd been expecting someone. Someone who never showed up.

Despite her own warnings last night, she'd expected Race to keep his word. She'd risen early, and instead of going to the bank in Columbia, as she should have done, she'd taken a bath and washed her hair. Although she'd never been vain, she knew her hair was one of her best assets. Since Race undoubtedly knew women more beautiful, more elegant than Dulcie could ever hope to be, she wanted to present her finer features in their best light.

She'd scarcely eaten all day. Between the hordes of butterflies zipping through her middle, and the fear of missing Race's arrival, she'd forgone all three meals. Granny had scolded, then scolded some more, but she'd finally persuaded Dulcie to eat a chunk of cheese and some fresh-baked bread. After that, her nerves had made her queasy, and she'd remained near the front window all day long.

She'd gotten nothing done. Not that there was much to do around the small house; neither Dulcie nor Granny K made much of a mess, and the house was always presentable. Regardless, she'd dusted the parlor furniture; she'd swept the floral-patterned carpet. She'd polished the wooden banister on the staircase. Most of all, she'd waited for Race.

"Did choo eat de last piece bread?" asked Granny from the doorway.

Startled, Dulcie turned and her feet slipped to the next step down. She swiped her eyes dry. "Oh hush, Granny. I'm disappointed, is all. Here, sit next to me. The porch steps are wide enough for the two of us."

Granny sat and lit her pipe. When the tobacco was burning, she turned to Dulcie. "Voulda been *besser* if de dressed-up pup sat here mit you."

Dulcie managed a soft chuckle.

"Unt I din't shoot his—"

"Granny!"

"Ach, that's more my Dulcie-girl. Choo cain't lose yer spirit. There's some man out dere vat's yours. I don't kenn ven he'll show, but yer cards don't a lonely life show. Unt yer heart line is strong unt deep."

Dulcie sighed. Granny and her magic. The tarot, the runes, and Dulcie's own hand provided Granny with reams of information about the future. Unfortunately, nothing she'd divined for Dulcie had ever come to pass. Yet. It was a long time since Dulcie had given credit to any of Granny's predictions.

Granny, of course, repeated over and over that Dulcie's life was to be a long, fruitful, and happy one. As if a doting grandmother would ever envision anything less for her grandchild!

"I wish you wouldn't talk about your magic," she said. "It's dangerous. Who knows what the wrong people would do if they learned you practice Hex-Craft."

"Don' know, don' care. If I kin help, I vill."

"I know that. And so does everyone who's known you

for a long time. But I would rather you hadn't brought up your supernatural interests when Race was here.''

''Ach! He din't kenn vat I vas talkin'. 'Sides, he never came back today. He doesn't care vat I do.''

''Yes, well, I *do* care what you do, especially if your actions bring trouble to you. I don't need to tell you about witch hunts. You know well enough.''

Granny expelled a prodigious cloud of smoke. ''Dulcie-girl, I jist pray unt give herbs vat make people *besser.* Vat's wrong mit dat?''

''Nothing. So long as the people who know you're doing it know that. Otherwise, some zealot could bring the law down on your head.''

''Don'cha vorry 'bout me. Vorry 'bout yerself. Vat ya gonna do 'bout the choc'lets?''

Just the mention of the bonbons brought back the strange conversation she and Race had had the day before. Had he ever been acting odd! Between his questions and moans and grimaces, one would have thought they'd been debating some political point. Besides, who could be *that* interested in candy? She was, because she planned to earn a living producing bonbons, but he was a lawyer. No matter how sweet a tooth a lawyer had, few probably ever thought about the making of candy, much less the person who made them. ''I'm going to Columbia tomorrow. I need money for ingredients. Then I'll make another batch and take it to Mr. Eby. I mean to rent that store of his.''

''Ye're determined?''

''Of course,'' Dulcie answered. She should never have let herself forget her goal just because she'd met a handsome, interesting, intelligent, fascinating— No! She would *not* waste any more time on Race Langston. ''Perhaps it's just as well he didn't come.''

''Vhy?''

With a sigh, Dulcie stood. She began to pace the length of the porch, trying to put her feelings into words. "Because I'm me, and he is he—"

"Unt sounds like a donkey heein' ta me. Donkeys ain't so smart. What choo said ain't neither."

"Oh, Granny, stop it! I'm not looking for a suitor. I'm too busy going into business. I don't have time to waste being called on." *Liar,* her conscience cried. *You were happy enough to wait all day for him.*

"An' if he back comes, you'll turn 'im avay?"

"Of course."

"Spit three times into the fire, Dulcie-girl, yer tellin' lies."

"No I'm not! I will certainly send Race Langston packing if he ever shows his face here again."

"Unt I'll keep my gun ready."

"Granny—"

"Now don'choo 'Granny' me. I be yer *Grossmutter,* and he hurt choo. Ain't givin' 'im another chance."

"You really found the gun?"

"Alvays do."

For a moment Dulcie entertained the thought of finding another hiding place for Granny's beloved shotgun. But when she caught sight of the stubborn glint in her grandmother's eyes, she realized that no matter where she hid the gun, Granny would always find it. She had her ways. To Granny, that gun meant security. It meant protection. And whether Dulcie liked it or not, she would always be what Granny most doggedly protected.

Maybe it would feel good watching Granny scare Race again. Maybe she would feel somewhat vindicated.

But for that to happen, Race still had to take the first step. He'd have to come call on Dulcie.

*   *   *

Early the next morning, Dulcie rose, went through the motions of her daily ablutions, and dressed in her most serious-looking clothes. She figured the navy blue serge skirt and her crisp white blouse with leg-o'-mutton sleeves would present a singularly sober image to Mr. Oberholtz, the banker. More than anything, she wanted to look responsible, trustworthy, and as mature as possible.

But the mature look continued to elude her, no matter what she tried. It probably had to do with her modest height, her blue eyes, and her curling blond hair. Since there was nothing she could do to change either her height or her eye color, she concentrated her efforts on taming her hair. Using a generous scoop of an odorous pomade, she wrinkled her nose and slicked her hair back into a severe knot at the base of her head. With firm motions, she anchored the bun with a multitude of hairpins, then ran her hands over the unattractive hairstyle.

If Race had seen her looking like this, they wouldn't have needed Granny's gun to chase him away! "Goodness, Dulcie," she said to her reflection in the washstand mirror, "you really look frightening. Prissy, bug-eyed, and all."

Without wasting another second, she ran downstairs, donned a plain navy felt hat, then hitched Molly to the repaired buckboard. In no time she reached Columbia.

"Good morning, Mr. Oberholtz," she said to the banker.

"'Morning, Miss Kramer." He raked her with a pickle-sour look, jabbed his bulbous nose higher in the air, and with a perfunctory wave gestured Dulcie into his office. "And how may I be of assistance?"

You could try a smile and friendliness, she thought, fighting not to voice her opinion. Taking a seat before the large mahogany desk, she waited until the banker was seated on the opposite side. "I need to discuss a business matter with you."

"Business . . . matter?" he asked, staring at Dulcie as if she'd suddenly sprouted two horns, a tail, and a black-and-white mottled hide.

Don't think me capable, do you? Just wait and see, she vowed. "Yes. Like my mother before me, I'm prepared to support my grandmother and myself by going into commerce."

"Ahem . . . And just *how* do you expect to do so? And why have you seen fit to come to me?"

Dulcie's expectations landed roughly somewhere near the soles of her repaired boots. "Well, sir, I'm negotiating with Mr. Martin Eby of Lancaster for the lease of his vacant store on Queen Street. The building is advantageously situated close to the railroad station, and the streetcar runs out front."

"Miss Kramer, that's all very well and good, but you still haven't told me what you're up to. Much less your reason for this visit."

With a quick prayer and a bracing breath, Dulcie rushed ahead. "Of course, sir. I inherited Maman's recipe for chocolate bonbons. She used to make them on consignment for friends and neighbors. These treats are special, and she was always well paid. I want to open a confectionery in Lancaster. After all, everyone knows how well Milton Hershey has done with his Lancaster Caramel Company."

"Are you . . . comparing yourself to an entrepreneur like Milton Hershey?"

The piercing black eyes made Dulcie want to squirm. She squelched the urge. "Why, no, sir. I merely pointed out that there's money to be made selling high-quality candies. And it's that potential I want to tap into."

Mr. Oberholtz stood, laced his pudgy fingers over his pronounced paunch, then walked out from behind his desk. "Let me get this straight," he said in a somewhat mocking voice. "You want to place yourself in a position to compete against Hershey's success. And you intend to do so by producing some fancy little treats. In addition to all *that*, since you're obviously in my office, you must be planning to ask for money to fund this impulsive plunge into the world of businessmen."

"Well, yes—I mean, no— What I mean is—"

"Yes, Miss Kramer, precisely what do you mean?"

Curse the tub of blubber! He'd taken Dulcie's words and turned them against her. On top of that, he'd insinuated that she was a bluestocking or some such suffragist sort, when all she wanted was to earn enough money to feed herself and Granny K. Maybe this time one of her grandmother's more ludicrous spells would have done some good. Dulcie wouldn't have felt nearly as intimidated if she thought she could turn Oberholtz into a toad or a slug or a mote of dust. She'd even be happy if a simple banishing spell were to work on him. But Dulcie didn't follow Granny's leanings; she attended Everleigh's Lutheran Church. And Pastor Eckert would frown on one of his parishioners turning to witchcraft for supernatural help in business.

"Mr. Oberholtz, I have no intention of challenging Mr. Hershey. He can continue to sell the world his caramels. I surely won't interfere with that. All I want to do is to produce elegant, French-style bonbons and sell them to the well-to-do of Lancaster."

"You don't think the rich in Lancaster eat caramels?"

What a pompous little tyrant! "Frankly, sir, I don't know and I don't care." Now where had that Granny-like response come from? Dulcie couldn't afford to offend the recalcitrant banker. She needed to win him over to her way of thinking. Honey always caught more flies than vinegar. And from what she could see, Mr. Oberholtz had already been soured in a crock of the latter.

Pasting a bright smile on her face, she tried again. "Does Mrs. Oberholtz like candies?"

Mr. Oberholtz coughed. He looked out the small window on the left wall of the lavishly appointed office. He frowned. He then took out a voluminous white handkerchief, wiped his suddenly damp-looking brow, then went back to sit in his black leather chair on the other side of the desk. Stuffing his hanky back in his coat pocket, he leaned toward Dulcie.

"What the devil does my wife have to do with any of this?"

"Absolutely nothing, sir. Does she like chocolates?"

"Ah . . . I don't know— I think so, yes . . ."

"And wouldn't she appreciate the finest quality possible?"

Again the banker held on to his response a bit more than necessary.

"Well, then," she said, suspecting Mr. Oberholtz had rarely thought of Mrs. Oberholtz's likes or dislikes. "Since you say she does like candies, and she clearly must have a discerning nature, she would be representative of my ideal customer. I intend to produce luxury chocolates on a limited basis. When your wife invites visitors, she serves them only the very best, right?"

"Yesss . . . but—"

"And you would agree it's the proper thing to do. Right?"

"Mm-hmm . . ."

"But does she have anywhere to purchase such confectionery delicacies at this present time?"

"Ah . . . well, maybe . . . I don't know, but—"

"Of course she doesn't. And that's the need I intend to meet. Mignone Kramer's Sweet Secrets Confectionery will provide the best families with superlative chocolates to serve when they wish to honor their friends and business associates with the finest.'' Dulcie figured she'd either win it all now, or she'd already lost the battle, so she barged ahead. ''And that's where you come in, sir. I'm sure you're always up-to-date on any new enterprises opening in this area. And you follow the business pulse of Lancaster, as well as that of our smaller towns. Wouldn't you want to play a part in the growing economy of Lancaster County? The bank would certainly profit from being associated with the most progressive enterprises, wouldn't you say?''

''Yes, but—''

''And that, Mr. Oberholtz, is where you come in. How would you like to lead the Columbia Savings and Trust Bank into the future? It only requires the simple matter of a business loan.''

Dead silence.

''Yes, indeed,'' she added in her most enthusiastic voice. ''The investment the bank makes in Mignone Kramer's Sweet Secrets Confectionery will yield attractive gains in repayment interest. I'm certain you can see the advisability in that sort of association. And truly, sir, these are the finest chocolates money can buy.''

Mr. Oberholtz's pudgy cheeks looked oddly flattened, and the twin red orbs where a thinner man would have cheekbones didn't augur success. Still, Dulcie felt she ought to give the matter one last try. ''We would of course have minor overhead expenses. You see, Granny and I can make the bonbons at home to eliminate the need for a stove, cooking equipment, and cooling racks. All we would have to pay out would be rent, the cost of ingredients, and whatever wrapping we choose to use.''

Abruptly the banker pushed away from the desk, stood, and began to pace again. He still didn't say a word.

It didn't look good for Dulcie's loan.

Now what? Should she press her suit? Should she remain

meek and mouselike in her chair? Would a strong, persuasive male—someone like Race Langston—leap up and declare the merit in his plans and challenge the unbeliever to prove the enterprise wouldn't succeed? Would Race have the courage to charge ahead, fueled by faith in his dreams?

Or was Dulcie, like Don Quixote, merely tilting at windmills? Was she seeking the impossible? Was that what she'd been doing when she dared believe in Race's apparent interest?

Oh, dear! There she was thinking of Race again. And at the worst possible moment. This was no time to think about a fancy, rich lawyer who lacked even the decency to keep a promi—

"Collateral!" thundered Mr. Oberholtz, startling Dulcie back from her wandering thoughts.

And it was just as well. She had matters of great importance to resolve. "Excuse—"

"No, no, no. No excuses here. I want to see just what you intend to use for collateral."

"Collateral?"

"Yes, Miss Kramer. What will you secure the loan with?"

Oh, dear. What did she have to put up for the loan? Nothing, she thought. If she'd had anything of value, she would already have sold it; she wouldn't have had to ask for arrogant Mr. Oberholtz's help. The only things she had were an ill-tempered elderly mare, an equally decrepit buckboard wagon, and one chocolate recipe—the only thing that held any hint of promise. And it didn't sound as if Mr. Oberholtz shared Dulcie's vision of that promise.

Beyond that, there was nothing else. Nothing, except the house . . .

Dared she risk the roof over their heads on her dreams of the future? Did she believe that strongly in herself?

"Yes!" she cried, then had to tamp down her spirit to continue in a more suitable tone of voice. "I have our house. I own it free and clear. I wish to take out a mortgage on the house."

Mr. Oberholtz looked flabbergasted. He halted his pacing, frowned, pursed his lips, then clasped his hands behind his back. The gesture left him looking like a plump partridge, and Dulcie had difficulty with the notion that such an innocuous-looking bird held her future in his hands.

"And just where do you plan to have your grandmother live?"

Dulcie sucked in a breath. "You see no future for my plans, do you? You don't believe I can repay the loan. You think you'd have to take the house from us."

The banker shrugged, then spread his hands in a gesture of helplessness.

"If I lose the house, I lose the house." Dulcie's middle clenched. "I would leave town, go West to find a teaching position. I'd take Granny with me."

"And how old is Ermentrude now? Seventy-five, eighty? She'd never survive the crossing, you foolish child."

"I beg to differ with you, sir," Dulcie said, rising and taking a firm stand. "I most certainly am not a child. And besides, wouldn't the bank profit from taking the house, then reselling it? It's certainly worth more than whatever loan I could persuade you to give me. And there's where your interest should lie."

Mr. Oberholtz's pudgy cheeks huffed in and out like a furnace bellows. "Is this candy foolishness the only thing you think of?" His features turned a violent shade of puce. "If that's the case, then you are indeed a foolish child, as I already stated. How could you expose Ermentrude to such a risk? Do you not even care if your grandmother lives or dies? I would place her in higher regard than a fanciful whim with absolutely no prospects.''

Dulcie'd had enough. ''I can see it will do me no good to continue this conversation. The only thing I wish to add is that it was Granny who suggested I come to you for assistance. She knows our options, and she believes in me. She's ready to move West, but she believes, as I do, that I would make good on that loan. With interest!''

''We can't do business on blind faith, Miss Kramer. A bank can only operate in the realm of the real, that which exists, what can be readily calculated by simple facts and figures. I won't let you run the risk of leaving your grandmother homeless.''

Dulcie straightened her spine to its firmest posture. She gathered her purse, her gloves, and the papers she'd brought to illustrate her projections. The papers she hadn't been given the opportunity to use. ''I have no intention of leaving my grandmother homeless. And sometimes, Mr. Oberholtz, a risk is a person's only choice. After all, if I cannot earn my living, the money my mother left will soon be gone, and we'll have no alternative but to sell the house. We would be just as homeless, as destitute as if I'd been unable to make good on a loan. As I see things, I have a better chance of success if I try to make a go of the confectionery than if I continue to withdraw what little we have left in the account.''

As Mr. Oberholtz's frown only deepened, Dulcie accepted that she'd never change his mind. Not now. But once she proved herself, he'd sing a different ditty. She yanked on her gloves. ''I won't waste another minute of your time, sir. Before I leave, however, as you well know, I need to withdraw from my account. If you would be so kind . . .''

''Certainly.''

Ten minutes later, Dulcie drove away from the bank, a

tidy sum in her purse, virtually nothing in her account, and a bitter taste in her mouth.

Matters were as grim as she'd feared. She'd lose the house if she couldn't make the confectionery pay. Then, without a house, she'd be forced to load whatever they could on the buckboard, harness Molly, and ride out with the sun.

It was a do-or-die situation, and Dulcie was afraid the do might prove impossible to reach.

After another harrowing night, one filled with fear for his father's health, Race lay numbly on his bed. He hadn't been able to keep his date with Dulcie yesterday. Mother had needed him; Father, too. Now Race had to face the formidable Mr. Hershey and explain what had happened. He could only hope that Milton would take Horace's recovery into account when Race approached him. And maybe, in view of Horace's precarious condition, Mr. Hershey might be more willing to let Race off the hook.

Still early, scarcely at dawn, Race gave up his efforts to rest. He rose and dressed, then went down to the kitchen. At this ludicrous hour, neither Pearl, the cook, nor Maudie, the downstairs maid, had arrived. Mother had finally taken the powders Dr. Murdoch had left her, knowing she'd never rest otherwise. Race was glad the medication had worked swiftly, effectively.

Mother needed her rest, and he'd hate to have to worry about her, too. She'd always been a strong, steady influence on the Langston family. He knew they would all have to draw encouragement from her to face whatever the future held.

With heavy tread, he gathered the coffeepot and the fragrant ground beans, then went to the sink for water. As he filled the container to the necessary proportions, he thought back on the last few moments he and Dulcie shared the night before last.

He couldn't help but regret the pain he'd undoubtedly caused her when he hadn't shown up. At no given moment could he have left the house. And he knew firsthand that the Kramer ladies didn't own a telephone. Sending a message hadn't occurred to him until late, at a time when it would have been highly improper and, he suspected, futile as well.

Since Father's pulse had remained unstable all day, nothing would have made Race leave his family. He hoped Dulcie would accept his explanation, once he was able to offer her one. After all, her devotion to her grandmother had been constantly in evidence when they'd spent time together.

Placing the coffeepot on the shiny black iron cookstove, Race lit the gas burner, then sat to wait. When things settled down some, he thought, he'd return to Everleigh and apologize to Dulcie. Although he doubted he'd win back her trust, he was interested enough to try, and regardless of the outcome, he at least wanted to explain what had happened.

He was especially disappointed, since he'd thought he could win Father's assistance in refusing to carry out Hershey's negotiations once he told him about Dulcie. Despite their reticence in displaying their feelings, he knew Mother and Father cared for each other. Thinking to appeal to his father's affections, Race had hoped emotion would succeed where reason had earlier failed.

Now, since Race held but scant hope of persuading Mr. Hershey, he was flat out of options. Although he was willing to try yet again to discourage Milton Hershey's insistence on Race's personal handling of his business, he held no hope of succeeding. Should he prove unable to do so, Race would undoubtedly have to return to Everleigh. Dulcie still owned the damn chocolate recipe. And so long as Race was responsible for obtaining the miserable thing, he could never pursue his feelings for her.

And what rare feelings those were! Dulcie had a lively temperament, plenty of daring, she demonstrated strong loyalties, something Race highly valued, and she was quick to smile and ready to laugh. Beyond those qualities was her innocent sensuality. It had come as a revelation to Race how quickly he'd become enflamed by a simple kiss.

Simple but potent. And he might never have the opportunity to experience it again.

As the coffeepot quit gurgling, Race stood and went to the butler's pantry for a cup. Back in the kitchen, he poured the coffee, then strode out the rear door. After closing it, he leaned back and watched the horizon grow rosier, brighter, as it welcomed the new day.

A hot shot of coffee scalded his mouth, but felt bracing going down. Something in this tangle of bad business ventures, new business ventures, old family secrets, and new family secrets, didn't quite fit. Everything that had happened so far had been ludicrous, silly even. And he was caught in the middle. Somehow, he'd have to unravel it.

Could he do it? Was this one of those rare opportunities Father had insinuated came infrequently into a man's life, bringing the chance to prove his own mettle?

Race suspected it was.

But he had no idea how he was going to face Father, Milton Hershey, perhaps Grandfather Richter, and even the delightful Dulcie Kramer. He felt strangely certain that nothing good could come of all this.

And it all lay squarely on his shoulders.

❖ 7 ❖

After a sizable breakfast, and with much trepidation, Race found himself back in the library, telephone receiver in hand. He still didn't relish speaking with Milton Hershey. Race had never been particularly comfortable around the intense man. Still, Milton had been a good friend to Horace, and Race was banking on that friendship.

He again applauded his father's progressive tendencies. Nothing on earth was less appealing than meeting Milton Hershey face-to-face right now. The man would be much too persuasive, too determined, for Race to even stand a chance. Thank goodness for the telephone.

He listened absently as the operator made the connection. Moments later, Milton answered.

He took a deep breath. "Race Langston here, sir."

That peculiar crackling of telephone communications nearly drowned out Hershey's response. But Race knew full well what the candy maker wanted to know. "Yes, sir. I did find the recipe," he said, hoping he chose the right words, hoping to sway Milton. "Actually, I found the new owner of the blasted thing. Turns out that Mignone Kramer recently died. Her daughter now owns the recipe."

Through the noise of the connection came more questions. "Yes, I'm sure," answered Race. "In fact, I've met the daughter. She has the recipe, but unfortunately she intends to become a confectioner. It seems Dul—Miss Kramer and her grandmother are in a situation of reduced resources. They feel they have no assets beyond the income they might earn by selling French-style bonbons."

Race fell silent while he listened to Hershey's response. Then, "I realize none of this has any bearing on your interests. However, I found it difficult in the extreme to negotiate with two bereaved women of scant means."

"That's why I authorized you to negotiate a fair contract," Hershey stated. "It's a very simple matter. They sell me the recipe, I eliminate competition before it begins, and you pay them a handsome sum of money. Everyone wins. I get what I want, and the Kramers turn a healthy profit without having to spend the time, funds, and effort needed to go into business."

Race thought it over, keeping Dulcie's enthusiasm and determination in mind. "I don't believe it would be quite so simple," he said. "Dul—Miss Kramer doesn't strike me as the sort who would take a challenge sitting down. She's opinionated and most determined to succeed. I think we'll have a dogfight on our hands if we try to buy the recipe. She considers the list of ingredients her inheritance."

Mr. Hershey offered additional arguments.

"I agree, sir," Race responded. "I don't consider sentimentality a solid basis for transacting business. But in all fairness to the Kramers, you obviously know the recipe has potential for success. Otherwise you wouldn't be so set on getting it. I can understand the hope it represents for them."

Race took out his handkerchief and wiped his damp forehead, then stuffed it back in a pocket. Didn't look good for his romantic interests. Milton Hershey was, if anything, even more firm in his insistence.

"You see, Mr. Hershey, it's like this," Race began, then felt a tremor of unease twist his insides. He didn't half like having to bare his personal feelings to a business acquaintance, but it didn't look as if he had any other choice. He went on, hoping that somewhere the confirmed bachelor hid a touch of romance. "I met Dulcie Kramer under rather odd circumstances. She'd been injured in an accident, and I came to her aid."

Dead silence.

The twisting in Race's middle resembled some barbaric form of torture. Still, Mr. Hershey seemed impervious to Race's plight, although he knew that Race had found yet another reason not to proceed with the negotiations.

There was no other hope. Race had to reveal his private feelings for Dulcie. And he suspected they'd be discounted as summarily as his other arguments had been.

He cleared his throat. "You see, sir, Dulcie and I became acquainted, and it seems a mutual, personal interest has grown between us. I would like to seriously court the young lady. I don't wish to get on her bad side by appearing to be interested in only a recipe she owns."

"Splendid!" exclaimed the entrepreneur. "By all means court her. Your interest in the young lady comes as a bonus. It will make the process less of a chore for you. Romance her, get the recipe, then marry the girl. Keep her too busy to think any further of entering the business world."

Now the twisting torment in Race's stomach turned to sour distaste. Only a confirmed bachelor, dried up and without a hint of emotion, would come up with such a repulsive idea. Race refused to entertain it. "Well, then, Mr. Hershey, you need to find yourself another emissary. I won't court a lady under such false pretenses. I can proceed no further on your behalf."

Again, that deadly silence prevailed.

Again, Race's heartbeat thundered.

Again, his forehead dampened.

"And you said Horace has taken a turn for the worse?" Mr. Hershey asked.

"Yes."

"I wouldn't want to excite him any further, would you, Race?"

"Not in the least, sir, but—"

"And should your grandfather sniff out what's happened, the results could be devastating, as far as your father's health is concerned, don't you think?"

Race sucked in a sharp breath. "Are you threatening me, sir?"

"Not at all, son. On the contrary, I'm trying to show you how important it is for us to complete these negotiations. And the best way to do it is so that everyone wins in the end. My proposal offers the best alternative."

Race gritted his teeth. "Sounds to me as if you're holding my father's health over my head. And all for the sake of a business deal."

"You could see it that way. But as I've already told you, I have important personal reasons why I want this matter handled by you, and only by you. Your father will understand those reasons once everything is resolved. Not only will he understand, he will support me, thank me, and congratulate me for what I'll have achieved. Even you will understand. You see, Race, Horace trusts me. I think, out of a son's respect for his father, you should do so as well."

"There's nothing more I can do or say, is there?"

"That sounds about right."

"Good day, then, Mr. Hershey."

"And a fruitful one for you, Race."

He hung up. Bile swirled in the back of his throat. How in hell could he court a woman—innocent Dulcie Kramer, at that—while still concealing ulterior motives? How would he ever convince her that his interest didn't come from his efforts on behalf of a client? That he hadn't even known who she was when he first met her, when he first realized how much she appealed to him?

As Race saw it, Milton Hershey had left him with only two choices, unpalatable ones at that. He could either act on Milton's proposition, or he could come clean with Dulcie, hoping somehow to prove the sincerity of his feelings. Neither option left him in a favorable position. In fact, Race would lose out, no matter which path he followed, no matter what the outcome. This fiasco was muddled as mud.

It was up to him. And he had no idea what to do next.

Late the next afternoon, Race found himself traveling down the old road to Everleigh. In a very short time he'd become amazingly familiar with the route. Over there was where the buckboard had lain, and across the way, behind a sturdy fence, four placid cows munched on the lush green grass at their feet. They were probably the same ones he'd seen the other time.

He still had no idea what he was going to do. The fact that he'd see Dulcie again kept him moving onward. Zephyr seemed to have learned the way, too.

Once in Everleigh, Race slowed his horse, dreading the upcoming visit. He hated deceit. He despised fraud. And unless he could bring himself to confess his situation to Dulcie, he would have to be guilty of both.

Willow Lane was as appealing as usual. Today, three boys spun hoops with sticks down the middle of the street, while one little girl sat amid a profusion of blossoms before the stone cottage, meticulously plucking every petal she could reach. Across the road, a tall, reed-thin woman with round spectacles swept her front stoop with furious shoves of the broom.

Race nudged Zephyr. Zephyr responded by moving a hair faster. Soon Race reached the Kramer home.

A chill swept his body as he caught sight of three people on the porch. Granny sat in her rigid, upright chair, pipe between tight lips, smoke chugging up around her like a just-stoked locomotive.

On the porch swing, Dulcie was doing some sort of needlework, keeping the rhythm going with a dainty tap of her foot.

What shocked and outraged Race was the beefy blond hayseed who straddled the porch balustrade, smirking at Dulcie, devouring her with his eyes. From the farmer's fixed expression, and the besotted smile that curved his fat pink lips, Race learned how smitten with Dulcie her caller was. The man's blue eyes burned with a spark of something less than noble.

That was bad, but what really provoked and alarmed him was Dulcie's attentiveness. She appeared riveted by whatever the rube was saying.

Remembering their kiss, Race only grew more irritated. And hell, yes, he was jealous! Did Dulcie kiss this fool as sweetly as she'd kissed Race that other night?

Could the man have a claim on her affections?

His pride stung, fear clasping his heart, Race came to the conclusion that it didn't matter what was between the farm boy and Dulcie. The only thing that mattered was that Race was falling for her, and he was willing to do whatever it took to win her.

Dismounting, he stopped cold for a moment. He'd come to discuss the chocolate recipe. Milton's interests should have been foremost in his mind. But the moment he saw Dulcie, all thought of business vanished. All Race could think of was how strongly he was attracted to her, how she'd pressed herself closer for yet another kiss, and how some other man was encroaching on territory he wanted to claim.

This was clearly not the best time to come clean with Dulcie. He would have to keep his other motive secret until he'd vanquished his rival. Only then, once he was sure of Dulcie's feelings for him, could he run the risk of angering her.

Decision made, Race strode up to the porch steps.

"Hell a' kitin', if it ain't Race! Come here unt goot day say."

Race was surprised by Granny K's enthusiastic greeting, but he wasn't about to do anything to change her mood. "Gladly, Granny. And how are you today?" he asked, bending close.

To his surprise, the old woman threw her arms around his neck and hugged him down to her bony chest. "Help me get shut-of dat svine, dere," she muttered under her breath. "I'd sooner you sit mit Dulcie than he come back again."

This was an interesting turn! He caught Granny's gaze and winked, letting her know where he stood. A wicked grin lit up her goblinlike face, and she turned to Dulcie's caller. "So, Kirk Slimebaugh—"

"Granny!" cried Dulcie from her perch on the swing. "Behave yourself. We have company."

Whereas she'd had a smile for her grandmother, and had shown attentive interest in the Slime character, Dulcie turned gelid-looking eyes in Race's direction. *Uh-oh.*

"Mr. Langston," she said, her voice dripping icicles. "What an *unexpected* surprise."

"Dulcie-girl!" Granny squawked. "You are so *fergesslich!* You alvays *fergess* ever'thing. Ve vere expectin' Race. Choo even cleaned house, unt vashed yer hair."

The furious flush on Dulcie's cheeks told Race she'd gone to some trouble waiting for him the day before. And he hadn't shown. He had quite a ways to go before she'd consider forgiving him.

At least Granny K was on his side. Race glanced her way to see if he could pick up his next cue.

"Go, go," she said, pointing with her pipe stem. "Go mit Dulcie sit, Race. Choo kenn she vants you. Go, now!"

Race grinned. And sat next to Dulcie.

The Slime person frowned. "I be here afor—"

"Kirk!" Granny cried out through her cloud of pipe smoke. "Sorry to hear choo must leave. Say hello to yer *Mutter* unt *Vater*."

The look of shock on Kirk's ruddy features struck Race as infinitely amusing. He resembled a newborn swine, all rosy, broad of cheek, and with a flatly rounded, upturned nose.

As the hayseed straddled the banister with his mammoth thighs, he teetered in and out, in danger of falling off altogether. However, his hefty bulk must have been on his side, for he swung one leg over the balustrade, then planted himself before Race.

Glaring, Race read the man's challenge. Not a word was needed, and Race suspected Kirk didn't know many. How could Dulcie tolerate the clod?

He slanted a look at her, but found nothing more than icy irritation on her face. He glanced again at the farmer before him, then again at Dulcie. Catching sight of her hand clasping and unclasping the rose fabric of her skirt close to his thigh, he had an idea. If his luck continued, Granny would play a most willing ally.

With a grin and a wink for Granny, he covered Dulcie's fingers and clasped them firmly in his hand. When she tugged, he smiled, leaned over, and pressed a kiss on her cheek.

The cheek grew hot and red.

The eyes grew icier.

The lips pruned.

"Mr. Langston, sir! If you please! Allow me to reject your advances. Unwelcome as they are," she added with a scowl that managed to sting. Race was afraid she'd meant that final comment seriously.

After tsk-tsking her displeasure, Granny snorted, then stood. "Dulcie, you must polite be. Race is our guest."

"Unt me?" demanded the blond behemoth.

"Choo go home, Kirk Slimebaugh. Go, go!" With no more warning, Granny swept the well-fed male off the porch.

Fighting to keep hold of Dulcie's hand, despite her vigorous efforts to thwart him, Race found his clasp weakened as he tried to stop his laughter. No sooner had Kirk disappeared down the lane, than Granny whooped a resounding victory cheer, and Race's chuckles broke free. Dulcie yanked her hand away.

Her vehemence was instantly sobering.

At his sudden silence, Granny turned and studied Dulcie's enraged expression. She then turned to Race, and he wasn't above adopting a poor-puppy-dog look.

Fickle as all females, she offered another cackle of mirth, then shook her head. "I go dinner make," she announced, then hefted up her ever-present crock and disappeared inside the door.

Awkward silence followed.

As soon as Granny's footsteps carried her out of hearing range, both Race and Dulcie stood, setting the porch swing a-jiggling.

"I'm so very sorry I couldn't—"

"I think it's time you left—"

Both stopped. A moment of silence slipped by. Then another. Quick glances were exchanged. The silence lengthened.

From inside the house Granny called out, "Do I need my shotgun agin? Such a bodderation! Talk, *talk*!" Irregular footsteps again were heard, this time approaching. "Ach! *Schtaerkeppich* you both be. Like a tick hangin' on a dog's behind. Talk, or I git my gun!"

"No gun, please!" Race's dismay leached warmth from his face. There went his only ally in Everleigh. Turning to Dulcie, he asked, "Fair-weather friend, isn't she?"

Tilting her nose upward, Dulcie stared him down. "More like you're the lesser of two evils, in her opinion."

"And in yours?"

Maintaining her regal stance, Dulcie gathered her needlework and folded it into a wicker basket near the swing. She picked up the hamper and slipped the handle over her forearm. She went toward the door, soft, rose-colored skirt swaying in alluring rhythm, then stopped. At the threshold, she looked sideways at him. "What do you think, Mr. Langston?"

Think, he urged the sodden lump that seemed to have suddenly taken residence inside his skull. Yes, what did he think? "I . . . I-I think you're jumping to conclusions too quickly. Why don't you ask what happened? I might have a valid reason for not showing up yesterday."

Dulcie stepped inside the house. *Sure you do, a horde of elegant socialites descended upon you, bent on reclaiming your straying interest.* "I don't have enough time to listen to stories, Mr. Langston. I'm very busy, especially since I'm launching a new business venture."

As Dulcie watched, Race's brown eyes closed for a moment, his features looking somewhat . . . pained? What could possibly be the problem with this man? At first he'd seemed dogged in his pursuit of her attentions. Then when she reciprocated and began to believe in the possibilities, he failed to come. Now, he'd returned, chased away a childhood schoolmate, and was acting as if he had a claim on her affections.

No, she thought. She certainly had no time for such games. "Mr. Langston, I—"

He blew out a gust of breath, obviously irritated by her failure to fall right into his hands. Dulcie felt pleased at having gotten a bit of her own back.

With an air of superiority, she waved him away. "No need to snort like a consumptive horse, Mr. Langston. And, please, I cannot waste any more time on useless chitchat."

As she watched, Race's face took on a fierce cast. His skin ruddied with what was obviously anger. His eyes narrowed. "I'm damnably sick of you calling me Mr. Langston. I think the kiss we shared at least dispenses with such formalities."

"You're the sorriest excuse for a gentleman, Race Langston!" she cried, feeling her discomfited blush from the crown of her head to the tips of her toes. "A gentleman would never remind a lady of a momentary lapse of propriety."

"I never cast myself in the role of gentleman. I said I was a lawyer, simply a man."

Oh, yes. Race Langston was indeed a man. A fine-looking specimen of a man, at that. Despite her anger, Dulcie was unable to halt the downward trip her gaze took, admiring every detail of Race's elegant masculinity. His shoulders were broad, wide enough to hold her, should the need arise. His torso was slender, no rolls of fat to proclaim him a sluggard. His legs were long, thighs muscular, not the massive slabs of flesh that Kirk Slimeba—*Schleinbaugh*—possessed. On her way back up, she took in Race's clean-cut features—a firm jaw, well-delineated lips, straight nose, broad forehead. And most compelling of all, those deep, dark, chocolate-colored eyes.

Eyes that were fastened on hers. Eyes that had no doubt mapped every move she took while on her visual journey. Eyes that were seeking her gaze, beckoning. Welcoming brown eyes.

Dulcie felt her resistance melt away. The depths of those eyes held more than frivolous flirting. They broadcast interest, yes, but also what looked like pain, fear, maybe even insecurity. They also appeared to reflect nothing but the deepest sincerity.

She set her basket down just inside the door. "I—please take a seat," she said, gesturing toward Granny's chair.

"No, join me here," he responded, sitting back down on the swing.

For a moment, Dulcie thought to deny his request. But again those eyes of his reached deep inside her. Race seemed to consider it essential for them to talk privately, and sitting close.

Dulcie had never been a coward, and she'd never been unfair. Who knows, he just might have a genuine reason for his failure to appear yesterday. She joined him on the swing.

"Look, I know you're angry," he said, "and I can understand why. If I'd been expecting someone who never showed up, I'd also be upset. But I would give that person a chance to explain."

Before Dulcie knew it, Race again took possession of her hand. His warmth shivered up her arm, then through her body, making her a touch light-headed, very willing to listen. The man was dangerous, her common sense warned.

He spoke again. "I really did plan to come. In fact, I was looking forward to seeing you again. As soon as I could.

But when I got home, an emergency took priority, and everything else had to wait.''

At her questioning glance, he shrugged. ''My father had a stroke six months ago. Shortly before I got home night before last, he began having chest pains, and his heartbeat grew erratic. His pulse remained unstable through all of yesterday, and only late last night did it begin to normalize.''

Race's voice had lowered, emotion underscoring every word. Everything he'd said rang with truth. Dulcie blushed again, this time in shame. Her impulsive nature had again gotten the better of her. She owed Race an apology.

But he wasn't waiting for one.

''My mother was understandably distraught, and I felt she needed me at her side just as much as I needed her company through those frightening hours. Even now, I don't know how he continues. I came to see you as soon as I could. I can't stay long. I just wanted you to know I didn't forget or consider our date unimportant.''

Race's words moved Dulcie. He was a rare man. He'd allowed her to see a hint of vulnerability. And yet, he remained as strong and masculine as ever. Tears of sympathy welled in her eyes.

She raised her hand to Race's cheek, offering compassion. ''I'm so sorry to hear that, Race. Especially since I've behaved like a spoiled child. You deserve my apology far more than I deserve yours. Please forgive my foolishness.''

Afraid he might see her tears, confuse her wish to comfort with pity, she lowered her head. Too, if he saw her tears he might think her a sentimental twit as well as an impulsive brat. But a warm finger curled under her chin, the finger that once wiped her cheek, that positioned her for her first kiss.

''Dulcie,'' he murmured.

''Yes.''

''Please look at me.''

"I can't."

A deep chuckle rumbled out. "I think we already had this conversation. And you certainly can look at me. Don't be afraid."

"I'm not afraid."

"Then . . . ?"

"I'm ashamed of my pettiness."

"Hush. You couldn't have known what happened. Besides, I'm here now. And I want to see your beautiful blue eyes."

The finger grew more insistent, and Dulcie let it have its way. She met Race's gaze, another of those penetrating looks of his, and she caught her breath. Warmth glowed in his eyes, a smile curved his lips, lips that came closer every second.

She realized he was giving her a chance to back away, to avoid the caress if she didn't want it. But she did. Want it. And she didn't back away. She grew impatient, halved the distance between them, met him midway.

The warmth of his lips again covered hers, gently rubbing, pressing against her. When the tickle of his tongue teased her mouth, she parted her lips. A glossing of her flesh followed, a tasting, a testing. Both hesitated, relishing the feelings they were sharing, fearing any action that might make the other back away.

Instead of backing away, Race reached up to Dulcie's hair and ran his fingers through the curls. He sifted through the strands and cupped the back of her head. Above all, he kissed her. A wondrous caress that warmed Dulcie's heart, as much as the heated shivers coursing her body warmed her flesh.

Dulcie's heart quickened its pace, thundering roughly, unevenly. *Thump, thump, thump.*

Suddenly Race let her go. He straightened, then whispered, "Granny!"

Her grandmother's uneven steps thumped closer still. So, it hadn't been her heart, after all. Glancing at Race, Dulcie almost laughed out loud at the look of craven fear on his face. It seemed Granny's intimidating tactics brought about resounding results!

Since she didn't want to call her grandmother's attention to lips that felt plumper than before, warmer than ever, she reached for her sewing basket, then groaned, remembering she'd left it inside the door.

"Vat, no talk?" Granny demanded from the doorway, gun hugged against her chest.

Race gulped and leapt to his feet. That damn shotgun again. The woman *hugged* the thing! To think he'd been clasped to that very chest when he arrived. Race wondered how he'd so suddenly lost favor with Granny. For it was clear that although she preferred Race to the Slime character, she didn't trust him an inch.

"Yes! Yes, of course we've been talking," he said, wondering what else to say. Might as well repeat his apologies. "I wanted both of you to know that I was unable to keep my promise to visit yesterday because my father, whose health is poor, took a turn for the worse."

"Vat's wrong mit 'im?"

"Well, six months ago, he suffered a stroke. Then the other night his heartbeat became erratic, unstable. Although he was better this morning, I'm not certain how he's doing now. I can't stay long, even though I'd certainly like to."

Granny stood for a moment, mulling over Race's words. The wrinkles on her forehead drooped close to the bridge of her nose, and her eyes crinkled. She was frowning, Race thought, remembering the first time he'd seen her. Funny how she'd grown on him. Today he hadn't even noticed that the denim overalls she wore sported rips that revealed bony knees.

"You vant I should try for 'im?"

"Huh?"

"Granny!" Dulcie cried, fear making her stomach plunge. Granny and her Hex-Craft! Why couldn't she just leave well enough alone? "Don't pay her any mind," she said to Race, taking his arm and pulling him toward the porch steps. With a glare at her grandmother and a furious shake of her head, she stopped Granny's approach.

"My ankle is much better," she continued, dragging Race behind her. "I think it would be good if I exercised it some. I don't want it to grow stiff or useless. Will you take a walk with me?"

Still turned toward Granny, eyes fixed on the older woman, he balked every step of the way. He was so heavy! Dulcie thought. And strong. And curious about what Granny had said. It showed on every feature of his face.

"Let's go for a walk, Race," Dulcie insisted, stepping down the first step.

"Wha—I—what did she say?" he asked, curiosity and bewilderment in his voice. "Try? What does that mean? What does she want to try?"

Dulcie gulped. Why did he insist on following her grandmother's ramblings? She thought he'd come to see *her*! Seemed the lawyer's curiosity didn't stay in Lancaster when he came to visit Everleigh. She would have to have another serious talk with Granny. But not before their walk.

"Come, Race, I want you to meet some of our neighbors."

Both arms hugging his biceps, Dulcie accomplished what she'd hoped to avoid three days ago when she rode home on Race's lap. Every neighbor on both sides of Willow Lane had come out, clearly knowing something interesting was happening at the Kramers' home.

Dulcie lifted her chin, pasted on a wide smile, and faced Granny's sewing-circle cronies with bravado.

❖ 8 ❖

"Good afternoon, Dulcie Kramer," called Myrna Whitaker as she swept the immaculate porch of her redbrick house.

"Afternoon, Mrs. Whitaker," Dulcie answered, resigned to her fate. "Here's someone I'd like you to meet."

With lean, spare gestures, the elderly woman dropped her broom and trotted out to where Dulcie and Race stood. "And who may *this* be?" she asked, peering over her round, wire-rimmed spectacles.

"I'm—"

"He's Race Langston, from Lancaster. A friend," Dulcie put in quickly, hoping to spend a minimum of time with the curious woman. She ignored Race's puzzled look.

Mrs. Whitaker peered through her spectacles at Race, her brows meeting as one over the bridge of her nose. "Seems I've seen 'im going by before," she said, obviously trying to pry details from Dulcie. "Not from Everleigh, ye say?"

Race smiled and began, "Ye—"

"You could have seen him," Dulcie hurried to say, cutting him off. "He's been by before." She ignored the scowl he gave her. "Well, seeing as you're busy cleaning this afternoon, we won't keep you any longer."

Slipping her hand into the crook at Race's elbow, Dulcie again picked up speed. When Race lagged behind, she paused to let him catch up. As she waited, hands linked around his arm, she spied Sarah Schwartz, who seemed to have deflowered her mother's pride and joy, her petunias. But no matter how hard Dulcie tugged, Race stood his ground. The look on his face brooked no argument.

She let go. "Yes?"

"Don't look so innocent, Miss Dulcie Kramer," he answered, then crossed his arms over his broad chest. His eyes blazed with unspoken questions.

"You don't care to continue our walk?" she tried again, then shook her head. "What would you like to do?"

"Lots. But we can start with a reasonable explanation for this sudden tour of your town. Why did you drag me away from your grandmother? Why didn't you let her answer my question? What was she talking about?"

Dulcie studied her companion for long moments. Her instincts told her he could be trusted, but . . . she didn't know him that well, and she really was responsible for her grandmother. Perhaps she could talk her way around this latest verbal blunder of Granny's.

She gingerly clasped both hands in the crook of Race's elbow again. He slanted a suspicious look her way. She smiled, aware that her dimples would show to great advantage. "Come," she urged, "let's keep walking while we talk."

He responded with a narrowed glance.

If she said enough, and said it fast, she might be able to get by without divulging too much. "Yes, well, I remember you mentioning how you liked Everleigh when you brought me home on your horse, and I thought this would be a fine time to show it to you. You know, a closer look. Besides, you didn't want to sit on our porch with Granny and her gun, did you? One never knows what will set her off next. And you do know how she can ramble on for hours.''

A wry twist lifted the corner of Race's mouth. ''You're right, I'm not fond of your grandmother's shotgun. But I don't mind when she rambles. Besides, she asked me a question, and I wanted to continue the conversation. I still want to know what she meant by 'try.' What did she want to try? And how did it have any relevance to my father?''

No wonder he'd become a lawyer! He was more persistent than a fly at a summer picnic. Looking both ways, she noticed Prudence Kleinschmidt stepping out of her fancy gray home. ''Hello, Prudence! I've someone with me I want you to meet.''

Prudence, the very image of a white-haired, blue-eyed, pink-cheeked grandmother, bustled her way to the white fence surrounding her yard. ''Dulcie, honey! I should say you *do* have someone *I'd* like to meet. Just who is this good-looking boy with you?''

Dulcie bit her lip to keep from laughing as Race stiffened at her side. ''Don't like being called a boy, do you?'' she asked under her breath.

''What do you think?'' he countered.

At that moment, saving Dulcie an answer, Prudence approached, then reached out to clasp Race's free hand in both of hers. With soft pats, she held on to him, all the while taking in every detail of his appearance. By tomorrow at this time, every member of the Everleigh Beneficial Association Quilting Bee would know each detail the gossipy widow had gleaned. Dulcie and Granny would immediately have to deflect the deluge of visitors who were certain to follow thereafter.

''My, my, my . . .'' Prudence said when done with her inspection, genuine appreciation for an attractive male coloring her tone. ''You sure are a well-made one.'' She turned

to Dulcie. ''Now, why didn't you tell me you were bein'
courted by such a beautiful man?''

Dulcie blushed. First Granny couldn't make up her mind
whether she wanted Dulcie to continue the friendship—and
more—with Race, or whether she was going to chase him
away. Now Prudence was putting them in yet another awkward position. ''Bet you've never had to deal with this sort
of thing in Lancaster,'' she said, again most quietly.

''Can't say I have, but I don't mi—''

Splat! went Prudence's chubby hand against Race's lean
one. ''Now, now. No whispering in front of me. I want to
know what you two are talking about.''

''Oh, well, it's—''

''Nothing much, jus—''

Dulcie looked at Race. Race glanced at Dulcie. Both
laughed.

Race winked. ''Seems we have a habit of doing this.''
Turning to Prudence, he added, ''We were commenting on
the peaceful pace of a charming small town like Everleigh.''

''Oh, Dulcie!'' gushed the widow. ''And he's ever so
perceptive. This one's a keeper.''

Mortified beyond belief, Dulcie wrested back the reins of
the discussion. ''We're on our way to the square. We'll see
you later, Prudence.''

''You certainly will, dear girl.''

Race chuckled. ''I'd say you've been warned.''

''You don't know the half of it!'' Dulcie said, then
groaned. ''She's one of Granny K's closest friends, an accomplished gossip, and loves men. I'm surprised she hasn't
remarried. The county's older bachelors have certainly done
their best to persuade her. I guess she just doesn't like to
narrow her field.''

''Hmmm . . . an elderly coquette.''

''Something like that.''

They fell silent for a moment, as they continued walking toward the center of Everleigh. Approaching the gazebo in the middle of Founders' Square, they heard the enthusiastic wielding of hammers. Dulcie glanced around and saw two of the Miller boys putting up stands for the upcoming Founders' Day celebration.

"What are they doing?" Race asked.

Should she . . . ? Dulcie took a bracing breath. "The stands are for our yearly festival. We celebrate the founding of the town with a community picnic, competitions and races, benefit raffles, and more food than you've ever seen in one place. The event starts not this Friday night, but the next, with a potluck supper at the Everleigh Lutheran Church."

With a mischievous smile, Race lifted an eyebrow. "And are out-of-towners welcome? Or is this a closed event?"

Dulcie donned a sassy smile. "Only the best can come. By invitation only."

"And where would a man go to get an invitation?"

"Oh, he can't just get one. They're quite hard to come by."

"Fascinating! Do give a clue . . ."

"Well, I could be persuaded . . ."

Race stepped back and studied Dulcie's satisfied smile. *Beautiful!* he thought. "Perhaps I should make use of my powers of persuasion. After all, I am a lawyer by trade."

"Heavens, don't I know! I yield, I yield!" Hands in the air, smile flashing dimples, Dulcie laughed. "Would you like to accompany me?"

"I thought you'd never ask!" Placing her soft warm hand back on his forearm, Race said, "Let's start back, shall we? I do need to get home to see about my father."

Dulcie immediately sobered. "Of course. I'm sorry we took so long."

"No, don't apologize. I did come to see you."

"I'm glad you did."

"So am I."

Smiling broadly, they retraced their way, and paused to let Dulcie introduce Race to Mary Margaret O'Murphy and Hubert Whitaker, both relatively innocuous sorts. Still, the curiosity in their eyes was not lost on Race. "Does everyone in town make it a point to know everyone else's business?"

" 'Fraid so," answered Dulcie. "There are times when all I want is to run to Lancaster and get away from the peering eyes." She fell silent. Then, "You know, although it can be a bother, at those times when it really counts, that meddling is what gets you through a tough spot. They care, and they feel connected, as if Everleigh were one extended family."

Race thought back on his relatives. This brand of open affection had somehow eluded the Langstons and the Richters. "You don't mind the lack of privacy?"

"Of course. Like today. By now I'd be willing to wager on the number of women who already know your name, height, approximate weight, hair and eye color, church membership, and chosen career."

Chuckling, Race shook his head. "*I'd* be a fool to take you up on a bet like that. And I don't consider myself a fool."

"Exactly!" Crossing the street just before they reached the Kramer home, Dulcie paused and faced Race. "When Maman died, everyone came to help. Some brought food, others helped with the casket, still others came to offer comfort and mourn with us." She looked up at the sky, eyes unfocused as she remembered. "And it's not just during bad times. Whenever there's a celebration, a wedding, a birth, everyone joins in. I guess Everleigh is a family. One I've always taken for granted, I'm afraid. I've looked toward the greener pastures of Lancaster.''

"You don't know how fortunate you are," Race said. "Lancaster is very busy, and a person can feel like a foreigner, even among acquaintances. Or during family gatherings. I've often felt alone, and if Mother weren't there, I'd be a stranger in their midst.''

"You're close to your mother?''

"We've recently become friends." The late-afternoon sun was still hot, but the lush wisteria vine climbing up the left side of the house offered shade. Race took Dulcie's hand and led her to the same private spot where he had first kissed her. "I'm glad you and I have become friends as well.''

"Mm-hm," Dulcie murmured, leaning against the clapboard siding. Her simple rose-colored dress contrasted vividly with the white wood at her back. Her blue eyes sparkled with interest, and if Race could trust his instincts around this woman, anticipation burned in her as well.

"I won't promise to return tomorrow," he said. "But I will come to the Founder's Day festivities. If my father's condition allows it, I'll see you before then. Likewise, if anything serious comes up, I'll make sure you receive word. I'll *never* let you down.''

Dulcie's smile deepened her dimples. The soft bloom of rose on her cheeks darkened, matching the cotton of her dress. A fine golden wisp slipped out from her pulled-back hairstyle and blew across her forehead. Race gently smoothed it back, relishing the silky feel of that lock.

"I'll be here," she said.

"Good." He kissed her. With infinite care he mapped out the contours of Dulcie's lips, the plump middle, the curving top. Then he sought deeper riches, and with a sigh she yielded to him. The delicate velvet of her tongue met his exploration.

Race deepened the kiss. Although still tender, the heat of passion tinted this caress a different shade of desire. The warm pressure of her breasts against Race's chest was unmistakably arousing, as was the length of her thighs pressed up against his. Her hands curled upward, and curious fingers sought the hair at the nape of his neck.

Those fingers, warm, gentle, innocent in their sensuality, ran through his hair, her touch yet another potent sensation. In response, Race shaped Dulcie's waist, then cautiously inched up. As he approached his twin goals, something moved on the other side of the shrub.

"Ee-yew! Dulcie's got a kissy-beau! Dulcie's got a kissy-beau!"

Billy Schofield's singsong voice startled Dulcie, and then she realized what the imp was broadcasting. "Oh, no! Billy! You come back here this very instant!"

"Uh-uh!" With a mean glare and blazing cheeks, Dulcie's tormentor began mincing his way down Willow Lane, swaying his scrawny posterior in an exaggerated parody of a feminine walk, smacking kisses in the air. "Dulcie's got a kissy-beau! *Smack, smack, smack!* Dulcie's got a kissy-beau. . . ."

Dulcie started off after her Sunday school student, the terror of the congregation, but soon noticed that every adult resident of Willow Lane had come outside in response to Billy's taunting tune.

The Whitakers, Prudence Kleinschmidt, Mary Margaret O'Murphy, and even Emma Schwartz, enormous in the last weeks of her pregnancy, stood watching the tableau with avid interest. Dulcie's cheeks burned, her earlobes tingled, and her scalp felt scalded. She wanted to die, so great was her chagrin.

From the end of Willow Lane, Billy's voice bounced back on a gust of wind. "Dulcie's got a kissy-beau. . . ." The last

Dulcie saw of the boy was when he turned her way and stuck his tongue out at her, anger evident on his freckled features.

Dulcie stopped in her tracks. She looked at Race, who wore a smug smile. Then she glanced at her curious neighbors. On some faces shock could be clearly read. "Oh, dear. I'm so sor—"

Myrna Whitaker cut Dulcie off. "Well, now Mary Margaret, didja hear that?"

"These young people today! What my father would have done to me doesn't bear retelling," offered Mary Margaret, appalled as a prim former schoolteacher would be.

"What'd the boy say?" asked Hubert, his hearing horn stuffed into his ear. "What'd the boy say?"

Prudence beamed at Dulcie and Race. "Always thought you were a smart one, Dulcie dear. Hang on to 'im!"

At that moment, Emma Schwartz spied the destruction her daughter had wrought. "Sarah Jane Schwartz! You get on inside right this minute. What were you thinking to ruin all Mama's flowers? Wait till your father gets home tonight. I better go get us a fresh switch, young lady." Pressing both fists into the small of her back, she trudged up her front steps, then turned toward Dulcie. "I warn you, Dulcie Kramer. Look at me real good. A girl has to watch out for these sweet-talking men!"

"Will she really beat that beautiful child?" Race asked, outrage making his voice quiver.

All that neighborly indignation had been wasted on the man. It seemed that once a lawyer, always a lawyer, bent on defending the innocent. Disgusted at his misplaced worry, Dulcie sniffed. "Fine one you are to worry about Sarah, who happens to be the most spoiled, well-loved child that ever lived. No one's laid a hand on her, nor will they. She's the apple of both parents' eyes. I'm the one who should arouse concern. Here I stand, facing scandal, and you don't even care.''

With a robust chuckle, Race winked at Dulcie. ''Trust me, sweetheart, you arouse plenty in me. And none of it can be labeled concern.''

Dulcie's blue eyes grew round. Her rosy lips formed a perfect O, and her cheeks pinkened to a luscious berry shade.

Knowing they were the prime item of interest, Race turned around and looked down the street. Although he hadn't planned it that way, it seemed he had effectively staked out a claim on Dulcie. When he turned back, he caught sight of Granny stepping out onto the porch, shotgun in hand, saggy wrinkles all in their frown position.

No fool, he glanced at Dulcie, saw irritation shove bemusement from her face, and decided to cut his losses. ''I really must go home. I need to check on my father's condition.'' With a quick wave, he trotted to the hitching post, gathered Zephyr's reins, then swung himself astride. ''I'll see you again as soon as I can. And definitely for Founders' Day.''

Before giving Dulcie a chance to take back her invitation, Race rode down Willow Lane as its inhabitants lined either side of the street, every eye fixed on his departing back.

Although his father's condition continued to improve, Race found himself rather busy with his practice. The Millers' will had to be duly witnessed and signed. Then for the Whorleys, the purchase of a lovely little cottage just beyond the northern limits of Lancaster had to be negotiated. Between meeting with the buyer and the seller, and staying close to home, Race found he didn't have enough time to slip in a visit to Dulcie until the Wednesday before Founders' Day.

As he approached Willow Lane, he found his pulse quickening, anticipation running rampant. This surfeit of emotion and expectation he was experiencing for Dulcie was certainly rare, not something that happened every day. He suspected his heart was already lost, and he wasn't quite ready to decide how he felt about that.

Hoping to talk Dulcie into an outing, he'd come in the Langstons' fine black Winton. Forward-thinking Horace bought the thousand-dollar "toy" last Christmas, more than likely before becoming embroiled in his business debacle. Race felt sure Dulcie would enjoy the sprightly automobile.

He stopped on the street outside the Kramer home and turned off the Winton's engine. Picking up a bouquet of white roses, he caught a hint of their spicy scent. He knocked on the door and fidgeted, passing the roses from hand to hand.

Dulcie came to see who'd arrived. "Race! What a wonderful surprise!"

"Well, I did tell you I'd try to return before Founders' Day."

"Yes, but I thought you'd be quite busy. How is your father?"

"Better, thank you. Here," he said, holding out another waxy-green florist's paper bundle. Dulcie unwrapped his offering, brought the delicate blossoms up to her face, and smiled.

"They smell wonderful," she said, again burying her face among the velvety petals. "Thank you."

"My pleasure. And speaking of pleasure, would you have some time to spare today? I have my father's new automobile and I thought it would be particularly nice to take a drive, seeing how beautiful the afternoon has become."

Dulcie thought a moment, then an idea occurred to her. "Did you have anywhere specific in mind for this drive?"

"No, not really, just to enjoy the fresh air, the sunny weather, your charming company."

Thinking back to the morning's activities, she went on. "Would you mind going to Lancaster?"

"Lancaster? Well, no . . . I guess if that's where you'd like to go, I don't have anything against it."

"Lovely!" she cried, then turned around and headed for the dining room. On the walnut table, she'd placed a generous-sized tin full of Maman's bonbons, ready to be taken to Mr. Eby. She could easily drop them off at his wife's millinery shop and still enjoy being with Race. "I'll be ready in a minute."

"I'll wait outside," Race said, wondering when Granny K would make her presence known. And he knew she would. He just had to stay on his guard to not be caught unawares. He returned to his father's pride and joy and began to crank the engine.

"I'm ready!" Dulcie chimed as she closed the front door behind her, her handbag batting against a royal-blue tin she carried.

"And not a moment too soon!" he exclaimed, extending his hand to help her. Surprisingly she hugged the tin to her chest and gave him her other hand. "Here," he said, wondering at her odd actions, "allow me."

From behind the automobile, Granny's voice boomed a song of doom. "Now vait chust vun minute. Vere do you think my Dulcie yer takin'?"

Visions of shotguns danced in Race's head. "No— nowhere. I mean, we're simply going for a drive. It's such a lovely afternoon, and all."

"Ja, lovely afternoon. But dat's a closed carriage. Ain't right fer Dulcie to go in there mit choo. Not alone."

From the stubborn jut of Granny K's chin, Race knew there would be no persuading her. Resignation came quickly. "Very well, I have no problem escorting both Kramer ladies to Lancaster."

He shrugged. If he had to take the grandmother to get the granddaughter, it was a small enough price to pay. "Let's be on our way. Would you like to drive down Queen Street? Toward Penn Square?"

Dulcie emitted a small gasp, then her eyes gleamed. "Perfect," she said with great emphasis.

Race shot her a questioning look, but only saw innocence. As he climbed into the automobile, he again took note of how different women were from men, particularly their ability to take on expressions as maddening as the artlessness Miss Dulcie Kramer's features wore. She was up to something.

Donning the black goggles he wore for driving, he noticed a wagon bouncing down Willow Lane, heading in their direction. He chose to wait, shutting off the engine, not wishing to spook the horse. Then he noticed Granny K's sudden animation.

"Vera!" Granny cried, waving furiously, shaking Horace Langston's most prized possession. A barrage of Pennsylvania German followed.

Granny K's friend Vera stopped her horse, looped the reins through the ring on the hitching post, then approached the automobile, healthy caution in her small dark eyes. The chattering never let up.

Then Granny rapped Race's head with her pipe. "Take Dulcie to Lancaster. Let me down. I gotta try for Vera. Her man no goot doing."

" 'Try'? What is this 'try,' Dulcie?" Race asked as he helped Granny down to the ground. He gladly handed the woman her shotgun. "And don't even think of changing the subject."

Dulcie watched Granny and Vera enter the Kramer home.

What should she do? She had to say *something*. Race came around to her side of the horseless carriage.

Oh, dear. "Don't pay her any attention. The older she gets, the more convinced she is of knowing everything about every subject of any importance. Many of her friends come to her with their troubles. She tries to help."

Dulcie bit her lip and crossed her fingers. She made quite a production of setting the tin of chocolates on her lap. She waved at Emma Schwartz, still pregnant, then turned back to Race.

Who was studying her as if she'd suddenly grown three heads.

"That's it?" he asked, his voice disbelieving. "That's all that 'trying' business is about? Giving homespun advice to her friends? Then why did you chase me off the other day? And why did you insist on ducking my questions?"

"My, my! You *are* a lawyer, aren't you?" Hoping to buy herself a few more seconds, she smiled. "You shoot out the questions at quite an impressive clip! That's a most valuable gift you have there. What a pity it would have been if you'd set your heart on a bookkeeping career. All that interrogating talent gone to waste."

Race's piercing stare narrowed with suspicion. *Oh-oh.* Her gamble hadn't paid off. She was going to have to give him an explanation of sorts. "Well, you see, Granny can become a nuisance when she tries to fix people's problems. And since she's certain she can, she never gives up. You know how persistent she can be."

Race only offered a noncommittal "Hmmm," then walked around the automobile and fiddled with the contraption.

Dulcie barged on. "Well, of course, you understand. Imagine how embarrassing it becomes when she meddles in a stranger's trouble."

"I guess the question is, how successful is she?"

It was Dulcie's turn to murmur a safe "Hmmm . . ."

Both fell silent as the vehicle rumbled back to life. By some exotic manipulation, Race jolted the automobile into motion. The noise of the machine made conversation difficult. Dulcie hoped her vague answers—not lies, mind you, just vague *non*answers—had been enough to satisfy Race.

She patted her tin of chocolates. It was most fortunate that Race had come to visit this afternoon. She'd been planning to go to Lancaster tomorrow, but with memories of her last trip still fresh in her mind, she'd leapt at the opportunity for a better mode of transportation. The Langstons' horseless carriage certainly delivered that. It was even exciting. And a bit frightening. Dulcie wasn't certain humans were meant to go quite so fast, but the ride was exhilarating.

As they drove through a kaleidoscope of Pennsylvania farm scenes—emerald pastures, black-and-white cows, red barns, white farmhouses, Delft-blue skies—the wind rushed past her cheeks, tousled her hair, then tossed tendrils down onto her forehead, across her lips. She laughed just for the sheer enjoyment of the experience. She noticed a similar expression on Race's handsome face.

Too soon, they reached Lancaster. Dulcie's pulse, already accelerated by the drive and Race's enervating presence, grew to a deliberate drum roll. This moment was of utmost importance. If Mr. Eby were to dislike her chocolate bonbons, he would never rent his vacant store to her. If she couldn't negotiate a reasonable rent, she'd be forced to discontinue her efforts. She still didn't want to move West.

As they drove past the railroad station on Queen Street, Dulcie gathered all her gumption. "Race," she called, raising her voice over the engine. "Could you stop near Katarina's European Millinery? There," she added, pointing, "on the right side of the street. I need to deliver this parcel."

Race's gaze retraced the path Dulcie's eyes took. He saw Katarina Eby's hat shop. *Ohmigod!*

It couldn't be . . . could it? He glanced at the tin innocently sitting on Dulcie's lap. What were the chances it held only trim for a hat? Laces? Ribbons?

From the way Dulcie clutched the container, one would think it carried her most prized possession. And *that* made the hairs on the back of Race's neck stand at attention. There was only one possible conclusion to come to. Dulcie had found a way to have Race bring her to deliver bonbon samples to Martin Eby.

Martin Eby. The businessman who'd told Milton Hershey he planned to rent a shop to a confectioner.

Stunned, Race brought the automobile to a screeching stop at the corner. Eby's building was only two doors away. Before he could gather his thoughts, Dulcie was out of the vehicle and sashaying into the millinery.

The entire situation stank of conflict of interest. And there was nothing Race could have done to prevent it. Should Milton Hershey learn that Race had actually transported the enemy to peddle her wares, hell would undoubtedly break loose.

Who'd have thought Dulcie Kramer's angelic exterior hid so much trouble?

❖ 9 ❖

Dumbstruck, Race sat in his father's automobile, waiting for Dulcie. No power on earth could have made him enter Katarina Eby's fussy little shop. Mrs. Eby and his mother served on various charitable committees together, and they had, over time, become friends. If Katarina or Martin noticed Race accompanying Dulcie, word would soon reach Milton Hershey.

What could he do now? His mind grappled with a bevy of options. Unfortunately no two agreed. He remained of two minds.

On the one hand, he felt guilty keeping secrets from Dulcie. It was bad enough that they'd met because he'd been hired to obtain something she had. Truly incriminating, though, were his subsequent returns to Everleigh, when he'd sought her out, kissed her even, while still hoping to obtain the recipe she considered crucial to her small family's livelihood. On the other hand, he *had* tried to tell Dulcie the truth, but each time it remotely looked like a good opportunity to do so, something had inevitably gone wrong.

How was he to persuade a woman, especially one as bright as Dulcie Kramer, that he'd returned to her side in response to the powerful attraction between them? How could he persuade her that he hadn't been romancing her simply for the sake of acquiring the damn chocolate bonbon recipe? How could he confess to working for the man who wanted to put Dulcie out of business even before she went into business in the first place?

Race felt backed into a corner with no way out. "Damn and blast that confounded Milton Hershey! And damn his canny business mind!"

With his father's health compromised, Race didn't dare approach the older Langston with his problems. Dr. Murdoch insisted that Horace be kept quiet, at peace, worry-free. If Race mentioned this situation to his father, his weakened heart might—

No! That wasn't the answer to Race's dilemma. He was a grown man who didn't need a parent to solve his problems. He wouldn't—couldn't—appeal to Horace for support in this matter.

If only he could come up with a different angle, a new argument, to persuade Milton Hershey to hire another carrier pigeon. This one was about to get his wing feathers drastically clipped.

Not that Race felt any better about keeping this latest development secret from both his father and Milton. Neither man would understand how Race had innocently blundered into this present complication in an already convoluted mess.

He really had no idea how to proceed. All he knew was that if he were to speak to Dulcie about Milton's interest in buying the bonbon recipe, he was sure to lose her. And Kirk "Slime" Schleinbaugh wasn't about to fade into the background. In fact, if Race were to be banished from the Kramer home—as he was certain would happen should Dulcie sniff out his ulterior motive—Kirk would merely take advantage of the opportunity.

If Race were absolutely honest, Kirk Schleinbaugh was not the ogrelike creature he preferred to think him. Kirk's Teutonic looks, his sun-bleached blond hair, blue eyes, rough-hewn facial features, and his powerful build would no doubt appeal to many a lovely lady. The man's homespun simplicity could even add to his charm. Besides, Kirk couldn't be too stupid; he was smart enough to want Dulcie.

And Dulcie might find enough to admire in Kirk.

Kirk also had the advantage of proximity to the object of their parallel affections. Whereas Race had a new practice to build in Lancaster, Kirk's farm was no doubt close to Everleigh. The farmer could visit Dulcie every day after he finished his chores. Race, however, was beginning to attract clients, and often enough his consultations extended into the evening hours. He wasn't free to spend much time with Dulcie.

Although he hated to admit it, Race was jealous of Kirk's long-time association with the Kramers. That history gave the man an impressive advantage in courting a woman's affections. Kirk and Dulcie no doubt had many shared memories. A determined suitor would make use of every possible link.

Then Race remembered Granny K. He did have an ace in the hole. Granny wasted no love on Kirk, and she seemed to encourage Race's pursuit of her granddaughter. Still, it was Dulcie who would ultimately choose between her two admirers. He didn't think Granny's support would mean much once Dulcie learned of his ties to Milton Hershey, and worse yet, when she learned what Hershey had in mind.

So, no, Race couldn't offer Dulcie money for her recipe, her inheritance, as she'd called it. He was right back where he'd started. He had to keep secrets from Dulcie, and his conscience flayed him for doing so. Guilt left a revolting aftertaste in his mouth.

In frustration, he slugged the steering wheel. "Damnation!"

Just then, the door to Katarina Eby's shop flew open. Dulcie fairly skipped out. "Oh, Race! You wouldn't believe my good fortune," she called as she hurried toward the automobile.

Race fortified himself with a deep breath. "Good fortune?"

"Well, yes," she said, opening the door. Race leaned across the passenger seat and extended a hand to assist her into the vehicle. She continued her animated chatter. "Mr. Eby happened to be at his wife's store right now. I'd brought him samples of my bonbons, and he absolutely loved them. In fact, he was so pleased with my product that he predicts Mignone Kramer's Sweet Secrets Confectionery will be a great success."

The sinking feeling in Race's gut mingled with the nauseating taste of guilt. His temples pounded viciously. Worse, he felt certain of only one thing. No matter what he did, this entire chocolate disaster was bound to rear up and smack him right between the eyes.

And he was helpless to stop it.

The best he could hope for was to outsmart Kirk Slimebaugh and hopefully win Dulcie's affections. Buying the recipe was, at present, impossible. "Tell me," he asked, "does that Kirk fellow know you're on the brink of entrepreneurship?"

"Kirk? I don't know." Dulcie shrugged. "It doesn't matter one way or the other. As I was saying, Mr. Eby was very enthusiastic about notifying his wife's best customers. He seemed to feel that the well-to-do ladies of Lancaster will rush to buy my bonbons."

"Have you known him long?" he asked.

"Mr. Eby?" she returned, sounding puzzled. "Of course not. I just met him two weeks ago."

"No, not Martin Eby," Race said, frustrated. "Kirk Slime—*Schlein*baugh."

"You want to know how long I've known Kirk?" At Race's nod, she frowned. "Why? He has nothing to do with my business. It's Mr. Eby who expects the hat shop's clientele to help my confectionery, and likewise my customers will probably patronize the millinery."

Race bit down on his impatience and curiosity. "Yes, yes. But you didn't answer. How long have you known Kirk?"

"Who cares how long I've known Kirk! It's my confectionery that matters. What is this sudden interest in Kirk Slime—*Schlein*baugh?"

"I'm just curious. Why won't you answer my questions about him?"

"Because he has nothing to do with my chocolate bonbons." Glancing out the window, Dulcie twirled a golden curl around her finger. "Hmm . . . you know? I'd better order large quantities of ingredients. They'll take time to arrive, and during that time I can ready the shop."

"Fine! Order your ingredients. Prepare your shop. But how long have you known Kirk Slime?"

"Race Langston! That is the rudest, meanest thing I've ever heard. Kirk is *not* slime. If you're so interested, I can tell you I've known him since I was born. Our families were friendly. We went to school together. He sat behind me."

Damn! It was worse than he'd thought. Childhood sweethearts. Race would have to be double-smart, work twice as hard, to win Dulcie's heart. His next question would surely awaken Miss Dulcie Kramer's spicy temper, but he really had to know. "Has he kissed you?"

Dulcie's jaw dropped open. The flush on her cheeks spread to her forehead, and Race would have sworn her delicate earlobes had also heated up. Then she pursed her lips in displeasure. She narrowed her gaze. "That, Mr. Langston, is none of your business. I wish to return home. Right this very moment, and with no further impertinent questions."

Hell, all he'd done was chase her away! But now, her reaction being so fiery, he *really* had to know. "Fine, I'll take you home. But first I need an answer."

"You have no right to ask me such personal questions. You have no claim on my affec—"

"That, Miss Kramer, is where I beg to differ with you. Those kisses we shared had layers of meaning. We each expressed certain feelings, and we both responded with equal passion. That intimacy gave me enough to claim."

If anything, Dulcie grew redder, angrier. "Since you insist on behaving boorishly, I will simply ignore you. Please start this vehicle."

She turned her back on him and faced Mr. Eby's building. Race's frustration, fear, and jealousy sent his hand out to grasp her shoulder. "Dammit, Dulcie, don't turn away from me. I really need to know."

When Race's hand covered her shoulder, Dulcie trembled. When his voice dropped from an autocratic pitch to that of an anxious suitor, she tamped down her outrage. When he gently squeezed, turning her back his way, she forgave him. "Kirk has never kissed me."

Race's sigh of relief was soul-deep. With a tentative pat to her shoulder, he took his hand away. "Forgive my persistence. It was just . . . the thought of another man kissing you the way I did was more than I could bear. Thank you for your honesty."

His apology was genuine. He really had been worried. And Dulcie was stunned by the depth of his need to know. Could Race care for her as much as she was growing to care for him? Could they truly have a future together?

Dulcie caught her bottom lip between her teeth. It was best if she didn't entertain such daydreams. It would do her no good to envision something that might never come to pass. She'd have to wait until the intense Mr. Race Langston made his next move.

But now she felt embarrassed. Admitting that Race was the only man she'd allowed such liberties revealed too much about her feelings. She hoped he didn't think she'd set out to "catch" him, as so many girls did. Dulcie was a businesswoman. She had a future in commerce.

She could scarcely contain her enthusiasm. "Oh, Race, I'm so excited! I'm so pleased with Mr. Eby's interest in my venture. It means so much to me. Especially since it's Maman's secret recipe I'll be using. And her name on the store sign. I miss her so much." Then she noticed Race's blanched features. "Race? Are you all right?"

He shot a nervous glance in her direction, avoided her questioning gaze, then opened the automobile's door. "Yes, yes," he answered with a careless wave. "I just have to check on the engine so we can return to Everleigh."

As she watched Race fiddle with the innards of the vehicle and listened to the mechanical spits and sputters it made, Dulcie decided she never wanted one of these monstrosities. Exciting though the ride into Lancaster had been, noisy machines like this one weren't for her. She'd stick with Old Molly, the horse's bad habits notwithstanding.

When the engine was chugging away, smoke billowing out the rear, Race sat behind the wheel and began the drive back. Although they'd been silent on their way to Lancaster, it had been an easy silence, both enjoying the ride and the pleasure of being together. Now, after that silly business about Kirk, the silence between Race and Dulcie felt strained. And she didn't know what to do about it.

Partway home, Race turned to Dulcie and, raising his voice, asked, "How often does Kirk come calling?"

Dulcie snorted. "Would you *please* stop talking about Kirk?" she yelled over the engine's rumble.

Race's jaw tightened. She ignored it.

He could remain surly. *She'd* rather relish her day's success. "Granny will be so excited about the confectionery. She's going to help me make the candies every morning."

Race nodded sharply. Dulcie tried again to establish a conversation. "I'd better start cleaning the shop tomorrow. It's going to take some work to have it ready. I plan to start selling chocolates the week after next."

This time Race's nod was even tighter.

Dulcie's patience took flight. "Oh, for goodness' sake! Have you forgotten how to carry on a conversation?"

"No," he bit off. "Since you want to talk, tell me this. If you're not allowing Kirk Slime any liberties, then why don't you send him packing when he comes to visit? He ogled you most improperly the other day."

Now that she had no patience left to call on, Dulcie grew irritated. "I already asked you to stop talking about Kirk," she said. "If you're so interested in him, then after you take me home, go visit the man. He'll likely think you stark, raving mad, as I'm beginning to do, but you're certainly free to befriend him."

"I don't want to befriend him! I just don't want him looking at you that way."

"What way?"

"As if he were about to devour you whole!"

"Oh, what nonsense! I'm tired of carrying on two separate conversations. I don't want to talk about Kirk Schleinbaugh, and you don't care about what matters to me. This outing is over, and quite a failure at that. Stop this vehicle! I wish to walk back home."

Race's eyebrows met. He shot her a dark look. "I took you from your home, and I'll escort you back."

"Oh, fine."

"Yes, fine. *Very* fine."

Both occupants of the Langstons' fine horseless carriage proceeded to stare forward. Not another word was exchanged, save two curt "goodbyes" upon arriving at the Kramer home.

The next day, Dulcie loaded a sturdy pail, a bag of rags, a mop, a broom, a feather duster, and a large block of strong yellow soap onto the recently repaired buckboard. As usual, Old Molly balked, but in the end Dulcie won out.

The outcome of her recent trips to Lancaster miserably clear in her mind, Dulcie took the Columbia Pike. In her usual cantankerous manner, Old Molly pulled to a halt each time another vehicle passed them. After a number of stops and starts, they reached the outskirts.

Dulcie left Molly at a livery she'd noticed the day before as she and Ra—*that man*—drove out of town. Loading her cleaning supplies into the pail, she then balanced her mop and broom on a shoulder. With her handbag bouncing from the arm holding the broom and mop, the pail swinging from the other, she clanked her way to the Ebys' building, not caring that she did indeed look a sight.

Using the key Mr. Eby had given her, she let herself into her store.

My store. Oh, that sounded good!

Dropping her burdens on the dusty floor, Dulcie studied the small room. It would do. She'd put shelves against that wall on the right to display freshly made goodies. A large, sturdy cabinet set close to the door would hold additional stock, and on its top she'd place a cash register.

Concentrating, she realized that if she painted the walls a

bright white, she could perhaps stencil an attractive pattern on the walls. Crisp curtains tied back on either side of the large front window would add welcome color. In the middle of the window she planned to set a table with samples of the gift tins of various sizes she also planned to sell.

It was going to be wonderful. *Magnifique!* as Maman would have said.

If only Race had cared enough—

No! Dulcie had lectured herself during the early hours before dawn. She would absolutely, positively not waste another second on thoughts of *that man*. His determined demand for information about Kirk Schleinbaugh, and his total lack of interest in her new venture, were reason enough to banish him from her thoughts.

So she began cleaning. And humming.

The day went fast. Before she even noticed, Katarina Eby had closed her shop. That had to have been around five, since that was the millinery's closing time. But Dulcie had worked on. It had felt so good to scrub away the dust of disuse from her store that she'd lost track of time. She'd polished windows, washed the back-room floor, and stripped cobwebs from concealed nooks.

On her way to the back room now, she was surprised to note how dark it was. Surely it was past eight already? But although the sky outside still bore the lavender gown of dusk, shadows shrouded the corners of her store. It was past time to go home.

As Dulcie gathered her cleaning supplies, she began humming again. After storing her housekeeping paraphernalia, she congratulated herself on a job well done. She gathered her handbag and locked the back door, then proceeded to the store front. A large human silhouette hid the front door.

"Aaaaaagh!" she shrieked, hand at her throat. "Who are you? What do you want?"

The shadow stepped forward, a hand extended toward her. "It's me. Race. You needn't have screamed."

Relief sapped the strength from her legs. She swooned. Race rushed up and prevented her fall. He righted her in the circle of his arms for a moment, and when she could again breathe, she took firm steps away from him. "What prompted you to skulk in my store?"

"I wasn't skulking, I was waiting for you."

With an expansive gesture, Dulcie sought to appear nonchalant. "Well, here I am. What do you want?"

"I came to apologize for my rude behavior yesterday afternoon."

Race's repentance punched a large hole in the fabric of Dulcie's anger. But she didn't wish to appear ingenuous. "Oh, so you *do* recognize your rudeness. Can I count on your improved behavior in the future?"

"Of course. That's why I came. I still want to escort you to the Founders' Day festivities. Will you allow me that?"

Race had to care about her—at least a little—otherwise why would he have returned? He'd humbled himself, something she'd heard men rarely ever did. She tried to calm her rapid heartbeat. "Mm-hmm. I'm looking forward to that."

Race appeared to relax, easing his posture from ramrod straight to a casual stance. Yes, thought Dulcie, he'd been worried. Worried she would reject him.

She smiled ruefully. "You're not the only one who got a scolding. Granny lectured me on my bad manners yesterday when you didn't come inside after bringing me home. She felt it highly improper of me not to invite you for some refreshment."

Race chuckled. "There'll be plenty of opportunities in the future. Both of you can count on that."

The warm glow in Race's dark eyes reached deep and touched Dulcie's emotions. He really was a beautiful man.

And he seemed smitten enough with her to be willing to take on the burden of charming her crazy grandmother. A ripple of excitement coiled through her. "I'd like to invite you for supper tonight."

Race's smiled melted away. "Oh, I'm sorry. I have an appointment with a client this evening. I'm working to establish my practice and can't afford to lose even one. This man has a large farm and various smaller properties he wants to sell. He needs me to prepare the necessary documents."

"Oh," Dulcie said, feeling silly. "I'm sorry, too. Especially for presuming you'd be free tonight. Well, Founders' Day will come soon enough day after tomorrow."

Race shook his head and approached her. "I'm afraid you're wrong. Even tomorrow wouldn't be soon enough. Not for me."

Slowly he reached out and wiped a smudge from her cheek. "Dust," he murmured, and drew closer.

Dulcie bit her bottom lip and stood statue-still.

"Dulcie," he whispered, then lowered his head.

Her heart beating loudly, so loudly she was sure Race could hear it, Dulcie watched his lips come close. Race was going to kiss her, and she wanted him to kiss her again. She wanted to see if the incredible sensations she remembered feeling before were real or merely a dream, a lovely fantasy. She parted her lips and waited.

Not for long. Soon he was there, his warm lips softly rubbing against hers. Nipping gently at her lower lip. Then his tongue touched her mouth, and the wet warmth tantalized her. He delineated her lips, a butterfly touch, the merest hint of a caress.

Dulcie sighed. Race's kiss. It was soft, gentle, drawing out responses from within her. But what she felt inside wasn't quite so subtle. It was more a burst of warmth throughout her body that then spread to her heart. Flashes of iridescent light flared behind her eyelids. Her pulse quickened, beating faster, faster, so fast that she felt dizzy, her thoughts and emotions all awhirl. Her body continued to tingle with fresh sparks of heat, more and more each time Race deepened the intensity of their kiss, in more and more private places. Heat swirled through her veins and pooled deep, low.

Curiosity, longing, desire had her slipping her tongue to touch Race's lips. Those clever lips that gave such plea—

"Wheeeew!"

The sudden piercing whistle brought Race rudely back from the paradise he'd escaped to while kissing the beautiful woman in his arms. With that rough interruption came the realization that they stood directly in front of the window, visible to anyone walking by. Since Lancaster was having lovely summer weather, many people were out for a twilight walk.

Race stepped away from Dulcie, wishing to spare her any additional embarrassment.

As Race backed away, Dulcie cast a quick glance to the window and, catching sight of the two adolescent faces scrunched up against the pane of glass, she felt a flush spread over her face. Oh, dear. How unseemly. Any number of passersby must have seen Race kissing her.

"You, there!" she cried. "Yes, you two scoundrels! Get away from my window. I just finished cleaning it."

"Ah-haah!" singsonged the heavyset one. "Musta been 'fore the sizzle we saw."

The skinny one with red hair and spectacles chortled. "An' now you gotta clean the steam off it!"

"Good!" cheered the fat one. Slapping each other's back in praise of their hateful comments, they strolled away toward Penn Square.

"Oh, dear," Dulcie moaned. "I'm ever so mortified. What could you possibly think of me?"

"I think you're a beautiful lady. And a passionate woman. The best combination possible. You're an absolute delight, and you've done nothing to change my high opinion of you."

Race came closer. Dulcie backed away. His legs were longer. He stood at her side. "And, Miss Dulcie Kramer, you'd better get used to being kissed, because I intend to do so as often as I can get away with it."

As Dulcie's jaw dropped in astonishment, Race winked and smiled.

"You were right," she murmured, waving her hand before her heated face. "Founders' Day won't come nearly soon enough."

Early Saturday morning, Dulcie finished frying large pieces of chicken. She'd already packed a crock with tangy potato salad, another one with coleslaw, and for dessert she'd cut generous wedges of molasses pie. The Kramer women's picnics usually drew high bids from the men, and every cent went to a good cause. Everleigh donated the proceeds of the box-lunch auction to an orphanage in Lancaster.

Dulcie put the chicken to cool, then stepped out back and through the half-door of the root cellar. She'd made lemonade last night and had left it in the cool depths of the storage place. In the dark, the odd odor of the cellar tickled her nose. It was a peculiar scent. The tang of onions and garlic mixed with the mellow fragrance of smoked ham and bacon, and before too long the spice of apples would add to the bouquet. In Lancaster County good eatings abounded.

"Dulcie-girl!"

Grabbing the two jugs of lemonade, Dulcie went back out and into the kitchen. "Yes, Granny. I'm just about ready."

Granny hitched up a shoulder strap of her faded overalls, then tucked her pipe stem over her ear. "Dat's vat you said ven I asked last."

Chuckling, Dulcie settled the lemonade in the two waiting baskets, then wrapped silverware and tin cups in crisp napkins. "This time, I *am* ready!" She closed the first hamper. "Here. Take yours. I'll carry mine."

"Goot. You said Race vould come?"

A ripple of excitement wriggled through Dulcie. Her cheeks grew warm. "That's what he said."

"But he said he vould other day come."

Although she'd been trying very hard not to remember that, Granny's comment planted doubt in Dulcie's expectations. But she refused to dwell on it. "I'm sure he'll be here today. And I hope he buys my basket. I'd love to share lunch with him."

"Lunch ain't all you vant to share mit 'im!"

"Oh, hush now, Granny. Come on, let's get to the square. I want to be there when Race arrives."

"Afraid of other girls?"

Dulcie's flush deepened. "Nonsense! I invited him. I should be there to greet him."

With a cackle, Granny slung her food basket over her arm. "You say too much, too loud. I know vat I know." And with a firm bob of her gray head, she clomped out the front door.

Dulcie followed, trying to stop the bothersome thoughts. Yes, Race would come today. Yes, he'd buy her lunch. And yes, they'd eat together. And of course it would be a wonderful day.

Closing the front door behind her, Dulcie donned a deliberately cheerful expression in anticipation of the greetings she would call out.

Heading for the square at the center of Everleigh, Dulcie

hummed a vague scrap of song. She caught sight of Sarah Schwartz and waved. Hubert Whitaker came outside, hearing horn in hand. "Good morning!" she yelled. "Isn't it a lovely day?"

"What you say? Imogene Hively is fey? I don't reckon. She's dull as a rusted nail."

Despite her nerves, Dulcie's laughter bubbled out. She nodded as she walked on by, knowing there was little she could do to elaborate. Hubert had long ago reached the point where he couldn't hear, and he seemed to like it that way. The horn was merely a sop to Doc Helmrich's pride and an appeasement for Myrna's wifely frustration.

Up ahead, on the edge of the square, she spied Billy Schofield. Hmmm, trouble was sure to follow. Arms around their shoulders, he was huddled with the youngest Miller boy, Ben, and Michael Druck. They were up to no good; they always were.

Glancing around at the people already gathered there, she spied a most anticipated coffee-brown head. "Race!" she called.

He looked straight at her, smiled, and made his way closer.

Then Billy saw Race. He turned to Dulcie, made a rude face, and glowered. Immediately he elbowed his companions. The three darted impudent looks in her direction, then began to prance on tiptoe, throwing kisses into the air. "Dulcie has a kissy-beau . . . Dulcie has a kissy-beau! *Smack, smack, smack!*"

At that very moment, just when Dulcie was praying for the ground to open and swallow her whole, she felt the uniquely warm, enervating touch of Race's hand at the small of her back. Cheeks burning, discomfiture reigning supreme, Dulcie looked from the boys to Race, then back to the boys again.

Behind the crowd staring from across the square, a familiar voice rang out. "Vat choo doin', Billy Schofield? Vant I should shoot you? My gun, I have it."

Race leaned closer to Dulcie's ear. "And I once worried she'd shoot me! I hope she peppers the little delinquent!"

"Oh, you—you male, you!" Dulcie sputtered. "You're all abominable from birth! Get away from me. I have better things to do than be publicly humiliated."

❖ *10* ❖

HE'D NEVER UNDERSTAND women. Never.

What had *he* done, anyway? The one in the wrong was that towheaded demon and his buddies. True, they'd taunted Dulcie because Billy caught Race kissing her in the privacy of a wisteria vine. But the little devil had no reason to be creeping around the Kramer home.

A puff of smoke blew up Race's nose.

"Now vat choo do?" Granny asked, standing before Race. "Vant I shoot you? Like Billy?"

"Honest," he answered, hands displayed in a gesture of innocence, "I did nothing. In fact, I told Dulcie I hoped you'd shoot that Billy full of holes. Then she got angry and ran off. I can't seem to find her."

"She vas chust embarrassed. De whole town Billy heard. Unt then you make fun. Ain't ready for it. Give her time, unt buy her box lunch."

"You want me to buy her a meal? Feed her?"

"Hell a' kitin'! You young'uns so *dummkup* be. I don' kenn vat you do mitout Granny." Shaking her head, and muttering in a dialect so heavy Race could make out none of what she was saying, Granny dragged him across the square and down a side street. "Listen goot. Give her time to *fergess* she's been set down plenty hard. Den choo buy *Dulcie's* basket unt mit her eat. Those *bissel rutz-naus,* dey embarrassed Dulcie. Der *vaters* oughta give 'em goot birchings on der *hinnerdales*!''

Race knew Granny was right. The boys had embarrassed Dulcie in front of the whole town. She'd need time to compose herself. And the three little snots did indeed deserve plenty birchings on their *hinnerdales*. But none of that helped him. He hadn't come to secure the punishment of the town's three hellions. Neither had he come to visit with Granny on some quiet side street.

He'd come to see Dulcie. And now she wanted nothing to do with him.

Perhaps Granny had the right idea. Perhaps if he let Dulcie spend time alone, her anger would lessen. Then he could follow Granny's suggestion, buy Dulcie's basket of food. ''Which is hers?''

Granny lit her pipe before answering. ''Mine unt Dulcie's are same. Big, mit red unt vite napkins. Dulcie's should sell first. Den mine.''

''Thank you. I'll try to identify it. I do want to share that lunch with her.''

''Unt she mit you!'' Granny countered, then cackled a laugh.

''Well, that's certainly good to know. After the way she ran off, I thought she'd never speak to me again.''

''She'll speak—unt more—mit you. But you mind vat I say. No more *schmutzing* behind the flowers!''

Race took out and waved his white handkerchief. ''No more schmootsing behind the flowers. I promise.''

With a final glare, Granny took off. She was a funny one, that Granny K. But she was right. Had Race not led Dulcie behind the wisteria, Billy would never have caught them. He thought on that for a moment.

"No regrets there, Granny!" he called out. Then with a smile, he sent a two-fingered salute to the old woman's retreating back.

When the sun reached the apex of the perfect blue sky, Race pushed away from the wall of the closed barbershop and approached the crowd around the gazebo in Founders' Square. A table laden with baskets and pails of every sort and size gave new meaning to the term "groaning board."

He remained on the edge of the throng, feeling as left out as if he were at a Richter family gathering. And he hated the feeling. Not only did he want to get back on Dulcie's good side because of his romantic interest, but because with her he felt as if he belonged. It was the oddest sensation, and he wasn't certain he wanted to feel such longing for another's presence, but there it was. He felt he belonged at Dulcie's side.

A ripple of applause broke out, and Race glanced toward the gazebo. An elderly gentleman, who, despite the humid heat, wore a black suit and a sparkling white shirt, stood before the table of lunches. He cleared his throat loud enough for Race to hear, then patted his flowing white beard.

"Ve ready to start?" he asked.

The crowd answered "Yes" as one.

"As alvays, ve start mit de Kramer lunches."

"Ja!" boomed a deep voice at Race's right. With a glance, he verified his suspicion. The Slime-man had shown up. And although Race had known in the back of his mind that Kirk Schleinbaugh would be present at this community event, he hadn't allowed the thought to disturb him. But now, as matters stood between Race and Dulcie, Kirk's presence carried an ominous threat.

Race *had* to buy that lunch.

He took a good look at the lunches. Dismay filled him. A veritable plethora of red and white fabric appeared to cover many of the baskets on the table. How would he ever identify Dulcie's?

As he watched, the black-garbed gentleman picked up an especially large basket. Like so many others, it was covered with a red-and-white napkin.

Then Race remembered Granny's words. *"Dulcie's should sell first."*

Crossing his arms over his chest, Race glanced toward Kirk and braced himself for what would surely be a battle of wits over a woman. Moments later, the gentleman in the gazebo began to chant unintelligibly.

Race frowned.

"Biddy, biddy, biddy . . ." the man continued to chant.

From the corner of his eye, Race saw Kirk raise his hand and nod. The man in the gazebo nodded back, then chanted again. Race had never seen this before. He assumed they were having what was better known in the area as a public vendue, but instead of auctioning livestock, the lunches were up for bid.

Screwing up his courage, somewhat daunted by the knowledge that he was an outsider, Race gestured to the auctioneer.

The white beard bobbed. Kirk glared at Race, then gestured again.

The white beard bobbed. Race glared at Kirk, then gestured again.

And so they went. Race hoped someone somewhere was keeping accurate count of how much he'd been bidding, as he had no idea what those "biddy, biddy, biddys" meant. He also hoped he had enough cash in his wallet.

Finally Kirk seemed to slow down. He didn't jump in with a bid quite as promptly as before. Race studied the blond man's broad face. A gloating look spread over the rough-hewn features.

Race smiled, then waggled his finger at the auctioneer.

The white beard bobbed.

Kirk smiled and kept still.

"*Biddy, biddy,* one. *Biddy, biddy,* two. *Biddy, biddy,* tree! Sold to stranger ower dere." And with a benevolent look lighting up his age-crinkled face, the man added, "Fer twelve dollars unt fifty cents. Most any lunch ever sell in dis town fer!"

Twelve dollars and fifty cents! No wonder everyone was staring at him. Kirk Slime certainly had good reason to smirk in triumph. Had he ever made a fool of Race!

The silence grew thick.

Taking his money clip from his trousers pocket, Race approached the gazebo. Suddenly to his left, a gun went off, shockingly loud in the stillness. Between two black-bonneted Mennonite farm women, Granny K appeared, limping toward the gazebo, shotgun waving over her head. "Dat's not Dulcie's lunch, Race. *Das ist* mine!"

The crowd gasped in unison, then chuckles sprouted around Race's rival. They took root, and soon the whole town bloomed with laughter.

Race knew that if he were one of them, he too would find the circumstances funny. But he wasn't anyone but himself, and he'd just bought an overpriced meal with Granny K and her loaded gun.

Putting on his best face, Race loped up the gazebo steps, hefted the weighty picnic-lunch basket, handed over his money, then went to stand beside Granny K. He crooked his elbow and waited until she slipped her arm through his. The pipe came, too.

"I intend to enjoy our meal, Granny," Race said gallantly.

"Ach!" the crone retorted. "Choo young'uns are *dumm-kup!* Couldn't find Dulcie's at the table afore de vendue?"

"I couldn't even get near the damn table! Besides, all the baskets had red-and-white napkins."

Granny shook her head. "Come, come. Dulcie alvays by river eat picnic. Choo vant to have a *sitz* her near. I vant'a vatch that *shkulduggl'r* Kirk. He's no goot."

Well, Race thought, couldn't get much clearer than that. Skulduggery, huh? Then he hadn't mistaken the lust in Kirk's eyes that day on the porch. And Granny didn't trust the fellow. That was good enough for him. "Show me the way."

Together, casting glances toward the gazebo, Race and Granny left the center of town by way of a broad side street. From behind them, he heard the older gentleman shout, *"Biddy, biddy,* one. *Biddy, biddy,* two. *Biddy, biddy,* tree! To Kirk Schleinbaugh, fer seventy-five cents."

So much for a battle of wits. He'd been soundly outmaneuvered. Outsmarted. And that didn't sit well with Race. He had to think. Surely with his training in law, his deductive powers, Race could anticipate Kirk's future actions and keep a step ahead of the farmer. He'd have to, since he couldn't stand the idea of Dulcie in Kirk's arms.

Still following Granny's lead, he went down the quiet street she'd chosen to take. Up ahead, he heard the rolling water of the Susquehanna River coming from beyond a stand of lush weeping willows. The trees offered welcome respite from the hot summer sun.

Once there, Granny grabbed the basket from Race, opened the lid, and spread an intricately pieced quilt on the grassless earth at the foot of a willow. Then she set the meal out for them. Race took in the beauty of the river's edge— the variegated greens of the trees, the rich fragrance of the loamy ground, the song of water bubbling brightly on its way. "Would have been the perfect place to eat with Dulcie."

Granny's gray bun bobbed in agreement. "But now she mit Kirk be. I vorry 'bout her."

"Me, too," he said, keeping an eye on the street they'd walked down.

Moments later, his vigilance yielded results. Chin held up in the air, and gaze affixed to the willows, Dulcie strode toward the river, Kirk Schleinbaugh at her side.

The blond man gave Race a triumphant smirk, then placed his broad palm at the small of Dulcie's back. As Race's temper began to boil, he observed Dulcie quickly step out of Kirk's reach.

Although Race took encouragement from Dulcie's evasion, he maintained his watchful pose. Kirk and Dulcie ducked under a particularly heavy willow, one right at the edge of the lapping water. Unfortunately the tree was so luxuriant, it completely concealed them.

"Damnation!"

"Das ist vat I chust said. I no Kirk trust. He ain't goot. But ve can't too close come. Dulcie vould angry be."

"Well," Race offered, "now that we both agree on the worthlessness of the man's character, let's eat. Perhaps they'll finish their meal quickly and without further incident."

"Here. Haf your chicken. Dulcie cooked it."

On her multicolored quilt, Granny had set out plates filled with golden chicken, creamy salads, rolls, and wedges of pie. The spread struck Race like a meal fit for a king. Sadly, this king was missing his queen.

Granny and Race ate silently, both keeping their attention on the tree farther down the river's shore. As soon as he deemed it socially acceptable, Race intended to reclaim Dulcie. After all, she had invited him to this disastrous event.

In a short time, the food was gone, and Race was sipping a final cupful of tart, cool lemonade. Beyond the lemonade, nothing else was particularly cold. Certainly not his disposition. Any wrong action from that Kirk creature would set off Race's leashed temper.

Suddenly, from the street that ran down to the stand of willows, came a woman's agitated voice. "Ermentrude! Ermentrude!"

Race turned and recognized the woman who'd distracted Granny the day he took Dulcie to Lancaster. She bustled closer, her somber purple dress ill-suited to the sultry weather. Consequently, her heavy-jowled face was flushed, and she perspired copiously.

"Vera," Granny said in response, waiting for the woman to reach her side. Pennsylvania German dialect ricocheted between the two women.

Then, turning to Race, Granny gestured toward the picnic debris. "Choo vait fer Dulcie. Den bring ever'ting home."

Race nodded, thinking. Granny had just done more than let him know she accepted his interest in Dulcie. She'd handed him something of great value: her trust. Moved by the gesture, he accepted the responsibility. Not only would he wait for Dulcie, but he'd make sure nothing happened to her. "Go on," he said. "I'll take care of everything."

Quickly he packed the dishes and utensils back into the picnic basket. As he ran yet another glance around the area they'd occupied, he noticed Granny's shotgun at the base of the tree, partly hidden by a fold in the quilt. Race was impressed by the depth of the woman's faith in him. She'd left her two treasures in his care.

Since he saw no sign of Dulcie and Kirk, he grudgingly gave them a few minutes more. He settled his back against a tree trunk, the basket, quilt, and gun within easy reach.

Now that there was trouble between him and Dulcie again, Race had no idea how he'd get around to concluding Milton Hershey's chocolate bonbon business. Especially since Kirk had upped the ante. Not that they were playing a game of cards, but still they were both competing for the same prize. At this moment, Kirk held the upper hand.

Making himself more comfortable by bending a knee, Race pulled a leaf off a low-hanging branch. He tapped it against his thigh, appreciating the bit of vegetation's flexibility. He wished Milton Hershey were half as tractable as the greenery was pliant. But the man had made abundantly clear his refusal to bend. Race would have to solve the dilemma without any hope of swaying his client.

Client! Hah. Theirs didn't feel like a normal attorney-client association. It felt more as if the candy maker were a master puppeteer, and Race a pile of sticks and threads, dancing at Milton's whim.

A balmy breeze trailed a willow branch across Race's face. He heard the slippery rustle of the wind as it wove a path through nearby trees, shrubs, and bushes. The soft ripple of the water added a splash to the rhythm overhead, and at a distance, something caught the air and gave it a voice. It sounded bright, high-pitched, excited. And it grew silent almost as quickly as it had begun its song.

The peace in the little town of Everleigh was something quite unique in Race's experience. He smiled without humor. He'd be hard-pressed to find such an idyllic spot in Lancaster. The thriving town had a busier pace, a brassier, more mechanical sound. And although he acknowledged the value of progress, he felt saddened to admit that progress brought with it a measure of loss.

What was taking Dulcie so long? he wondered. He pulled out his pocket watch. It was nearly two o'clock. More than time enough for Dulcie and Kirk to have finished their meal.

He ran a finger under his collar, studying the obstructive willow, hoping for a glimpse of blue dress.

When the song of the wind played out again, Race stood. His patience had run out. He'd leave Granny's picnic belongings where they were under the tree. But he was going to reclaim Miss Dulcie Kramer.

He again heard the bell-like sound of the breeze, but unlike the two earlier times, this time it ended on a far sharper note. He was thrown for a second. Had it indeed been the wind?

Since the sound had come from the general area where Kirk and Dulcie had disappeared behind the willow, Race approached quietly, trying to again hear the sound. Maybe he'd be able to identify it, whether it was the wind or—

"No!"

Dulcie! It had been Dulcie's voice, and it seemed as if his more vile suspicions about Kirk were proving only too well founded.

In scant steps he broke through the shield of branches. Before him, he found his worst nightmare come true. On a quilt beneath the tree was a jar of lemonade, a dish piled high with chicken bones, and Dulcie pinned down by Kirk's massive bulk.

She struggled frantically, seeking to wrest her hands from his grip, her legs kicking from under the tossed-up skirt, her head turned to avoid the aim of Kirk's lips.

Without a word, Race lunged toward the farmer, shoving him off Dulcie. Glancing at her as Kirk lay dazed, Race found reason to commit murder. Dulcie's lace-trimmed sky-blue dress was ripped down the front, her corset lacings torn, baring an abundance of creamy flesh across her chest and all the way to her waist. Sobbing, shaking, she sought to cover herself.

With a growl, and without giving his opponent a chance

to recover, Race grabbed Kirk's shirt and hauled him up off the ground. His fury gave him strength he'd never known he possessed, but it was strength he needed.

Swinging his arm back, Race plowed his fist forward and hit his target. Kirk's nose cracked. The blond behemoth grunted.

Race followed that first punch with a battery of others. Finally, when his knuckles could take no more punishment, he thrust Kirk away.

Moaning, the blond man crept off.

Cradling his battered hand, Race approached Dulcie. What would he do if she was so distraught that she wouldn't let him near? Obviously Kirk had ruined her dress. Race doubted her trust had survived the brutal attack.

"Dulcie," he whispered.

She whimpered in response as she tried to cover herself, never once letting her hands still. Catching the torn fabric of her bodice, she tugged and pulled in an effort to repair the damage. Failure to do so seemed to deepen her misery.

He repeated her name and drew closer. She reacted to his voice, glancing his way. Her blue eyes widened. Her reddened lips mouthed his name.

"Let me help you," he murmured.

Dulcie hiccuped, and fresh tears formed on her eyelashes. Race held his breath. When she only stared at his outstretched hand, tears flooding her face, he whispered, "Don't be scared. I only want to help you."

Then violent sobs ripped through her, convulsing her. Her hand shook, but she placed her fingers across his. Slowly, soothingly, Race wrapped his free arm around her shoulders. Her fingers clutched his. The sobs gentled, but the tears continued to flow.

Race began to rub her shoulder. Then he slipped his hand out from under hers to retrieve his handkerchief. With the white square of linen, he gathered every drop of Dulcie's pain. As the sobs came at longer and longer intervals, she took the handkerchief from him and leaned back against his supporting arm. She shook out the linen square and tried to use the fabric to cover herself.

"Let me help you," he offered yet again.

Dulcie's head jerked with a couple of nods. She yielded the handkerchief when he reached for it. He set it down, folding it into a triangle, and laid it over his lap. With his free hand, he grasped one torn edge of the bodice.

Uneven footsteps pounded behind him. Race turned, ready to seek help, to demand the full justice of the law. The words froze on his tongue, however, when he read the expressions of Granny K, that Vera woman, the elderly coquette, and three other old women he'd never seen before.

"Deflowerer!"

"Criminal!"

"Debaucher!"

"Oh, oh—scandalous!"

"Vat choo do dat fer, Race?" demanded Granny, a look of betrayal deepening her wrinkles. She dropped down beside Dulcie and swatted his offending hand away from her granddaughter's bosom. "I tell you ta vatch her. I cain't trust Kirk Slimebaugh, so I trusted choo. An' fer nothin'. What have choo done to my Dulcie?"

"But—but—it's not what it seems!"

"Ach! All men say same ven dey in *hase-wasser*. I no vant to hear no more horse *misht!*"

"Granny!" Dulcie cried. "Race is *not* in hot water. And he's not speaking horse manure! It wasn't him. He didn't do this," she said, waving at her ruined dress.

More running was heard. Male shouts drowned out the sound of the river. Then the low-hanging willow branches were again pulled aside.

The auctioneer, a bald-headed, paunchy fellow bearing Granny's shotgun, and a man in a clerical collar descended upon the miserable tableau under the tree.

Although no explanation seemed necessary, the handful of older women began cackling all at once, bringing to Race's mind hens who'd captured a marauding wolf in their midst.

But he was no wolf. He'd come to Dulcie's rescue. And he was being judged by the unscrupulous actions of another man.

Race stood. Enough was enough. He knew Dulcie needed attention, but not in the form of the hubbub the elders of Everleigh had brought down upon her. "Excuse me," he said, then shook his head. At this rate they'd never hear him. "EXCUSE ME!" he bellowed, and felt satisfaction at the sudden silence.

"It seems to me that all this arguing is useless," he said, appealing to his listeners' common sense and compassion. "Could we please take Dulcie home now? You can continue your discussion after she's been taken care of."

The old women clucked their accusations.

Granny slanted Race a poisonous glare.

The auctioneer reddened above his white beard.

The man in the clerical collar pulled a Bible from his jacket pocket.

The paunchy, bald-headed fellow raised Granny's gun and aimed dead center at Race's crotch.

❖ *11* ❖

DULCIE'S STOMACH LURCHED. "Mayor Winebrenner! Race did nothing, *nothing*. Please put the gun down. It was Kirk who ripped my dress."

The chattering stopped when she mentioned her attacker's name. All the faces around her displayed evidence of weighing her words. Then, one by one, her would-be rescuers shook their heads.

Granny lit her pipe, then considered Race and Dulcie through the smoke. "Naw," she muttered. "I don't like Kirk Slime, but Race's hands on yer bosoms vere. Not Kirk's."

A ripple of agreement coursed among the crowd.

"'Sides," added Mr. Winebrenner, Everleigh's mayor, "Kirk'd never do such a disgrace. Kirk Schleinbaugh is my vife's cousin's boy. I know him vell. He vou'n't never attack Dulcie."

In frustration, Dulcie blew a curl off her forehead. "Then you can't know him too well. *I* thought I knew him. But when we finished eating, he decided I was dessert! He started smacking great sloppy kisses all over my face, and when I tried to leave, he grabbed my dress, pulled until it ripped, then threw me on the ground. After that, he jumped on me so I couldn't move. I . . . I was really scared."

Just remembering made her shudder. But she had more to say. "Then Race arrived. He knocked Kirk off me and flattened his face. Kirk crawled away howling. Race *helped* me. He would never hurt me," she added with a smile for her knight in dented armor.

He smiled crookedly and said in a gentle voice, "I don't need you to defend me, Dulcie." Then he faced his accusers. His voice hardened. "It's simple. All we need do is find Kirk. One look at his face will show you how I did this to my knuckles." He displayed his bleeding, battered hand.

"Ach! Gott im Himmel!"

"Fer goodness' sake—"

"He beat Kirk ta git ta Dulcie."

Clucks and tsk-tsks joined the disbelievers' chorus. Only Granny K kept silent. She sucked on her pipe, never looking away from Race. Dulcie hoped her grandmother would see the truth for what it was, but surrounded by so many nay-sayers, she feared Granny might be swayed by their emotions rather than follow her intuition.

Granny approached Race. Standing a foot or more shorter than him, she had to crane her neck way back. With a final puff to the pipe, she narrowed her eyelids, her small eyes peering into him with razor-sharp incisiveness. Dulcie shuddered, glad she wasn't on the receiving end of that look.

It was unfair, she acknowledged. And she'd brought all this upon Race with her reaction to her earlier humiliation. If she hadn't been piqued at him, she'd never have let him end up with Granny's picnic lunch. They would have eaten together, enjoyed the beautiful summer day, and perhaps played some of the games that had been organized for the festivities. But because she ran away rather than face em-barrassing questions and looks, she'd eaten lunch with Kirk, who'd smelled suspiciously of moonshine when he'd approached her. Perhaps the 'shine had riled him up, or perhaps Dulcie's obvious disinterest had stung his masculine pride, or perhaps he'd been celebrating his victory over Race. Dulcie didn't know.

She only knew one thing. Kirk had become a giant eight-handed spider, pawing at her body, pinning her down, his knee thrusting between her legs, his mouth landing foul kisses wherever it reached.

Were it not for Race's intervention, Dulcie had no doubt she would have been violated. He deserved none of the accusations being leveled at him. "You *must* listen to me, Granny!" she pleaded in the ominous silence. "If Race hadn't come when he did, Kirk would . . . he would have . . ." Fear and revulsion clogged her throat. "Raped me," she whispered.

A shocked gasp arose from the people crowding around them. They formed an audience that had mushroomed as the citizens of Everleigh had sniffed out a scandal. But they didn't matter to Dulcie. Only Race and Granny K did.

Studying Race's face, Granny seemed intent on learning the truth. "I'm goin' home," she suddenly said, whipping around, grabbing her shotgun. "I'll try fer seein' the truth."

Mayor Winebrenner puffed out his chest. "Go, go. I'll take care of everything."

"There's nothing to take care of here," Dulcie tried again. "*Kirk Schleinbaugh* was the one who hurt me. He ripped my dress, he forced himself on me, and wouldn't let me alone, no matter how hard I fought him. Race Langston is a lawyer. He's not a criminal. And he has *never* done anything improper."

"Oh, yeah?" questioned Billy Schofield.

Dulcie groaned, blushing furiously. "Oh, yeah, Billy. Race has done nothing wrong."

"I seen 'im kiss ya, all squishy and fer a real long time,"

he said with relish. "Ya know, right behind that wisteria bush ya got climbing up the side of yer house."

This time it was Race who groaned. Dulcie was certain she'd soon die of embarrassment. But before that happened, she wouldn't be so lily-livered as to let Race bear the blame of even that minor transgression.

"Yes," she said, facing her neighbors, her hands pressing Race's handkerchief over her tattered bodice. "Race kissed me behind the wisteria at home." A gasp rose heavenward from the throng. "But he never *forced* himself on me. That was a kiss I—I welcomed."

She turned toward Race, wanting to see if he understood what she'd admitted. Sure enough, a deep, warm glow heated his gaze, and a gentle smile curved his lips.

From the back of the crowd a woman cried, "Hussy!"

Dulcie held herself straighter. "I'm no such thing. Just a woman, and one who was glad to share a kiss with a very proper gentleman."

Old Mrs. Overmeyer, standing inch-deep in river water, pointed at Dulcie. "Chezebel! Delilah! Vanton creetchure!" She hiked up her somber navy dress and black apron, both dripping rivulets, and stomped toward Dulcie, black bonnet bouncing on her head. "So dat's vat fer choo defend him! Choo *liked* vat he doin' vas!"

"No—yes—that's not at all what I said!"

Mrs. Overmeyer waddled over to Race. "Tell me. Did choo kiss Dulcie Kramer?"

From where she stood, Dulcie watched Race's shoulders rise and fall with his deep breath. "Yes," he said, "but—"

Mrs. Overmeyer's bonnet swung from side to side. "No, no, no, no, no! No but. Choo kissed her. She say no to kissing?"

"No. She—"

"Choo don't talk to me back!" bit off the old tartar. Race

was rapidly losing his temper, but he remained determined to clear up the misunderstanding. He'd let the woman ask her questions. Maybe after she was satisfied, she'd be willing to listen to reason.

"So," sang the martinet, "choo kissed Dulcie, Dulcie no say no. Choo came mit Dulcie under the tree. Ermentrude, Prudence, unt de others saw choo, her dress opened, yer hands on Dulcie's bosoms. Ain't dat right?"

Dammit all anyway! If he said no, he'd be lying. If he said yes, it would be equal to confessing to a crime he didn't commit. And Dulcie, damn all these curious buzzards, was half undressed, fully miserable, and tilting at the giant windmill of their self-righteousness in her efforts to champion Race.

In the deathly silence, an obnoxious chant arose. "Dulcie has a kissy-beau, Dulcie has a kissy-beau. . . ."

And like nothing else that had happened before, that child's taunt seemed to damn Race for destroying the innocence of an entire town.

Except that he hadn't done it. And aside from Dulcie, no one believed him. But he wasn't going to take it without fighting back! "It was Kirk Schleinbaugh who bought Dulcie's picnic and ate with her. I sat with her grandmother. And it was Kirk who attacked Dulcie. I heard her cry for help. *I* fought Kirk off her. *I* sent him packing. I'm only guilty of liking Dulcie Kramer, kissing her, and buying her grandmother's picnic basket instead of hers."

Mayor Winebrenner grew red in the face. "Don't choo talk dat vay 'bout my vife's cousin's boy. Kirk Schleinbaugh ist from Everleigh. He live neighbors to us. Ve know him. He vould never, never so foul a thing do."

"But he did—"

"He did this—"

Both Race and Dulcie stopped. They shared glances,

shrugged, obviously wondering how to clear up the situation.

"It seems to me," Dulcie offered, "that we can get to the truth here if someone finds Kirk. See if he's bruised, bleeding. Ask him where his injuries came from."

"Ach!" spat Granny, parting the crowd like Moses did the Red Sea. "Race whumped 'im but goot. Race looks bad in the hand, Kirk looks bad in the face. Vat matters is vhy, unt vat ve're goin' ta do 'bout it. *Dat's* vat ve must kenn."

At the somewhat reasonable tone of Granny's voice, Dulcie sagged with relief. Perhaps her grandmother would listen. And more importantly, perhaps Dulcie could escape the curious eyes, pointing fingers, and knowing smirks of her neighbors.

Emotionally drained, she began to shiver. Her tremors grew into violent shudders. She felt humiliated, exhausted, and knew she couldn't take much more of this public interrogation.

"Gra—Granny," she said, her voice breaking with the strength of her body's quaking. "Could we . . . please . . . go home?"

Like a down blanket, silence muffled the discussions, the whispers, the criticisms. One by one, those gathered around the willow tree watched Dulcie droop, then collapse. They watched Race reach her before anyone else moved, watched him gather her in his arms. He picked her up, everyone still staring at him, and held her against his chest. He raked those around them with a murderous glare.

"Your 'concern' smells worse than an angry polecat," he said. "If any of you dares say he or she cares for Dulcie Kramer, you'll have me to persuade. And I'd take a lot of persuading. No one's thought about Dulcie's embarrassment. No one's thought to offer her covering beyond what my handkerchief offers. No one's thought to check her for scrapes, scratches, or bruises. All you've thought of was satisfying your curiosity, and joining in mistaken accusations.''

Race took steps toward the street, holding his precious bundle close. He noted that the suddenly shamed citizens of Everleigh melted out of his path quicker and far more easily than if they'd been ice chips on this sunny day.

A measure of satisfaction warmed his heart. ''I'm taking her home. And I heartily suggest the rest of you get back to your business. I'll leave her in her grandmother's care, but no one better come sniffing around the Kramer home with more rash judgments and offensive questions.'' Now that he'd started, Race gathered a head of steam. He rolled ahead on his verbal track. ''Just tell me one thing. How many of you have never, *never* stolen or surrendered to a secret kiss?''

Gasps were heard. The ensuing silence was disturbed only by the gurgling of the Susquehanna. ''Just as I thought,'' he said, taking steps toward the street. He turned back for the last time. ''I think, Reverend, you could look for the verse in that handy Bible that addresses this matter. Something about logs and specks in people's eyes. You know the one I mean, it's all about finger-pointing.''

Without waiting, Race strode away.

Once he reached Willow Lane, Race allowed his pace to slow. Although he didn't think Dulcie had actually fainted dead away, her weakened state was undeniable. He glanced down and found her eyes still closed.

He said nothing, wanting to capture the sensation of Dulcie in his arms, to imprint in his heart and mind the joy of protecting her. He wondered how long she'd allow him the privilege.

Not long. ''Why are you carrying me?''

Race studied Dulcie's pale face, cradled against his shoulder. "Because someone had to. You swooned."

At his words, she stiffened. Oh-oh, he'd said the wrong thing.

"I'll have you know *I* do not swoon. Other girls might, but it's an affectation a lady never resorts to. Maman made sure I learned that lesson well."

Chuckling, he tightened his grip on her wriggling body. "Let me remind you," he said, "that save for *my* handkerchief and the way I'm holding you, you'd be baring a lot more of your beautiful flesh. I'm preserving your modesty."

"And I'm profoundly grateful. Now will you *please* set me down?"

Knowing that further argument would only make the situation worse, Race complied. He let her legs swing down, then he eased her onto her feet. With his arms around her still, he separated their bodies. He took away one of his arms. Then the other.

A heartbeat later, she was on her way back down to the ground.

Race again broke her fall. "May I now have the pleasure of carrying you home?"

She muttered something that sounded like, "Do what you have to."

Damn, she was stubborn! At least until he got her home, discretion would serve him best, he decided.

Moments later, the sound of an approaching buggy caught Race's attention. Then he heard a low, feminine voice call out. "Dulcie, Dulcie, Dulcie! What a delightful way to travel. You simply *must* tell me how you do it. Two grown men fighting for you like dogs over a gnawed-on bone."

Race bit down on his tongue.

Dulcie stuck her chin on Race's shoulder. "Well, Isabella,'' she drawled, ''can't be due to bitch-in-heat behavior. You have me beat there.''

Race stumbled, nearly dropping Dulcie. He'd never heard her use a word like that. But there it was, bouncing between them on Willow Lane. Ever so slowly, his grasp firm around the scrapper in his arms, he turned toward the newcomer.

At the same time, the young woman stood. And damn! was she *ever* something to look at. From the elegant, ostrich-feather-bedecked hat on her midnight curls, to her fashionable, lace-garnished black boots, this was a woman in all that the word encompassed. Brilliant green eyes glittered at Race, and although he told himself she couldn't possibly do that at will, somehow his gut insisted otherwise. With a pouty smile on full, ruby lips, she moved to disembark, then fluttered lush ebony lashes at Race.

She wanted *him* to assist her!

But he had Dulcie in his arms. Dulcie, who was twisting and turning and twitching and trying to get out of his hold. ''Let me go!'' she demanded.

Race ignored her.

She punched his shoulder.

''Ouch!'' he cried, and with some maneuvering he manacled her loose hand with his. Renewing her efforts to escape, and cursing most vividly, she grew redder by the minute. She also looked ready to take on Isabella.

For his own protection, he held on tighter. ''Now, stop that, you hellion,'' he whispered. To the vision in scarlet satin, he said, ''As you can see, I have my hands full. By the way, I'm Race Langston. From Lancaster.''

Dulcie quit pummeling him and, yanking his ears, made Race face her. ''She knows. She spends her days mucking around in town gossip.''

Narrowing her gaze, Isabella blatantly ignored Dulcie.

"So I've heard," she murmured, her emerald gaze raking Race.

In a well-rehearsed move, she lowered herself to her knees, as if to make the conversation more intimate, then leaned forward. The shiny fabric of her dress pulled tight across her truly prodigious bosom. Black velvet piping framed the deep vee of milk-white skin bared by her bodice. "I wanted to make sure you were welcomed properly," she added.

"Oh, you cheap little—"

Race released Dulcie's wrist to clap his hand over her mouth. He sent Isabella a taut smile. Where had this temptress come from? Surely she couldn't hail from Everleigh? "Oh, I've been welcomed, all right."

Dulcie began kicking. Regardless of where Isabella came from, he hoped she returned before her ham-handed seduction efforts made him laugh out loud or Dulcie's wrestling unmanned him.

Women were hell. He held a tigress in his arms, and Lord have mercy on the man who landed within reach of Isabella's talon-tipped claws! She'd shred him to bits, devour him, spit out his bones, then go look for her next course.

His hellion bit his hand.

"What'd you do that for?" he yowled.

Dulcie renewed her efforts. *"Msrumg flmenv sgaedrd msnsdut qysjnxh hwenr!"*

Race smiled weakly at Isabella, but kept his fingers over Dulcie's lethal teeth.

Oozing her curve-lavished figure back onto the bench of the buggy, Isabella sent him an outrageous wink. "I'm so glad to meet you, Race. Perhaps we can get better acquainted sometime soon. It'll truly be a pleasure."

"Hmmm . . ." he murmured noncommittally. She was an audacious piece of work, all right. Thank goodness he'd found Dulcie before meeting up with this man-eater. Beautiful and sensually appealing to any healthy male, Isabella promised a fast trip down destruction lane. He'd had a neat escape, if he said so himself.

He glanced at his escape route. Her sky-blue eyes were opened to their widest, her earlobes were fiery red, and she was snuffling like an enraged bull. The aftermath of Isabella's appearance would be no more pleasant than the encounter itself.

"Well, Dulcie," the source of Race's and Dulcie's current irritation offered. "I'll leave you in Race's capable hands. I must see to the poor soul this . . . mmm . . . warrior vanquished for you. Poor Kirk, with his broken heart and battered face, needs a woman's tender touch. Goodbye!"

Cracking the reins, Isabella turned her horse toward town.

Race retrieved his mangled hand.

Curses peppered out from Dulcie's mouth like so much buckshot.

Race's jaw dropped. She really had an astonishing vocabulary! And she was mad enough to use it. Sagely, he set her down, then offered soothingly, "Easy, Dulcie."

"Easy nothing!" she spat back, again pounding on Race's shoulder with impressive vigor. Using his hands as a shield, he fended off her subsequent blows.

Dulcie resorted to the only weapon he'd left her. "That dog in heat is nothing but trash!" she argued. "She's been batting her eyelashes to get her way since we were both six years old and starting school. Only difference is, she now has those watermelons on her chest to go with the tease-and-tickle eyes."

Race knew precisely what part of Dulcie's diatribe to ignore. "You mean she's from Everleigh?"

"Unfortunately."

"Well, how the hell did she turn out like . . . like *that*?"

''Too much money. No mother. Busy father. I don't know for sure, but I figure that must be it. She's scary!''

''I'll say!''

''Oh, you mean you didn't care for her melons?''

Where the hell did Dulcie come up with a question like that? Race carefully studied her stony expression. Could Miss Dulcie Kramer, who only a short while ago had been labeled a wanton and a hussy, be feeling unsure of her own appeal? Was she actually jealous?

He tucked the thought away to consider it with more care at a later time. ''Well, now, Miss Dulcie Kramer, don't you think I've seen enough 'melons' for one day? How about getting you home so you can cover the mighty fine bosom I stole a glimpse of earlier?''

''You—you—'' As her face reddened, she seemed to become more tongue-tied. Then she shoved him out of her way. ''You fancy talker, you! You're just awful. What a shocking thing to say!''

And the woman who'd been on the verge of collapse gathered her blue skirts and stomped off ahead of Race.

He watched her, enjoying the stimulating rear view. Skirts whipping up around her shins, Dulcie gave Race tempting glimpses of trim ankles, curvy calves, and the pristine froth of lacy petticoats. Her hips swung smartly, her shoulders were squared. She held her head high, and with one hand she hugged his handkerchief to her chest, the other one holding her skirts just out of range of her feet.

Race chuckled, certain she'd lambast him if she knew his thoughts. But they were his, private, and he savored them. Just as he savored the warm feelings he got in Dulcie's presence, when thinking of her, and even when he was angry at her.

At the Kramer house, Dulcie made short work of the porch steps. She flung open the door and, without waiting for him, vanished inside. At least she hadn't locked him out, he thought. He wasn't about to leave her alone. Not even alone with Granny. Although Dulcie's anger seemed to strengthen her, she had swooned, and when her fury dwindled, it could leach out all her oomph.

Although Granny believed he'd betrayed her trust, Race knew better. He would indeed follow through on his promises. His honor was at stake.

Entering the house, he smelled the now-familiar smoke. "Granny?"

"*Ja.*"

"I brought Dulcie home."

"I saw."

"I'm going to stay until I'm sure she's recovered."

"Hmmm . . ."

What the hell! Had Granny's sound represented assent or dissent? He made his own choice and went farther into the parlor. He dodged the man-traps in the fussy room and sat on the sturdy settee, making himself comfortable.

The silence thickened. It soon raged louder than an oncoming locomotive. Race swallowed uncomfortably. He craned his neck and ran a finger inside his stiff collar.

Granny puffed on.

The ormolu clock on the fireplace mantel bonged the hour. Muffled sounds came from upstairs. Soft scuffs, the closing of a door, whispery rustlings. How long could it take Dulcie to change out of her ruined clothes?

Perhaps well into the next century, if she'd seen him enter the house!

As he reviewed his options, footsteps sounded on the porch steps. Vigorous knocking rattled the door. When Granny went to rise from her straight-backed wooden chair, Race waved her back down. "Allow me. I'm closer."

She bobbed her head. Smoke haloed her face.

Race opened the door and found himself facing Mayor Winebrenner, the Bible-toting preacher, and the fat old lady in navy blue and black who'd started the name-calling down by the river. Swell. Things were improving by the minute, his more sarcastic subconscious piped in.

As Race turned to allow the contingent of jurors into the Kramer home, Granny began spitting gobs of excited Pennsylvania German dialect. From the expression on the waddling tartar's face, Race assumed she didn't like what Granny was saying. With a bob of her crisp black bonnet, she barked back.

Then the two men joined the verbal fray. Race felt dizzy from following the volleys of discussion around the room. He gave up, retreated to his corner on the settee, and settled down to wait out the match. Moments later, wearing the most ludicrous costume he'd ever seen, the object of the controversy sailed down the stairs.

As hot a summer day as it was, Dulcie wore a high-necked blouse, topped by a boxy wine-colored jacket. The shapeless matching skirt hid her curves, and from under its hem he caught a glimpse of what had to be a pair of Granny's overalls.

If not for the tenderness and sympathy that welled up in Race as he viewed Dulcie's fabric armor for what it truly was, he would have found her getup humorous. More than ever he wanted to protect her, soothe her hurts, bring a smile back to her lips and the sparkle to her blue eyes.

Quietly he rose and, skirting the vociferous gathering of elderly pedants, he reached Dulcie. He held out his hand, holding his breath, and sighed in relief when she trusted him with her fingers. As he tugged her closer, he realized the room was again held in the clutches of an oppressive silence.

"Choo see?" demanded the blackbird. "They're again touchin'. Disgustin'! Unt immoral."

Race shot a look at Granny. Her face seemed hewn out of stone. Licks of smoke dallied around her head.

Then, most unexpectedly, Mayor Winebrenner leapt toward the table where Granny had left her shotgun, grabbed the weapon, and braced it against his shoulder.

"Dammit all to hell!" Race cried out. "Does this town have only one way to resolve its problems—with a shotgun?"

Dulcie squeezed his fingers. He yelped and gave her an accusatory glare. Mayor Winebrenner approached. "Choo've disgraced Dulcie Kramer. She's one of us, unt ve take care of our own. Vat choo now gonna do?"

In a deliberately slow movement, the mayor leveled the shotgun at Race's chest. This time there'd be no easy escape. The affront these people believed he'd committed was a particularly vile one. And they intended to right the wrong.

As Race thought and thought, he noticed Granny slip her pipe behind her ear. "Choo see, Race," she said, "Everleigh is like family. Ve all take care of each other. Dulcie has dishonored been. Don't matter *who's* guilty. Ve all tink of vat's best fer Dulcie, ve care fer her. Dere's only one ting choo can do to fix dis mess."

Only one thing . . .

Was she saying what Race thought she was saying? He scanned the other faces gathered around. Grim expressions spoke volumes. Dulcie's lowered chin and protective garments broadcast her shame.

They meant it.

Although his intentions toward Dulcie had always been honorable, Race hadn't reached the point of considering matrimony. He reassessed the expressions around him and found only implacable determination.

Then he saw Granny's eye twitch. Or had it been a wink meant for him?

The shotgun approached.

It couldn't have been a wink. And even if it was, it hadn't been meant for him. He was the guilty party, in their opinion.

He glanced at Granny again. With no change in her expression, the eyelid dipped again. Race took hope, thinking it a wink, one to reassure him of her support. Support for what? A shotgun wedding?

Mayor Winebrenner came closer, shotgun at the ready.

Marriage.

To Dulcie.

Although the idea was hardly repulsive, it was somewhat premature. They hardly knew each other. Sorting through the collage of images in his mind, he remembered bandaging her ankle and stealing the sweetest kisses. He remembered comforting her the moment before the picnic site turned into Armageddon. He remembered the relief he'd felt when he compared Isabella to Dulcie and knew, beyond a shadow of a doubt, the depth of his feelings for one and distaste for the other.

The barrel of the shotgun goosed Race's spine.

Would they really kill him for a couple of stolen kisses? Was he willing to risk it?

He glanced at Dulcie. She lifted her chin, a mutinous gleam in her eyes. Race knew fear. Just as she had with Isabella, Dulcie looked ready to plunge into the verbal fracas with a salvo of her own. He had to prevent that. He had to save her—himself, too. "Will you marry me?"

"Hell, no!"

❖ *12* ❖

"WHY THE HELL not?"

"Because I won't marry someone who proposes while a gun's pointed at his rear."

"And who *will* you marry? Kirk? The one who mauled you, then ran away?"

Dulcie fell silent. In a town as small as Everleigh, indiscretions could be catastrophic. In fact, she was sure that many were already proclaiming her a bad influence on the morals of the town. She also knew that, if she didn't marry, she might as well move out West. She'd have virtually no place in Everleigh. But despite her lively performance today, Granny's health was worsening by the day, and Dulcie didn't want to leave home.

Race was right. She never wanted to see Kirk again in her entire life, much less marry him. And if she managed to persuade Pastor Eckert, Mayor Winebrenner, Mrs. Overmeyer, and Granny that it had indeed been Kirk who'd molested her, they might see him as a better choice for a spouse than an outsider like Race.

She wouldn't.

But no self-respecting woman wanted to force a man to marry her. And since Dulcie knew she bore no blame in what had happened, she didn't feel the need to be restored to someone else's idea of respectability. She didn't need a man to make her acceptable. She was the victim here, and she was strong enough to prevail on her own. She was about to become a businesswoman.

She nudged her chin up a notch. "No, Race. You know I won't do that. And you should also know that I won't be forced into anything." She turned toward Mayor Winebrenner. "You heard him. He proposed. He did what you wanted him to do. I refused him. You can put the gun down and go back home."

"B-but yer reputa—"

"What about my reputation?"

"Vell . . . ah," he mumbled, growing redder, but also taking the shotgun away from Race's spine. "No decent man from Everleigh vill vant to marry mit a girl who . . ."

"Who what?" she prodded.

With his free hand, the mayor waved lamely.

Pastor Eckert cleared his throat. "What our esteemed mayor means is that gossip will flourish, and you've been compromised, Dulcie. That stain follows a woman forever. Your only hope for respectability is marriage. *Immediate* marriage."

The more they insisted, the firmer her resolve grew. "Compromised? Respectability? Kirk Schleinbaugh is the one who snubs respectability."

"Ach! Ridiculous," Granny declared. "Dis ist the most *unfershtendich* thing I ever heard. Race likes Dulcie, Dulcie likes Race. Dulcie's reputachon ist all *booghered up*. It makes a body tired to hear sich goin's-on. Choo two must marry. I read de runes."

"Granny!" Dulcie cried, despairing of ever guessing what her grandmother might say next. "Stop this foolishness. You know very well that Kirk hurt me, Race saved me, and that this nonsense about marriage is absurd. We don't need to get married. *I* don't want to get married.''

Mrs. Overmeyer sniffed. ''Chust as I said. Dulcie Kramer is not'ing but a Chezebel. Shameless.''

''Now wait a moment, please,'' Race finally cried out. ''The name-calling is unnecessary. Dulcie has done nothing wrong. But she's about to.''

Dulcie spun around and glared at Race. ''What does *that* mean?''

He glared back. ''As a woman about to open a new business, you need to maintain a scrupulous reputation.''

''My reputation is not at issue here. In Lancaster no one knows me. They don't care about what entertains folks in Everleigh. If the gossips must gossip, then gossip they will. I don't want to waste my time, much less ruin my life, by agreeing to a preposterous marriage.''

To her surprise, Race looked hurt. ''You really think marrying me will ruin your life?''

Dulcie reddened. No. Marriage to Race would likely enrich the life of any woman. And, yes, she'd toyed with the idea of a future with him, knowing how easily she'd come to care for him. She was even willing to admit that love had blossomed in her heart.

She'd dreamed of becoming the love of his life.

But that was where her problem lay. She wanted, not his honorable actions or his dutiful performance, but his love. If she were to force this marriage on him, he'd likely never fall in love with her. One-sided love would never satisfy her.

Although her heart beat a resounding ''Yes,'' she met Race's gaze and said, ''No. Marrying you won't ruin my life. *Forcing* you into a future not of your own choosing would. I'll never create a prison for my spouse.''

''I wouldn't be imprisoned by marrying you.''

"Neither would you be fulfilled if that yoke were imposed upon you."

"What if I voluntarily don the yoke?"

"I think it's too late for that."

"Too late?"

"Yes."

"And how?"

"You've already had a gun held to your back."

"It's not there anymore, and I'm still asking you to marry me."

"The gun is merely symbolic."

"Felt pretty real to me. Marry me."

"No."

Granny spat smoke like a bellows stirs ashes. "Dis ist so *ferhoodled!* I ain't vatchin' no more." She gesticulated at the gloomy chorus. "Go, go. Dulcie ist my *granddatter*, unt I must make goot all dis."

With obvious reluctance, the three did as she said. Once they'd left the porch steps, Granny returned to the parlor.

Dulcie kept an eye on her grandmother. This latest action strongly suggested that Granny K had a plan. And as history proved, Granny's plans often became *hinnersfeddersht*, hind end backward, as she liked to say.

Dulcie didn't like the smell of this new development. Best thing to do was wait her grandmother out.

Tension mounted in the silent parlor. Granny even let her pipe go out. As if by predetermined consensus, all three sat down. The house creaked. The clock ticked.

Dulcie grew restless. She stole a peek at Race.

His jaw was squared. His brow, runneled by a frown.

Dulcie glanced at Granny. A hand in the pocket of her overalls, she sat motionless. Her face revealed none of her thoughts. Her eyes were shut.

Then Dulcie spied movement in the pocket Granny had

her hand in. The familiar rolling motion immediately brought dread into Dulcie's middle. She'd seen Granny do this millions of time, just before she took out the black satin pouch where she kept her rune stones.

The last thing Dulcie wanted was for Granny to pull out her divining tools and prove to Race that he'd landed in a pit of heathens, which was exactly what Granny considered herself, a Germanic Heathen.

She went to her grandmother's side. "Why don't you go rest a bit?"

"Rest? I vill rest plenty soon enough."

Dulcie reined in her impatience. She lowered her voice. "Very well, go to your room and cast the runes there. Just don't do it where Race can see you."

Granny opened her eyes. The fire in them caught Dulcie by surprise. "It's not'ing dishonorable I do de runes mit. Vhy hide?"

Dulcie shot a quick look at Race. He seemed consumed by his own thoughts. "Because people who don't know you, don't know that you mean no harm. They're scared of those who practice the old religion, and who like to look into the future. They fear what they don't know."

"Ach, Dulcie-girl, choo only say dat 'cause yer humoring me. Choo know not'ing 'bout it."

"True. And I don't want to know more than I already know. But I also won't try to change what's been with you far longer than I have."

Granny again met Dulcie's gaze. A different, disturbing light burned in her grandmother's eyes. Dulcie shivered.

"Ach! I vill to my room go." With effort, Granny stood. She leaned heavily on Dulcie and sighed. "I been here a long time. I get tired. Very tired."

At her grim words, Dulcie placed an arm around her grandmother's shoulders. She hugged her, careful of Granny's rheumatism-plagued bones. "Hush, don't talk like that. It's just been a bad day. That's why I want you to rest. You'll feel better afterward."

Shrugging, Granny said, "*Ja*. But vat choo gonna do"— she jerked her head toward Race—"him mit?"

Dulcie sighed. "I don't really know, Granny. This is one of those times I wish I had a special gift to trust in. I wish I could see what will be best for us all."

"Cast de runes, child."

"No. I really can't put faith in a handful of stones." She led Granny to the stairs. "Now, don't you worry about me, reading the runes, or anything else. I'm no longer a child. I must start taking care of my life."

Granny again gave her one of those indecipherable looks. It left Dulcie feeling even more unsettled than before. She paused on the first riser. Turning to Race, she said, "I'll be right back. I'm just helping her to her room."

Race nodded absently.

"Hell a' kitin'! Where's my jug?"

"Where did you leave it?" Dulcie asked reasonably.

"If I kenn, I vould get it."

Race stood. "I'll get her jug." Taking steps toward Granny's favorite straight-backed chair, he bent to the floor next to it, and hefted up the item in question. As Dulcie watched, he tried unobtrusively to sniff its contents, but gave up when he caught her eyeing him.

His cheekbones glowed ruddy. "Here," he muttered, then went back to where he'd been sitting.

Dulcie fought the urge to laugh. She knew what he thought was in Granny's ever-present jug. Everyone thought the same. But she knew that if anyone suspected it was an infusion of vervain to help rid her grandmother of kidney stones, Granny would likely deny it. She took enormous pleasure in knowing she was the object of everyone's speculation.

Minutes later, Dulcie returned to the parlor. She glanced warily at Race, not knowing what to do next. If nothing else, the day had been one humiliating disaster after the other. But he seemed relatively at ease. He'd leaned his head against the overstuffed sofa back and appeared to be dozing. She was anything but calm.

"Race."

"Hmmm?"

"Oh! I thought you'd fallen asleep."

"Today?"

"I guess it hasn't been the most soothing of days."

"Are you going to marry me?"

"No, but—"

Restrained knocking at the door interrupted her. Who on earth could be so insensitive as to come calling? It had to be Mrs. Overmeyer. The old sourpuss had probably forgotten to level another epithet at Dulcie's loose morals.

She squared her shoulders and opened the door. "Oh! Emma. What . . . what can I do to help? Is it the baby?"

A warm pan was extended toward Dulcie. She was so surprised, she nearly dropped the fragrant container. Stepping out of Emma's way, she watched the pregnant woman shuffle in. Carrying a child looked to be excruciatingly uncomfortable.

"No, dear," Emma said, her brown eyes offering comfort. "I came to see if there was anything I could do for you. Today was foul, and you must be hurting in more ways than one."

"Oh, Emma. You really didn't have to put yourself out. Granny and I, we can manage between the two of us."

"I didn't put myself out at all. I'd started a kettle of stew before the festivities, and since it had simmered all this time, it was ready when I came back. I divided it, figuring neither you nor Granny needed to bother with cooking.''

Her friend's kindness overwhelmed Dulcie. Tears welled in her eyes. ''Thank you ever so much,'' she whispered, a sob lodged in her throat. ''This is the nicest thing anyone's ever done for me. And I do understand what you're saying.''

''Mm-hm,'' responded her neighbor, lifting her chin. ''Kirk Schleinbaugh should be gelded. If Race hadn't been there . . . And what about other girls? Those who innocently go with him and don't have a Race waiting to rescue them?'' Emma's eyes now blazed with outrage. ''I think you'll soon see that what many said down by the river was said without thought. Shock often makes people lose their wits and babble like fools. I can't for a minute believe that Prudence, Mary Margaret O'Murphy—anyone in town, for that matter—would side with Mayor Winebrenner and Mrs. Overmeyer.''

''I'd like to think so—''

Again Dulcie was cut off by footsteps announcing another arrival. She found Prudence Kleinschmidt and Mary Margaret O'Murphy waiting on the porch, anxious expressions on their aged faces. ''May we come in?'' asked Miss O'Murphy.

Dulcie nodded and stepped out of their way. By the time she closed the door, she noticed that Emma had sat next to Race, and the two were whispering like long-time friends.

''What may I do for—''

''Nothing, Dulcine—''

''Then why are you here?'' Dulcie cut in before Miss O'Murphy finished voicing her embarrassing name.

Dulcie's former schoolteacher frowned. ''Now, dear,'' she said in her familiar, teacherish manner. ''I taught you not to interrupt. I'll understand this time, since it's been such a harrowing day, but please retain your pride in your education."

Mary Margaret had been Dulcie's second-staunchest supporter when she'd begun to study for her teaching certification—Maman, of course, being the first. She'd been dismayed by the abrupt end Mignone's death put to Dulcie's training. She mourned not only the passing of one of her closest friends, but also the death of Dulcie's dream.

"Yes, Miss O'Murphy, I do pride myself in my accomplishments. I am, however, distraught, as you can imagine."

"Of course, sugar," crooned Prudence. She leaned toward Dulcie and took her hand in both her pudgy ones. She punctuated her words with powder-puff pats. "Mary Margaret and I came to take charge of things so you and Ermentrude can catch some restorative sleep."

In that velvet-covered steamroller fashion she had, Prudence led Dulcie to the stairs. She turned to speak to her companion, and only then noticed Emma and Race, who were still discussing something in quiet tones. "Why, Emma Schwartz! What on earth are you doing gallivanting around town with that child almost here? Don't you think we have enough worrying to do with these two Kramer women? And where is that rogue, Nathaniel?"

"Hello, Prudence, I'm happy to see you, too. Nathaniel had to go into Columbia to see about the storage of some molds for the foundry. I wasn't gallivanting anywhere. I was sitting, having a nice chat with Race. And I came because I too was worried about Granny K and Dulcie."

"Well, dear child, now that Mary Margaret and I are here, you can take the two of you home, put your feet up, and wait until that baby decides to come join us out here."

Race chuckled, his eyes bearing a hint of the humor Dulcie had so much enjoyed since they'd met. She hadn't realized how much she'd missed it recently.

With great difficulty, and the support of Race's arm, Emma stood. "I'll go relieve Mama. She's been watching Sarah for a time now. That child can exhaust the most energetic human in only minutes."

Emma came up to Dulcie and surprised her by putting her arms around her. Dulcie again felt the knot wedge in her throat. She hugged her friend back. "Oh! Your baby kicked me!"

"Dulcie, my dear, you have no idea how well this rascal kicks." Emma paused by the door and winked. "But you won't have long to wait. You'll soon be married, settled, and sporting a figure like mine."

Dulcie blushed and didn't know where to look. After Emma left, Prudence gave her another little prod in the behind, and Mary Margaret O'Murphy descended upon Race. Oh, dear. Poor man had no idea how expertly he was about to be manipulated.

As she started to intercept her neighbor, she caught a glimpse of a buggy pulling up in front of the house. Then she heard a familiar voice.

Outside, Vera Oberholtz called, "Ermentrude! Ermentrude!" Heavy footsteps crossed the porch, and Vera let herself in.

A flurry of Pennsylvania German burst from the new arrival, and although Dulcie understood the dialect, she'd never felt quite comfortable speaking it. "Why, thank you, Vera," she said in English. "Granny and I do appreciate your concern and support. As you can see, however, we have all the help we could ever need."

"Dis ist goot. But vait, I back be coming." She stormed outside, and in seconds returned. "Here. This fer choo."

Dulcie grabbed the brown-paper–wrapped bundle the woman shoved at her middle. She loosened the cord that neatly tied it, and discarded the wrapper. Stunned, she plopped down on a stair step. The most exquisite, ivory-colored, butter-rich satin poured over her lap. She looked up. "Mrs. Oberholtz?"

"Fer vedding, *ja?*"

Before Dulcie could catch her breath to answer, Race slipped between the two women, sat next to Dulcie, and wrapped an arm about her shoulders.

"Ja, ja," he said, nodding.

"But, Race! I've told you no any number of times."

"And since I've asked you any number of more times, I'll keep on asking until you say yes to shut me up."

"Why, that's even more preposterous than marrying for the sake of a reputation!" She glanced around, seeking support, and suddenly realized the three women had vanished from the parlor.

"Dulcie," Race said, his voice low. "Am I so repulsive that you won't even consider marrying me?"

Her heart twisted at the emotion in his words. "No, you're not repulsive at all!"

"Would you believe that I knew I wanted nothing so much as to marry you the first time you said no?"

Dulcie gave him a crooked smile. "That's not a good reason, either."

"What would you consider a good reason?"

She scuffed the floor with the toe of her boot. "Oh, it sounds childish, but . . . I want to marry someone I love, someone who loves me."

"Would you believe me if I told you I lo—"

She placed a hand over Race's lips. He took the opportunity to kiss it. "No!" she cried, drawing back, curling her fingers over the caress. "Don't say that. I couldn't stand it if you said those words simply in reaction to this afternoon's events. It would hurt twice as much when you realized you really didn't."

"Then perhaps this will persuade you." His lips caught hers, surprising her. Gently, with a most tender passion, Race wooed a response from her. And she yielded. The tenderness and passion grew, and all at once became desire. A yearning for Race filled her, for his kiss, for his embrace, for the man who would sacrifice a bit of his future for her sake.

He nibbled on her bottom lip. "Sweet," he murmured in her ear. He nuzzled her neck. "The sweetest of sweets."

He recaptured her lips. The damp velvet of his tongue dipped in, and again she experienced the warming of her limbs, the heating of her flesh. A heaviness low in her body surprised her with its intensity. She pressed herself to Race, knowing he could ease her need.

When the pressure of his lips lessened, Dulcie burrowed her face in his chest.

"Marry me."

At that moment, still under the effect of that kiss, Dulcie would have agreed to anything. Anything at all. And especially to Race's plea. Still more, to the desires of her heart. "Yes, I'll marry you."

"Choo see?" singsonged Granny from the upstairs landing, a wicked sparkle in her eyes. "Like I said, ever'ting vork out fine. Ve haf a vedding to make ready."

It wasn't until he found himself halfway home that Race remembered Milton Snavely Hershey. Not only did he remember the man, but his memory brought back those accursed phone calls. Especially the one in which the candy maker suggested that Race marry Dulcie and keep her too busy to compete against Milton for chocolate-lovers.

Ten grisly days later, Race stood in the Kramer parlor, dressed in his finest suit, the stiff collar biting into his neck. He could feel his parents' eyes boring holes in his back. To say they hadn't taken the news of his upcoming nuptials particularly well was a gross understatement. And Grandfather Richter had stated he didn't know anyone so common as to marry some dairymaid he'd compromised.

Milton, on the other hand, had vigorously pumped Race's arm in congratulation for his astute business instincts. That man, the one with all the sharp instincts, had lacked the brass to mention the mitigating presence of Kirk or the shotgun-wielding mayor.

Race did tell his mother about Dulcie's attack. He also confessed to having deep feelings for his bride-to-be. And although he'd refrained from saying the word ''love'' to anyone but Dulcie, his mother had clearly understood Race's situation. After that, she'd set aside her maternal concerns and staunchly backed him during the awful discussions he and Father had. She'd somehow kept Father's heart from giving the family another scare.

Now Race's parents sat in the Kramers' parlor, together with Everleigh's residents, waiting for Pastor Eckert to join him and Dulcie in holy matrimony.

Each time he thought of marrying Dulcie, he felt a pulse of excitement, and he relished the promise it held. Eternity, with Dulcie at his side, stretched out before him. And if anyone had thought to ask, he would have confessed to the anticipation he felt right now.

True, he was also filled with trepidation, especially since his bride believed he was marrying her out of a sense of duty, a strong attraction, or the desire to stifle the gossip about her attack. Dulcie would take time to persuade. Race wanted them married and with that long future assured.

The pastor's wife sat at the piano, playing hymns. The garments worn by the guests whispered as they entered the parlor and took seats. Flowers had been cut and arranged on the mantel. The pastor stood to a side, Race beside the cleric. They waited.

All that was needed was—

A vision in lush cream satin appeared on the stairs. Dulcie descended regally, as she'd said she intended to make memories for the future. Race's heart had taken hope from her words.

Dulcie's dress was simple. The satin bodice was fitted, and with every breath she took, it caught the warm sunlight entering through the windows. A yoke of lace lavished the satin at shoulders and chest with its luxury, then curled up in a crisp ruff. A velvet ribbon held a cameo at the base of her throat. The skirt was fitted to her waist, then flared out in graceful folds.

She was the most beautiful sight Race had ever seen.

Dulcie reached Race's side. His eyes taking in the loveliness of his bride, Race heard the pastor begin the ceremony.

After a solemn blessing, the bridal couple exchanged simple, binding vows. In the silence of a summer afternoon, Race Langston and Dulcie Kramer became husband and wife.

❖ *13* ❖

Dᴜʟᴄɪᴇ's ꜰᴏɴᴅᴇsᴛ ᴅʀᴇᴀᴍ had come true. Sort of.

As she went up the stairs to her bedroom, she heard Race call out farewells to the last of their wedding guests.

Race. Race Langston was her husband. She, his wife.

Through the open bedroom window, the rumble of the last departing buggies filled the quiet room. But only for moments. The farther the vehicles went, the deeper the silence in the house grew. And darkness had come.

It was night. Her wedding night.

As a country girl, Dulcie had a fairly good idea of the basic mechanics of mating. Dogs, pigs, cats, cows, horses; they were unavoidable sights and sounds on the farm-studded countryside of Lancaster County. None of those members of the animal kingdom remotely resembled Race, however, and she had no idea what to expect from this unusual wedding night.

Unusual? That barely hinted at the truth. She was married to a stranger who'd share a bed with her for the rest of their lives. She was married, and she'd only met his parents this afternoon. She was married, and during the last ten days, while everyone in town helped prepare for the most elaborate wedding Everleigh had ever seen, she'd hardly spoken to, much less kissed or embraced, this man who'd just become her mate.

And, she thought as she heard him come up the stairs, she was married to Race Langston, the man she loved. But she knew nothing of his feelings for her. Well, she knew he liked her, and he certainly had liked kissing her, but how deep did that "like" go? Could it someday turn to love?

Please, God, let that happen.

The bedroom door swung in. Race entered. Dulcie laced her fingers behind her back, hoping to hide how badly she was shaking. "It was a nice wedding, don't you think?"

Race glanced up. Their gazes collided. Just as abruptly, both looked away. Oh, dear. How uncomfortable this all felt. And from what Dulcie could see, Race didn't feel any more at ease with their situation than she did. At least they had *that* in common.

She smiled. "I emptied my mother's chiffonier for your things. I hope you have enough space."

Race shot a glance toward the piece of furniture and nodded absently. He then parted the unbuttoned sides of his jacket and slipped his hands in his pockets. He strode to the window.

Moonlight poured in, surrounding him. In his dark suit, limned by the silvery light, Race looked tall and strong, every inch a man. That masculinity drew Dulcie, just as surely as it made her hesitate. What did she know about men?

True, she wasn't supposed to know a great deal, although at times she feared she'd learned too much during that episode by the river with the drunken Kirk. But this was Race. And if there was one thing she knew, it was that her new husband would never hurt her. With that conviction, she approached him.

"I like your mother," she said. "She reminds me of Maman. Oh, I know they look nothing alike, and your mother doesn't speak with a French accent, but something in her eyes put me in mind of my mother. She must be wondering why on earth I kept looking at her all afternoon.''

Without turning, Race said, ''I'm glad you liked her. She's become a friend to me as well as a mother in the past few years. I would hate it if you two hadn't gotten on well.''

''Rest assured, that'll never happen.'' Then her playful side gave her a nudge. ''I'll even find some way to make your father smile.''

That made him spin! ''Oh, you must understand, my father's been ill, and he's had a troublesome business venture on his mind for a while now. To top it all off, I came home and announced I was marrying what to them was a total stranger. He's still trying to take it all in.''

Dulcie laid her hand on his forearm. ''I know that, silly. That's why I'm determined to find some way to cheer him up.''

''You and Granny K!''

''Can you believe she asked for some of his pipe tobacco? I didn't know whether to throttle her or rush him back to Lancaster!''

Race chuckled. ''But you noticed, didn't you? He shared.''

''Um-hmmm. We Kramer women have our ways!''

''You're not a Kramer woman any longer. You're Mrs. Race Langston.''

''Oh, now wait one moment. I'll take the 'Langston,' thank you very much, but I haven't changed my name to Race. I'm Mrs. Dulcie Langston.''

''As long as the Langston stays, I don't care what you call yourself.''

''Dulcie will do.'' Then, narrowing her gaze, Dulcie walked toward the side of the bed, never looking away from him. She sat. A sharp pain on her buttock made her leap right back up. "Oh, dear," she murmured, and moved the offending rose aside. Race looked at her questioningly, but she gave him a guileless smile.

Sitting again, she went on. "Now, it strikes me as very odd that Pastor Eckert happened to mumble when it came to your name. I don't know if he actually said 'Race Langston.' Why would that be?"

To her amazement and surprise, Race turned beet-red. He pulled his hands from his pockets and began to pace, gesticulating in jagged spurts of motion. "I have no idea what you're talking about. I heard him, everyone else heard him. We're married. No one can question whether he said my name or not. *I* said my name, and I vowed that this union was forever, in illness and in health, as long as we both shall live. So did you. We are married. Before man and God."

As his voice roughened and his fervor deepened, Dulcie knew what was wrong. "I wasn't denying our marriage. I'd never do that. I was there, next to you. I made those same vows."

A thrill of excitement rippled through her as she remembered the fire in his eyes when he'd turned to her and pledged his troth. Every fiber of her being had resonated with that heat, with the love she felt. What she didn't know was what that hunger meant to him. She didn't dare ask.

To lighten the moment, she said, "I wanted to determine if your name is Horace after all."

Again, his face reddened. "What do you think?"

"That the name Horace doesn't suit you."

One dark eyebrow rose, and at the same time a corner of his mouth kicked up.

"Really," she insisted. "I'm not even sure it suits your father."

''Pray tell, why not? It seems to have gotten him this far in life.''

Sudden heat in her cheeks had her fanning them. ''Well, I don't mean to be rude or anything, but your father is a very distinguished-looking gentleman, not stodgy at all. Horace is a stodgy name. Oh, and he's very handsome, I might add.''

Race's other brow bobbed up.

''Well, of course he is! He looks just the way I expect you'll look when you're his age.''

''Sooo . . . I'm handsome, you say.''

''Oh, stop! You know you are!''

''I like knowing my wife thinks so.''

Dulcie lowered her head. ''I have, since I first saw you.''

A pair of black shoes appeared in her line of vision. ''You know what?'' he asked. She shrugged. ''From the moment I saw your posterior—''

''Race!''

''Dulcie!''

''You're incorrigible!''

''Ah, but would you want me to change?''

Silence.

With a finger beneath her chin, Race tilted Dulcie's face. Their eyes met. Stillness, thick and rich, enveloped them. Moonlight pooled in a circle on the bed. The scent of white roses filled Dulcie's senses, and she remembered the crushed blossom. She felt as fragile as the flower.

As Race looked into her eyes, Dulcie knew that there was more in him for her. More feelings, more friendship, and much, much more passion than she could even imagine. Another shiver ran down her spine, leaving her skin tingling. Anticipation burned in her, warring with her natural reserve.

Race leaned closer, pressing his cheek against hers. ''You're like satin, you know.''

She arched her neck and returned the caress with her cheek. "You're not."

A chuckle rumbled from deep within Race. "I'm not supposed to be."

"I know."

Race cupped her head in his hand. Pulling her close, he nuzzled her temple. "You're as fragrant as a rose."

"That's because I just sat on one."

Race leaned away. When she saw how puzzled he looked, she realized how foolish her response had sounded. She lowered her lashes, feeling more awkward than ever.

Race pulled her close again. "Dulcie," he whispered, nuzzling her ear. "It's me. Race. I'm your husband. Are you afraid of me?"

She shook her head, but nothing short of the Apocalypse would have made her meet the warmth in those brown eyes.

"If you're not afraid, why won't you look at me?"

"I . . . I feel strange, nervous and awkward . . . and there's more that I can't identify."

"I know. I feel the same."

"You do?" she asked, her eyes popping open.

Ruddy color tinted his cheekbones again. "Yes . . . I do. I mean, it's not something I would tell just anybody or anything. But you're my wife. And . . . and I think you deserve to know. I'm no skirt-chaser. I'll never be one, so you don't need to worry about fidelity. I never was interested in frivolous attachments of the fleshly sort. I mean—"

Dulcie curved her hand about his jawline. "Are you trying to tell me you—"

"Yes, Dulcie. This is as new to me as it is to you."

"Oh!"

"Yes, oh!"

Their exclamations hung on the calmness of the summer night. In the moonlight, brown eyes and blue held firm, sharing warmth, hinting at secrets that both were too afraid to voice, revealing what drew one to the other.

"Dulcie . . ." he whispered, and brought his lips to hers.

Tentatively he kissed her. His lips rocked over hers, a gentle, caring sort of caress. One that spoke of deep feelings, but didn't divulge their fullness. To this she could respond. She met him halfway.

The warmth of Race's mouth spread through her. Flickers of fire ran in her veins, awakening her senses, setting her skin aflame. Then the tip of his tongue outlined her lips. His touch set off sparkles of effervescence that caused her to melt in his arms.

She wanted more.

He had a neverending supply of kisses, caresses, desire. Warm shivers ran through her. A roaring filled her ears. The world fell away, and they were all that remained. Race and Dulcie, husband and wife.

Yearning filled her heart. It grew, then pooled as a foreign quickening deep inside her, kindling an unmistakable ache. Race deepened the kiss, and her reaction was earth-shattering. The power of his touch went far beyond anything she could have anticipated. Longing for Race, for closeness, for the passion she knew he also felt, filled her.

The kiss continued, and Dulcie reveled in his nearness. Pressing closer, she absorbed his heat. She savored his scent, his taste, his strength. She whimpered as the sensations intensified. Feelings, emotions, responses she'd never felt before. Sweetness with the nip of heat. It all swirled deep inside her, leaving her light-headed, but still seeking more.

When Dulcie yielded to his kiss, Race's blood burned with need for his wife. Sweet, sensual Dulcie, who tasted of innocence and desire. As he deepened his kisses, each one a more drugging caress than the last, he pulled the pins from her hair. He wanted to feel that glorious wealth of gold on his skin. He longed to bury his face in those curls, to revel in the scent of Dulcie, floral and delicate.

His every muscle straining toward her, he took his lips from hers, then strung a chain of kisses to her neck. He unraveled the knot of silky blond hair, then brought handfuls of it forward. Sighing deeply, he buried his face in its satiny, sensual luxury.

"Race . . ."

Her breathy voice, far weaker than usual, trembled with the same thrill he felt at being this close. He pulled back. A soft smile gleamed up at him, and her velvety cheeks glowed with a rosy flush. She was the most beautiful woman alive, certainly the loveliest he'd ever seen.

And she was ". . . my wife."

"Mm-hmm," she murmured, sounding like a cat feasting on cream.

At the evidence of her shared desire, Race grew bolder and brought his hand to the row of satin-covered buttons that ranged her spine. Awkwardly he tried to unfasten them, catching the soft fabric on his rough fingers. "Damn!"

Dulcie chuckled, something no woman should ever do to a man this aroused, Race thought. He was burning for her, and she was laughing! How he wished they'd had the time for a normal courtship, for the delightful moments of discovery, learning the caresses each preferred. How much more joyous tonight would have been. But then he remembered the circumstances surrounding their marriage.

A shudder ran through him. Guilt crossed his conscience. He'd still made no mention of the damn chocolate recipe, much less of his connection to Milton Hershey.

He suddenly felt sick. Sick with guilt. How could he claim his bride without confessing? How could he take her innocence while keeping secrets? What kind of loving could they share?

Dulcie moaned deep in her throat. Her hands crept around his neck, and her fingers toyed with the hair on his collar. He surrendered to her touch. He kissed her and trembled, not in a shudder, but from an electric jolt of need, of craving for his wife's love.

For that was just what Race wanted, to imprint on Dulcie the intensity of his love, to woo her response, to feel her love in ways that said nothing else would ever matter. Regardless what the future held.

Dulcie pulled away. As he felt emptiness in his arms, Race opened his eyes, a question on his lips. But the warmth of her gaze met his. He saw there a depth of feeling that he couldn't measure, powerful emotions that gave him hope for the future. His heart sped up. Then it stopped altogether when, with a knowing look, she smiled and turned her back to him, lifting a cascade of curls in her arms.

Race nearly died of apoplexy. Her delicate neck was exposed, feminine and graceful. He kissed it. But that hadn't caused his shock. It was the row of buttons she'd just asked him to undo!

Feeling the same pride he'd felt by the river when Granny K had offered him her trust, Race accepted Dulcie's gift of her most prized possession. Herself.

Soon she'd be his wife in every way. Moments from now they'd come together in a reverent act. They'd become one.

He set to his task. Now that he could see what he was doing, he found the buttons easy to separate from the satin loops. In moments, Dulcie's gown slid off her shoulders, revealing a lacy concoction that teased him with glimpses of her skin.

He slid the long sleeves down her arms. The bodice followed, then caught at her rounded hips. He grasped Dulcie's shoulders gently, turning her around. His hands curled around her hips and pushed the dress to the floor. When he looked up, he noticed the straight line of her shoulders, the tilt of her head. Her expression revealed pride in her femininity and allure.

''Oh, Dulcie . . . you're so beautiful, so feminine . . .''

With shaking fingers, Race opened the satin ribbons that held that gossamer lace together. The soft fabric parted, revealing the laced front of her corset. Impatient, he groaned, releasing the lacings, setting her free of her garments. Then he slid her stockings down her legs and onto the froth of underclothes and wedding gown on the floor.

He might not be experienced, but common sense and powerful instincts led him. Kneeling at her feet, he dared to finally gaze upon his bride's body. He rose slowly, not wanting to scare her. His eyes mapped out each creamy curve, each luscious fullness. She was the embodiment of woman, and she was his.

When Race looked up from where he knelt at her feet, Dulcie feared she would swoon. No one had ever viewed her like this, and she supposed she ought to feel self-conscious. Besides, Granny K had made her a quantity of nightgowns, and they were only steps away in her armoire. She could always use one to cover her nakedness. But the appreciation she read on every line of Race's dear face only made her feel proud of herself.

Unfortunately, she didn't know what to do next.

Fortunately, the following instant Race became a blur of activity. He toed off his shoes, tugged off his tie, then sent it soaring toward the chiffonier. His jacket flew to a plum-colored armchair in the corner, and his belt dropped to the floor.

Dulcie felt the most brazen urge to laugh. Here she stood, naked as the day she was born, while before her the most attractive man she'd ever seen fought to strip himself of

every thread on his body. And having the devil of a time.
One could say he was distracted.

Funny though it seemed, she dared not laugh. She didn't
want to turn her wedding night into a farce. But as Race's
big fingers fought the jet studs holding his white shirt together, it became obvious that haste was making him waste
time. And if he didn't pay more attention to what he was
doing, he'd likely find himself manacled by his clothes.

"Let me," she said, curbing her humor, indulging her
curiosity.

Race stood stock-still. But beneath the tension, there was
heat, a leashed power that lured Dulcie closer. She flicked
open the studs on his shirt and, with hands that trembled,
slid the garment from his shoulders. She uncovered a broad
chest, well muscled, and dusted with a scattering of dark
hair. Before she thought better of it, she placed her hand on
him.

He sucked in a breath.

She pressed her hand more fully against his flesh, feeling
a faint trembling that matched her own. He was as affected
by their nearness as she was, and the knowledge filled her
with tenderness.

His gaze remained riveted on her.

There he stood, her hand on his chest, wearing only a pair
of black trousers. He was hers—and suddenly her courage
abandoned her. She remembered how exposed she was, and
she lost the impulse that had led her to attempt to disrobe
him.

"Race," she whispered, pressing herself closer, then
moving back and turning away when he hissed at the contact.

"Yes."

"I . . . I can't do this."

"You what?"

"I-I can't take your trousers off."

Relieved, Race allowed himself to breathe again. He'd feared she'd decided to refuse consummation, and to a man in a condition as dire as his, that would have constituted hell on earth. "I can."

Her head bobbed in affirmation.

Seconds later, he was nude, and he closed the distance between them. He gently wrapped his arms about her waist, pulling her to him. At the moment of full contact, she stiffened. Then, in a fluid flow their bodies met.

Race savored the vibrant desire between them. "My wife . . ."

"My husband . . ."

Turning her in his arms, he pressed a kiss to her forehead, hoping he could control his rampant need. He felt unsure of himself, lacking prior experience, yet somehow even that felt right to him. They both came to this as equals, honestly, and with a natural passion they would explore together.

He hoped his lack of expertise wouldn't cause him to scare her, much less hurt her. After all, the urges within him were stunningly strong, powerful and demanding. Surrendering to that demand, he slid one hand down her arm, catching her fingers in his. Leading her to the bed, he offered a prayer for patience and control. But the moment his eyes again caught sight of Dulcie's breasts, full and rose-tipped, he found himself unable to finish that prayer.

They sank together onto the bed. Race shifted to his side, resting his weight on his elbow. With trembling fingers, he caressed Dulcie, leaving trails of fire over every nerve he touched. He kissed her lips, her cheeks, her eyes. He kissed his way to the hollow of her throat, tasting her tenderly.

And then he buried his face in the bounty of her breasts. He rubbed the roughness of his cheeks against her, breathed moist heat on her flesh. His hand cupped one firm mound, and Dulcie gasped at the pleasure the contact brought her. She arched her back, needing to get as close to Race as she could. When his warm lips covered the sensitive crest, Dulcie's world turned over in a dizzy flurry of heat, need, and love.

She loved him. She loved the way he looked and the way he spoke. She loved how he kissed her, how he touched her, as if she were the most precious thing in the world.

He smoothed his hand downward, over her belly and between her legs. At first she clamped her thighs tight. In response, Race's lips returned to hers and kissed her so passionately that she forgot the reserve that had made her close up against him.

He touched her. Fire raced through her body, exploding at their point of contact. She'd never imagined she would experience such pleasure. She'd never known a man's touch could feel so good, so right. "Race . . . oh, Race . . ."

His caresses intensified, deepened. Dulcie felt her body's hunger, and Race continued to feed it. When she thought she'd surely die from the wild torment he created, he rose above her and whispered her name. Dragging her eyes open, she looked into his.

"You're mine," he said.

As they joined, she felt pain at the invasion of his flesh. Staring through tears into his eyes, she felt him still within her, tensing with the effort he expended. When she tried to smile, he began to move again, gently at first, kissing her lips and cheeks and chin.

As passion again blazed through her body, she began to move with Race, meeting his every motion with one of her own. Flames blazed within her. Desire spun into need. Need soared, raging toward completion.

She could take no more of this loving torment.

And then, at that highest pinnacle, she felt herself explode in a burst of thunder, a rainbow of colors, a deluge of passion. A cry tore out from within her, and seconds later, Race echoed her sounds of joy when he stiffened in her arms.

Together, they spun into eternity.

The days that followed their wedding slipped by like links on a chain. Race and Dulcie entwined their thoughts, their dreams, their desire into a neverending thread of gold. Their closeness deepened; the physical joy they found together blossomed into hours of delicious discoveries that created memories that would last forever.

Soon they communicated with only a glance, a tilt of a smile, a butterfly-light touch. They fell ever more deeply in love with each other, yet neither voiced those binding words, as they didn't know what the other felt in return.

Although at times Race was riddled with doubts and guilt due to his terrible secret, the happiness in his marriage constantly soothed the ragged edges of fear. He allowed himself to be lulled by the satiation of his deepest longings, his most gripping desires.

A few days after the wedding, Pastor Eckert, knowing of Dulcie's abilities with candy, asked the newlyweds to chaperone a taffy-pull party for the young unmarried of the Everleigh Lutheran Church. Race and Dulcie quickly accepted, as Race wanted to make a place for himself among her neighbors.

Before the young people arrived at the church fellowship room, Race helped Dulcie cook the candy. He carried the heavy kettle to the enormous black iron stove. When she poured water into the sugar, he stirred the two ingredients with a large paddle. She worked her candy-making magic and added extracts to the mixture to give the finished product even better flavor.

During the entire time, a comfortable quiet reigned between them, broken by occasional requests for help and bits and snips of commentaries. Time passed in gratifying accord, underscoring how suitable their union was.

Soon the peace was broken by the arrival of the others. High-pitched feminine voices blended with the deeper murmurs of the young men, and laughter rang out above the conversations.

After Dulcie took the kettle off the stove, she doffed her apron and dragged Race by the hand into the midst of the group. "I'd like you to meet my husband, Race," she said to anyone and everyone she came across.

Race relished the warmth of her soft hand tightly holding his.

The candy was forgotten while it cooled to the necessary temperature for pulling, and someone produced a fiddle. A harmonica followed, and moments later everyone paired off. The dancing began.

Race swirled his wife through dance after dance, keeping pace with the lively music. At every turn he caught sight of her sparkling blue eyes, her rose-tinted cheeks, her sugar-plum lips. Her delicate blond beauty was set off by a peri-winkle-blue dress that showed a hint of creamy flesh at the top of the bodice. Her enthusiasm was palpable. Her happiness touched all who approached her. Race knew he belonged to Dulcie.

He was the happiest man alive.

The luckiest one, too.

Without a word, but after a conspiratorial wink, he tugged on her hand, then rushed her back to the kitchen. Under the pretext of checking the taffy, he led her next to the stove and with his body pressed her against the wall. An arm over her head braced him; with his other hand he cupped her chin. "You're mine," he whispered, then caught her lips in a devastating kiss.

A kiss she returned, her passion rising apace with his, her desire as vibrant as his own. They belonged together, had been made one for the other, and with every breath he drew, he sought to further join them in the lasting bonds of love.

But he still dared not speak it.

He had yet to confess.

So he revealed his love with actions, with kisses, with tenderness and passion, and all-encompassing need. And if his instincts didn't mislead him, he would swear Dulcie loved him as deeply as he loved her.

Still, he needed to hear her speak her love for him, to vow that nothing would ever separate them. Until he coaxed that confession from her lips, he wouldn't speak of Milton Hershey or chocolates. He couldn't risk losing the woman he loved.

''Where's the taffy?'' a male voice boomed from the door. ''Ohhhh! It's not the taffy that's cooking in the kitchen. It's the newlyweds!''

Mr. and Mrs. Race Langston flew apart, blushing. In seconds the kitchen filled with young people, all teasing good-naturedly.

''Here,'' Race said, handing first a folded towel, then the kettle of candy to Richard Maier, the one who'd interrupted. ''You can keep the candy. I'll continue savoring my bride!''

Male cheers roared.

''Race!'' Dulcie chided, again reddening.

''Dulcie!'' he retorted with a wicked gleam in his brown eyes.

The tension between them grew. Desire crackled in the air around them. They drew closer, as if held by a binding chain. The revelers, some indulgent, others envious, went back to the evening's entertainment, leaving Race and Dulcie to their mutual need.

Race caught her up in a tight embrace and returned to

kissing his wife. He'd given away the candy, but for himself he'd retained the very best. Dulcie was a delicacy infinitely sweeter than any candy.

The kiss went on and on. It multiplied into infinite caresses. More passionate kisses followed. Race knew that life couldn't get much better than this. Needing to control his rampant desire, he dragged his lips from Dulcie's.

She glanced up, and their gazes met.

"I love you."

❖ 14 ❖

Race's heart took flight. "Say it again," he demanded, needing to hear those words more than to draw his next breath.

The color in Dulcie's cheeks deepened. A telltale shine sparkled in her eyes. She smiled and said, "I love you."

"Oh, Dulcie . . ." His arms clamped fervently about her body. "Sweetheart . . ."

His voice was rough, and his heart beat loud and strong. His wife loved him! As he loved her.

He needed her. He needed to love her to where she'd never harbor doubts about his love. Until she could sustain her faith and hope for their marriage beyond the words he'd soon need to speak. But not now. Now he needed hours of intimacy, hours where nothing existed but the two of them and their powerful passion, their limitless love.

With a quick kiss to her reddened lips, he caught her fingers with his, and pulled her toward the door. The back door.

"What are you doing?" she asked, balking.

"I don't know about you, but I prefer privacy. I want you, on our bed, with forever to love you every way we both desire."

Dulcie waved her hand at her face. "Oh, my, Race. Just the tone of your voice is enough to scald me!"

With a sideways glance, he opened the door. "Now, don't try and tell me you object. I know I'm not alone on that bed we scorch night after night. And I've heard you cry out for more."

"You *are* incorrigible!"

"I'll ask you again. Would you want me to change?"

Standing at the threshold, Dulcie studied her handsome husband. His looks appealed to her more than ever, but now that she knew what lay behind his fiery gaze, she responded. Her body quivered with need as strong as his. They were, in fact, perfectly matched.

"Never!" she cried, darting out the door. "I'll race you home!"

The next morning, Dulcie woke up slowly, her body satiated and her heart content. She took her time bathing and dressing, already missing Race. He'd gone to Lancaster to meet a client. The man could only see him on a Saturday.

Her inner joy propelled her through the morning, carrying her into the afternoon. After the midday meal, she gathered her sewing basket and Granny K's bag of fabric remnants. She was expected at Emma Schwartz's home, where Granny's sewing circle had invited all the women of Everleigh for a quilting bee.

Dulcie smiled. It seemed that in their efforts to protect her and to ensure that Race did right by her, the residents of Everleigh had forgotten her encounter with Kirk by the river. Everyone had rallied round her. Her wedding had been beautiful and the celebration afterward had been fun for everyone.

Everyone but Kirk. No one had seen the brute since Founders' Day.

Well, no one but Isabella, and Dulcie never counted her anyway. The dark beauty could have Kirk. Ever since Isabella had realized he might have something there for her, she'd been trying to get inside Kirk's trousers. She often made reference to Kirk's "delicious animal essence" and couldn't understand why he hadn't yet surrendered to her. She considered herself higher "quality" than a farmer, and frequently argued that Kirk should realize the honor her attentions represented.

Isabella should have had a switch applied to her rear more often, Dulcie thought. But there hadn't been anyone to administer discipline.

Joe—as everyone called Giuseppe Morelli—owned the Ironfast Furnace Company, one of the most lucrative enterprises in the area. He'd worked alongside his immigrant father in various forges around Lancaster County. When the elder Morelli died, an ironmaster took the youth under his wing and trained him. When the man died, Joe was named sole heir. One thing led to the next, and capitalizing on a need, Joe opened the furnace company. Ever since, the man had seemed endowed with a golden touch.

Isabella's mother had died of influenza, leaving the child in the care of housekeepers and nannies. Joe had spared no expense when it came to his daughter's wants. The only whim he'd been unable to satisfy was her unrequited desire for Kirk Schleinbaugh. For years now, Isabella had waged an ardent campaign for the man who'd made no secret of his feelings for Dulcie.

"They deserve each other," Dulcie muttered. "And good riddance, too!"

Walking out, she heard birds singing, and the soft breeze that dallied in the branches overhead played its accompaniment. The hot scent of summer soil was spiced with the fragrant roses that bloomed in Granny's flower beds. A brilliant blue sky peeked through the canopy of trees, and up ahead, petunias, marigolds, phlox, and peonies dappled color around the various homes.

Dulcie knew life was wonderful, and she was the luckiest woman alive. She lived in a town that cared for its residents, the town being nothing more than what the people themselves made it. Her grandmother wouldn't have to endure a voyage West, since the confectionery was about to open, and according to Granny's divining methods, the enterprise was fated to be a great success. Granny never tired of reminding Dulcie that she'd read the future accurately. She basked in her frequent ''I told you so's'' and claimed the runes had told her Dulcie and Race were meant for each other.

Dulcie agreed. They *were* a perfect match. She didn't credit the runes, however, but she'd never get a word in edgewise if she tried to argue with her grandmother on that point.

It didn't particularly matter how they'd come together. What mattered was their marriage and the future that lay before them.

Dulcie climbed the front steps of the Schwartz home and placed a hand over her womb. Please God, she *would* soon sport a figure like Emma's. She could think of nothing more magnificent than creating a child from the exquisite loving she and Race shared.

Her heart skipped a beat. It could already have happened! What a joy that would be.

Wearing a secretive, satisfied smile, she knocked on the door before pushing it open and joining the women inside.

Cheers and words of welcome greeted her, as she was the honored guest. Emma waddled over. ''I'm so happy for you,'' she said, breathless from the strain of walking for two.

''You know,'' Dulcie said, ''I am, too!''

"And well you should be. Look at the lovely man you married."

Dulcie felt a prickle of heat in her cheeks. Oh, yes, she *had* looked—and plenty—at her husband. How well she knew how lovely the man really was! But that remained her secret, hers and his.

"Mm-hmm," she murmured with feeling, that smug smile back on her lips. Next thing she knew, Emma's elbow jabbed at her side. When she went to object, she caught the devilish gleam in her friend's gaze.

Dulcie laughed. There was nothing else to do, since each had communicated a private, womanly knowledge both now shared. Emma laughed, too.

"All right you two," called Prudence, "time to work! You don't want to be the only one who doesn't work on your wedding quilt, do you, Dulcie?"

Controlling her laughter, Dulcie hurried to where fabric of every color imaginable was spread out on Emma's dining-room table. She added Granny's scraps to the abundance. "Where should I start, Pru?"

"You can join the group piecing already. And mind you, keep your stitches neat and small!"

Dulcie and Emma glanced at each other across the room, and both chuckled again. Dulcie sat down to sew, while Emma slipped into the kitchen.

Moments later, Dulcie felt herself the object of scrutiny. Glancing sideways, she noticed Erika Stoltzfus eyeing her closely. Squashing a childish urge to stick her tongue out at Isabella Morelli's closest friend, Dulcie wondered if her nemesis would be coming. Although Isabella had never sewn a stitch, it wasn't inconceivable that she'd come to collect more gossip ammunition.

Oh, well, she wouldn't let either woman ruin her day.

Time was spent productively. Some women plied their

scissors, cutting precise shapes from the wealth of colorful fabric. Others, like Dulcie, sewed the pieces together, finally joining them to form interlocking rings against a white background.

They were making a quilt for Dulcie and Race. Prudence, Granny, and Mary Margaret O'Murphy, the eternal agitators of the Everleigh Beneficial Association Quilting Bee, had insisted that nothing but a Wedding Ring–pattern quilt would do. Every time she glanced at the beautiful needlework they were doing, Dulcie caught her breath. Even though her wedding had been of the shotgun variety, these women were treating her as they did any other Everleigh bride.

The afternoon flew by on the wings of busy needles and animated chatter. Bit by bit the quilt grew.

Hours later, Dulcie grew thirsty, and knowing that Emma had set the women's refreshment largess on the kitchen table, Dulcie excused herself from her piecing partners, and went for something to quench her thirst.

As she stepped into Emma's cheerful kitchen, Dulcie caught a glimpse of lavender skirt slipping out the back door. Hmmm . . . Erika Stoltzfus had worn a lavender dress. Was she leaving because Isabella hadn't shown up?

Oh, who cares? What mattered was the love and caring Dulcie was being shown. Besides, she was dying for something cool to drink. She looked around for the beverages.

Across the back wall of Emma's bright kitchen, a generous window allowed the sun to kiss the porcelain sink with sparkles of light. Crisp red and white checked curtains edged with eyelet lace framed the window. A massive black iron stove sat at her right, a fat squat icebox to her left. The center of the generous room was occupied by an oak table that, at the moment, displayed every conceivable form of treat.

Nibbling on a snickerdoodle cookie, Dulcie studied the

other offerings. A trace of the scent of fried funnel cakes still hung in the air, although the last crumb had been enjoyed a while ago. At the end of the table nearest the icebox, a punch bowl seemed to have been recently replenished. Right beside it, Dulcie found what she'd hoped for. A large pitcher was filled with thick, creamy buttermilk, its sides sweating as the cold beverage chilled the crockery from inside and the summer heat lapped it on the outside.

Glasses were arranged on a wide shelf by the sink, and Dulcie took the buttermilk with her to pour it there. As she approached the sink and the open window above, she caught the sound of what seemed like a furtive conversation. She wondered who was on the Schwartzes' back porch, but didn't dwell on the matter. The buttermilk was as cold as she'd expected and, with its tart tang, went down refreshingly.

Then she heard her name spoken. It blew in on a puff of breeze. She set down the pitcher to approach the window and the adjacent back door. The hiss of gossip continued.

"You should see the airs she's putting on," said Erika. "And you can come in, you know."

"Oh, but of course she's putting on airs! What did you expect?" asked Isabella Morelli. "And, no, I couldn't *abide* sitting in there, listening to the praises of that insipid little Dutch girl. Besides, you already told me the good stuff you heard inside."

"Hmmph!" Nothing good was going on out there. Dulcie strained to hear more.

"Fool that she is," continued Isabella, "she doesn't realize that yummy man was only courting her for her chocolate recipe. After all, he proposed with a gun at his back."

Dulcie's hands trembled. She set the glass down in the sink. Dear God, it couldn't be true . . . could it?

What would Race have wanted with her family recipe,

anyway? Besides, he loved her. True, he hadn't said so, but would a man treat a woman the way he treated her without love to prompt his actions?

She forced herself to ignore the buzz of thoughts in her head and leaned against the closed door.

"Why would a lawyer want a chocolate recipe?" asked Erika.

"Oh, for nothing. *He* doesn't want it. He was hired to either buy or seduce the recipe from her. His main interest is to make sure her store fails so she doesn't steal his client's future customers."

Erika gasped. "Where did you hear that?"

Yes, Dulcie thought, where *had* Isabella learned that? She held her breath, intent on catching even the quietest whisper.

"My cousin Vincent works at the Lancaster Caramel Company. He heard Horace Langston speaking with Milton Hershey about the chocolates."

Dulcie whimpered and covered her ears. The breath left her lungs. Shards of pain pierced her heart, and she felt dizzy. Limp, she slid down the door to the floor, where she huddled, hugging her knees to her chest.

It had all been a lie. The flowers he'd brought, the visits, the indulgent way he'd seemed to accept Granny's eccentricities. Everything. None of it had been real.

Her throat burned, and hot tears runneled her cheeks. If that were so, then none of his kisses or tenderness had been real. And that meant that their lovemaking, as passionate and emotional as it had seemed, had been no more genuine than the rest.

He'd betrayed her trust.

He'd betrayed their vows. The vows he'd so vehemently insisted were real. His intensity had challenged her to restate those vows. And she had. Dear God, she'd made those vows, meant every word she'd spoken, every kiss she'd given.

Beyond kisses, she'd generously given herself to him, body and soul. How could he have touched her so intimately, so lovingly, and meant nothing by it? She'd returned the caresses, the passion, and the love she'd sworn she'd seen in his eyes. And it turned out that she'd seen only what she'd wanted to see.

A sob rose from her breast; she couldn't hold it back. If she concentrated, she could still feel Race's hands on her body, heating her, inciting her passion, then fulfilling her every need. And the lovemaking that had so thoroughly satisfied her, that she had treasured in her heart, had meant nothing to her husband.

Husband. Ha! A confidence man was what he was, a creative genius who'd painted a reality that hadn't existed at all. And yes, like the fool Isabella had called her, she'd happily put her heart and hopes in his hands. She'd given him everything she'd had to give, counting on the chimera of his love.

It seemed Mignone Kramer had been right all those years ago, when she'd named her only daughter after the nonexistent lady of Don Quixote's dreams. Dulcie had thought herself a bride, a wife. Now she had no idea what she was. She'd been as foolish as the misguided knight who'd seen giants in place of windmills.

Yes, Dulcie had tilted at a windmill. She'd thought she'd discovered love; but it was betrayal behind the mirage. Tears drenching her face, Dulcie cringed and thought how wretched she felt, especially by comparison to how she'd felt earlier that day.

Footsteps approached. The kitchen door swung in. ''Dulcie?'' called Emma. ''Are you in here?''

Oh, no! She had to leave. She had to get out of here

before everyone found her weeping in a corner of the
Schwartzes' kitchen. A sudden, monstrous thought came to
her. Did everyone know Race had played her false? Was
that why they'd insisted he marry her? Did everyone figure
that with her reputation compromised, and lacking her
blasted family recipe, she'd just wither and die?

She really *had* to get out of here. By dint of will Dulcie
rose, slapping the tears from her cheeks. Catching sight of
her, Emma gasped. "What's happened?"

Dulcie shook her head. She didn't trust herself to say
much. 'Nothing. I-I must get home."

Without waiting for further questions, Dulcie slipped
around Emma's expanded girth and ran through the doorway. She didn't stop to respond to the quilters' many calls.
She had only one goal in mind. She had to get out of there.

Running wildly down the street, she noticed the sun,
which was starting to slide down the canopy of sky above.
Dusk would soon arrive. Then night. Race was due back
shortly. What if he returned earlier than expected?

More tears filled Dulcie's eyes. What would she do if he
was already back? What could she say to her husband, her
lover who really wasn't? How she wished she'd never heard
Isabella. How she wished none of it were true—

Well, now, she suddenly thought. What if . . . what if Isabella had just been making up stories about Dulcie? It
wouldn't have been the first time. And who was Dulcie going to trust? Isabella or Race?

Maybe . . . maybe she'd jumped to unfair conclusions.
Dear God, please let it be so.

Slowing her breakneck speed, she ran up the porch steps
and went inside. Granny was still at the quilting bee, which
was all for the good. Dulcie needed time to compose herself.
She didn't want to look like a madwoman when Race came

home. And she had no courage left to face both Granny and Race at the same time.

In the bedroom, Dulcie's strength drained away. She collapsed on the bed, the bed she shared with Race. Fear, anger, and hurt filled her heart. She wasn't even sure how best to confront her husband. And she really did have to remove the evidence of her tears.

But was she done crying? It depended on Race.

Shoving a hank of loosened hair behind her ear, with her other hand she mopped away the tears on her cheeks. Then, out of the corner of her eye, she noticed something dark sticking out from under the bed. She wriggled on her stomach closer to the edge, and realized it was Race's portfolio.

He must have been in a hurry and missed it. Why else would he leave it behind when he'd gone to town on business? Could Isabella be onto something, after all?

"No," she scolded herself. "Don't try to second-guess everything. Calm down and get ready for when Race comes home."

She scooted to the edge of the bed and picked up the leather case. The clasp had been left open, and a flood of papers poured out onto the floor. "Oh, horsefeathers!" Now she had to pick them all up. She just hoped Race didn't return while she was still all rumpled and teary—

She froze. *"No!"* she whimpered. It couldn't be. Across the top of one of those frightfully businesslike documents she read "Kramer's Sweet Secrets."

She straightened slowly, reading farther down the page. It only took seconds to realize she held a contract to sell Milton Snavely Hershey her secret recipe. At the bottom of the page, Mr. Hershey had already signed. Signed and dated his signature, which harked back to the infamous day of the skunk!

So it was true. Isabella hadn't been lying. Race had only wanted Maman's secret recipe.

Mr. Hershey must be quite worried about Dulcie's potential to compete for customers. Although she was pleased to note that, her tiny burst of pride was vastly overshadowed by the bitter gall of betrayal.

Betrayed. All the intimate words Race had whispered, all those kisses and tingling caresses, even his lovemaking had been nothing but a cruel sham.

She hoped he'd been well paid. After all, forcing himself to wed a country bumpkin like herself was a most extreme step to take on behalf of a client, no matter how wealthy or influential Milton Hershey was.

No wonder Race had always looked pained when she discussed her plans for the confectionery. She'd reminded him of a job he still had to do. And how did he think he'd get the recipe from her? When she was all soft and sated on their bed? Had he thought she'd agree to anything after he pleasured her?

Dulcie felt ill to her stomach. The pain in her heart was vicious. But she had one more thing to do. She had to confront Race with the evidence she'd found. And she'd be damned if he'd find her looking like this!

Quickly, she changed from her calico dress into her best royal-blue linen church dress. With rough strokes she unraveled the coil she'd made with her braid. She wanted to wear it in a more imposing style, something that gave her, if nothing else, the illusion of a few more inches in height.

The water in the pitcher on her washstand felt summer-warm. Running downstairs, she went to the kitchen and chipped a chunk of ice from the block in the icebox. Back upstairs, she plopped it in with the water she poured into the basin. Wetting a fresh washcloth with the cooled water, she pressed it against her swollen eyes.

When they no longer hurt so much, she removed the compress and took a good long look in the mirror. While she'd never be a ravishing beauty like Isabella, Dulcie judged herself quite passable. Her hair was a nice gold color. Her blue eyes, although still a bit puffy, were nice, too. Her figure had certainly seemed to please Race every time he'd lost himself in its exploration, and if she held her shoulders and chin high enough and firm enough, she could get through just about anything.

As she studied her reflection, she heard hoofbeats outside. Giant bats suddenly took off inside her stomach. Dark and voracious, they flapped harsh wings against her innards, again making her feel queasy. Oh, dear. Maybe she couldn't really face her husband after all.

The front door opened, and she heard his footsteps on the stairs. "Dulcie!" he called. "I'm home."

❖ 15 ❖

Dᴜʟᴄɪᴇ ᴡᴇɴᴛ ᴛᴏ stand by the bed, where she'd dropped the offending papers. Lacing her hands across her middle, she took a deep breath. "I'm upstairs."

Race must have taken the steps two by two, because in no time he burst through the doorway. "You'll never believe it. I forgot my portfolio. But, oh, I've missed you!" he exclaimed, then came to embrace her, his lips aiming for hers.

She turned away to avert the contact, then stepped back and faced him again. He looked startled by her actions, and she could swear her refusal had hurt him. Something instinctive, deep in her heart, urged her to go to him, to hug him, kiss him, enjoy his company as usual. But then she told herself they had the papers to contend with.

As far as she was concerned, no amount of rejection on her part could equal the fact that he'd been less than honest with her all along. "You've lied to me," she said, not giving him time to question her. "When were you planning to ask for the chocolate recipe?"

Race froze in place, his jaw flapping open. "H-how did you—"

If she hadn't been so angry, so hurt, she would have

thought he looked funny standing there like a giant catfish, jawing silently. But as it was, her heart was broken, especially since his lack of denial said more than words ever could. "Did you think you could steal from me without my noticing?"

"You're not so stupid—"

"I sure was! Imagine how very stupid I was, that I began to believe our marriage had a chance."

"But that's not stupid! Our marriage—"

"Spare me the protestations, Race," she cut in, then crossed her arms over her chest, wishing she could squeeze the pain from her heart. "There is no marriage. You know perfectly well that lawyers have ways to wriggle clients out of a nuptial noose. There's a particularly appropriate one for us. It's the one that deals with marrying under false pretenses. In the end, it's as if the marriage never was."

"B-but—"

"No, thank you. I don't want explanations. Just answers." She picked up the incriminating documents. "Did you draft these—these contracts? Did you have them when you carried me home on your horse? Did you have them when you kissed me? Proposed? Married me? You obviously had them when you took me to bed."

"Y-yes, but—"

"I don't want to hear any more." She shoved the papers into his stomach, and experienced a jolt of satisfaction when he gasped from the blow. "I don't even want to see you. Leave! Go back to your rich family and your big-city ways."

Race flung the papers back on the bed and approached Dulcie, his hands extended toward her. She stuck her arm, palm out, in front of her. "Don't come closer. I want you out of my house, out of my life, you . . . you lying city swell."

"But I don't want to leave. You're my wife, Dulcie. We're married. Remember? Those were vows we took. Until death do us part."

Tears stung Dulcie's eyes. She turned her back on Race, not wanting him to see her pain. "Don't speak to me of vows, Race Langston. You never meant a word you said. All you wanted was the money Milton Hershey is paying you." She paused to clear away the knot in her throat. "Let me tell you something. I'm a simple person. From Everleigh. Where people don't use other people to make money. You can think me foolish, or dull-witted and countrified, but I'm proud of who I am. I'm proud of my small-town ideas and outlook and actions. Those small-town notions were what made my neighbors rally around me when they thought you'd dishonored me."

Squaring her shoulders, she turned around. She raked him with her gaze and saw him clench his jaw. His cheeks burned red, and his eyes registered hurt. Again feeling that inner softening, she fought it with another glance at the crushed papers. "Please leave," she said. "I don't want my grandmother to see you again. She cares for you, and I don't want her hurt any more than she has been up to now."

"Now *you* listen to *me*," he responded through gritted teeth. "I don't believe at any time I have actually lied to you. Yes, I kept some things silent. But I had my reasons."

When she snorted and rolled her eyes, muscles again worked in his cheek, and he took an ominous step closer. "Hear me out. I have *never* done anything to hurt your grandmother. I like her. What's more, I respect her. As far as our marriage is concerned, I'm going to hold you to those vows. You are my wife."

As Race said "wife," Dulcie's wayward heart sped up its beat. Amazing how even after learning of Race's deceit, that fickle organ could still feel love for him. But she couldn't give in. No matter how earnest he sounded.

"Tell me," she demanded. "Did you or did you not come to Everleigh to keep my chocolate bonbons from competing against Milton Hershey's candies? Yes or no will do."

Race grabbed the papers, then clenched his fists. The damned contract for the double-damned chocolates became a wadded ball. He wished he could make it disappear. He wanted to deny his connection to Milton Hershey. He wished he could tell Dulcie his motives had been only the purest, but since he held the condemning evidence in his hand, he couldn't offer a blatant lie.

"Go," she whispered.

A pang of guilt punched Race in the gut. He'd much rather see Dulcie as a spitfire than the bruised summer flower she so resembled now. It was clear that the sight of him was more than she could bear, which hurt him to the core. So he'd leave. But not for good.

"Very well," he said. "But you will listen to what I have to say. Then I'll go." He kept his gaze on her, hoping to see a sign of yielding. There was none. "I take our vows seriously. I'm a fairly serious sort, especially when it comes to something like marriage. In spite of how this looks, I value my integrity. When I vowed to love you until the day I die, that's what I meant. I will love you forever."

He'd hoped she'd respond to his confession of love, but if anything, her chin burrowed deeper into her chest. She looked diminished, and he ached to see her looking so. "I don't care if you believe me or not. Just believe this. We're married. Forever. And I love you. No matter how long it takes, I'll prove myself to you."

She turned her back to him.

Race winced, closing his eyes against the sting of tears. It stunned him to realize he was on the verge of weeping. Save for the threat to his father's health, nothing had ever had the power to move him so strongly. But she could. He loved her, and she meant the world to him. He would do whatever it took to convince her of his love.

He prayed it wouldn't cost him his father's life.

The horrible encounter with Dulcie had lasted only minutes. Race had trouble accepting that such a short span of time could so devastate a man's life. It could, but only if the man allowed it. And Race refused to surrender. Dulcie was his. His wife. His future.

With a pat to the animal's neck, Race urged Zephyr to pick up his pace. They had no time to waste. He meant to go directly to Milton Hershey's home. He would tell the man what havoc his determination had wrought in Race's life. He'd rip up the crumpled contract he carried in his jacket pocket and leave the scraps with the obstinate candy maker.

Then he'd do what he should have done from the start. He'd demand total honesty and disclosure from his father. Race could offer no real help until he had all the facts. Then he could work to resolve Horace's business fiasco, even if it pitted him against his domineering grandfather. The man who'd called Dulcie a dairymaid.

The old battleax had better stop aiming blows at Dulcie, Race thought. She might be from the country, but that had no bearing whatsoever on who she really was. She was the woman he'd fallen in love with. The woman with whom he would spend the rest of his life.

He'd let no one stand in his way.

Not Milton Snavely Hershey.

Not Horace Langston III.

Not Edward Richter.

Not even Dulcie Kramer Langston herself.

*   *   *

Nothing went according to plan. Milton hadn't been home, so Race was forced to keep the crushed contract and head for his parents' house. It didn't matter who he dealt with first. Milton and Horace and Edward were formidable, each in his own right.

He left Zephyr with Harris, a mumbled greeting all he could offer his friend. He hurried across the lawn and, once inside, headed straight for the library. A knock yielded his father's response.

"We must talk," Race said, his manner far from what he'd hoped for. But he was desperate. And a desperate man didn't bother with niceties. "I need to know everything about your failed business venture. What it entailed. How much money—to the penny—was lost. What business assets can be liquidated. Who your partners were. I can't help if I'm kept blind."

Horace pointed to the overstuffed armchair across from his desk. "Sit down, son. You remind me of that chestnut beast of yours after he's gone on a hard run. You're nearly frothing at the mouth."

"I have no time to waste. This . . . mess is about to cost me the most important part of my life. And I don't mean to let that happen. Not if I can at all help it, and from what you've told me, I'm the only one who can do anything about it. Start at the beginning and tell all."

Horace's brown eyes darted toward his large oak file chest. "This could take time."

"If I don't resolve this nightmare quickly, I'll have nothing more than time to kill for the rest of my life."

"You needn't sound so melodramatic."

"I'd hardly call one's wife annulling one's marriage mere melodrama."

Horace's eyebrows drew together. Frown lines deepened

the creases on his forehead. "Why on earth would that child do such a thing? She seemed reasonable."

"She learned of my relationship with Milton Hershey and didn't appreciate being wooed, then wed, for the sake of a damned family recipe."

"Don't curse, dear," offered his mother from the doorway. "Pray tell, what is going on here? And where would Dulcie get such a foolish notion?"

"Good," Race said. "I'm glad you're here. We're going to get a few things out in the open. Then I'll decide where we go from there. Please make yourself comfortable, Mother. I suspect this will be a long night."

Pulling the wad of paper that threatened his marriage from his jacket pocket, Race threw it on his father's desk. He then dropped into the large mulberry chair Horace had indicated. Mother took the matching seat next to Race. "Everything, Father. From the start."

Horace cleared his throat. He shifted. He clasped his hands, then opened them again. He picked up a dried-out pen and tapped the instrument against the edge of the desk. "I didn't expect you to drag your mother into this."

Race glanced at his mother, who was avidly following the interplay between her husband and son. He'd envied Dulcie her comfortable openness with Granny K. If he truly wanted that for his family, he was going to have to bring it about himself. It was up to him.

He took a deep breath for courage. "I'm dragging no one, Father. We're a family. Whatever happens to one of us affects the others. And I'm tired of all the deuced secrecy this . . . this . . . Hell, I don't even know what to call this ridiculous situation. A chocolate recipe, for goodness' sake!"

Mother looked enthralled. "Chocolate?"

"Just wait, Mother. I've a feeling this will get stranger

and more convoluted before I unravel the knotty muddle Father and Milton Hershey have made.''

''No, son,'' said Horace. ''Milton has nothing to do with it. He simply came to my rescue. Listen carefully, because I'll only explain once. Once will be humiliation enough.''

Horace stood and, clasping his hands at his back, strode to the tall window behind the desk. Through the sparkling pane Race could make out the silhouette of the rosebushes in his mother's garden. Just the thought of that flower's scent made him ache for Dulcie and the tender love they'd found in each other's arms.

''Marthe's well aware that there's no love lost between your grandfather and me,'' Horace said, addressing Race without turning. ''He's always believed your mother married well beneath her—''

''Oh, stop that, Horace,'' Marthe interrupted in her soft yet firm voice. ''You know how I feel about Father's ridiculous opinions. You shouldn't let his foolishness get the best of you.''

Horace laughed without humor. ''You could say this time he'll get the best of me. You see, darling, for years I've done what he wanted, when he wanted it done, how he wanted it done, even when it wasn't the best way to do things. God knows I've tried to be the perfect son-in-law and employee. But God also knows, Edward's never forgiven me for dashing his hopes of marrying you to Old Philadelphia money.''

''Pshaw!'' she said, waving his comment aside. ''I would never have married some nasty old gob of money.''

Race's eyes widened, and his eyebrows met his hairline. He'd *never* heard his mother speak so coarsely. What's more, she seemed to appreciate the opportunity to vent her thoughts!

The elder Langston came around the desk. ''This really

has nothing to do with you, Marthe. It's always been between Edward and me.'' He went to his wife and laid a
hand on her slender shoulder. ''For whatever it's worth, I
needed to accomplish *something* of my own. I studied various business ventures I'd heard about, and decided to take
a portion of department store profits and invest them. I—
foolishly—thought I could turn that money around and
show a healthy profit. I backed the wrong horse, however.''

''You invested in racehorses?'' Race asked, stunned.
''But . . . why? You've always disapproved of gambling. I
don't understand.''

''No, son. I didn't invest in horses. I still hold nothing
but contempt for games of chance. I must admit, however,
that my failed investment is best called a gamble.''

Race had no patience left. They were still skirting the
issue. ''Father, I meant what I said when I first arrived.
Every detail, if you please. I don't have all night to spend
chatting or philosophizing with you. Investment ventures are
nothing more than legitimate gambles. Highly costly ones,
at times.''

''Indeed,'' Horace responded. ''You want details, I'll
give you details.'' He strode to the file chest, opened the
top drawer, and withdrew a fat envelope. He handed it to
Race. ''Here it is. Every last, miserable detail.''

As Race rifled through the thick sheaf of papers, his
mother turned to Horace. ''How did you ever get Father to
invest profits outside Richter's Department Store?''

''That, Marthe, was my first mistake.''

''Your first mistake?''

''Yes. You see, I-I took the money without letting him
know. I was assured that the investment would pay off in
only a few months' time, and I acted on that expectation.
But everything went wrong.''

Horace paused, and Race heard his father sigh. He'd

learned more by keeping quiet while his parents spoke than by direct questioning. Perhaps Mother would extract the information he needed. He continued perusing the bewildering array of vague agreements, bills of sale, and other strange documents, an ear cocked toward his parents.

"What went wrong, then, dear?"

"That was my second mistake. I failed to fully investigate all aspects of the business."

"But Horace dear, what on earth was the business? What were you putting the money—"

"Peacocks?" Race leapt up. "I'll be damned if I can believe it! Please tell me this is a mistake."

"Sorry, son, I can't do that."

Mother stood. She looked at Father, then glanced at Race. "What peacocks? What *are* you talking about?"

Studying his father, Race read clearly how miserable the man felt. "You invested a minor fortune in . . . peacocks?"

Horace colored and nodded.

"In Pennsylvania?"

Another nod.

"Weren't you aware that they're native to Southern Asia? The East Indies? They hail from warmer climates."

"I know now."

Marthe Langston grabbed her husband's shirtsleeve. "Horace Langston! What on earth did you want with peacocks in the first place?"

Horace walked back to his chair, then crumpled down in it. "I wanted nothing to do with peacocks. I merely wanted a constant and inexpensive source of peacock feathers for the store. They're all the rage. And I hoped the feathers could be marketed to other enterprises. That would have enabled me to turn the money around with a healthy profit. I meant to show Edward I could do it. And ultimately I wanted the money to start over, on my own. I wanted to finally be my own man.''

"Oh, love.'' Marthe sighed.

"But peacocks, Father? I've seen no fakirs on Queen Street or Penn Square. Racehorses would have worked.''

"As I told you before, a desperate man is capable of foolish acts.''

Race paused. Yes, he knew all about desperation. He was about to sell his soul to Milton Hershey to bail his father out. He would take on the repayment of Father's outlandish disaster. He'd pay Hershey those thousands upon thousands of dollars the man had given Horace to cover his loss. If things didn't work out favorably, Race would likely live his life under Hershey's financial thumb, much as Horace had done with Edward.

"Tell me, Father, how can an otherwise intelligent man be persuaded to think peacocks can survive Pennsylvania winters?''

"Need I really go into all the grisly details?'' Race nodded. Horace squared his shoulders. "I was told by the zoologist I consulted that a barn would suffice in winter. Wretchedly, we learned it didn't. No sooner had January's snows come, than one by one the peafowl caught cold. The money went the way of the dying birds.''

The telephone rang. Ready to tear his hair out in frustration, Race answered the contraption since he was expecting a call from Milton. "Hello,'' he said. "Hershey! I'm certainly glad to hear from you.''

Race listened to inane greetings and took note of the man's good wishes for Horace's continued recovery. "That's all fine, sir. But an urgent situation has arisen. I cannot carry out your negotiations. You must allow me to pay you back in regular monetary allotments.''

"How many times need I tell you I have personal reasons for—"

"No more," Race said, cutting off the confectioner, "since they're now superseded by my own personal reasons. I'll explain. As you're aware, I've recently married Dulcie Kramer. When she learned of my involvement with you, she decided to declare our marriage null and void. That's something I'll never allow. As you can see, I can no longer represent you in the matter of the chocolates."

"I . . . see . . ."

"Do you, sir? And will you desist in holding your assistance over my father's head?"

Across the telephone line, Race heard Hershey clear his throat. "Well, now, son, I held nothing over your father's head. I never intended to demand repayment. When I needed his help, your father backed me without question. When he had a need, I did the same. Knowing how difficult it's been for him to remain in Edward's employ, however, I wanted to hire you to handle a fairly simple matter so I could recommend your work to everyone I deal with. I wanted to help make a success of your practice."

"You mean you wanted me to buy that damn recipe for my own benefit?"

The telephone crackled noisily. "In an odd sort of sense. Perhaps if you look at it with humor . . ."

Race saw red. "I see nothing humorous in this situation. I might lose my wife for the sake of a recipe you don't even want! And all because of a roost of dead peacocks!"

A pause. Then, "I never said I didn't want the recipe," said Milton, his words distinct, his diction slow and cautious. "In fact, I want it more than ever. I've heard the candies your wife makes put my chocolate to shame."

"No. I want nothing to do with chocolate. I'll repay every cent that went to rescue my father from Edward Richter's fury, but I want nothing more of those damned chocolate bonbons.''

Race could almost hear the thoughts barreling around Mr. Hershey's head. "Tell you what," the man finally said. "Let's agree to talk at length about this tomorrow. Get a good night's rest, and matters will surely look better afterward."

"Frankly, sir, I don't see how they have a chance in hell of doing that. You still want that chocolate recipe, and my father is still scared to death that Edward might learn he's lost thousands in store dollars—''

The library door crashed against the wall. "Who lost thousands from my store?'' roared Edward Richter as he stormed into the room, eyes black as night, white hair bristling with life.

Race glanced at Horace, who paled. "We'll meet tomorrow, Milton. There's trouble here—''

The receiver spat more crackling sounds. ". . . hear Edward in a foul mood," Milton said. "We'll speak tomorrow."

"Fine." Race watched his father and grandfather stare each other down. Marthe flitted between the two men, more agitated than he'd ever seen her. "Tomorrow."

Returning the earpiece to its hook, he studied the family muddle before him. Common sense was needed. "Why don't we all take seats and discuss this rationally?"

Edward whirled toward his grandson, lean cheeks streaked with red. "I *am* discussing this rationally. What the hell has he done with my money?"

Horace stood behind the desk and, holding onto a veneer of dignity, faced his father-in-law. "I've already replaced the funds I used to make an investment. One that failed."

"How much?" Edward insisted, his bass voice deadly low.

"Fifty thousand dollars."

Jerking as if bitten by one of Horace's dead peacocks, Edward's expression turned murderous. He smacked both fists on Horace's desk, his lean, spare body adopting a vulture's pose. "You took fifty thousand dollars from my store?"

"Yes, and I replaced—"

"Fifty thousand dollars?"

"Father!" Marthe cried, pulling on Edward's jacket. "Please don't bellow. Sit down so we can do as Race said. It's not often you stop by, so let's discuss this rationally."

Edward patted his daughter's head, then said, "Later, dearest, Papa has business to attend to."

Horace abandoned his bunker behind the desk and went to Marthe's side. "Edward, Marthe is forty-five years old. Don't pat my wife on the head as if she were an infant." He turned to Marthe. "Why don't you go make some coffee? We're going to need it."

Marthe glared back. "You just said it. I'm forty-five years old. This is my family falling apart. None of you are going to settle down long enough to drink coffee, so don't patronize me!"

Race's jaw dropped. That was his mother? His elegant, soft-spoken mother? Things were certainly changing in the Langston home.

Marthe returned to her armchair, a mutinous look on her still unlined face, her arms like steel bands across her chest.

Edward stared at his daughter, dumbstruck.

Horace ran with the opportunity. "I took fifty thousand dollars, Edward. I was at the end of my tether. For twenty-eight years you've made me pay for marrying your daughter. Have you ever asked her if she was satisfied with her bargain?"

Marthe again leapt up. "Horace—"

Edward cut her off. "I should hope she's satisfied. But you, you stole from me. Do you understand that? You diverted funds from my business to line your own pocket."

Race lunged in at Edward's pause. "Father never intended to harm you. He was trying to reap a profit with his investment, in the hope that you would allow him to keep some of the money he'd made. Besides, he's already returned the money, sir. You can't call it theft since you have experienced no loss."

Edward sputtered, then, glaring at Horace, said, "I can call it what I damn well please. You stole my daughter and now my money. I call that theft." Running his hand through his heavy thatch of snow-white hair, he turned on Race. "And you! You had to stoop even lower than your mother. A milkmaid. Bah!"

He stalked to the door. "I told you then and I'll say it again, Horace Langston. You're not nearly good enough for my daughter."

"Father!"

As he left the room, Edward waved dismissively. "I have no daughter! No daughter of mine would marry a swindler. I tried, Marthe. I tried to warn you years ago. But you refused to listen. It took some time, but you've finally proven me right. I wash my hands of all of you. You'll hear from the police in the morning."

At Edward's words, Horace gasped, clutching his chest. He swayed and stumbled into Race's vacant chair.

❖ 16 ❖

As Race walked out, Dulcie's heart wanted to follow. But her pain, the reality of his betrayal, proved strong enough to halt her steps. He hadn't meant any of the things he'd said, she thought. He hadn't meant his vows, either.

As she mulled over his treachery, a tiny twitch of conscience brought to mind the earnest expression on Race's face when he'd told her he loved her. She remembered the strong, steady voice with which he'd taken his marriage vows. Her heart recalled the intensity of his lovemaking, his tenderness toward her, the way he'd kissed and held and touched her.

That foolish, foolish heart refused to believe what her eyes had read. It rejected all thought of deceit on Race's part.

But fact prevailed over fickle emotion.

Loud, uneven footsteps pounded on the porch. Hinges whined as the door opened roughly. "Hell a' kitin', Dulcinea-girl! Vat is here happening? Vere vas Race going?"

Oh, no. Not so soon. Dulcie wasn't ready to discuss what had led to Race's departure. She wasn't ready to face how naïve she'd been. She wasn't ready to share her heartache.

"Dulcie!" Granny cried again. "I kenn yer here. If choo don't down come, I vill up go!"

"No, Granny, you don't need to come upstairs." Granny tried to maneuver the stairs only once a day, usually at bedtime. Dulcie didn't want her to make an attempt when she was obviously upset. "I'm coming down."

When Dulcie reached the parlor, she found Granny on her straight-backed chair, her pipe puffing like a mill smokestack. Instantly her gaze was drawn to the green settee, where Race had so often sat. She remembered him picking his way around Maman's furnishings. She remembered him stealing kisses on that green sofa when Granny K wasn't looking. She remembered him following her around the room, determined to distract her from whatever she'd been doing.

Pain pierced her heart. Memories of a brief taste of heaven. That's all she had left. It hadn't been a marriage. Just the vague illusion of something that would never come to pass.

"Race is gone," she said, as much for her own benefit as to answer Granny's question. "I know you've grown fond of him, but I've just learned that his interest in me wasn't that of a man looking for a wife. He only wanted to buy my chocolate recipe for Milton Hershey, a candy maker who doesn't want me competing with his candies."

"Vat? Choo mean Race is gone . . . fer alvays?"

The bewilderment on her grandmother's face was easy for Dulcie to understand. Had she not seen the contract herself, had she not witnessed Race's inability to deny her charges, she would have felt the same. Questions would have filled her, and she would likely have accepted any explanation Race concocted. Painful though it was, she was better off knowing the truth.

"Yes, Granny. Race never wanted to marry me. Not really. He thought I was a simple country girl he could bedazzle with his city ways. All he wanted was Maman's bonbon recipe."

A virulent stream of German curses gushed out of Granny's mouth. "Dis ist foolishness. The runes no lie. Choo unt Race must married stay. Go to Lancaster *shnell,* right avay! Talk *fershtendich* mit him. Sensible talk, Dulcie. He's yer man, yer husband. Go, go *shnell!*"

Dulcie took a fortifying breath. "Oh, Granny. If it were only that easy. I can't go after him. He lied to me. He lied to you. We're not even really married."

"Ach! Dis ist so *ferhoodled! Ja,* yer married. The runes say choo marry mit Race. Pastor Eckert married choo mit Race. *Das ist alles.*" Waving Dulcie away, Granny stood, hitched the shoulder strap of her overalls higher on her shoulder, then swooped up her jug. "I spell go cast. Choo tink, unt I vill try fer choo. Den bed I go."

Although she held no faith in Granny's supernatural endeavors, Dulcie knew her grandmother would feel better by doing something familiar and meaningful to her. "You do that, Granny. I'll sit on the porch a while, then go to bed. Pleasant dreams."

Muttering about nightmares, Granny pulled herself up the stairs with the help of the banister and disappeared into her room. After the door slammed behind the older woman, the overwhelming silence of the house crashed down on Dulcie. It felt barren, dead, mournful. When Race had been there, the air had fairly crackled with energy, the attraction between the two of them almost palpable.

For the first time in her life, Dulcie understood loneliness. It didn't merely stem from being alone. It came with the realization that the one person who really mattered, the one who gave you reason for living, was no longer there. Loneliness was a void, darker than the darkest night Dulcie had ever known.

Her pain was almost visceral. It cut through any effort to forget it. It filled her eyes with tears, a weakness she wished she didn't have to yield to. But her feelings for Race ran too deeply for her to take his deceit lightly.

Walking out onto the porch, Dulcie shivered when an owl hooted. A cool breeze stroked her tear-stung eyes, playing in her hair, then wafting on its way. Like Race. He'd come, filled an empty space she hadn't even known she had, and then when she began to count on his presence, she learned he hadn't come to stay, he'd only lingered before heading toward the rest of his life.

Tears again wet her cheeks. As she so often had, Dulcie sought refuge on the old porch swing. As a child, every time she'd scraped a knee, been disappointed, or in a huff, she'd sat there, letting the rhythmic motion soothe her feelings. She'd sat for hours on the swing the day they'd buried Maman, tears flowing from sore, anguished eyes. She'd fallen asleep and woken only when the weak spring dawn had blushed in the eastern sky.

And now, heartbroken, her marriage a sham, she sat on the old swing and set it to rocking with her toes.

Dulcie was so engrossed in her thoughts that she failed to notice she had company. It was only when Emma Schwartz laid a comforting hand on her shoulder that she looked up.

"What happened?" her friend asked.

"Oh, Emma, I've been such a fool. I fell for a lie and a handsome face."

"Race?"

"Who else? I've never thought of myself as easy to fool, but I was taken in by his elegance, his attentions, his kisses, and his promises."

Emma lowered her ungainly body onto the swing next to Dulcie. "What are you talking about? I've never seen a more smitten newlywed than Race."

"Just goes to show how good an actor he is. He fooled everyone!"

Taking Dulcie's hand in hers, Emma squeezed. "Dulcie, dear, how could Race fool everyone? I don't understand."

"He never wanted to marry me. He only wanted my chocolate recipe."

"That's the silliest thing I ever heard. Why would he want it?"

"It's not silly at all! *Race* didn't want it, his client, Milton Hershey, did."

"The candy-making man in Lancaster?"

"That very one. Race only wooed me to get the recipe. I was such a fool that I fell for his act. The whole town did. Imagine how he must have laughed when the mayor played right into his hands and demanded that Race do right by me. It was like handing a lamb to the fox."

Emma pressed a fist to one side of the mountain of unborn child in her lap, then wiggled in search of a more comfortable position. "That is too the silliest thing I've ever heard! There's not a man alive who'd marry a woman just so he could get his hands on a recipe. Imagine, what tailor would marry a dressmaker only for her talent in cutting patterns? What shoemaker would marry a cobbler just to learn how she fixes ladies' heels? It makes no sense."

"I'll admit your comparisons sound stupid," Dulcie said. "But our situation isn't like that. I found the contract he wrote the day Old Molly was spooked by the skunk. All that time he courted me under false pretenses. All that time he kept his reasons secret. All that time he could have told me, but never did."

"You've worked yourself up into a twitteration, and you don't make sense! When you ran from my kitchen I knew, of course, that something was wrong. And looking out the kitchen window, I realized who was behind your misery.

Isabella Morelli has been under your skin since the two of you met. I can't figure out what she still has against you, now that you're married and Kirk Schleinbaugh won't come within miles of you or Race."

Dulcie used the hem of her dress to wipe her cheeks. "Oh, Emma, Isabella is the least of my troubles. In fact, she helped me. She knew Race was only after my recipe."

"If you repeat that cockeyed notion again, I'll leave you to your misery!"

"It might be best for you. You and the little one need your sleep."

"Yes, silly. And so do you. Besides, what are friends for, if not to share each other's miseries?"

"Ha!" Dulcie crowed. "Sleep. That'll never come. All I see when I close my eyes is the snake I married taking phony vows in front of the entire town. That, or his face when he made lo—" She blushed furiously when she caught Emma's knowing wink. "Never mind that. He even had the audacity to try to romance me into discounting what I'd learned. He's despicable!"

"What did he do?"

"He said he loved me!"

"Oh, yes. Of course. The man is a diabolical fiend because he tried to talk some sense into you."

"All right," Dulcie conceded. "We're not going to agree, and it's only getting later. Go to bed, Emma Schwartz!" Standing, Dulcie squared her shoulders, then helped Emma rise. "Besides, you weren't there. You didn't see the contract, you didn't hear him confess that he'd come to Everleigh for the recipe. I did. Go home, Nathaniel and Sarah need you."

"Yes, it's late. I'll be going soon enough. And you need a friend, too." As she spoke, Emma slid her arm around Dulcie's shoulders. "Yes, I believe he came to Everleigh for a recipe. But then . . ." Emma paused before the porch steps.

"Then what?" asked Dulcie.

Emma smiled, the moonlight illuminating her face. "Then Race met you. He fell in love."

Dulcie stood on the porch, watching her friend carefully return home. Could Emma be right? If she were, wouldn't Race have refused to continue working for the Lancaster candy maker when he learned how much Dulcie was counting on her recipe? Wouldn't he have tried to help her succeed if he'd really loved her?

Had he loved her even a little?

In the days that followed, Dulcie concentrated on work. She dueled with dirt, vanquished cobwebs, decimated dust. And that was just at home. Every morning, after grappling with whatever housework she found at the Kramer house, she packed up her supplies and headed for her store.

There she waxed the floor and vinegared the windows. She painted the walls, then trimmed them with stenciled flowers. She measured the display window and made cheery red and white checked curtains. Then, when everything was as it should be, she received the ingredients she'd ordered. She was ready to launch her new enterprise.

The morning of the grand opening, Dulcie and Granny got up before dawn and turned sugar, cocoa, flavorings, and a dash of rich milk into the most sinfully delicious goodies anyone had ever tasted. They made trays and trays of the round brown morsels.

Packing the bonbons in flat, stackable wooden boxes Dulcie had constructed—with help from Emma's able husband—she was soon ready to go. She put the boxes on the floor of the buckboard, gave Old Molly a stern warning, then turned to Granny, knowing she wouldn't get away without a charm for prosperity. Granny proceeded true to form.

"Three sisters rode across de land
Each mit pieces of gold in their hands
De first one said, 'She needs one'
De second said, 'She gets some'
De third said, 'She has plenty, chust as she vished,
Plenty of gold to fill her dish!' "

Dulcie remained with her head dutifully bowed until Granny was done. Recognizing the love her grandmother had just expressed made it easier for Dulcie to shake off the uneasiness she felt when Granny practiced her pagan faith on her behalf. Then she wrapped her arms around her grandmother. "I love you, Granny K."

"*Ja*, I kenn dat. Go! Unt tink about choor husband."

Dulcie laughed without humor. Once Granny made up her mind, she was unmovable. "Don't wait supper for me. I'll just warm something when I get home."

With a nod and a wave, Granny shooed her on her way. Dulcie was glad she'd risen early. Just past dawn, the Columbia Pike was still empty; Old Molly had no excuse to put on her antics. Soon Dulcie reached Lancaster, and as she headed toward the livery, excitement bubbled up inside her for the first time since she'd sent Race away.

At the livery, the owner, Mr. Müller, refused to let her carry the boxes of chocolates by herself. He called one of his stable boys and, offering him a coin, sent Dulcie and her helper on their way.

At the store, Dulcie set a rusty flatiron on the floor by the door to keep it from closing. She wanted to make buying her bonbons an effortless endeavor.

"Good morning, Dulcie!" called Mrs. Eby as she opened the millinery.

With a wave, Dulcie asked, "Isn't it a lovely day?"

Katarina Eby stuck her head outside, threatening the security of the hat bedecked with flowers and stuffed blue jays that she wore. As the birds looked poised to take flight, carrying the hat with them, the milliner clutched one of the unfortunate creatures, restoring the contraption to its vantage point. Dulcie fought to stifle a laugh.

After much consideration, the hatmaker shrugged. "From what I can see, it looks to be another of our hot and humid days. I wonder if anyone will venture out on a scorcher like today?"

Refusing to let something as fickle as the weather ruin her store opening, Dulcie smiled. "Just you wait and see. They'll be lining up in droves! I took out an advertisement in the *Lancaster Intelligencer*. Every customer, whether they buy or not, gets to sample the candies."

The stable boy, who stood just inside the confectionery, arms full of delicacies, cleared his throat, then sent a cajoling smile to Dulcie.

Laughing, she said, "Yes, yes. Of course I'll give you a chocolate. You've been most helpful. There," she added, pointing to the large display table, "that's where the boxes go."

The youth complied, then opened his eyes wide when Dulcie uncovered the bonbons. "Thanks!" he said, then tore out of the store.

"Mrs. Eby!" Dulcie called. "Would you care to sample a chocolate?"

Hatless, Mrs. Eby bustled in. "I've been dying to try one. My husband wouldn't share the other ones you brought."

"Then you deserve two."

And with that, two customers entered the millinery, and a gentleman the confectionery. "Can you pack the chocolates in a gift tin?"

"Yes, sir!" Dulcie answered, making her first sale.

The day flew by, not giving Dulcie a moment to entertain

troublesome thoughts. At half past five, the steady stream of customers dwindled to a trickle, and Dulcie began to prepare for closing. She'd almost sold out the chocolates. And she'd made back close to what she'd paid for her stock of ingredients!

If business continued this strong, soon Dulcie would be able to buy a large stove to cook the candies at the store instead of at home. That would take some of the work off Granny's shoulders. Not that Dulcie put the older woman to work; it was a matter of Granny holding the reins of all that went on in the Kramer home. And Dulcie wanted her grandmother to take things easier. Granny's kidneys were faulty, and rheumatism crippled her more each day.

Why, if she could maintain such interest in her product, Dulcie would never again have to think of moving out West! The Kramer women could stay at home, in Everleigh, where they belonged.

Hanging up her apron, Dulcie collected the stack of empty candy boxes. As she went toward the front door, she saw movement outside her display window. She paused, waiting to see if another customer would straggle in. When no one did, she shrugged and went on. Again the furtive motion caught her attention, and she set the boxes on the floor. Approaching the window, she hid behind the curtain. At the last moment, she yanked the curtain back and caught the two adolescents who'd spied on her and Race the day he'd kissed her in full view through the window.

The youths stared, then shook their heads, as if disappointed that nothing titillating was likely to happen. They ran off, laughing.

Inside the store, tears scalded Dulcie's eyes. That kiss had been so tender, so powerful. It had seemed to say so much without words. And yet, in the end Race had made a fool of her.

Efforts to forget him had come to naught. At night she still cried herself to sleep, her hand holding tight to the pillow Race had used. She'd given up her hours on the swing. It too bore memories of the man she loved—the man who didn't love her.

She'd thought that hours of hard work in the store would keep remembrance and pain at bay. But here she stood, dusk approaching, and the sight of two boys was enough to catapult her back into the misery she'd tried to escape.

But was there escape from a broken heart? Was there ever a moment one felt oneself healed of the pain? Could she forget her love for Race? The man to whom she'd given her heart, her soul, her self?

Sobbing, she sat on the floor next to her candy boxes. "Damn you, Race Langston! Why'd you ever have to be so . . . so . . . Oh, damn!"

The torrent of tears poured out; loud sobs ripped from her throat. This was the first time she'd given her anguish free rein. At home, Granny had watched her with worry in her eyes. Emma had kept her company, despite the swollen ankles and short breath of late pregnancy. Even Mrs. Eby must have sensed something was wrong, since she'd spent an inordinate amount of time helping Dulcie and, more frequently, just talking.

Today Dulcie was alone. For a moment she thought she'd head home before it grew too dark. But the tears kept flowing, her sobs wouldn't quit, and she felt too miserable to walk to the livery just then.

She cried until all the dreams she'd dreamt of a future with Race came, then left. She cried until one by one her hopes fled, leaving her emptier than she'd ever been. She'd thought that opening her store would fill the spot in her life Race had vacated. But here she sat, her store a reality, a taste of success under her belt, and still she ached.

Unmindful of where she was, she lay back on the floor and stared at the blank ceiling. The white expanse above her looked invitingly vacant and new. That was what she wanted, she thought. A new start, a blank page she could fill with bright feelings and easy emotions. No more of this turbulent love for a man she couldn't have. She fought to turn her mind into that clean canvas, emotion-free.

After a while, she realized that her tears had stopped. Evening had painted the sky indigo-blue. Granny must be worried.

She gathered up her boxes again and closed the store. Quickly she went down Queen Street to the livery and once there hurried to Old Molly, who snuffled in her crotchety way.

"Oh, no, you don't," Dulcie muttered at her ornery horse. "I must get home as soon as possible. I don't have time for any of your tricks. Granny needs me home."

Dropping the boxes on the floor of the buckboard, Dulcie waved farewell to Mr. Müller, who'd given her a low monthly rate for keeping Molly during working hours. She was soon on the Columbia Pike.

By the time Dulcie got home, it was night, a moonlit night she wished she could share with Race. As it had on their wedding night, it sparkled with silver-dusted light. She'd forever associate moonlight with passion. With passion and love.

The next morning, Dulcie and Granny repeated yesterday's routine, and before long, Dulcie found herself approaching Lancaster. With a hello for the livery owner and a smile for Bobby, her helper, she set off on Queen Street heading for her store.

As they approached the Eby Building, she noticed a crowd gathered at the nearest street corner and smoke billowing above the spectators' heads. Oh, dear. It looked as if something up ahead, close to her store, had caught fire.

Although the entire block of buildings wouldn't go up in flames, thanks to an ordinance requiring brick or stone construction in Lancaster, the interior of the structure would surely be gutted by what appeared to be a furious blaze.

She heard the clanging of a bell and spotted a steam-powered fire wagon approaching. The crowd thinned to allow the firemen through. Dulcie caught a glimpse of black smoke and licking flames.

"Here," Bobby cried, pushing the boxes at Dulcie. "I gotta get back to work."

And with a juicy story to tell! When she turned her attention back to the commotion, she caught a glimpse of gray smoke shrouding the façade of the building next to her store. "Goodness!" she cried. "That looks awfully close to my store."

A portly gentleman, holding a rolled *Intelligencer* under his arm, turned her way. "You have a store near the Eby Building?"

"Actually, *in* the Eby Building. I opened a confectionery next to Mrs. Eby's hat shop."

"Oh, dear," he answered, concern underscoring a sympathetic expression. "I'm afraid I have bad news. The Eby Building's on fire."

"No," Dulcie whispered, shaking her head in disbelief. She refused to consider the possibility. "It can't be. I just opened my store yesterday. Everything was fine when I left last night. Are you sure?"

"Here," said the gentleman, "stand in front of me. You'll see better."

Dulcie moved, and while she tried to keep the chocolates from being jostled, she stood on tiptoe to get a better view. Her heart plummeted. The man was right. The wooden sign above the main door had ignited, and as flames spilled out the shattered windows, they licked the bricks, painting them black. A bucket brigade had been started, and men in shirt-sleeves sought to control the power of the hungry blaze.

Both windows were gone; both stores were ruined. "How—how could this happen?" she asked.

The stout man put a comforting hand on her shoulder. "From what I've heard, it's thought that feather and fur trimmings in the hat shop somehow caught fire. There was much to feed the flame, and the wooden floors and walls burned, too. It's a pity."

Pity? It wasn't a pity. It was devastation of the worst kind! All Dulcie and Granny had in material worth had been poured into the store and their product. All they had now was the house, the buckboard, Old Molly, and boxes of expensive chocolates with nowhere to sell them.

Up ahead, it looked as if the firemen were winning the battle against the ravaging fire. Once the onlookers realized that the most dramatic part of the event was over, they began to disperse. Soon a path opened before Dulcie, and she drew closer to her store. Coal and cinders were all that remained in the wake of the blaze.

And the ashes of her dreams.

A block down Queen Street, Race watched Dulcie approach the devastated Eby Building. She paused, holding on to a stack of thin wooden boxes he assumed held her chocolates. Then, as the crowd thinned, she crossed the street. He saw her speak with a fireman. The man shook his head, and Dulcie's shoulders sagged.

She sank down on the sidewalk, still holding onto her candies. Her head bowed. She covered her face with her hands, and Race felt his wife's misery in his heart. He'd give anything to comfort her, to make the store whole again, to revive her dream.

But he feared she'd send him away, reject him once again. He wasn't ready to tackle her anger and misconceptions. And surely this wasn't the most advantageous time to fight for his marriage.

Still, against logic, he felt drawn to her side to tell her how sorry he was her store had burned, especially so soon after her spectacular opening. Everyone in Lancaster had been praising her bonbons.

Slowly Race approached. Across the street from where Dulcie still sat, he paused, waiting for traffic to allow him to cross. His heart pounded in his chest, his palms grew damp, and anticipation burned in his gut. He welcomed the opportunity to speak to Dulcie. He missed her so much.

As he stepped into the street, she lifted her head, her gaze homing in on him. Tears had swollen her eyes; angry red splotches marred her skin. Her mouth formed an *O*, and she shook her head. Race froze.

She didn't even want him near.

A sword of pain sliced through him, stealing all hope. Dulcie didn't want him. Even at a moment of anguish and loss. He'd lost his wife.

Torturing himself with the sight of the woman he loved, the woman who'd just rejected him again, Race watched her stand, square her shoulders, then march down Queen Street. When she'd gone about one block, she paused.

She cast a glance in his direction, and despite the distance, their gazes caught. Wretched blue eyes stared into ravaged brown ones. For a moment, Race read longing in his wife's eyes. Then she tipped her chin toward the sky and resumed her stride.

A smile began to lift Race's lips. Yes, she'd turned her back on him. She'd refused the comfort he would gladly have lavished on her. But in an unguarded moment she'd given him back what he'd needed most.

Hope.

❖ 17 ❖

"Oh, Granny, I'm so tired, and everything is so mixed up!" Dulcie cried hours later.

Since she'd come home, she'd considered all sorts of ideas and possibilities for the future, but in the end, none had seemed workable. At each pass, she faced the same reality. They had a rickety buckboard wagon, a recalcitrant old mare, a house in a town where most residents inherited their homes, and no money. Were she to try to sell the house, she knew she'd have few prospects. Newcomers rarely came to Everleigh, so a sale wasn't likely to happen soon, if ever, and surely it wouldn't yield a high price.

Still, something deep in Dulcie kept her from deciding to move West. It seemed so . . . final, somehow. Almost like jumping off a precipice into a velvet-thick darkness. Although she'd never considered herself a coward, the black unknown made her pull up just short of taking that leap.

Maybe it was due to an overly sentimental nature. Or maybe she *did* have a cowardly stripe somewhere down her back. Or maybe it was sheer, ornery stubbornness. She just didn't want to move West.

It was too far from Race.

That thought set her stomach to churning with conflicting

emotions. The unguarded moment when she'd met his gaze across a smoky Lancaster street had revived responses she'd thought she'd never experience again. The feelings—good as well as bad—rushed back, leaving her breathless and with a soul-deep yearning for her husband.

Her estranged husband.

After a lengthy silence, Granny tossed back a generous glug of her kidney tonic. "Ach! Vas thirsty. Choo kenn, Dulcinea, choo should mit yer man talk. Him in Lancaster, choo in Everleigh ist no goot. Race loves choo. De runes say so."

I wish it was that simple, she thought. "I can't, Granny. I'm sure Race would do whatever he could to help us. He seems to have a well-developed sense of duty. At least toward a client. I would imagine he'd behave likewise in the case of his wife's family. That is, if he even considers me his wife. That's exactly why I can't turn to him. A marriage based on trickery is no marriage at all."

Shaking her head, Granny stood. "Ach! Dis ist *lobbich*, silly. Talk mit Race. Clear up dis . . . dis . . . mess. Runes no lie. Choo two are married. Married, married, married."

With a disgusted snort, Granny pulled her pipe out from behind her ear, lit it, then grabbed her jug and clumped toward the kitchen, muttering too low for Dulcie to catch what she was saying.

It didn't matter. Dulcie knew how Granny felt about her aborted marriage. In fact, Dulcie knew only too well how Granny felt about *everything*. Ermentrude Kramer wasn't one to keep her opinions to herself. Still, despite her love for her grandmother, Dulcie couldn't quite bring herself to trust Granny's divining methods. She believed the future was what you made of what God gave you. No stones, no tea leaves, not even a crystal ball could foresee something she had yet to make happen.

A twitch of her conscience brought to mind that up to now, Granny's predictions had never been wrong—for other folks, if not for Dulcie. She'd always contended that once Granny told someone what she saw in their future, that person went and worked to make the vision come true. Still, there was that perfect record, that confounded reliability.

According to Granny, Race and Dulcie were fated to a blissful marriage. But Dulcie couldn't see it. Just as she couldn't see what she should do next to bring a financially fit future into being. This rare case of wishy-washiness was driving her mad!

But that was better than letting her memories take over. She refused to waste any more time crying for a man who'd used her, dreaming of wonders that could never be, loving someone who didn't love her.

She followed her grandmother to the kitchen. "I still believe that given a chance, I could support us by selling Maman's bonbons."

Without missing a beat, Granny scrubbed a pot, dunked it into the rinse water, set it upside down to dry on a clean kitchen towel, then took a puff from her pipe and a swig from her jug. *"Ja."*

"But my store burned down!"

Granny repeated her actions. *"Ja."*

Dulcie wrinkled her nose. Granny was being purposely dull-witted. "All right. If you agree with me about the possibilities for the chocolates, tell me what your stones and tea leaves and crystal ball have to say about my lack of a store."

"Think, Dulcie. Choo found a store, it burned. Find another."

"Find another store! Have you any idea how difficult it was to find one so well situated, *then* persuade the owner of the building to lease me the property?"

"But choo a store found. One store, 'nother store. Same diff'rence. Go ask choor man to help find a store."

"Oh, Granny!" Dulcie wailed in frustration. "Please stop trying to send me to Race. I *can't* do that—"

"Unt vy not? Choo vould move us mit Indians, but choo no talk yer husband mit? *Das ist* stoopid!"

As Dulcie struggled to find yet another reason why she couldn't go to Race for help, she watched Granny's motions become grander, rougher, each pot clanking against the porcelain sink, each plate coming close to shattering. She sighed. "You've made your point, Granny. Somehow I'll find another store. You can stop smashing the sink now."

Granny's gray bun bobbled in assent. A satisfied grunt followed.

Yes, Dulcie would seek another store. Although she had virtually no hope of finding another vacancy, she had no alternative but to look. She couldn't just give up. Just as she couldn't turn to Race.

Why she felt she had to succeed without his help, she didn't know. She just knew she couldn't turn to him. In fact, he was the enemy. Or at the very least, the enemy's emissary.

As it was dark and she felt drained, Dulcie went upstairs and got ready for bed. Sitting before her vanity table in her nightgown, she brushed her hair, remembering how much Race loved to play with the curling ends. It was so hard to forget him, to ignore her love for him. But somehow she had to find the strength to do so. And she would have to toughen up. She couldn't go all silly and dreamy, then heartbroken and tearful each time she set eyes on the man. After all, she was determined to remain in his—no, *this* part of the country. If she eventually found it impossible to forget him, or to ignore his presence, she could then reconsider moving to the We—

No. She might as well admit it. She could no more move out West than she could cut from her heart her love for Race. She simply had to find a solution to her problems. She had to be stronger, smarter, more like Maman had been.

Thinking of her mother, it occurred to her that she didn't actually need a store of her own to sell her products. Maman had worked here at home. Women had brought their fabrics and their needs to her, and Mignone had worked her needlework magic in her room down the hall.

While Dulcie couldn't imagine selling chocolates from home, she realized she didn't need to become a shopkeeper to do so. What if . . .

What if she could sell her treats on consignment? In someone else's store? After all, the larger department stores in Lancaster and York offered locally made items for sale in their suitable departments. And in Lancaster, no store was larger, or more frequented, than Richter's Department Store.

They even had a specialty foods department!

Dropping her hairbrush on the vanity table, Dulcie rose and began to pace. It could work. It would certainly be easier on Granny and her to make the bonbons, then let a clerk at a department store sell them. It would also be better if she didn't go into Lancaster every day; it would cut her risk of meeting up with Race.

The more she thought it over, the more she liked the idea. And she had plenty of chocolates ready-made. All she had to do was return to Lancaster in the morning and present her proposal to someone in authority at Richter's. Surely the candies were good enough to sell themselves, at least to the store representative.

Feeling hope for the first time since that morning before the fire, Dulcie turned out the oil lamp and climbed into bed. Through the window, silver rays lit the empty half of the bed, pooling on Race's pillow. In the privacy of her room and the loneliness of the overlarge bed, Dulcie allowed herself to grieve for her ruined marriage. She missed Race. She would always miss him.

Running her hand over the mattress, she remembered how warm it had felt while they'd loved and slept on this bed. Their passion had turned up the heat on balmy summer nights, never cooling, never losing its power.

A tear escaped the corner of her eye and slipped into her hair.

Race and moonlight. Moonlight and passion. Passion and love. All three were part of a whole, the fabric of her feelings for the man she'd loved and lost.

But she wouldn't lose her future. She'd just have to build a new one, one full of success rather than passion. One lacking the sweet secrets of love.

A future without Race.

Early the next day, Dulcie donned a white cotton blouse with leg-o'-mutton sleeves and her navy serge skirt. She hoped the outfit had better luck at Richter's than it had had with Mr. Oberholtz. Slicking down her natural waves, she then pulled her hair back. Her youth would work against her, so she sought to present a sensible front to the management of Richter's Department Store.

Downstairs, Granny had a bowl of oats cooked with honey and dried apples waiting for her. This was normally one of Dulcie's favorite ways to start the day, but this morning she was so nervous, her stomach rioted each time she even thought of eating. She couldn't run the risk of arriving in Lancaster with an unsteady stomach.

"Not today," she told Granny, who frowned, shook her head, then took the bowl away from the table. "I'm sorry. I-I feel all jumpy and unsettled. I couldn't possibly eat. Maybe once I've solved the matter of the bonbons."

"Fine," Granny spat out. "But choo ain't gonna come clean up ta Lancaster *ferhext*. Granny vill cast a banishing spell for choo."

Resigned to her fate, Dulcie groaned. She wouldn't get out of the house until Granny cast a spell to eliminate whatever hex she believed Dulcie was under. "Very well, Granny. Let's have the spell."

Clumping unevenly, Granny bustled in the kitchen, gathering her Pow-Wowing necessities. Into a clean white conjuring bag she put Saint-John's-wort, basil, angelica, yarrow, rosemary, rue, vervain, and asafetida. At the last inclusion Dulcie wrinkled her nose. Asafetida was exceptionally foul-smelling.

Then Granny placed a loaf of freshly baked brown bread at the center of the kitchen table. Next to it she set a long, sharply gleaming knife. Dulcie watched as Granny cast her magick circle. After the circle was drawn, she began the actual spell by walking counterclockwise—*widdershins,* as Granny called it—around Dulcie. In the silence of the morning, her words rang clear.

> *"Dulcie strolled through a red forest*
> *Unt in de red forest dere vas a red barn*
> *In de red barn dere vas a red table, surrounded by*
>   *red straw*
> *On de red table lay a red knife*
> *Beside de red knife vas a loaf of red bread*
> *Cut de red bread*
> *De evil attached to Dulcie ist dead."*

As Granny intoned the last words, she lifted the knife and brought it forcefully down, stabbing the brown bread.

*"Say dead.
Now it be so."*

Granny closed the magick circle she'd opened, and grounded the energy she'd just raised. "*Now* choo to Lancaster go. De hex on choo is banished."

Not that Dulcie had ever thought that her misfortunes were caused by a curse someone had put on her; still, Granny felt better having done what she could to help her, so Dulcie thanked her for her efforts. "I do believe this idea of selling the candies on consignment is even more likely to succeed than the confectionery would have."

Granny shrugged, lighting her pipe. She puffed for a few moments, then studied Dulcie through narrowed eyes. "Choo must talk mit Race. De soonest ist *besser.*"

Refusing to be drawn into that discussion again, Dulcie picked up the two gift tins she'd prepared and went toward the front door. "I don't know when I'll be back. Don't worry if I'm late."

"I no vorry no more. I banished all spells."

Chuckling, Dulcie stepped outside. "Thanks, Granny. Since you say so, I'm sure to succeed."

As she coaxed Old Molly onto the Columbia Pike, Dulcie concentrated on what she would say to the management of a large, successful department store, and sway them to her way of thinking. Fortunately she had the opening-day success of her confectionery to back her up. She had done a good business, even though it lasted only one day. And since Richter's catered to the well-to-do of Lancaster, her deluxe treats would fit right in with the general appeal of their specialty foods department. If they sold locally produced, chocolate-covered caramels—Milton Hershey's chocolate-covered caramels—they could certainly find customers for her fancy French bonbons.

As she neared Lancaster, she grew more and more optimistic about this latest plan. It seemed almost too good to be true, but she chided herself for such a negative train of thought.

"You *will* succeed. You *will* find a way to support yourself and Granny. You will *not* consider defeat," she stated out loud. Over and over she repeated the litany, the butterflies in her stomach settling a bit more each time she heard her firm words.

At Müller's Livery, she left Molly in Bobby's care, then set off down Queen Street toward Richter's in the center of town. Once she found herself before the many-storied building, the sparkle of the pristine windows and the well-polished brass fittings on the doors made her waver momentarily. Yes, it was a wildly successful emporium. And, too, it presented its success most boldly. Dulcie produced the most impossibly perfect chocolates, however, and Richter's Department Store should give itself the chance to sell the finest in confectionery.

Or so she told herself, especially when the butterflies in her stomach began growing to buzzard size. "Onward," she ordered her balking feet.

She found her way to the specialty foods department and was glad to see that the clerk was a motherly sort, somewhat reminiscent of Prudence Kleinschmidt, Dulcie's widowed neighbor. "May I help you?" the lady asked.

"Perhaps I can help you," Dulcie answered. "I have with me a sampling of the most exquisite chocolate bonbons known to mankind. I'm interested in discussing the possibility of selling them on consignment from your department."

For a moment the clerk looked stunned. Then a smile curved her lips. Finally a knowing gleam lit her kind gray eyes. "You must be Mignone Kramer."

"No, Mignone was my mother. She passed away recently." Hoping to sound more mature, Dulcie gave her married name. "I'm Dulcie Kramer Langston, and I did run Mignone Kramer's Sweet Secrets Confectionery for its launch and unfortunate demise."

"I'm Mrs. Marquardt, and as you can see, I run the specialty foods department. Give me a moment to find one of my clerks, and you and I can discuss your candies at that table over there."

Dulcie's pulse sped as Mrs. Marquardt expressed a serious interest in her chocolates. Everything was going to work out! She could just feel it. Life would soon become so much simpler for Granny K and herself. In the giddiness of hope, Dulcie allowed herself to relax in one of the chairs by the table.

Moments later, Mrs. Marquardt returned. "Let me see what you have there, Miss Langston."

Opening one of the gift tins, Dulcie said, "It's *Mrs.* Langston, but please call me Dulcie."

Mrs. Marquardt's eyes lit up when she saw the attractive arrangement of candies Dulcie had prepared. But it wasn't until the lady took a bite of a bonbon that Dulcie knew the deal was done. Mrs. Marquardt's eyes twinkled, and her smile spoke for itself.

"Tell me, Dulcie, how do you propose to provide us with a steady supply? Do you have a kitchen nearby?"

"Not in town, but I do live close enough that I can bring to town enough for a few days each time I come. We could set up a regular delivery schedule."

"Hmmm . . ." Mrs. Marquardt tapped her short-nailed fingers on the tabletop. She took another bonbon and savored the chocolate. "We already carry Mr. Hershey's chocolate-covered caramels, so I'm not certain we would have sufficient demand for both confections."

Dulcie gasped. Not that Hershey man again! "Why, the two candies are completely different. They don't taste anything alike. Besides, you do want to offer your customers a choice. When caramels aren't elegant enough, the chocolate bonbons could be just the thing."

Mrs. Marquardt studied Dulcie. "You wouldn't be looking for a clerking position, would you? I've a feeling you could sell an Amish dairyman a daily surplus of fresh cream!"

A smile tilted the corners of Dulcie's lips. Moments later, she saw admiration and approval in the older woman's eyes. A chuckle bubbled up from deep inside her, and soon both women were laughing.

"Tell you what we can do," offered Mrs. Marquardt. "I like the bonbons, and I'm sure I could sell them quite briskly. I don't have the authority to offer you a contract for your product. Mr. Richter, though, certainly can. I believe he's already in his office. Follow me and bring your candies. We have one store owner to persuade."

Dulcie smiled her gratitude, especially since Mrs. Marquardt had so easily assumed part ownership of Dulcie's crusade. They walked down a long corridor to a set of stairs at the back of the store building. Up they went, Dulcie's anticipation multiplying. Buoyed by her success with Mrs. Marquardt, she figured Mr. Richter would be easily swayed by the quality of her product and his employee's enthusiasm for the chocolates.

After climbing various flights, they found themselves in another long corridor, this one carpeted with a flowered runner. The deep reds and creams of the blossoms enhanced the rich tones of the black walnut-paneled walls. Brass and cut-crystal gaslights illuminated the hall.

At the end of the corridor, Dulcie took in a large desk, four burgundy leather wing chairs, and the brocade draperies adorning two tall windows. A door to the right side of this waiting area bore a small brass plaque engraved with the name Edward W. Richter.

A thin, nervous-looking young man stood up behind the desk when he saw Dulcie and Mrs. Marquardt approaching.

"Good morning, Theodore," Mrs. Marquardt said. "Could you please let Mr. Richter know that I need to discuss an important matter with him?"

"Ce-certain—certainly!" he stammered, then bumped his chair against the wood-paneled wall. "Oh, no!" he groaned, pulling the chair back to its proper position. In doing so, he caught his coat sleeve on a pen set and spilled ink over a stack of important-looking papers. Dulcie felt for the young man. But there was nothing she could do that wouldn't make matters worse.

Mrs. Marquardt tsk-tsked, then said soothingly, "Why don't I let him know I'm here while you tend to your paperwork? I'm sorry we disturbed you."

Theodore grabbed the ink-sodden mess and stuffed it into a trash receptacle by his desk, scurrying like a frightened mouse. Dulcie pitied the young man and hoped he'd soon find himself a position where he felt more at ease than he obviously did here.

Was Theodore's jumpy behavior indicative of Mr. Richter's character, she wondered as Mrs. Marquardt rapped her knuckles on the store owner's office door. A gruff "Yes" sounded from within the room.

"May I come in, Mr. Richter?" Mrs. Marquardt asked when she opened the door.

"Of course, but you must be brief. My calendar is full today."

Dulcie felt the fluttering of butterflies in her stomach, and her hands chilled. With a quick prayer for divine help, she followed Mrs. Marquardt into the most lavishly appointed

room she'd ever seen. The walls were paneled in the same
black walnut as the hall and waiting area outside, and the
pattern on the hall carpet runner was repeated on the luxurious Persian rug that covered the floor. More of those burgundy leather chairs made a semicircle in front of a
burnished, red-toned table, behind which stood a tall, thin
man with a thick mane of white hair.

"What is the problem, Mrs. Marquardt?" he asked.

"May I?" Mrs. Marquardt asked, gesturing toward one
of the chairs. As Mr. Richter nodded, the two women sat.
"There's no problem at all, sir. In fact, I'm bringing you a
most attractive proposition."

When she paused to allow him comment, he murmured,
"I see."

Mrs. Marquardt continued. "This young lady has a wonderful product I believe would enhance our stock of fine
confections."

A spark of interest brightened intense brown eyes. Beautiful eyes, Dulcie thought, almost as beautiful as Race's.
Then she chided herself for the foolishness of allowing herself to think of her husband at a time like this. She couldn't
let thoughts of their estrangement ruin her chances at Richter's Department Store.

Mrs. Marquardt continued extolling the virtues of Dulcie's bonbons, and Mr. Richter's interest clearly grew the
more he heard about them. "Very well," he finally said.
"I'd like to try these confections you describe so elo-
quently."

Dulcie took the initiative. "Of course, Mr. Richter. Here,
this is a sample of the gift tins I use to pack the bonbons.
And please, help yourself to as many as you need to make
up your mind."

Edward Richter did as Dulcie suggested. When he bit into

the first chocolate, the room grew silent. Tension built. A verdict was imminent.

Mr. Richter sat behind his desk. Dulcie's stomach tightened.

He took another bonbon. He chewed and savored it.

Minutes ticked by, the grandfather clock against the left wall marking them loudly. Aside from the sound of time creeping by, the room remained still.

Mr. Richter took yet another chocolate, and Dulcie felt like shaking the man. How could he sit there, knowing how anxious she was, and not say one word! He hadn't made a sound of pleasure or displeasure as he chewed the chocolates like a cow would its cud. Any moment now, Dulcie expected the man would moo his opinion at her.

"Excellent!" he exclaimed, startling the two women. "I believe you're quite correct, Mrs. Marquardt. These delicious morsels would indeed make a marvelous addition to our stock of fine edibles."

Dulcie sagged back into her chair, then leapt up. This was a proud moment in her life. She was about to embark on a new business venture. She couldn't be looking like a lump of horse *misht,* as Granny would say. "I'm very pleased you like my product. Could we discuss a contract for a steady supply of Mignone Kramer's Bonbons?"

"Of course, Mignone Kramer," Mr. Richter said, extending his hand.

Dulcie placed her fingers in his large paw. "Mignone is my late mother—"

"Oh, forgive my distraction, sir," Mrs. Marquardt cut in. "I was so excited by the opportunity to sell these exceptional treats that I forgot to introduce the two of you. Mr. Richter, this is Dulcie Kramer Langston. Dulcie, Mr. Edward Richter, owner of the store."

"Pleased to meet you, sir," Dulcie answered, despite his tightened grip on her hand.

Mr. Richter's brow furrowed. His eyes narrowed. He studied Dulcie. The smile he'd worn melted off his lips, and something like anger sharpened the effect of his gaze. "Are you perchance related to the Horace Langstons?" he asked at length.

Dulcie winced at the name. Would she ever be free of Race's memory? Probably not.

She nodded reluctantly, cursing the odd impulse that had egged her to add his surname to hers. "I'm Race Langston's . . . wife."

As if the gaslights in the room had been suddenly turned off, Mr. Richter's gaze grew shuttered, his expression stormy and dark. His voice boomed out. "Young lady! How dare you show your face here? Don't you know I've disowned my daughter for marrying that worthless fool, Horace? I want nothing to do with the lot of you."

Tall and lean, Race's grandfather was a most imposing person, especially when enraged. Dulcie again cursed the fate that had led her down an old country road at the same time a skunk tried to cross it.

Before she could think of an appropriate answer, Mr. Richter continued in the same offensive vein. "I most assuredly want nothing to do with the milkmaid wife of that good-for-nothing grandson of mine! No matter how tasty your products are, you will never do business with Richter's Department Store. Furthermore, every store in Lancaster avoids challenging me, and that's what they'd be doing if they were to contract for your candies. I'll make certain that is the case."

Dulcie's skin grew clammy. Her body chilled. The anger and disdain in Mr. Richter's expression were truly frightening. More so was the finality of what he'd said. He had the means to keep Dulcie from doing business in Lancaster. His money and power would buy the compliance of anyone who might think to deal with her.

All because she'd married Race. Even though they were estranged.

Edward Richter waved the back of his hand at her. "Go on, go on! Go back where you came from. The Langstons are nothing to me."

First Race had stolen Dulcie's heart. Now it seemed he'd also stolen her future.

❖ *18* ❖

Forcing her spine into a straight line and with her shoulders squared, Dulcie left Edward Richter's luxurious office, propelled by her pride. Outside the store, she measured her steps, placing one foot ahead of the other, allowing herself no thought than that she must go home.

Home. She'd have to store enough memories of Everleigh to carry her through her unsettled future. After having her latest hopes so thoroughly dashed by her husband's grandfather, Dulcie knew she had no prospects save moving West. And she wasn't sure she was strong enough to do so.

Especially since she didn't want to.

At the livery she called for Bobby, who soon brought Molly around. Lacking cash, Dulcie gave the boy the tin of bonbons that hadn't been opened at Richter's Department Store. What was she going to do with all that expensive leftover candy? Should she try to sell it in Everleigh?

No. Their neighbors would make the effort to buy the chocolates, not because they wanted them, but because they'd do whatever they could to help Dulcie and Granny K. The thought of being forced to accept charity sickened Dulcie. She well knew no one in Everleigh could take on the support of two destitute women. The best thing to do was to speak to Mary Margaret O'Murphy and see if the former teacher knew of any open positions, preferably out West.

On the way to Everleigh, when tears tried to form, Dulcie pulled over to the side of the road, pinched her eyes tightly shut, and took deep breaths. She had to compose herself. Much remained to be done. Only in the privacy of her bedroom could she let herself examine her battered soul.

This was undoubtedly the lowest point in Dulcie's life. Even when Maman died it hadn't felt like the end of the world. She'd been understandably sad, and she knew the sense of loss left by her mother's death would never disappear, but at that time Dulcie hadn't known how bad things could get. Time certainly had taken care of teaching her that little lesson. Still grieving for her mother, heartbroken, and defeated at every effort to rise above her reduced circumstances, today she'd finally been rendered hopeless. Matters couldn't get worse.

Dulcie picked up the reins and got Molly going again.

At least she could count on Granny. Her grandmother was sure to provide the soothing and sympathy her bruised sensibilities needed. If anything were to happen to Granny K . . . No! No matter what happened, Dulcie would obtain Granny's safety and comfort. She would make sure her grandmother's age-diminished strength wasn't taxed any more than was absolutely necessary.

Although Dulcie couldn't generate much enthusiasm for the unavoidable departure from Everleigh, she made herself think of those details she'd have to see to before they could make that move. She had no time to waste.

Nearing town, Dulcie considered the differences between Everleigh and Lancaster. In Everleigh, everyone gathered around her when she'd been wronged, demanding restitution. True, they'd confronted the wrong man, but their intentions had always been the best. In Lancaster, Edward Richter's money and prestige could buy the destruction of a person's dreams. Lancaster wasn't for her.

Fine, she thought. Lancaster didn't suit, and they couldn't stay in Everleigh, unless they were willing to accept charity. Dulcie hated the bitter taste of debt, and that was what charity always led to.

Times were tough. She accepted that. Money was tight, even at the banks. After her last encounter with Mr. Oberholtz, Dulcie doubted she could wheedle her way to mortgaging the Kramer home. Selling the property was her only option, if not a good one.

If they could find a buyer.

Time had come to face facts. She couldn't afford sentimentality; she couldn't afford to be choosy. A new life in a new town where she wouldn't be waylaid by painful memories might be just what the two Kramer women needed. Well, the three of them. She couldn't forget Molly.

Dulcie counted her resources. The house. The buckboard. The mare. Her three questionable assets added up to more headaches than solutions. After all, Molly was an unlikely nest egg.

Although Granny was paid for her Witchcraft and Pow-Wowing, it didn't add up to a steady source of income. The ham, potatoes, eggs, and cheese were wonderful, but they came with no reliable regularity.

Dulcie had no idea what she'd do next. But she would come up with something. She had to.

The longing in Dulcie's eyes yesterday morning had hit Race like a runaway locomotive. She loved him, dammit! And she was his wife. Nothing was ever going to change that. Not even if his hellion hired herself a shyster and tried to sue Race for a disgracing divorce.

He'd lost an entire night of sleep remembering the poignancy of that look, and his own response to the evidence of his wife's feelings. The only conclusion he could come to was that he'd let nothing on earth keep them apart. Somehow he'd break through the wall of hurt, anger, and disappointment Dulcie had erected. They were meant to be together, and he was going to do whatever it took to secure that future!

To that purpose, Race had Harris bring Zephyr around. Then he left for Everleigh, traveling by way of the old road where he and Dulcie had met. Sometimes it seemed as if they'd known each other forever. Other times, Race realized that their problems stemmed from their shortened courtship and interrupted marriage. The only way to remedy that was to remain in close contact with his wife. No matter how angry Dulcie was, no matter how doggedly she sent him away, Race was going to plant himself in her path. He was glad he'd left his belongings in the Kramer house when Dulcie sent him away. He was coming to stay, and sooner or later he'd prove to her they were meant for each other. Preferably sooner.

Upon arriving at the Kramer home, Race found Granny K spewing smoke rings and swigging whatever it was she kept in the ever-present jug. " 'Morning, Granny!''

''Race!'' she cried, a grin splitting her wrinkled face. ''I'm so glad choo dropped up ta see me!''

''Well, Granny, I came to see Dulcie. But I'm glad to see you, too.''

Granny snorted. ''I kenn choo come fer Dulcie. Choo cain't stay away fer goot.''

Race smiled, looping Zephyr's reins through the ring on the hitching post. ''I never meant to disappear. Dulcie and I are married. When she stops being stubborn and gets over her anger, she'll come around.''

"Ja," Granny chimed in, her gray bun bouncing in agreement. "De runes say dat, too."

"The runes?"

"Ja, de runes. Choo kenn de runes?"

"Can't say I do. What are they?"

"Come. I vill show you de runes."

From a pocket in her overalls, Granny withdrew a black bag. Opening it, she dropped smooth pebbles into her cupped hand. Each one bore a different etched and painted symbol. Curiosity piqued, Race picked one up. "What are they for?"

"Ta see de fuchure! De runes say choo unt Dulcie vould marry. Unt choo did. De runes say choo unt Dulcie vill a fine life have together mit. Unt choo vill. But now ve must make Dulcie sense see."

Race chuckled. Yes, he had to make Dulcie accept what was a matter of fact, simple common sense. No matter how much faith Granny put in her pebbles, however, Race couldn't see how they could further his plans. But he'd do whatever it took to win Dulcie back, and if indulging Granny K's eccentricities would gain him a powerful ally, it was little enough to do. "So," he said, "what do the runes say I should do next?"

"De runes no say vat choo do next. Dey say vat vill be." Granny stuck her pipe behind her ear and began to rise. Race hurried to help her, and she gave him her impish grin. "Choo are goot fer me, too. Since my boy died—choo kenn, Dulcie's *vater*—I alvays vanted a grandson. I got choo now."

At Granny's words, warmth spread through Race. After the recent difficulties his family had faced, he needed to feel wanted, if not loved. Granny's astringent affection was just the sort of mothering he needed.

"And I have you," he murmured, his arm embracing her

frail shoulders. Clearing his throat of the emotion there, he went on. "What do I have to do to change your grand-daughter's mind about me?"

Leading him to the stairs, Granny shrugged. "Choo have to chust love her. Unt not let her *lobbich* be."

"Lobbich?"

"Ja. Silly." Granny wrestled her way onto the first step. "Come mit me. I must fer choo try."

Again that mysterious trying business! This time, Race thought with a smile, Dulcie wasn't around to distract him and keep him from satisfying his curiosity. He joined Granny on the steps. "What does that mean?"

"Hmph! Dulcie not tell choo. She thinks Pow-Wow unt magick are *shrecklich.* Frightful. But de Ol' Relichion ain't bad. It's de vay ve used to do in de Black Forest."

"What is this Old Religion?"

"Ach! 'Tis de Craft. *Ja, ja.* De Vitchcraft."

Race lifted a skeptical eyebrow. "You said . . . witch-craft?"

"Ja. 'Tis of de land, de trees, fire, *wasser,* air. De God unt de Goddess. Magick."

With an arm around the old woman, Race took them both upstairs. They continued down the hall to Granny's room. When she opened the door, a spicy, earthy scent tickled his nostrils. Walking in, he identified the source of the fragrance. Everywhere he looked, there were bunches of dried leaves and sticks and roots. Perhaps what Granny called witchcraft was more a knowledge of herbal medicine.

He hoped. This was suddenly getting . . . spooky.

"Sit!" she ordered.

He did, studying her every move.

In her usual rapid-fire way, she limped around the room collecting scraps of cloth, string, and bits and pieces of her herbal arsenal. She approached, then set her odds and ends on a table next to Race's chair. What was she up to? No one needed an herbal tonic. It was his marriage that was diseased.

Granny then played with the runes for a while, and before long, she stood before him again, murmuring musically. Only then did Race notice the knife she held. She began to walk clockwise around him, holding the cleaver in the air.

Maybe Granny *did* dabble in witchcraft. He only hoped she wasn't after *his* blood for her next potion.

She placed the knife on the table and grew silent. Spreading out the white bit of cloth, she mounded the dead vegetation on one half of the fabric. With a red string, she drew the cotton into a pouch, then knotted the strand.

From a cupboard next to the table, she took a brown clay bowl. Into the bowl she poured a measure of brownish grainy stuff. It looked like . . . dirty sugar? Again turning to the storage chest, she took out a small pouch, and sprinkled the dried leaves it contained on top of the grains in the bowl. A savory scent reached his nostrils, but gave him not a clue as to what Granny was up to.

On a scrap of paper she then wrote his name and buried it in the spiced grains. Solemnly she drew a cross on the surface of the mixture. Finally she stood a brown-colored candle in the middle of the bowl.

Granny faced Race. She laid hands on him. In a clear voice, she spoke the words.

> *"Thine cussedness I vill ofercome*
> *In days of nine mit de setting sun*
> *I'll have thy friendship in my hand*
> *Through thick unt thin it vill stand.*
> *I choose not to harm but to heal de vound*
> *Love comes now by the Vitches' Tune!*
> *So be it!"*

Knife in hand, she again drew invisible markings in the air and sketched the circle she'd made earlier. "Dere! De spell is cast. Choo now can go make right ev'r'ting."

Race hesitated. Granny clearly believed she'd cast a spell on him. Somehow she thought he needed otherworldly assistance to gain someone's friendship. Something about a wound that needed healing. True, there were problems between him and Dulcie, and their marriage could do with some healing, but he'd be damned if he'd let Dulcie contrive a mere friendship between them! They were married. Two made one, eternal partners, lovers forever.

"Granny," he said hesitantly, "I don't want Dulcie's friendship. I want my wife back."

Then Race realized what he was doing. He was questioning the suitability of the spell Ermentrude Kramer had just cast on him! What was happening to him? Where was his logic? If he didn't watch himself, he'd soon become as eccentric as Granny K!

While storing the items she'd used, Granny answered. "No matter. De spell ain't fer Dulcie's *Freundschaft*. Ven I read de runes, I read trouble mit someone in choor family. Dat's vat fer de spell ist. Not fer choor marriage."

A friendship. With someone in his family. Did Granny mean his grandfather? Was that the wound she'd spoken of?

Good heavens, she'd cast a spell on the Langstons and the Richters! The very notion was hilarious in its absurdity. Except . . . How could she possibly know— No, of course she couldn't know. It wasn't possible. Just coincidence. Right?

He'd told no one about the rift in his family.

Chills running down his spine, Race stood. "Er . . . I must be on my way. I'll be back soon. You can count on that. I-I have an appointment later today. When I come back, it will be to stay."

He hoped Dulcie would be there. Right now, her efforts to distract him from Granny's peculiarities didn't seem as irritating as they once had. In fact, he wished she'd been around to prevent what had just taken place. He reminded himself that witchcraft and magic were mere superstitions.

Granny put a glowing match to her pipe, and soon smoke curled around her head. "*Besser* do dat. *Schnell*. Dulcie vants to move Vest."

"What!" He couldn't have heard right. "Dulcie wants to go West?"

"*Ja*. No store, no money, no Everleigh. Dulcie vants a teacher be out Vest. Mit Indians."

Outraged, Race was torn. Should he leave and compose himself? Prepare for battling Dulcie's anger? Or should he just stay and outstubborn her?

"Unt, Race. Choo must choor *Grossvater* talk. Soon."

Race's chills chased out his outrage. His hands grew clammy. *His grandfather*. Granny had said his grandfather. Could those rune stones actually have shown her ... the truth?

He refused to consider the possibility. It was past time to go. "Yes, well, I'll speak with him when I have an opportunity. Please tell Dulcie I came to see her, that I'm sorry I missed her."

"*Ja*, I tell Dulcie. Don't *fergess* choor *Grossvater* talk mit."

Race descended the stairs at a trot. Something really strange and wholly inexplicable had happened in that fragrant room.

"Race!" Granny called out.

He hesitated. He really wanted to get away. He needed to regain perspective. Hell, maybe even his sanity. "Yes ... ?"

"Here, choo must yer conjuring bag mit choo take. I put celandine mit. It vill help choor *ferhoodled* family!" She held out the red-string–tied white cotton pouch she'd prepared in her room.

A conjuring bag. A witch's concoction. Would she now tap him with a magic wand and turn him into something warty and slimy?

With a shudder, Race glanced at Granny and noticed the gleam of wisdom in her gaze. It gave him pause. He also knew he had to stay on her good side if he hoped to win Dulcie back. Somehow he'd have to overcome his instinctive misgivings of the unknown. He again took to the stairs, slowly retracing his steps. "Thank you . . . I guess."

Granny's cackle rasped down his spine. "Ve talk ven choo come back."

This time Race rushed out to the porch and down the walkway to where Zephyr waited. He wanted to give Granny no reason to think he might need another spell. The one she'd cast on him was one spell too many. Besides, who knew? She might offer him eye of newt or blood of bat. Leaves and twigs suddenly suited him just fine.

He mounted Zephyr, stuffing the objectionable object deep into his jacket pocket. Granny's unexplained knowledge of his family situation still perturbed him. He'd said nothing to her about the problems his unusual courtship of Dulcie had unleashed. Still, she'd somehow tied the two situations together. Correctly, as it turned out.

And what about his hellion wife? Now that she'd turned his whole life upside down, she was flirting with the idea of a move West? Over his dead body!

The conjuring bag crackled in his pocket. Well, maybe his dead body was going too far. Especially if his wife's grandmother was a witch. But if Granny was a witch, and what she'd said was right, did he really have to face his grandfather?

If Granny *was* a witch? He really was losing his mind!

Still, as much as the talk of spells and witchcraft bothered him, he'd rather become Granny's apprentice than speak with Edward Richter again.

As Dulcie rode past Founders' Square, she glanced toward the gazebo, and what she saw there gave her pause. Tied to a hitching post, and filled to overflowing, the Schleinbaughs' wagon waited for its driver, who was otherwise occupied in the gazebo. In an emerald silk suit, Isabella sat next to Kirk, flirting outrageously. What really surprised Dulcie was the look of rapt attention and fascination on her erstwhile suitor's face. It looked as if Isabella had finally caught her man.

If anything, the happiness of Dulcie's two tormentors only increased her sense of personal loss. She wished them well.

Turning onto Willow Lane, Dulcie pulled back on Molly's reins. She recognized the enormous horse coming her way. She knew the rider, too. And it looked as if they were leaving the Kramer house.

"How dare he?" she muttered, lifting her chin. How dare he come nosing around her home? She hoped Granny had set him straight. Especially since after today, she planned never to set eyes on him again.

Zephyr came closer. Molly skittered sideways, jiggling the buckboard. Dulcie yanked hard on the reins, narrowly avoiding Emma's recovering petunias. Even her husband's horse was treacherous!

Dulcie allowed herself a glance at Race. An odd expression twisted his features before he silently mouthed her name. Without conscious effort, her gaze met his. Again, as they had done yesterday morning, brown eyes clung to blue in silent communication. Longing and desire grew.

But while mesmerized by what she saw in the depths of

her husband's gaze, Dulcie remembered the pain she'd felt when she'd learned of Race's deception. She relived the loneliness she'd known since then and plummeted back into the void he left when he stole her dreams.

Again, tears welled up. She still felt so much for him. She feared she always would. Her pain grew sharper, more piercing. She gasped when she realized that without Race, her future might turn out to be cold, lonely, barren.

She'd never settle for a one-sided marriage, and her hope of winning Race's love had died.

With superhuman effort, she dragged her eyelids down, closing out the sight of the only man she'd ever love. She breathed slowly, deeply, hearing the thunder of her broken heart. It was time to go forward, to step into her future, no matter how bleak it looked. Race Langston belonged to her past. She was bound for new horizons, a new town, a new start. She didn't need him in that new life.

Opening her eyes again, Dulcie tugged on Molly's reins and continued home. Behind her, she heard him call her name. She went on.

"Granny!" Dulcie cried when she saw her grandmother on the porch. "Can you believe the gall of that man? Just who does he think he is, coming around here after all he's done?"

After a swig from her jug, Granny tsk-tsked. "He tinks he's choor husband, unt dat's vat he ist."

"No he's not! He only wanted my bonbon recipe. He never wanted *me*."

"Ach, Dulcie, dis ist stoopid. Race loves choo, unt choo love him. Vat choo gonna do, marry mit Kirk Schleinbaugh?"

A shudder of revulsion ran through her. "Of course not! Besides, our marriage is a fake. I can have it annulled. I'm glad you sent him away."

"But I didn't. I gave 'im a conjuring bag, unt I cast a spell for his family's troubles."

Dulcie stared at her grandmother in disbelief. "You mean you didn't send him away? You *invited* him into the house?"

Granny nodded, her mouth clamped around the stem of her pipe. She crossed her arms over her chest and lifted her chin. *"Ja."*

Dulcie's head began to spin. "How could you, Granny? After what he did to me? I never thought *you* would betray me."

She collapsed onto the porch swing. First she'd lost Maman, then she'd lost her heart to Race. After that, she lost Race himself, and now she'd lost Granny, too.

It hurt. It hurt so much to feel so alone. . . .

Around her, everything seemed different. The midday sun shone a brassy yellow. The scent of late summer flowers cloyed her senses. A crow squawked somewhere behind the house, and Dulcie felt the loss of her last ounce of strength. She'd been robbed of all that mattered to her. She'd been left with nothing.

Moments later, sounds of running dragged Dulcie from her misery. Then a child's voice called out. "Granny K! Granny K!"

"Vat choo vant, Sarah Schvartz?"

Slowly Dulcie turned to see Emma's little girl running as fast as her pudgy legs could carry her, two glossy brown braids slapping her back.

"What's wrong, Sarah?" Dulcie asked.

"It's Mama! Mama's having the baby! And Papa's not home!"

Dulcie leapt up. "Oh, dear! I'll go stay with her while you go fetch Dr. Helmrich. Hurry! I'll make sure your mama's comfortable." Dulcie gladly set aside her sense of loss.

She still had Emma's friendship, and now Emma was in labor. That was far more urgent than the rotten state of Dulcie's heart.

Turning to Granny, she realized her grandmother had disappeared. Then she saw her clumping back from the kitchen, a leather pouch in hand. "Come, come, Dulcinea! Ve must Emma help. Choo can sorry feel later."

Dulcie didn't stop to argue. And she was glad Granny had gathered her bagful of herbs. If there was any way to ease Emma's delivery, Granny would see to it. She'd never let anyone suffer unnecessarily.

As she ran up Willow Lane, a strange thought crossed Dulcie's mind. Why had Granny offered to help Race, knowing it would hurt Dulcie? This was the first time her grandmother had ever sided with someone else against her. Then she remembered how much Granny liked Race. Was Granny suffering from conflicting loyalties?

Running up the front steps of the Schwartzes' home, Dulcie set aside her personal woes. Emma needed her, and Dulcie would never fail her friend.

Not like Race, she thought, pausing just inside the Schwartzes' front door. He once promised never to let her down again. But he had. He'd betrayed her.

"Dulcinea-girl!"

"Coming, Granny." Dulcie shook off the hurt and ran up the stairs and into Emma's room. She went to the bedside, noting Emma's flush, her furrowed brow, and her brave attempt at a smile. "I'm so glad you came," Emma said.

Dulcie squeezed her friend's fingers. "You knew I would."

Then Emma turned redder still and started to gasp in spurts. Her shoulders rose off the pillow, and her knees bent, tenting the summer-thin blanket on the bed. Granny took the opportunity to check Emma's condition. "Choor ready, Emma-girl. Vy choo no send fer me before?"

With a noisy sigh Emma sank back against the pillows. "There was nothing you could do earlier. As you can see, I'm getting ready to . . ." Emma's face reddened even more.

Granny whipped around Dulcie and took a towel from a stack of linens Emma had obviously set out in preparation for the arrival of her second child. Heavy footsteps sounded downstairs.

"Emma!" called Nathaniel Schwartz.

"We're all upstairs," Dulcie called, since Emma couldn't answer just then. "The baby's coming."

The house shook with the urgency of his climb up the stairs. "Is she—Emma!" The anxious look on his rugged features disappeared when he saw his wife smile. He knelt by the top of the bed, taking her hand in both his. "*Liebchen,* are you all right?"

Dulcie watched the tender moment, noting Nathaniel's love for his wife. It was a powerful moment, theirs a powerful love. If only . . .

Emma gritted her teeth. Her body convulsed. "Nathaniel Schwartz," she forced out, "if you ever lay another finger on me, I promise I'll cut your—"

"Ach, Emma! Push, don't fight. Dulcie! Varm *wasser, schnell!*"

Dulcie ran down the stairs and found a large pot of water steaming at the back of the stove. A clean enamel pail sat on a shelf nearby. Carefully she poured hot water into the pail, then added cold until it felt right. Granny had assisted in many a birthing, and Dulcie had helped since she'd turned fourteen.

Lifting the pail, she headed for Emma's room. Halfway there, she heard her friend cry out in a guttural groan. She paused to offer a prayer. Seconds later, she heard the thin wail of a newborn—one of the most welcome sounds on earth.

Resuming her climb, Dulcie smiled, then nearly tripped when Sarah flew up the stairs past her. "Slow down, Sarah! The baby was just born."

Sarah ignored Dulcie.

Dulcie entered the room and came to a standstill. What she saw deserved admiration and respect. At the head of the bed, Nathaniel sat close to his wife, his arm around her shoulders. Emma, looking tired, damp, and pale, wore the most exquisite expression of love on her pretty features. Curled up beside her, Sarah peeked at the bundle at Emma's breast. A tiny red fist flailed softly.

Tears misted Dulcie's eyes. The pain she'd felt earlier returned, pummeling her temples. Before her lay what she'd wanted, what she'd lost. Only at that moment did she recognize the enormity of her loss. A sob escaped her lips.

Emma glanced up. Their gazes met. "Don't be stubborn. He loves you. It doesn't matter how you came together. What matters is that you did."

Tears overflowed Dulcie's eyes. Emma's face blurred. Through her misery, she heard her friend again. "Don't hold so tight to your pride. It won't bring you love."

❖ *19* ❖

So SHE WAS planning a move West. Was he so easy to forget?

If that was the case, Race was ready to remedy it. He'd stay in Lancaster long enough to gather the few items he never took to Everleigh after the wedding, then, sparing minutes at his office to gather files he was working on, he could return to Dulcie by late evening.

Then he'd challenge her plans.

"Back early today," commented Harris, exiting the carriage house. "Is business doing poorly?"

Shaking his head, Race said, "Just a short visit." He handed over Zephyr's reins. "I'll be going home to Everleigh before dark." Stating his intentions boosted Race's efforts to shake off the jitters he'd fought since the eerie incident with Granny K.

But, no, he wouldn't dwell on it. It was time to concentrate on his marriage and his legal practice. In precisely that order. He could afford no distractions.

Race let himself into the house. From the vestibule, he noticed the open library door. Then he heard his mother's sobs and his father's comforting response. Now what?

He stepped into the book-lined room, lit by one gaslight.

There, he saw his mother holding a sheet of paper in her trembling hand. "What's that you have there?"

She lifted red, tearing eyes to meet his. "Oh, Race! This is awful, hideous. Look what your grandfather sent by messenger only moments ago."

Race took the page with great misgiving. Anything having to do with Edward Richter was of reptilian shrewdness, and produced venomous effects. As he scanned the cramped writing, one word jumped out. "Embezzlement."

That snake was threatening to press criminal charges against Horace. What a miserable old coot! "There's really nothing he can do to Father," Race said, placing a hand on his mother's shaking shoulder.

"Why, what do you mean?" she asked.

Father cleared his throat. "Yes, son, what exactly do you mean?"

"There's nothing Grandfather can do since you replaced the funds you took. He must experience a loss to press charges. You *did* put the money back, didn't you?"

"Of course! As soon as Milton signed the bank check."

"He can't prosecute if he hasn't been injured. By replacing the money, you put Grandfather back where he started. He hasn't got a case."

"Are you sure?" Mother asked, her expression hopeful.

Race knelt at her side. "Yes, Mother, I'm sure. I do know *something* about the law," he added with a wry smile. "Don't worry about this any longer. I'll take care of it." Turning to Horace, Race said, "Why not take Mother to the sun room? Both of you could do with a rest."

"Good idea, son. But are you sure you won't need me?"

Go choor Grossvater *talk mit*. Granny K's words returned to Race's mind. Perhaps she'd been right. It seemed he couldn't avoid his grandfather. "I'm certain."

When his parents left the room, Race closed the door. He

didn't want them to hear should the discussion with Edward Richter turn heated. He approached the telephone, his grandfather's message in hand.

As the operator made the connection, the familiar crackle of the telephone chattered in his ear. Moments later, Edward's priggish secretary, Theodore Madison, answered the call. Race identified himself and asked for his grandfather, sparing no time for pleasantries.

Grandfather's abrupt "Yes" assaulted his ear.

"It's Race Langston. I'd like an explanation for this threat to my father."

"What damn-fool explanation do you want, boy? I'm taking that good-for-nothing father of yours to jail."

"And how do you presume to do so?"

"You can read, can't you? He embezzled fifty thousand dollars!"

"And can you provide evidence to the authorities?"

"I need no evidence. I'm Edward Richter."

"But you're not above the law."

Angry sputtering battered Race's ear. He held the receiver away.

"Dammit, boy, first he stole my daughter, then he stole my money!"

Race paused . . . *stole my daughter . . . my daughter . . .* His grandfather's reproachful words reverberated in his mind. Was that the cause of all those years of enmity? A father suffering from the inevitable maturing of his child?

That sort of pain could only happen where there was great love. Race knew. He'd lost Dulcie's trust, and his loss cut through even his normal common sense. Before Dulcie came into his life, he would have laughed if anyone had suggested he'd someday entertain a superstition. Yet here he stood, hand rhythmically squeezing a damnable witch's amulet! No wonder Edward behaved so foolishly. No wonder he was blind to his daughter's happiness with the man she loved. Matters of the heart rendered all men fools.

With the benefit of new understanding, Race tempered his words. "I'd like to discuss this further, sir, but I'd rather do it in person."

Silence. Then Edward cleared his throat. "*I'd* rather not, but do as you will."

"I'll come by shortly."

After he cut the connection, Race hesitated only long enough to devise a plan of action. He had to speak with Edward, but besides speaking, he had to build a bridge that would enable father, daughter, and son-in-law to meet. Granny's voice again invaded his thoughts. He held his family's future in his hands.

His family. Mother, Father, Edward Richter, and himself. He had to bring them all together. Only then could the rift begin to heal. For a moment he questioned his impulse. Could Father's health handle the emotional upheaval? Would his heart fail him again?

They'd been fortunate the last time. After Edward stormed from the house, Mother had marshaled Horace to bed and, with Dr. Murdoch's full support, had kept him bedridden. His heartbeat had normalized.

Thinking further, Race realized that the strain of worry, his mother's anguish, and the loss of his manager's position at the store would have at least as damaging an effect on Horace's heart as any confrontation. So Race weighed his two options. His heart leaned toward the one that promised the greatest reward. He'd take the risk.

Just as his love for Dulcie had driven him back to her home, where Granny had forced him to think about his troubled family, Race had to trust that love would smooth the way to understanding and reconciliation within his family. It could work. Then he'd be free to return to his bride's side. He'd have righted the wrongs his love for Dulcie had brought about.

Besides, he hated being called a boy. He'd make sure that after today his grandfather never used that word to demean him again.

Anticipating his renewed honeymoon, Race left the formal library and headed for the sun room. With his parents he emerged from the back of the house and went directly to the carriage house. Soon the three were in the Langstons' elegant rig, knowing how much Edward despised automobiles, on their way to Richter's Department Store.

In the waiting room outside his grandfather's office, Race suggested his parents wait in Theodore's twittering company. Speaking to Edward was bound to be a ticklish matter, and he wanted to prevent anything from going wrong. Race dared not let the two older men come face-to-face until he'd smoothed the waters.

What troubled him was that he had no assurance of success.

"Is he alone?" Race asked Theodore.

Theodore nodded, then dropped his pen. He bobbed down to retrieve it from the floor, and on his way up, he smacked his head on the edge of the desk. When he went to rub his injury, he forgot he still held the pen, and a splotch of ink plopped down on his beaklike nose.

"Oh! Oh, oh, oh!" he moaned. "If you'll . . . excuse me . . . I must—must clean up. Oh, oh . . ."

Race remembered a moment of tension when he'd come close to experiencing Theodore's nervous ineptitude. He'd been dealing with Milton Hershey, and he'd known his future was on the line. For the first time, he experienced sympathy for his grandfather's secretary.

"Come in when you no longer hear him roaring," he told his parents with a wry grin. He then knocked on Edward's closed door. At the responding bellow, he entered the lion's den.

His grandfather glanced up, then reddened and looked away. He waved Race toward a chair. "What have you to say for yourself, boy? Especially after trying to trick me with that milkmaid of yours!"

Trick? *His* milkmaid? "What does Dulcie have to do with this?"

"Hell, I don't know! *You* tell *me* why she came and begged me to sell her sweets in the store."

"What are you talking about? Dulcie Kramer is constitutionally incapable of begging. That woman has pride enough for three!"

Edward's cheeks again colored. "Well, er, maybe 'begging' is a bit strong. But she was here and she brought a tin of fancy chocolates. She tried to trick me by calling herself Mignone Something-or-other."

"She wouldn't have called herself Mignone. That's her late mother."

"I know now. But I had to dig the information out of her."

Something wasn't quite right here. "Is that *precisely* how it happened?"

Edward began to bluster. "Well, er, maybe not quite so."

"And you're sure it was my wife?"

"How many chocolate-toting Dulcie Kramer Langston milkmaids do *you* know, boy?"

Fortunately only one! "So she offered her bonbons on consignment. What did you tell her?"

"I sent the brazen chit packing!"

Race winced. No wonder Dulcie cut him cold when they crossed paths earlier that day. "When did all this happen?"

Edward stood and held a doily-trimmed tin out to Race. One of the tins Dulcie had so proudly described. "Here, have a chocolate. They're the best damn candies I've ever tasted. Oh, yes, she came by earlier this morning.''

Ouch! Although he wanted to rush to his wife's side, to comfort her in her disappointment, Race still had another matter to address. ''Let's leave my wife's enterprise to the side for a moment,'' he suggested. ''Let's discuss this problem between you and Father. Mother, too.''

''There's no problem,'' Edward stated, gesturing dramatically. ''Your mother's a fool who married another fool and had a third fool for a son.''

His grandfather's petty words would have hurt only hours earlier. Now Race understood the cause of Edward's bitterness. ''You really think Mother's a fool? A daughter of yours . . . a fool?''

''She left home and married Horace Langston.''

''That makes her a fool? Has she been miserable? Wanted for anything?''

Edward turned away. He stood before a tall narrow window and looked outside. His shoulders slumped. ''No,'' he said in a foreign, quiet voice. ''But I have. I've been miserable and lonely and missing my little girl.''

''She hasn't been a little girl for a long time.''

''I know. Even when I didn't want to know.''

Race felt a hand on his shoulder. He turned and saw his mother. She placed a finger over her lips, and he nodded in response.

''I've only been across town, Papa.'' Edward turned sharply and met his daughter's gaze. She went on. ''I didn't abandon you. I . . . just fell in love. There was no reason for your loneliness. We would gladly have welcomed you. I've always loved you, and Horace has spent a lifetime seeking your acceptance and approval. Won't you help us put an end to all this pain?''

"I doubt Horace can forgive so many years of petty behavior."

"I'd like to try," Horace said, appearing in the open doorway. He then strode to Edward. For a moment, a tense, silent moment, Edward Richter stared at his son-in-law's outstretched hand. Then cautiously he met it with his.

As the two men shook hands, Race embraced his mother, who smiled at him through a flood of tears.

They all talked. Mother laughed and cried. Race smiled. He felt the beginnings of a new closeness for his family. He wasn't so naïve as to hope that a simple handshake between Horace and Edward could settle their differences. It would take a long time to fashion bonds like those that tied Granny K and Dulcie—if they ever did.

The thought of his wife had Race glancing out the office window. "Look how late it is! The sun's about to set."

Amid a chorus of exclamations, Race realized it was too late to rush back to Everleigh. Fine. He'd stay the night in Lancaster, but come tomorrow morning, thankfully a Saturday, he planned to take root at Dulcie's side. And nothing, not pride, not fear, not even anger, would push him away. They were married, and that was that.

After an awkward, overly polite supper in the Langstons' cavernous dining room, Race bid Edward and his parents good night. He retired to the room that had been his since early childhood. Although he felt a sense of sadness, he knew the time was right for him to leave. He was no longer a child.

He began to gather those items he wished to take with him to Everleigh, and on his desk he found a letter waiting for him.

It was from Milton Hershey. Curious, Race ripped open the envelope.

Esteemed Race:

Although I apologized for the unfortunate results of my attempts to help both you and your father, I know I've hardly said enough. I'd like to clarify my current stance, if you please.

First, I think you have the makings of a fine attorney, and I'd like to retain your services if you could set aside any unpleasant memories and ill will toward me. We can continue discussing the repayment of the fifty thousand.

As to the chocolate matter, I've been entertaining the idea of purchasing property outside the city of Lancaster, and building there the sort of factory I will need to bring my ideas to fruition. Although I'm still set on producing chocolates, I would especially like to make them affordable to everyone. In other words, I want to deal with vast quantities.

Your wife's exquisite confections would therefore present no competition to the chocolates I aim to produce. She can certainly continue to market her luxury confections, and I'll concentrate on serving the masses.

I again apologize for the trouble I unwittingly caused you and your new bride, and certainly hope all is settled between you.

Please let me know if you're amenable to handling certain legal matters for me.

Sincerely,
Milton S. Hershey

As full of turmoil as it had been, the day had also been productive, Race conceded. Now he could go to Dulcie, having obtained what should have been hers from the start: the opportunity to succeed in a project that meant so much to her.

Satisfied with the day's accomplishments, Race soon

dozed and dreamt of a sweet reunion. He slept well and awoke rested and exhilarated, anticipation fueling his steps.

Downstairs he avoided the breakfast room, not willing to stay separated from his wife a moment longer. As he opened the door, however, Edward Richter called his name.

"You're still here, Grandfather?"

"Call me Edward, son. 'Grandfather' makes me feel like a stranger."

Race smiled, understanding all too well. "Pleasure, Edward."

"Where are you off to?"

"Home. Everleigh and my wife."

Edward shook a finger at Race. "You tell her to make sure she has a dozen cases of bonbons at the store first thing Monday morning." His brown eyes twinkled with mischief. "And if she'd like, she can either work for me at the store, or for your father in his new venture. He'll be opening a bookstore, The New Leaf."

Race chuckled, pleased with the developments. Then he remembered a thought he'd had last night. "Only if I can steal Theodore Madison. He's had enough fear to last a lifetime."

Edward waved. "Take him, take him. His jumpiness makes me nervous."

Race chose to maintain a discreet smile and withhold comment. "I doubt I'll be back until next week. Hope to see you then, sir."

"Bring your wife. She's . . . fascinating."

"Wouldn't come without her." Race held out his hand.

Edward took the proffered olive branch, then pulled on Race and upped the ante. A manly embrace followed, both men growing misty-eyed. "Thank you, son," Edward whispered.

"Anytime, Edward. Anytime."

Race went for Zephyr, humming a happy tune. Life was good. And it was about to get much, much better.

Early Saturday morning, Dulcie left the house before Granny woke up. Today was bound to be difficult. The Everleigh Lutheran Church was holding a bazaar to raise money for the mission field. Dulcie had donated the wedding ring quilt the women of Everleigh had made for her and Race. It was to be auctioned off.

Slowly she walked to the church, approached the altar, and sat in one of the front pews. She had no idea how many more times she'd sit in the little church where her faith had been nurtured since childhood. She'd spoken with the mayor, Pastor Eckert, Doc Helmrich, and anybody else she could think of. Although none of them knew any potential buyers for the Kramer home, they'd agreed to be on the lookout. None of them had had any suggestions to help her avoid the move West.

She knelt, bowed her head, and prayed for strength in the days to come, for wisdom to discern what was best, for inner peace, and especially for healing. Her broken heart had yet to accept what Dulcie knew. Her future had no place for Race Langston.

She'd disappear. Let him use his legal expertise and declare her a deserting spouse. She couldn't bear the continued reminders of her failed marriage. She couldn't stand to remember loving Race.

As the tears flowed, Dulcie heard the door to the sanctuary open. She bowed her head even more and hoped the other supplicant had the decency to grant her privacy. But it was not to be. The rustle of garments at her side made her glance that way.

"Billy! What are you doing in church today? It's not Sunday."

Billy's fair skin reddened, and he scuffed a shoe against the kneeler. "I saw you come in here, an' I wanted to talk to you."

What could this imp be up to? Getting him to Sunday school was struggle enough. He'd entered the house of God willingly. "What did you want to discuss?" she asked, and surreptitiously wiped her eyes.

"That rotten, stinkin', two-faced, stuck-up city swell ya married! I knew he wuz gonna make ya cry. I knew he wuz no good. But now he's gone, an' . . . I—I love ya, an' if ya'll give me a coupla years, I'll marry ya an' make ya smile."

Dulcie's heart flip-flopped. "Oh, Billy," she murmured, reaching for his hand. "How I wish you were a couple of years older. Believe me, I'd snap up the best husband that ever was. But now I'm going West, to Washington State, somewhere north of Seattle. I'm going to teach school there—"

"Aw, take me wid ya, pleeze? I'll be your best student."

Dulcie choked back a sob and a laugh. This was so sweet, and salved her pride, but it was making the future loom too real for a day like today. "I don't think your ma and pa would appreciate me taking you so far away."

"But I'm big an' strong an' kin help you an' Granny. You need me more'n Ma an' Pa does. They got the others."

"But they have only one of you. And I know they need you something fierce. Besides, who's going to carve this All Hallows' Eve contest-winning pumpkin?"

Billy mulled this over. "All right. I guess I'm not big *enough*. But I'll come fer ya, just wait 'n' see."

Sparing no more time for his romantic pursuits, the boy ran off, most likely to seek Ben Miller and Michael Druck, and then to find mischief. Smiling ruefully, Dulcie had a very clear picture of what had caused Billy's obnoxious behavior toward her and Race. The boy had been jealous, heartbroken. But now it seemed she'd set his heart on the path to recovery. She wished she could as easily set aside her own heartache.

But she couldn't. She knew she'd never make it through the day if she remained where she could hear the bustle of the bazaar, the calling of the auctioneer. She'd told Granny she'd spend the day reading a book about the West down by the river, and so she left the church by the back door. She hoped the song of the Susquehanna would help soothe her battered senses.

She no longer held hope for healing her heart.

Coming into Everleigh, Race noted the air of festivity around the square. Another celebration? he wondered.

As he scanned the crowd he caught sight of a familiar gray bun through pipe smoke. He waved to catch her attention. "Granny!"

A grin hiked up her wrinkles. "Race! I thought choo vere last night coming home."

He smiled wryly. "I had to talk to my grandfather."

"Goot, goot. Now, choo must to river go. Dulcie ist crying dere. Oh, unt yer vedding quilt. She gave it to church to auctioned be."

"What quilt? And why is there an auction? Another Founders' Day?"

"Naw, Dulcie's church vants money fer missions. She don't vant quilt mitout husband."

Race frowned. None of this made much sense, but seeing how well Granny's record was running, he'd comply with her commands. He shuddered, however, at the memory of his last vendue. "Tell you what, Granny. I'll go to the river if you'll buy me the quilt. Here's my money clip. If Dulcie couldn't stand to keep that quilt without keeping me, I know I *need* to keep it from being sold.''

Granny nodded, sucking on her pipe. ''I liked choo ven choo first came, I like choo more now. Go get Dulcie. Today be fer fun, not fer cryin'.''

Laughing, Race turned toward the side street that led to the fateful stand of willows, but before he got there, he heard his name. Pausing, he felt a tug on his sleeve. ''Emma!''

''Yes, it's me. And Nathan,'' she added, displaying her blue-blanketed offspring. ''Race, you must do something. Anything. Just don't let her move to Washington State. Please.''

Race felt a knot at his throat. He had another champion in this tiny town. The small-town welcome was again reaching out. ''I'm going to her now. I won't let you down.''

Emma stood on tiptoe and kissed Race's cheek. ''She's my best friend. I can't lose her. I'd like to keep you here, too.''

''Consider it done.'' Striding toward the rolling water, Race knew he'd done the right thing by coming back. Everleigh certainly felt more like home than Lancaster did. Sure, he'd keep his office there; Everleigh wasn't large enough for an attorney. Nights, though, he'd come home to Dulcie.

He spied her sitting under a willow tree, an open book on her lap, her head against the tree trunk, tears flowing down her cheeks. Although he never wanted to see her suffer, those tears told him more than words ever could. ''Dulcie . . .''

''Oh!'' She rose with a wobble, and rubbed her palms against her cheeks. Race caught both hands in his, then pulled her close to kiss the tears away. Well before he was done, she stiffened and crushed her boot heel on his tender toes.

''Ouch!'' Race hopped back, keeping his weight off his

injured foot. "Why'd you do that? I was only kissing you."

"That's why, you lying, cheating, double-faced traitor! Oh, yes, and a thief, too. It wasn't enough to steal my heart. You had to steal my hopes and my future. It's your fault I have to move to Washington State."

"No, by God, you're not moving, you wild woman! Hellion! You're not going anywhere but home with me. That was my second mistake. I should have stayed put and made you see reason."

"What was your first mistake, marrying me?"

Under the taut bravado, Race heard the quiver of pain. "No, Dulcie, never that. In fact, that's the best thing I've ever done." He owed her an explanation, but he didn't know where to start. Too much was riding on his words. "My first mistake was to let Father and Hershey talk me into negotiating the purchase of your chocolate recipe. At that time, I still behaved like a son, a child who always obeys adults. I had to grow up. And I did."

Race stepped closer to his wife. He breathed easier when she didn't back away. "In the end, I have those three crusty curmudgeons and Granny to thank for opening my eyes. I had to prove to myself that I could handle anything that came up. I interceded with my grandfather on behalf of my parents and brought about a reconciliation that was years in the coming."

"Your pompous, autocratic, despotic grandfather? That monster listened to you?"

"I'm sure you'll see him differently when I tell you he wants a dozen cases of bonbons at the store first thing Monday morning. It's his way of apologizing."

Dulcie's jaw dropped. Race took advantage of her speechlessness. "And I'm to bring you to Lancaster next time I go."

He took another step, then another. She didn't move.

Wrapping his arms around her, he pulled her close. "I never wanted to keep any secrets from you. I argued over and over with Milton, trying to show him I couldn't represent him to you. I only wanted to represent myself. I wanted to court you, not buy you out. And in the end, I learned that Milton only wanted to give me the opportunity to solve a legal matter so he could recommend me to other potential clients. Ironic, isn't it?"

"Diabolical," she muttered, still withholding forgiveness.

Not that he'd expected this to be easy. Time to play his trump card. "You know what? It seems Hershey does indeed have big plans. So big, he's planning to buy land and build himself a factory. He has decided to concentrate on the mass production of milk chocolate. In a letter to me, he admitted your luxury treats will pose him no competition after all."

"Are you serious?" she asked, hope, fear, anger, and something sweeter in her expression.

"Of course I am. I'm here, aren't I?" He ran his hand over her hair, tangling his fingers in the loose curls. "I love you, Dulcie. I always have. I never wanted that recipe. I never wanted to work for Milton Hershey. All I've wanted all this time is you. I'm sorry—sorrier than you'll ever know—that I kept secrets from you. I had a reason, a valid one, or so I thought. I was afraid my father's heart wouldn't take the strain of fighting my grandfather. But in the end, he looks stronger, revitalized. He's going after what he really wants."

"I'm glad," she said softly. "I liked him, even though he seemed to be in such low spirits at our wedding."

"He's not low now!" Race took a deep breath. "Forgive me?"

"I-I'm not sure."

Race remembered another time when persuasion had been

needed. "Then perhaps this will persuade you," he murmured, tilting her face up to his.

It wasn't a gentle kiss. It wasn't tentative at all. It was the kiss of a man who, fearful of losing his woman, showed her more than words could tell.

She quivered in his arms. She yielded, then met his passion equally, kissing him back. The kiss continued, endless, potent, ripe with promise, full of love. "I love you, Dulcie, sweetheart. I'll always love you—"

"Hell a' kitin'!" Granny called. "Yer *schmutzing* already! Here, yer quilt take, unt yer money, too! Choo two vill no more fight, right?"

Race met Dulcie's gaze and knew without a doubt that she was his. He also read the laughter and mischief he'd always seen there, the laughter and mischief he so loved. He chuckled, and she joined him.

"No!" both cried in unison.

Then the sound of yelling caught their attention. What Dulcie saw when she turned around had her laughing even more. A rolling pin held high in the air, square-cut Vera Oberholtz chased her partridgelike banker husband down the street. A Pennsylvania German argument filled the air.

Behind Vera, crying "Oh my, oh my" came Prudence Kleinschmidt, wringing her hands. "It was all innocent," she then cried in defense.

Dulcie laughed till she cried.

"What is it?" Race asked. "What's going on?"

"It's . . . too . . . funny. Seems Mr. Oberholtz has been stepping out on the side, softening Prudence with gifts of flowers and candies, and Vera has suspected his philandering for a while. That's what she consulted Granny about. Pru insists it was just a harmless flirtation."

"Looks like that spell didn't work."

Dulcie's eyes widened. "You know."

"Mm-hmm."

"And what have you done about it? What'll you do?"

"Do? Why nothing, of course. It's just Granny's way."

Dulcie pressed her face into Race's chest, breathing deeply of his special citrus-and-man scent.

"Dulcinea-girl. Take the quilt unt my jug. I must a murder stop." Shoving the items at Race and Dulcie, she limped off after the romantic triangle.

Triumphantly Race spun away, jug in hand. He put it up to his lips, leaned his head back, and gulped away. Seconds later, he straightened, his face all apucker, and sprayed the willow.

"What the hell is this? I expected moonshine."

Dulcie couldn't stop laughing. She gasped in the hope of getting air in her lungs, then held her middle and laughed some more. He was so disappointed in the contents of Granny's jug! "It-it's a tonic for her kidneys. And it's foul!"

Race swiped his mouth, then froze. "Dulcinea?"

"Uh-oh." She tried a winning smile.

"As in *Don Quixote*? The peasant he thought was a lady? The one he fought windmills for?"

Dulcie nodded. She stole a glance. He was smiling. "Seems fitting," he said. "I just fought Grandfather and Milton Hershey for you."

"Wait a minute there! I remember tilting at those giants myself."

Race cocked his head. He thought for a moment. "Most appropriate. They turned out to be nothing more than windmills, after all."

"They looked quite alarming to me. I even fought Mr. Oberholtz!"

"Not much of a fight, if you ask me."

They laughed. They hugged, their Wedding Ring quilt

wrapped around them. They kissed, and the passion soared, caught fire, ran wild.

"Damn, I love you," he croaked out. "And I want you all to myself. Come on, let's go try out our quilt!"

Dulcie smiled through tears of happiness. His idea had much merit. She remembered the night of the taffy pull.

Throwing the quilt over his head, she cried, "Race you home!"

AUTHOR'S NOTE

Milton Snavely Hershey was unquestionably a fascinating man. And while he lived in South-Central Pennsylvania and founded not only Hershey Foods Corporation, but also the town of Hershey, the situations in *Candy Kiss* are a product of my imagination. Knowing of Mr. Hershey's charitable nature, which led him to establish the Milton Hershey School for underprivileged children, I created circumstances where he might have been likely to try to help a friend's son.

In the mid-to-late 1890s, Hershey began to plan the production of milk chocolate for which he is now known internationally. He founded the town of Hershey, Pennsylvania, in 1909 to house the employees at his chocolate factory.

Race, Dulcie, and Granny K are, of course, fictional.

The local Pennsylvania-German speech patterns are charming, musical, a touch foreign, and completely fascinating. South-Central Pennsylvania, with its farms and rolling hills, is a beautiful part of this country, and wonderfully rich in history.

Finally, my research into HexCraft and Pagan faiths was based on the following books:

Hexcraft, Dutch Country Pow-Wow Magick, by Silver

RavenWolf, Llewellyn Publications, St. Paul, Minnesota.

To Ride A Silver Broomstick, by Silver RavenWolf, Llewellyn Publications, St. Paul, Minnesota.

WICCA Craft, The Modern Witch's Book of Herbs, Magick, and Dreams, by Gerina Dunwich, Citadel Press/Carol Publishing Group, New York, New York.

Living WICCA, by Scott Cunningham, Llewellyn Publications, St. Paul, Minnesota.

I particularly appreciate the wealth of information provided by Silver RavenWolf, especially the personal experiences she related to me.